The Delany Bennets

DESIREE R. KANNEL

Black Rose Writing | Texas

The author grants the final approval for this literary material.

First printing

This is a work of fiction. Names, characters, businesses, places, events, and incidents are either the products of the author's imagination or used in a fictitious manner. Any resemblance to actual persons, living or dead, or actual events is purely coincidental.

ISBN: 978-1-68513-289-7
PUBLISHED BY BLACK ROSE WRITING
www.blackrosewriting.com

Printed in the United States of America
Suggested Retail Price (SRP) $24.95

The Delany Bennets is printed in Baskerville

*As a planet-friendly publisher, Black Rose Writing does its best to eliminate unnecessary waste to reduce paper usage and energy costs, while never compromising the reading experience. As a result, the final word count vs. page count may not meet common expectations.

Cover design by Ivanna Nashkolna

To Kristin R. who helped me jumpstart
this project back in 2018. I did it!

This book would not have been possible without the rap music guidance and inspiration I received from Talford and Sara C.

The Delany
Bennets

Ashley!
Thanks so much!
Happy Reading!

CHAPTER 1

SUMMER INTO FALL, 1999

There was a lot of pink. And not the soft lemonade pink, or the classic rose pink. This was pink as in bubble gum; the hue typically seen ballooning out of a six-year-old's mouth. Macy, the bride, fell in love with the color at a young age, carried it through adolescence, and now infused it into every aspect of her wedding day. All the guests had … opinions, but only one of them spoke openly.

"God! How *un*original!" Mrs. Hattie Bennet gasped at the sight of the pink tableware. She picked up a pink plastic flute and frowned. "*Really?*"

Lizzy, her second eldest, glanced nervously. "Mother," she whispered. "Someone might hear you."

Mrs. Bennet, never one to turn away from a challenge, doubled down. "And so what if they did?" she responded. "It's not like what *I* say means anything to anybody." She took a sip of sparkling cider from the plastic flute. "If it did," she continued, wrinkling her nose at the offensive tableware, "then they would have *never* provided such tacky—"

"That's enough, Mrs. B," her husband said to his wife and his daughters. "We're not here to judge the table settings. We're here to celebrate young Macy's wedding."

The Bennet family, all seven of them, occupied a table near the back of the banquet hall, but with a good view of the dance floor and the wedding party. The Bennets of Longbourne House currently consists of five daughters, four grown, one entering her final year of high school, and the parents, Mr. Harold Bennet and Mrs. Hattie Bennet. Married almost thirty years, the couple affectionately call each other Mr. and Mrs. B, along with other classic terms of endearment. Macy, the bride, is the granddaughter of Mr. and Mrs. Bennet's long-time friend, Mrs. Claire Hoffman.

Mr. Bennet looked around the table at his daughters and offered each a reassuring smile. He knew, although only two would admit it, that his girls were having a difficult time celebrating the occasion. Three of his five had reached the age when family and close friends felt it their duty to wonder, then inquire about something he felt was none of their business.

"Time to think about marriage."

"Don't wait too long."

And his least favorite: *"Girls like you can't be too picky."*

Humph! *Girls like you.*

Any man would be lucky to have one of his daughters. Well, not *any* man, but he related to his daughters' plight.

"You're a fine one to talk," his wife said. "You're at that university every day, and not one—not one—eligible man have you brought home or introduced to your daughters?"

"Mrs. B, I'm there to tend to the grounds, not find husbands for my daughters."

Mrs. Bennet waved her hand at the celebration before her. "*That* should be Jane or Lizzy," she whined. "Instead, here we all sit; the Bennets and their unattached daughters." The dance floor cleared, and the DJ announced the beginning of the father-daughter dance. Macy glided onto the floor, her proud father holding her hand and leading her like she was royalty. The guests clapped as *You Light Up My Life* wafted through the speakers. Lizzy gave her sister a playful nudge as the two eldest Bennet sisters grinned.

The rest of the reception went on pretty much as everyone expected. After the father-daughter dance, the newlyweds wowed everyone with a well-rehearsed dance sequence, which was met with hearty applause, except from Mrs. Bennet, who mumbled at how she thought the spectacle vulgar and show-offie.

Jane and Lizzy sat quietly with their parents, only now and then accepting an offer to dance, mostly from men they already knew. Merryton, North Carolina was a small town, and with Martin Delany University as a major employer, most of its citizens were related via employer and/or family. After the cake cutting, the DJ launched into a repertoire of contemporary and old school selections, music easy and fun to dance to. Lizzy smiled and nodded at the tracks booming from the huge speakers. "Your handiwork?" Jane said to her sister, who only smiled and nodded.

Despite the disastrous play of *You Light Up My Life*, the rest of the reception music was spot-on. The DJ, a student from the university, had consulted with Lizzy beforehand. And why wouldn't she? Professor Elizabeth Bennet was the authority on music, specifically hip hop and R & B. She's also one of the more popular professors at Martin Delany University. Besides teaching English Composition and literature courses, she's also known as the Hip Hop professor, leading undergrad courses in a deconstructive study of rap music.

The DJ was winding down the lyrics to *I'm Every Woman* by Chaka Khan, and Lizzy could hear the soft beat of the next track, *I'm Your Baby Tonight*, fading in. She smiled as Macy and her new husband twirled around the dance floor.

"And what are you so happy about, Miss Lizzy?" Mrs. Bennet leaned across the table. "That should be you up there, you know."

Lizzy took a deep sigh. She was just about at her fill of her mother for one evening. It was bad enough that the whole family still lived together, but spending her precious Saturday evenings was a bit too much. Kitty and Lydia, the two youngest, had abandoned the family table long ago.

Lizzy and Jane had income enough to afford their own place, but with heavy student loan debts, living at home allowed them the chance to pay off quickly. Plus Longbourne House, the family home, was more convenient. For now. Lizzy nudged Jane and was about to suggest the pair leave when Joyce Gardiner came up to the table, dressed all out in her Sunday-come-to-meeting outfit: lavender dress suit, with matching sequin on the collar and hem. On her head perched an oversized pillbox hat that perfectly matched her dress. She looked like someone had dipped her in a vat of lavender paint. Joyce pulled out a chair and sat down. Lizzy noted beads of perspiration on her forehead.

"Oh, thank goodness you all are still here," she said, taking a big gulp of air after her last word.

"My goodness, Joyce," Mrs. Bennet said. "What's got you so hot and bothered?" She handed her sister a pink napkin to wipe her brow, but she brushed it away.

"Never mind that, girl." She leaned forward and motioned for the others to join her. Mrs. Bennet and Mary did without hesitation, Jane and Lizzy stayed where they were, content to just watch, and Mr. Bennet busied himself with another piece of wedding cake.

"Sister," she said, "have you heard the news?!"

Mrs. Bennet rolled her eyes. "You know I have not, Joyce. That's why you practically ran over here to tell us."

Joyce tried to look angry, but the deliciousness of her tidbit of gossip must have been too good to let her elder sister ruin it, so she continued.

"There's a new professor set to begin next semester and you'll never guess who!" Before anyone could guess, she continued. "Dr. William Darcy!"

Lizzy and Jane looked at each other. Their mother looked momentarily perplexed, but it didn't last long. "You don't mean *that* Dr. Darcy? The one who was on the cover of *Ebony Magazine*?"

Joyce had taken a bite of cake from Lydia's abandoned plate and could only nod her head. After she swallowed, she continued.

"Yes! That Dr. Darcy. President Lucas worked extra hard to get someone like *him* to come to our little university, and I don't even want to think about how much he agreed to pay him, but coming he is, Sister." She leaned back and smiled while the remaining Bennets took in the news. Mrs. Bennet got to work.

"Did you hear that Mr. B? Dr. William Darcy will teach at Delany this semester." She leaned back and smiled at her two eldest. "What a wonderful opportunity for our girls."

Her husband finished his last bit of cake, licked the pink plastic spoon, and said, "Our girls? Why our girls, Mrs. B?"

A look of exasperation ran across his wife's face. "What do you mean, 'why'. Oh please, even you can't be daft enough to not see how I'm thinking he could marry one of our girls."

Joyce laughed. Jane and Lizzy winced.

"And don't say a word, Joyce. You were thinking the same thing. That's why you ran over here." The sly smile that spread exposed Joyce's agreement.

But Mr. Bennet remained unconvinced. "Why on earth would you think that the famous Doctor-Professor Darcy would come to our little university just so he could marry one of our daughters?"

Mrs. Bennet rolled her eyes. "Of course he's not coming here for *that*. But it *could* happen." She clicked her tongue. "You just make sure you introduce yourself to him as soon as that campus opens back up. Introduce him, then after a suitable amount of time, invite him over to dinner." She tilted her head in thought. "No, not dinner. Too pushy. Make it lunch. Yes! A small Sunday lunch. He'll appreciate that; a nice extension of Southern hospitality and charm." Mrs. Bennet leaned back in her chair, quite proud of her plan.

Her husband laughed. "Mrs. B," he said, "I intend to do no such thing. I'm the groundskeeper and the only professor I hang around with is this one sitting next to me." He reached over and gave Lizzy a loving pat on the shoulder. "And she can find her own husband without any help from me. Or you."

The look she gave her husband told him that the conversation was far from over. Joyce picked up on the tension too and quietly excused herself. Jane and Lizzy resumed their plan to leave and joined their aunt.

"Poor mother," Jane said as they made their way to the lobby area. "I hope Father is not too hard on her."

"Oh, they'll be all right. You know our mother. Worrying about her daughters is her number one hobby."

"Have you heard of Dr. Darcy?"

"Who hasn't?" Lizzy answered. "He's one of the top Black professors in the country. Economics, which means our paths will hardly cross."

Jane nodded. "Makes me wonder why he's coming here, then."

"Why else?" Lizzy answered with a playful smile. "It is a truth universally acknowledged that a single Black male professor in possession of a good fortune *must* be in want of a wife."

CHAPTER 2

The Monday after the wedding, Mr. Bennet left Longbourne House earlier than usual. He liked to walk from his home on the lower campus grounds to his office in the old Frederick Douglass Building. When the students and staff return, he'll use the motorized garden cart to get to and from work. But now, with his campus all to himself, he liked to walk and take his time, marveling at nature's handiwork. He handles a full-time landscaping crew of 10, and when part-time workers come in, usually right after winter—with new plantings and cleaning at high levels—he'll be responsible for up to 25 workers. Although the campus' scholarly offerings had changed significantly since its opening, the care and upkeep of the lawns and gardens remained the same. With one family working on the landscape, marvelous and unique beauty was sure to follow. Harold Bennet was the 4th generation landscape manager, and he learned everything he needed to learn from his father, just as his father had, and his father before him and so on down from the first Bennet, August.

A group of formerly enslaved men started the college in the small town of Merryton, North Carolina, in 1875. All had been the property of the Willoughby plantation in Augusta, Georgia. Around 1857, they banded together and escaped. As free men in the North, they educated themselves, started new families, and taught other freed men and women. After the Civil War, they banded together again and resettled their school in Merryton. Some ventured further south to their old plantations in search of families they had left behind. One man they hoped to find was a fieldhand by the name of August. Also enslaved at the Willoughby plantation, August had sacrificed himself by acting as a decoy, turning the overseer away from the fleeing men and women. Almost 10 years later, they found August among a handful of the newly freed and convinced him to come back with them. He had nothing keeping him in Georgia since the master had sold off his wife and children as punishment for trying to escape.

In his new home of Merryton, North Carolina, August attended reading and writing classes, but he was more interested in helping to build the school. He worked with a Quaker named Bennet Longbourne who was also helping to make the university a reality. After a few years, Bennet and August completed housing for the university president and faculty. Grateful for his labor and the sacrifice he had made for them at the Willoughby plantation, the university's founders also had a separate house built for August. And to solidify the relationship, they amended the university bylaws, adding a mandate stating August and his descendants would always have a home and work at the school. As for August, his experience with Bennet Longbourne taught him that not all white men were evil. After his mentor died, August took his last name, and called his new home Longbourne.

In 1885, they officially named the college Martin Delany University, after the physician and Black Nationalist.

.   .   .

Mr. Bennet entered his office, which was behind a brick wall that separated the university's works and storage yard from the large and beautiful Ancestors Garden. The wall directly opposite his office front door held pictures of the previous groundskeepers. His picture, the only one in color, hung right next to his father's. He removed his cap and tossed it on the desk. His crew was not due for another 30 minutes, which gave him time to pull out the campus map and begin marking the areas they needed to work on. He had made a mental note about the faulty irrigation points in front of the library. He hoped it would not turn out to be a big issue. The entire system was long overdue for an upgrade.

A few minutes later, his office door opened. At the sight of the early morning visitor, he stood up. "Good morning, Dr. Lucas. What brings you to my humble little office?"

Dr. Lucas gave a lopsided smile and motioned for Mr. Bennet to sit back down. "No need for formalities now. Just us two, you know." The two had grown up together but followed decidedly different paths.

"Got any coffee for an old friend?" Dr. Lucas asked.

The two men chatted for a while, mostly about Macy's wedding, their daughters, and Merryton gossip. Dr. Lucas, like Mr. Bennet, had only daughters; his two to the Bennet's five. Charlotte, Dr. Lucas' eldest, was Lizzy's best friend.

After a few minutes, the conversation dwindled to an awkward silence. Mr. Bennet could tell something was on his friend's mind. Being president of the university was no simple task.

Dr. Lucas drained his coffee, straightened up, and said, "Look, Harold, there's no easy way to say this." He paused. "I'm sure you've heard the rumors," he continued, but then shook his head. "Of course, you haven't. Out here in your little hideaway."

This last comment made Mr. Bennet nod in agreement. He did like his solitude and next to being alone in his office, he preferred his private den at home.

"Well, it is hard for a man living with six women to find a bit of peace. Mrs. B rarely comes here anymore." He smiled, looking around the small office. "It's not much, but ..."

Dr. Lucas stood up so suddenly that it startled his friend. "Damn it, Harold! Why didn't you and Hattie make plans to do something else? To *live* somewhere else?"

"What do you mean? Why would we do that? You know my family's history better than anybody."

A wave of sadness passed over Dr. Lucas's face. "History? You haven't been relying on history, have you, Harold? You can't expect that a promise made over 100 years ago would last forever. Could you?"

Mr. Bennet took a sharp inhale, stood up, and reminded his friend that what he called a mere 'promise' was much more than that. It was a mutual agreement in which both sides benefited. "No one can say that the Bennet men ever got more than they gave," he said.

Dr. Lucas held up his hand. "You don't have to convince me." He pointed to himself. "Everything you just said is pretty close to the argument I made at the last board meeting." He held up his hands in a gesture of helplessness. "But these are new times, and a lot of the younger board members don't think as we do."

Mr. Bennet sat back down, feeling a sudden sense of dread. His friend remained standing and finally shared the reason for this early morning visit.

Twenty minutes later, Jake, one of his workers, came in to find his boss sitting at his desk, staring into a cold cup of coffee.

■   ■   ■

Harold Bennet was not the only Bennet who enjoyed the solitary campus. Professor Elizabeth Bennet entered the Ancestors Garden area. Being the groundskeeper's daughter may not be the most prestigious connection, but it gave her access to areas otherwise off-limits. Like this magnificent garden, locked behind a 6-foot gate whenever school was not in session. On one end of the garden was a simple labyrinth, made of boxwood bushes almost 6 feet tall. Twenty years ago, when the shrubs reached a height that allowed for great hiding places, the university almost removed the boxwoods, claiming them as a health and safety hazard. But both her grandfather and father had fought hard to keep them and instead convinced the board to secure the space with gates and security cameras. But Elizabeth never worried about her safety while there. The area emitted a sense of peace and safety.

Elizabeth wasn't going into the maze today. On her mind was the arduous task of planning for the new semester. She sighed as she walked through the garden towards her favorite bench. One of the few wooden ones remaining, and the square brass plaque set in the cement before it let everyone know why.

Twig Book Shop #106
306 Pearl Parkway #106
San Antonio, TX 78215
(210) 826-6411

17:06:29
76693757

10/24/2023
Terminal ID No.:

Credit Sale:

Transaction #:   Visa
Card Type: *************5581
Account: Chip
Entry:

Amount: USD$77.86

Host Ref. Number: 329722002113
Auth. Code: 031118
Batch Number: 737
Response: APPROVAL 031118
                         Issuer
                 A0000000031010
                 VISA DEBIT
Mode:
AID:
APPLAB:
        CUSTOMER COPY

Sit and spell.

August 12, 1900

This bench stands in memory of

August Kennet

Original groundskeeper and dedicated friend of

Martin Shaw University

1870–1977

As always, Elizabeth gave a respectful pause and nod as she stepped over the memorial. She settled into the well-worn bench, pulled a notebook and pen freshly from her book bag, opened it on her lap, and got to work. This syllabus won't write itself, she thought with a laugh.

As was the case of any teacher, she had a full load—five courses. Three of them didn't need too much prep. Those would be her sophomore composition classes, along with Intro to African American Literature, but she took the most time, care, and pride in planning her Rap & Hip Hop Studies class. And this semester, because of its popularity, she had two sections to prep for. Thinking back on how just four years ago, Lizzy had to beg forgiveness for including *Tupac Shakur* and *Public Enemy* in her literature syllabus, she couldn't believe that she now had a semester-long course on the subject. Ever since she was a teen and heard rap artists' brash voices and bold lyrics, she saw that there was something special about the music. Rap is probably the only genre that touches every issue in the Black community: racism, crime, police brutality, and even welfare. The constant influx of new music and artists meant she had to stay on top of it all and make sure her syllabus reflected current trends. And with the revolutionary release of Missy Elliott's second album, *Da Real World*, and the hit single, *She's a Bitch*, there was sure to be some lively classroom discussions. She leaned back and smiled. While others dismissed such lyrics as vulgar, demeaning, and misogynistic, Professor Bennet, the Hip Hop professor, understood another side of the groundbreaking music, and made it her mission to change people's minds. And, understanding the publish-or-perish aspects of higher academia, on her office desk computer were drafts and endless notes for an academic paper she was preparing for submission.

And somewhere else on that computer was a file containing her PhD program research. Next year, she told herself before switching on her CD player.

Above her, in the adjacent Economics building, a young, handsome, Black professor, new to the campus, looks down into the Ancestors' Garden and maze. He understood the locals called it a labyrinth, but he wasn't willing to give such a label. From his 4th-floor vantage point, he could make out at least two entrances and the iron gate surrounding the area. *Do they keep gold there?* he thought with a smirk a moment before his peripheral vision pulled his gaze to another part of the garden. Although only able to make out her figure, he was more intrigued than attracted to the woman that appeared before him. Tall, voluptuous figure, and with a mass of black, curly hair that bounced when she walked. Over her arm hung a brown leather satchel. She sat down on a bench and placed a CD player on her lap. I hope she is not a student, was his first thought.

CHAPTER 3

Charles Bingley followed his friend, William Darcy, through the first floor of the estate that was to be his new home, at least for the next few months. The real estate agent, to gloss over the plantation's horrid past, claimed the property possessed a Southern mystique, but after decades of neglect, any mystique had vanished. Despite that, he had signed on the dotted line in part because he knew his older sister, Caroline, would relish the chance to turn the former slave plantation into a Black-owned architectural wonder. She was practically giddy thinking about using Black dollars to revive the place. Now, several months later, he looks around in wonder at the job she accomplished.

"Well, I see what's kept your sister so occupied," William Darcy said as they made their way upstairs.

The second floor was just as impressive. "And," Charles said, walking into another room, "we thought this would make a nice home office for you."

It was one of the larger rooms, partially furnished with bookcases, a large desk and chair. The exterior wall held French doors leading out to a small balcony that overlooked the tennis court and swimming pool. It was the best room on the second floor. "Shouldn't this be your room, my friend? You being the new 'master' and all."

Charles laughed. "Well, maybe, but let's just say it's my way of thanking you for joining me on this little Southern adventure."

Both men stepped out onto the balcony. What appeared to be a cornfield was off in the distance. Rows of slim green stalks stood tall, soaking up the afternoon sun and waiting for the inevitable harvest. Tractors and other big machinery lined the road alongside the crops. "Good god, Bingley, I knew you always had an unhealthy obsession with country living and such, but don't you think investing a million dollars to indulge yourself is a bit much?"

Charles laughed. "I *wish* it was only one mill. Caroline went way over budget. Thompson's going to have a heart attack."

"I'm surprised he's lasted this long," Darcy said. "Most of the Bingley family accountants quit in frustration after a year."

"Ha ha," Charles said. "We can't all be financial know-it-alls like you."

Darcy took another look around. "But seriously, the boredom will drive you mad before Thanksgiving break. What do you even have in common with country folk?"

"My family owns wineries, Darce, which *is* farming. Isn't it? Besides, I find the idea of owning a former plantation both exciting and ironic." He gave a hollow laugh. "Do you even think our ancestors could imagine that one day a Black man would actually *own* the plantation? And have white workers." He clapped his old friend on the back. "It really was too good of a prospect to pass on."

The pair took a quick turn through the rest of the upstairs before heading downstairs. Darcy finally admitted that the home held a particular aesthetic, although he much preferred his own home. A pre-war duplex penthouse his father named Pemberly, in San Francisco's Pacific Heights. Most evenings offered a fantastic view of the Golden Gate Bridge.

"Where has your sister gone off to?" Darcy asked.

"She's meeting with the groundskeepers. We have something called Apple Scabs that needs to be taken care of."

Darcy's eyes widen. "Caroline? And tree diseases?" he laughed. "Looks like she's taken to Netherfield, too."

"Well, you know Caroline. If it involves spending our money, she's all in."

Bingley moved to change the subject. "Look, it's a bit of a drive from the University, and my sister can be sort of . . . you know. But I hope the place works out for you." Bingley gave his friend a playful nudge. "You'll need somewhere to escape from all those country bumpkins."

Despite his resolve to stay serious, Darcy smiled. William Darcy and Charles Bingley first met at the Chadwick boarding school at 12 years of age. Although schools such as Chadwick had formally eliminated their segregation practices, they had yet to admit any African American students. The Darcys and Bingleys were among the wealthiest African American families in the US and not from sports, music, or dumb luck. Bingley's family owned wineries and other enterprises throughout the US, South Africa, and Europe, while Darcy's family had made the bulk of their fortune through a mixture of shrewd investments and innovations. They were only sons, with parents now passed away. Now at 31 and 32, both were well into marriageable age, which was a fact often brought up to them by aunts, and, in Bingley's case, his sister.

Happily situated at his tenured position at Berkeley, Dr. Darcy did not need to seek another position, especially here. But two things happened. The first was his department chair urging him to take a long overdue sabbatical. The second was after he discovered his friend's intention to purchase the Netherfield plantation. Netherfield is located near Martin Delany University, and Darcy had been looking for an excuse to spend time at the university. Delany was home to an economics professor whose research on poverty and economic inequality in minority communities had impressed Darcy. Although poverty was a stranger to him, he had an uncommon empathy for those born less fortunate. Spending his sabbatical studying with a colleague at Delany would be an efficient way to use his time. Darcy was nothing if not efficient.

On its surface, the friendship between the two heirs seemed unlikely. While Darcy was all formality and stiffness, everyone knew Charles Bingley for his uncensored friendliness and good cheer. He made friends wherever he went, and acquaintances were always glad to see him. Even when he was with "that Darcy dude." While Darcy kept his circle tight, Bingley had the uncommon trait of being able to connect and carry a conversation with anyone, from any station. He could converse and laugh with the migrant grape pickers and their families and then feel just at ease in a boardroom full of wealthy executives. While Darcy approaches a newcomer with a suspicious gaze and folded arms, Bingley is all smiles and an outstretched hand. But Bingley knew something about William Darcy that few had had the privilege of knowing, mainly because none stayed around long enough. That is that once you earned William Darcy's trust, you became a friend for life.

And, while Darcy had his reasons for coming to Netherfield Plantation, Bingley also had an ulterior motive. Having recently gone through an emotional and tragic ordeal involving someone they both thought they could trust, Bingley believed Darcy needed a break from his usual surroundings. A reset, as some would call it.

The two men walked out onto the huge front porch. They both saw Caroline standing at the entrance to the tennis court. She was talking with a woman whom Bingley didn't recognize. When Caroline noticed them on the porch, she waved, signaling them to join her.

"Charles, this is Linda Grant, from *North Carolina Homes Magazine*. She wants to do a layout of Netherfield."

Linda Grant extended her hand. "Nice to meet you Mr. Bingley, and …?"

"William Darcy," Caroline supplied. "He'll be teaching at Martin Delany University this year."

Linda Grant's blue eyes grew round behind her gold-rimmed glasses. "Is that so?" she said. "You must be the new basketball coach everyone's been talking about."

"No," Darcy said, his voice flat. "I'm the new economics professor that I am sure no one is talking about."

"*Dr.* Darcy is on sabbatical from Berkeley," Caroline said. "A university. In California. I'm sure you've heard of it."

Linda Grant gave an awkward smile before apologizing. "You know us Southerners," she said. "We got sports on the brain."

"Apparently so," Darcy said.

Linda stuck her hand into her bag and pulled out a business card. Handing it to Caroline. "Well, I will contact you as soon as the photographer is free. We'd love to do a feature on the home and how you brought it back to life!" She turned and hurried towards the carport.

"Well, Miss Ca-ro-line, it looks like you've done gone and made a name for yourself here in good old North Carolin-ee," Charles said in his best attempt at a Southern accent.

She waved off her brother's attempt at a compliment. "What have you two been up to?" she asked.

"Just showing our new roommate around the place."

"Oh, good," Caroline said. She glanced up at the massive house. "Lord knows we have the space."

Darcy turned to his friends. "Of course. I couldn't imagine myself being in any other place." A thought came to him. "And now it's my turn to ask a favor. There is a school tradition of having a pre-convocation a few days before the start of each year. They introduce new faculty and present the year's … oh, I don't know … goals? Anyway, there is a luncheon on the grounds afterward."

"Sounds fascinating," Charles replied without a hint of sarcasm.

"You can't be serious, man. I had no intention of going, but Dr. Lucas made it sound like I had to."

"What? Why not? Should be fun," he smiled. "And a great way to meet the ladies."

Meet the ladies. There was one particular lady Darcy wouldn't mind meeting. He found he could not erase the image of the young woman he had seen in the gardens.

Caroline noticed what appeared to be a mild look of satisfaction on Darcy's face as he took in the scenery. She took his arm and smiled. "Don't worry, William. The year will fly by and then you'll be back to your precious Berkley and spreadsheets and whatnots."

Darcy shrugged. "If you say so, Caroline."

"Oh, come on, you two," Charles said. "Who knows what adventures await us? Here's to country life!"

Darcy laughed. "Whatever that may be."

CHAPTER 4

It had been two days since Dr. Lucas' visit. Mr. Bennet was good at keeping things to himself, but holding this bit of information was causing him to feel an unfamiliar sense of angst.

"I tried to fight for you, Harold, but this is something those new folks have been pushing for. And since this is the first time there isn't a male to take over—" Dr. Lucas had told him.

"It doesn't have to be a man, you know."

"Yes, yes, I know. And *you* know what I mean, but because no Bennet heir wants to carry on the tradition, now is as good a time as any to make changes."

Mr. Bennet felt a sudden sense of dread and unease wash over him. Having a Plan B, as his friend had called it, was something that, although he knew he should do, never seemed to find the time or motivation to do. And now it was too late.

"When do these 'new folks' plan to kick me out?" he asked. "What about Longbourne? They can't mean to have us lose the house, too?" He met this additional thought with a bit of panic.

Dr. Lucas raised a hand to calm his friend. "You can stay in the house until you . . . no longer need it," he added, shifting his eyes around the room to avoid eye contact.

"'No longer need it?' What the hell does that mean, John? When I'm dead?" The shock and horror of the realization made his face hot.

"Well ... yes, that's exactly what it means."

"And my family? What about my wife and daughters?"

"Oh, Harold, you talk like this is the old Regency period. Your girls are perfectly able to take care of themselves. At least Jane, Elizabeth, and Mary can and together they will make sure that the younger ones and your wife will be cared for." He smiled and tried to reassure his old friend. "And if they don't, I promise you I will."

This made his friend laugh. "You? You'll be dead too, John. Don't kid yourself."

"I'm going to let that pass." Dr. Lucas sighed. "You must feel as if this came out of left field, but you can't be that surprised. How many other universities do you know that manage their grounds? None. It will be hard at first, but in the long run, better for the university."

Mr. Bennet wanted to add, *what about me,* but didn't? He was too proud to play the pity card. Instead, he thanked his friend for coming over to break the news.

"No official announcement yet, and we won't until you're ready, Harold. Discuss this with your family and when you are ready, let me know." He turned to leave. "And don't worry, the university will give you a great send-off."

. . .

It hadn't been his intention to head out to Netherfield, but his old truck seemed to just take him there. It was a drive he enjoyed though, with its sprawling, dark green landscapes dotted with chestnut trees here and there. In a few months, fall will erupt on the scene, casting shades of yellows, golds, and reds as far as the eye can see. Fall was his favorite time of year; it signaled the end of a growing season and the beginning of calm while Mother Nature took a much-needed break.

As he turned the last bend that would lead him into the boundaries of Netherfield, he mused how, according to Dr. Lucas, he would enter his own season of rest soon. Of course, he had thought of retirement before, but always in an *I don't have to think of that yet* sort of way. But that, of course, all shifted.

Mr. Bennet referred to his children as five of the silliest girls in Merryton. Those close to him understood it to be his unique term of endearment, but those unfamiliar found the slander shocking.

His oldest two, Jane and Elizabeth, or Lizzy, were far from silly and his favorites. Lizzy a bit more than Jane, although what father would admit such a thing? Both exhibited above-average intelligence, but his Lizzy had a bit more of the street smarts that would help her make it in the world. Jane, well, her naiveté could be her undoing. Thank God, she confided in her sister. Hopefully, Lizzy would be the one to keep her grounded.

Then there was Mary. What she may lack in attractiveness, she tried to make up with her passions, which were (unfortunately) bugs and insects. Mr. Bennet smiles thinking about how, as a child, she would follow him around the grounds with a net and small cage, ready to trap and collect the various creatures she came across. Her profession was male dominated, but they tended to prefer the insects over his Mary.

He reserved his biggest worry for Kitty. For the life of him, he couldn't understand how she chose Lydia (truly the silliest daughter) as her confidant and running partner. Kitty was two years older; shouldn't it have been the other way around?

The thought of his two youngest re-ignited his resolve to do whatever he could to help his daughters secure their future. A husband was not necessary, but it could provide an extra layer of protection.

As he approached the large estate, he turned and drove into the circular driveway. Back in the day, an iron gate blocked drivers from entering, but years of neglect rendered it a useless eyesore. The city had it removed a few years ago. Mr. Bennet pulled his old truck up the drive and parked. His gaze immediately took in the new landscaping and outdoor work. He nodded in approval and before he could wonder who was responsible, a truck belonging to Magic Landscaping came from behind the mansion and drove towards the main road. He snickered. Those guys were located over an hour away in Raleigh and had outrageous fees, especially to unsuspecting newcomers. Walking up to the massive wrap-around porch, he reminded himself that he was there to introduce himself and, if it seemed appropriate, offer his services to help with the grounds. For example, he could recommend a more local and affordable groundskeeping service.

Nothing unusual about that, he thought as he ascended the porch stairs.

.   .   .

Mrs. Bennet and her daughters looked up from their tasks as their father entered the sitting room. Although summer, the family had gotten used to the no-TV-on-weeknights rule and often found other interests to amuse themselves. Mostly reading, although the two youngest, Kitty and Lydia, would spend equal amounts of time thumbing through fashion magazines and doing their nails.

"And what brings you in here, Mr. B? Don't tell me you've run out of books."

Kitty and Lydia snickered, causing Lizzy to flash them a look of warning.

Mr. Bennet ignored his wife's jab and sat down in the chair next to hers. "Why, my dear wife, anyone would think you are not happy to see your dear husband?"

Mrs. Bennet pulled a stitch through before setting her embroidery project in her lap. "I would be glad to see you *if* you had some good news."

"Good news?" her husband replied with a raised eyebrow.

"Oh, you always love to tease me, don't you?" she answered. "I heard from the Lucases that Professor Darcy has arrived. *And* that he brought a friend with him. A Mr. Charles Bingley. The Bingleys are the ones who bought that old plantation. Apparently, they are 'fixing it up', according to Mrs. Lucas. Sounds like a waste of money to me."

He nodded. "Yes. That is … mostly true. Oh, and it's Dr. Darcy, not—"

"And," his wife continued with some flourish, "Dr. Lucas has already been around to see them twice, and he brought his daughters with him the second time around."

Mr. Bennet didn't bother to point out to his wife that it was perfectly reasonable for the president of the university to go see his new professor. Especially someone as well-known as Dr. Darcy.

Instead, he merely leaned back into his chair and placed his entwined fingers across his middle. "Is that so?" he asked. The others in the room noticed his hint of mischievousness, but his wife was too busy nursing her anger and disappointment to notice.

"Yes, that is so. And no doubt he did not hesitate to parade Charlotte in front of them like some sort of prized peacock or something."

Lizzy spoke up, feeling the need to defend her good friend. "Mother, I doubt Charlotte would put up with such a thing."

But her mother wasn't having it. "You'd be surprised what women will 'put up with' when a catch like that Professor— *Doctor*—Darcy is around. And his friend, Mr. Bingley? Why, I heard he's nearly as rich as Darcy."

"Did you, Mrs. B?"

"Yes, I did. And before you accuse me of being a snoop, I was just doing what any mother would think to do." She glared at her husband. "Which is more than I can say for you."

Mr. Bennet glanced around the small room. When he was growing up, his mother had claimed the space for herself and used it for sewing and reading. With just men in the house, she needed a room of her own. After he got married, his parents lived with them until they both passed away. At that time, it was only Jane and Elizabeth. His wife decided she would continue the tradition and keep the room for herself, but after Kitty was born, the need for more family space caused her to give up the room. Looking at it now, Mr. Bennet suppressed a gasp when he realized his was the last family of Bennets who would have the privilege of calling Longbourne home.

"Is something the matter, Father?"

He looked up to see Lizzy watching him.

"Everything is fine," he said, shaking his head to gather his thoughts. Taking another look around the room, he added. "But where is our Jane tonight? Not working again?"

Lizzy sighed. "I'm afraid so. There's a staff shortage right now."

"I hope they pay her overtime," Mrs. Bennet said as she resumed her needlepoint. She was working on an intricate flower pattern that would later become a pillow cover. She was quite good and often mused about giving lessons or selling her work. Examples of her handiwork were throughout the house, and Lizzy and Jane would often ask her to make things for their coworkers. Every new mother in the Liberal Arts Department received a handmade gift for their new nursery.

Before Lizzy could respond, Lydia stood up to go. "*Of course,* she gets overtime, mother." Lydia sang out. "Our sister is going to be rolling in dough, and the first thing I'm going to ask her for is a new pair of Guess Jeans."

"No, you won't Lydia. You're still on restriction, remember?" her father said. "No new clothes until school starts."

Lydia stomped her feet. "But I need something to wear to the convocation!"

Mr. Bennet sat up straight and looked his youngest in the eye. Never in his life had he laid a hand on his girls, and he didn't want to start now, but this one — "Lydia, dear," her mother said, breaking his thoughts, "when you raise your voice like that, you sound like you don't have any manners. Remember, no man wants a lady who is loud and irritable."

Mary finally lifted her head from her insect cases. "You sound like a tree full of cicadas!"

"Yes, mother," Lydia said before plopping down on the sofa. She turned to Mary and rolled her eyes. "I'd rather sound like one than look like one!"

"That's enough, you two," Mr. Bennet said. "As with every other year, the Bennets will be at the annual convocation. With or without new jeans."

Mrs. Bennet let loose one of her signature sighs. "Oh, why bother," she said. "We've met everyone. The speeches will all be the same, and the food hasn't been decent since they switched caterers a few years ago."

Lydia reminded her she had wanted Lizzy to meet that rich professor.

"Like it even matters," her mother replied. "Everyone knows how snooty those economic professors are. Without a formal introduction, our Lizzy has no chance of meeting him, so why should she even go?" She glared at her husband. "And your father has made it crystal clear that he will *not* help us." She turned back to her daughters. "And I so wanted at least one of you to be married or engaged before the end of the century."

Mr. Bennet chuckled. "You are not going, Lizzy? That's too bad. Had I known, I wouldn't have bothered going out to Netherfield and introducing myself to the new professor." He ignored his wife's gasp. "I told him all about you and to look out for you during the convocation." He winked at his daughter.

"Oh, Mr. B!" His wife was up and heading towards him, arms outstretched and ready to catch him in a mushy bear hug, the kind he hated. "You always like to tease me," she said before peppering his cheek with kisses. After she released him, she turned back to her daughters. "Isn't your father too funny, girls? Lizzy, let's go upstairs and pick out what you'll wear to the convocation." Before Lizzy could say yes or no, her mother grabbed her by the wrist and pulled her up. "Mary, come with us. We may need you to run your sister's outfit to the cleaners."

"Why me?" she complained. "You may not understand, Mother, but I have important things to do too."

She waved her daughter's concern away. "What? Those books about insects? Yuck! I told you no man is going to want a woman who spends her time crawling around in the gardens looking for bugs."

Mary gave her father an imploring look, but all he could offer was a sympathetic smile with his eyes saying, *just go along; it's easier that way.*

CHAPTER 5

The great day came, and it was everything Professor Elizabeth Bennet loved about academia. Everyone put on their best business attire for the affair, and colleagues greeted each other with hugs, talk about summer, and well wishes for the semester ahead.

Walking up the auditorium steps, Lizzy saw her father standing on the other side of the quad. He liked to watch from afar. He and his crew had been working tirelessly, getting the campus ready for the onslaught. She waved. He waved back.

"Your father does us proud every year." Dr. Laura Wright walked up beside Lizzy. "The whole campus is glowing green and bright and gorgeous." Lizzy smiled and leaned in to hug her friend.

Dr. Wright smiled back and looked over at her friend. "Your hair looks gorgeous! I like it at this length. Do not cut it!"

Lizzy laughed. "I don't plan to, but the upkeep is taking more time than I like." She pulled her fingers through the soft black curls. "But enough about *me*. When did you get back and how was Congo?"

"It was fabulous. And very fruitful." Dr. Wright winked.

Dr. Wright went to Africa to study ancient tribal chants, drumming, and oral storytelling traditions. Lizzy was curious to hear her findings, knowing that rap stems from these ancient traditions. The two educators had theorized that the current hip-hop genre has its roots in the music from that continent. "A biological connection, and if we can prove that, hello MacArthur!" they had dreamed one evening over drinks a few semesters ago.

Lizzy welcomed the probable thesis. She welcomed *anything* that added legitimacy to her area of study.

"Oh, no!" Dr. Wright stopped dead in her tracks. Her eyes froze on someone emerging from the other side of the auditorium. "That must be the famous Dr. Darcy. He's not close, but I can tell from this distance that he is one handsome Black man."

Lizzy turned and strained her neck to get a glimpse. Despite all her words of disinterest, she showered on her mother, she had to admit that it was a curious situation.

Dr. William Darcy, the famous economics professor, was at least a head taller than the people who had gathered around him. His dark gray and perfectly fitted suit jacket and a crisp blue tie, perfectly knotted, stood out against a bright white shirt. Although she couldn't see it, Lizzy assumed it was monogrammed; he seemed like a person who would wear nothing less. Someone spoke to him, and he leaned his head down slightly towards the speaker. That's when their eyes met and she thought she saw his eyes widen, as if in recognition. But why? She was certain that they had never met before.

Dr. Wright nudged her. "Stop ogling," she teased. "I see the rest of our gang over there."

Lizzy slowly turned her eyes away from the new professor. Before she could object, Dr. Wright grabbed her arm and pulled her along. The liberal arts folks gravitated to the upper seats of the auditorium, and that was where the two headed.

There were about 10 minutes before the parade of speeches and announcements, so the liberal arts gang chit-chatted and caught each other up on their summer doings. It surprised her to hear more than one compliment on the college gardens and grounds. She had noticed her father working extra hard these past few weeks, but nothing out of the ordinary. She took each compliment with grace, proud of her father's work and the legacy he continued.

The low murmurs that floated through the packed auditorium came to a halt as the house lights dimmed. The velvet maroon curtains glided open, revealing a podium with a half circle of chairs behind it. Just like last year, and every year before, Lizzy thought. She settled back in her seat to get comfortable. She, and the rest of the Delany University staff and faculty, had about 45 minutes ahead of them.

The university's band revved up, playing the school's anthem, and then the parade of Deans entered, all decked out in their scholarly robes and regalia. Lizzy knew them all and watched as they glided across the stage and took their seats. The first rows of the auditorium filled up too, but with the new faculty that each school's dean would introduce. Of this group, Lizzy recognized two, the new English professors.

After Dr. Lucas spoke, the Dean of each college would speak next with a two-fold objective: first to sing the college's praises–alumni accomplishments, grants, awards, and faculty successes; and second, to introduce new faculty.

Because of the luck of the alphabet, Lizzy's college was next to last, followed by the College of Natural Science and Math. About five years ago, the economics department separated from the liberal arts department, adding another college to the campus.

Dr. Baei, Dean of Economics, stood up after the dance department finished. From her spot in the nose-bleed seats, Lizzy could tell something was off about the elderly professor. Supposedly, he was contemplating retirement this year, but the odds were against it. Dr. Baei, the first Iranian American to hold a leadership position at Delany, would probably have to be carried out. After he announced the award of a huge grant to study something Lizzy knew absolutely nothing about, Dr. Baei shifted from one foot to the other and began his new faculty introductions.

"This semester, we are very fortunate to have the addition of Dr. William Darcy, on sabbatical from UC Berkley. He is bringing his study of microeconomics concerning poverty and resilience in the African American community." The audience mumbled. After his introduction, Dr. Darcy stood up, turned, and gave a slight bow to the audience. He sat down almost as fast as he stood. Professor Wright leaned over and whispered in Lizzy's ear. "Well, that was interesting."

After the remaining schools did their introductions, Dr. Lucas went back to the podium. "Before we adjourn, I want to reassure everyone that the university has been working overtime to make sure we have a safe and event-free transition into the new millennium. I do not have to tell you all how rampant Y2K hysteria is right now, and I expect there will be many questions and concerns from our students. Be sure to keep up with emails and other communications on the subject. And," he paused for dramatic effect, "the board has decided to allow the student body to put on a small, and vetted Y2K celebration. I hope you will consider volunteering to help with the logistics." An audible groan followed, along with a few chuckles.

To wrap up the convocation, everyone stood to sing the school's pride song while the Delany mascot, a rhinoceros everyone called Randy, pranced around the stage, doing his best to cheer the crowd. "Go fighting rhinos!"

"Is it me, or do these things seem longer every year?" Behind her, Professor Davis, who taught women's lit, stood up and arched her back in what looked like a very satisfying stretch.

Dr. Wright laughed. "Is it me, or do you ask that same question every year?" The trio laughed as they made their way to the aisle, down the stairs, and into the lobby. People were already spilling out and onto the lower campus field—an open space surrounded by the baseball and softball fields and the running tracks. The football stadium was off-site. Although she couldn't see him anymore, Lizzy knew her father was somewhere around, making sure that the mass of white marque tents were secured, and that no patches of too-wet grass would trap an unsuspecting colleague. The grass they all walked on, Bahia, according to her father, seemed to glow green. As expected, the tent that held the food was the busiest. "Let's wait," someone said. Silently, Lizzy agreed.

She excused herself from her colleagues and went in search of her family. Strictly speaking, the Bennets were not part of the staff, but everyone welcomed them to this annual event.

"Lizzy!"

She looked up to see Kitty and Lydia heading her way. Thankfully, both dressed properly for the occasion. Lydia spoke first.

"Oh Gawd," she moaned. "Dr. Lucas gets more boring each year."

Kitty giggled.

"Lower your voice, you two, and besides, you don't *have* to be here."

Lydia shrugged. "We know, but honestly, what else is there to do in this town?"

Plenty, Lizzy thought. She glanced around and saw her mother chatting with Dr. Wright.

"Where's Jane?"

"No idea," her sisters answered in unison. "Mary is somewhere, hanging out with the other bug people," Kitty added.

"Ick!" Lydia squirmed. "How embarrassing to have a sister like that!" She would have continued except for her older sister's warning look. Lydia and her aversion to academics and decorum is well known, and their parents *she'll grow out of it* prediction, was looking less and less likely.

Lizzy checked her watch, wondering where Jane was. They had plans to meet up with Charlotte after the luncheon and take in a movie, *The Sixth Sense.* "Go get our parents, find a table, and wait for me. I need to find Jane."

With nothing else to do, the two youngest Bennet sisters did as they were told.

Jane. Jane. Where can you be? Lizzy wondered, searching the crowd.

∙   ∙   ∙

EARLIER THAT DAY

"Don't you look lovely?" Caroline said.

Darcy smiled and gave a slight nod to acknowledge the compliment. He pulled out a chair to sit down. "You did a good job here, Caroline. I can hardly tell that this space used to look like something from the pre-civil war days."

Caroline sighed. "Yes. Now time to turn the focus on finding decent help, especially someone to take care of the grounds. The last thing I need is for all the money spent on plants, trees, grass, and shrubbery to go to waste." She groaned, but both her brother and Darcy knew that she secretly looked forward to the task. Next to shopping in Paris, Caroline enjoyed planning and ordering people around, and with a project as big as remodeling an 18th-century plantation, she would have plenty of opportunities to do both.

"Speaking of grounds," Charles said, pouring himself another cup of coffee. "What did you think of Mr. Bennet? His family's history is fascinating."

Darcy scoffed. "What's so fascinating about being an indentured servant all these years?"

Bingley set his cup down with a bit of force. "What do you mean 'indentured servant'? I didn't get that at all."

"Well, what else would you call it?" Darcy asked. "Stuck at the same position for generations, unable to move up or out."

Bingley scoffed at his friend's assessment of the situation. "From what I could tell, it has been a mutually beneficial agreement. I've never seen a man prouder or more satisfied with his work. And don't forget the housing. Longbourne sounded like a lovely little estate."

"Ha!" Caroline said. "With five daughters, it can't be that 'little.' I found it interesting how he made sure to mention them. *All of them.* Didn't you, Darcy?"

Darcy turned to gaze out the window. The sun was well past rising and cast a yellow-white glow over the fields. The landscape had immediately taken him, having come from a state that was in a perpetual drought, causing all green things to stay brown and dry. But here, the reliable rain kept everything green and lush. Like new. But back to his friend. He didn't have the time to explain the complicated economic and social issues around this so-called legacy agreement between the university and the Bennet family. The founders may have been grateful to the first Bennet, but by their "generous" actions, they did nothing but ensure that their benefactor would stay in the lower position they placed him in. Dr. Darcy could only guess at their original motive, but he hoped it wasn't that.

"No more interesting than any other father speaking about his offspring," Darcy answered.

Before Caroline could respond, a youngish and petite Black woman entered, carrying a tray filled with their breakfast.

"Thank you, Corrine," Caroline said. She introduced the young lady and added that she would come in during the week to help in the kitchen and do light cleaning. "But we will need to get a full crew in here at least once a month, though. Plus a gardener, and someone to look after you two. Possibly even a chauffeur."

"If you don't mind my saying," Corrine said as she laid the breakfast dishes on the table, "The Bennets know practically *everyone* in the neighborhood, seeing how they are a legacy family and all. You could ask them."

"You're acquainted with the family?"

Corrine laughed. "Who isn't? My brother went to school with Jane and called himself having a crush on her, but so did every other boy at school."

"Interesting ..." Charles muttered. Across the table, Darcy flashed a warning look.

Caroline turned to Darcy. "Didn't he say one of them was a professor at Delany?"

He nodded. "Not in my department, though, so I doubt our paths will ever cross."

"Oh, the whole family will be at the pre-con," Corrine said. "The Bennets would never miss that."

Darcy poured himself another cup of coffee. "Well, problem solved, Caroline. You can chat with them later today. I'm sure there will be plenty of time afterward."

"Today won't work. I already have a packed afternoon."

"You won't be coming to the luncheon?" Darcy asked.

"I'm coming, but will have to leave right after, I'm afraid."

Darcy nodded. With Caroline there, the likelihood of being ambushed by the single women diminished. He wasn't being conceited in this thought. Darcy believed that most, if not all, of the attention he received from ladies was due mainly to his status and wealth. Most never bothered to get to know him.

"Speaking of appointments," Charles said. "I need to go downtown and file some papers at the courthouse." He turned to Corrine. "What's the traffic like this time of day?"

She giggled. "Traffic? Man, you can really tell that you all are *not* from around here. You may get stuck behind a tractor or a herd of sheep, but once you pass the Hurley farm, you don't have to worry about no 'traffic.'"

Caroline gave her a look of caution, which the young girl completely missed. Bingley laughed it off. "Well, that's one more thing I love about this place."

Forty minutes later, the two gentlemen exited the mansion and walked to their cars. Darcy warned his friend not to be late, and Bingley promised he wouldn't.

.   .   .

Bingley got turned around as soon as he reached the city center. On the drive into town, he encountered one tractor, but no sheep, which disappointed him a bit. A sign about three miles back was the last bit of direction he saw. As he drove up and down the streets, almost going the wrong way on several one-ways, he realized he was getting more and more lost and would be late—if not miss—the convocation. "Damn!" Bingley muttered. "Darce is going to kill me."

After driving down the same street twice, he turned his BMW onto a small side street and immediately knew he had made a mistake. After a few blocks, the clean, quaint, and touristy charm of the city vanished. Trash choked the gutters, and now and then he'd notice a single shoe among the debris. The people populating the sidewalks looked like they needed a hot bath and a new set of clothes. Preferably ones that fit. To his shock, the scene reminded him of the slums in Hong Kong he had seen two summers ago, again quite by accident. *Is this America?* he thought before realizing that this is what Dr. Darcy's studies were mainly about: poverty, and the factors that keep so many stuck in it.

Bingley had just made a mental note to tell Darce about his discovery when he heard a loud pop, followed by the thump-thump-thump that could only mean a flat tire.

He pulled over and looked at his cell phone, only to see *No Service* flash across the screen. Looking around, he noticed a small crowd of people standing in front of what appeared to be the cleanest building on the block. A sign above the entrance read, *Westside Health Clinic.*

Charles got out of his BMW Z8 Roadster and tried to ignore the stares as he walked towards the clinic. He looked at his key fob and stopped before pressing the lock button. The idea of pressing the lock button, which would cause the car to emit that chirp-chirp sound, seemed rude to him. He turned around to manually lock the car, not noticing the small child who had crept up behind him. Both tumbled to the hard concrete, with Charles instinctively shifting his body to protect the child from harm. A lady broke free from the line of people outside the clinic and ran towards them.

"Bobby!" she scolded. "I told you not to bother that man." She bent down to scoop up the child, a boy with smooth, dark brown skin, eyes with black clear pupils, and long lashes. His hair looked freshly cut, cleanly cropped on the sides, with a small scroll cut above his right ear. What a beautiful child, Charles thought.

"I'm so sorry, Sir," the woman said. She reached out a hand. "Let me help you."

Charles accepted the outstretched hand with his own, but then immediately pulled it back. The woman's eyes widened, then stopped when she heard his wince of pain.

She narrowed her eyes to get a closer look. "Oh dear," she said. "You're bleeding. And a lot."

In trying to save the young boy, Charles had turned his left side towards the sidewalk and fell on some jagged chunks of a broken beer bottle. He looked at his upper arm to see at least four pieces of thick brown glass sticking through his white linen shirt and into this brown flesh. Blood was soaking the rest of his shirt's arm and dripping onto the dirty concrete below. "Oh shit," he whispered. And then he passed out.

.   .   .

Charles Bingley shut his eyes a second after he opened them. The harsh light blinded him and caused his head to throb. Eyes closed, he didn't move and tried to calm his mind. At the present moment, he understood more about where he was not than where he was. For example, he knew by the feeling of confinement and the hardness of the surface, that he was not at home in his own bed. The cacophony of voices and unfamiliar sounds around him were also proof that he was somewhere other than his lovely, quiet, and luxurious mansion.

"Don't touch me!"

"Calm down, we are not going to hurt you!"

"Devils! All of you!"

"He's spitting. Go get another orderly, stat!"

Now he knew he wasn't at home. Unless his sister or Darcy were watching some subpar medical drama.

He tried to shift a bit to get more comfortable, causing his left arm to hit something. The pain was slight but immediate. He squeezed his eyes tighter when it all came back to him. The last thing he remembered was a bright-faced little boy—almost cherub-like—and a woman, both looking down on him. And the blood. And the pain. Then darkness. He groaned when the realization of what had happened came back.

"Looks like the rich guy is up."

"Don't call him that," said another voice. This one female and gentle sounding.

Charles tightened up at the sound and could sense someone hovering over him. The faint smell of lavender came through, causing his eyes to flutter, but remain closed.

She reached up to place a gentle hand on his right shoulder. "Mr. Bingley? Can you hear me?"

Her voice wafted down upon him like a shower of serenity, washing away his previous feelings of unease and fear. He wanted to open his eyes, but was afraid of what he would see. How could any image match the beauty of that voice?

"You got a pretty nasty cut, Mr. Bingley, and you lost a bit of blood so you may feel woozy. Is there someone we can call?"

He wondered why they hadn't used his mobile phone, but then remembered he left it in the car. When he didn't answer, he felt her move away from him.

"Looks like the pain shot still has him knocked out. Let's give him another thirty minutes."

The other voice sounded irritated. "Our shift ended ten minutes ago, Miss Jane, and I cannot afford to piss my babysitter off again."

Miss Jane.

His savior sighed.

"I know, Karen. You go. I'll wait here until he wakes, and we can find someone to come pick him up."

"But you'll miss the luncheon," Karen, the gruff one, said.

"Do you know how many Delany convocation luncheons I've attended?" she laughed. "The one next year will be just like this one."

Charles tried to remain still. Luncheon? Was she due to be at the same event he was? And in what capacity? Student? Professor? Or, worse, the *wife* of a student or professor?

He must have appeared agitated because in the next moment, he felt a hand on his forehead, then move to the large patch on his arm. "No fever and no bleeding," Jane said.

Karen warned her not to stay too long, then he heard her leave.

Jane checked his IV and vital signs. He could hear the scritch-scratch of her pen, probably recording the data she had just collected. Then it was quiet. He counted to ten and slowly opened his eyes.

His eyelids fluttered open and closed for a few seconds until his pupils could adjust to the harsh lighting. *Cut his arm*, he thought, then wondered about the boy, hoping he was safe. From his vantage point, he could see a white wall covered with health posters. Warnings against drinking while pregnant, and smoking were the subjects of two of the posters. The others contained information on vaccines and where to get free condoms. They listed that one in about a dozen different languages. On the wall to his left hung a panoramic picture of what he assumed was the university, along with portraits of Martin Luther King and Malcolm X.

His back was stiff from lying on the hard hospital gurney. He scrunched his shoulders to ease the discomfort. It didn't work, so he tried moving his head from side to side and that's when he saw her.

"I thought you were awake."

The voice.

Before he could say anything, Jane walked towards him, a triumphant smile on her face. "No sense in trying to play possum here," she said, bending over to pull the top half of the gurney into an upright position. "We're pretty good at spotting the fakes." Once up, she slid her hand under the pillow and adjusted it. "Better?" she asked, taking a step back.

"Yes," Charles mumbled, and then, "Thank you."

Jane's face became serious. "Can you tell me your name?"

"Charles Bingley."

She nodded, then informed him of what had happened after the fall. "We here at Westside are used to bloody conflicts, so you couldn't have picked a better place to fall and cut your arm."

It was a joke, and normally he would have joined in on the fun, but he was having a hard time collecting his thoughts. Jane, he would later admit to himself, was the most beautiful woman he had ever seen. And he could tell right away that it was a beauty that went well below the surface. She practically glowed with goodness.

"How long have I been here?" he asked.

She checked his chart. "Almost two hours now. The sedative the doctor gave you knocked you out, I'm afraid. You were pretty agitated when they brought you in—"

"Who brought me in?"

"A few men from outside carried you inside," she answered. "Everyone was concerned."

"Everyone?"

"Well, everyone out on the street who witnessed what happened. You're quite the hero, you know. Protecting little Bobby from that glass the way you did."

Charles, grateful for the memory jog, asked if the boy was all right.

"Oh, yes," Jane replied. "Thanks to you."

Jane noticed and wondered about the wave of relief that came over his features. "Are you acquainted with the family?" she asked.

He shook his head. "Of course not. This is my very first time here. In this neighborhood." He was quiet after that, not sure what else he could say. Maybe his head was still woozy from whatever sedative they gave him, but he was having a hard time making sense of all that had happened and was happening.

He had a million questions, most of them *not* related to his care. He decided that the best way forward was to let her ask all the questions. When he answered, he would try not to sound stupid.

It took about five minutes for Jane to collect all the information she needed to complete his chart. His IV had emptied, so she busied herself with removing the needle and line. "I'll ask the doctor to come to give you a final look over and then you are free to go. But you shouldn't drive. Is there someone we can call to come to collect you?"

He said he could call his sister, which seemed to make her happy.

Before she left the room, he asked, "What about payment? Will you bill me?"

She gave a small laugh. "Why, Mr. Bingley, you are in luck. We offer all services at the Westside clinic free of charge."

After they properly discharged Charles, they took him to the waiting room. He sat in one of the few empty seats. On his left was a large Hispanic woman, a new mother. He realized this after she unceremoniously pulled a huge, engorged breast from its bra and presented it to her baby, who latched on and was now greedily and noisily enjoying his afternoon meal. On his right was an elderly

African American man who looked like he had worked hard labor every day of his life. Calloused hands clasped together on bony knees, his small head bent over, chin pressing into his chest. He was asleep.

Charles sat as still as possible, not wanting to disturb either of his seatmates. A sheath of papers lay in his lap, and the doctor had made them put his injured arm in a sling, securing it to his waist. "You'll need to be careful and keep that arm fairly stable for at least a week. You can come back then to have the stitches removed." Charles thought it was a bit much, but allowed them to secure his arm. It actually felt better that way.

The clock on the wall above the receptionist's window let him know just how late he was. He had left his mobile phone in the car, and there it was, probably with at least half a dozen missed calls from Darcy.

"OH MY GOD!"

The sound was unmistakable and when Charles turned towards the shrill voice, he saw his sister coming towards him, not bothering to hide the look of disgust on her face. He suddenly felt embarrassed.

"Are you insane, Charles? What in heaven's name are you doing here?"

He stood up, causing the sleeping man to wake. He yawned, glanced at the two people before him, snorted, then went back to sleep.

"Really, Charles," Caroline continued, "I knew you coming to this god-forsaken part of the country was a mistake, but had no idea you'd get into trouble so soon."

She looked around at the crowded waiting room and frowned. Later, Charles would wonder at the lack of empathy his sister displayed, but at that moment, Nurse Jane entered the scene, and all he wanted to do was get his sister out of there before she could say anything embarrassing or offensive.

"Is this your ride, then?" Jane asked. She had changed from her uniform and was wearing a lovely summer dress, off-white with a splattering of wildflowers. He thought how beautiful it looked against her soft brown skin. Her hair was still pulled up in a bun and he couldn't stop himself from imagining how it would look let loose and falling over her shoulders.

Caroline stepped back and glared at Jane. "Excuse me," she said. "I'm his sister; not his 'ride'."

If Jane found offense, she didn't let it show. "It's good you came," she said. "Your brother shouldn't drive. Probably for a few days, I'd say."

"And you are?" Caroline asked.

Charles answered for her. "This is Jane, my nurse. She took excellent care of me." He smiled at Jane and was happy to see a flustered look cross her features.

"Oh. The nurse."

"Yes," Jane said. "Your brother got a nasty cut on his upper left arm. The doctor cleaned it up and put in about six stitches." She stopped when Caroline gasped.

"But how ...?" Caroline began. Charles stopped her, saying that he would explain it all to her later. "Now, how are we getting home?" he asked, and then, "My car!"

He hadn't thought about his BMW since he entered the clinic, but he now remembered it was unlocked and with a flat tire. He knew enough about the neighborhood to know that a car like his was the same as dangling a bag of money in front of that crowd he saw outside the clinic. Jane must have noticed his concern. "Your car is safe and sound," she said. Then, motioning them to follow, she walked towards the clinic's doors. "After your brother's act of bravery, the neighbors took it upon themselves to be his personal property guard."

Outside, the first thing Charles noticed was that the crowd had thinned. His car hadn't moved. He looked towards it, half expecting the hubcaps to be gone and windows busted. But what he saw instead surprised and delighted him.

The little boy he had rescued came towards him, running at first, until a word of caution from his mom stopped him. "Slow down, Bobby! You want to knock him over again?"

Bobby stopped and turned back to his mother. "Sorry." He turned back towards Charles. "We've been watching your car for you," he said with a big grin.

Charles stepped towards him, but a whiff of wooziness stopped him. Jane immediately took his good arm to settle him. "Careful, now. You really are not tolerant of any type of sedatives, are you?"

"Of course, he isn't," Caroline said. "Our Charles can hardly handle a Tylenol."

Charles tried to hide his embarrassment. "I'm fine, really," he said. "Now, young man," he said, turning his attention back to the child. "You've been standing watch all this time?"

Bobby nodded. "Not just me," he said. "We all helped out." He waved to the small crowd. A young man came forward. "We all saw how you protected little Bobby here."

Charles tried to smile but had trouble taking in what they were saying. He was more used to being known as the party boy or Mr. Devil-May-Care. The young man pointed to the flat tire. "If you pop the trunk, I can put your spare on for you, if you like."

"That won't be necessary," Caroline said, stepping forward. "I've already arranged for someone—a professional—to take care of our car."

Charles was the only Bingley that noticed the sudden shift in the air, changing from friendly to offended. To his relief, the young man simplied smiled and laughed. "Whatever you say, ma'am."

Charles thanked him and everyone else before telling his sister it was time to go. "The car will be fine," he said to her protest. He nodded to Jane as they walked past her on the way to Caroline's Mercedes. It was a silent drive back to Netherfield.

CHAPTER 6

After her third turn through the luncheon area, Lizzy gave up on finding Jane, most likely because of an emergency at the clinic. She would get the details at home.

With no one else she was particularly interested in seeing, she made her way to the table her family was occupying, taking a detour to the dessert tent.

Grabbing a small, clear plastic plate, she hovered around the tiered dessert trays, trying to decide between the eclairs and petite fours, when she looked up and saw Dr. William Darcy on the other side of the table. His hands were empty, making her wonder what he was doing there. She offered a small welcome smile before returning her attention to the sweets.

"There you are, Dr. Darcy." Dr. Lucas's familiar voice came from behind Lizzy, who turned to greet him. "And our Miss Lizzy—I mean—Professor Bennet," he said with a smile. Dr. Lucas reached out to give her a quick hug. "Another year, another opening convocation, eh, Lizzy?"

"Yep. And they get better each year."

"Hilarious," he replied, joining in the joke. He looked across the table at Darcy. "And have you met our visiting professor, Dr. Darcy? We are expecting great things from him and the other econ professors."

Lizzy shifted her plate to her other side, and held out her right hand for him to shake. He hesitated a few seconds, making her wonder if he would return the gesture.

He did, although his grip was what people would call weak. He mumbled a "Hello," and quickly dropped her hand. It was an awkward moment.

"Professor Bennet is another one of our campus jewels," Dr. Lucas said. "Her studies in hip hop and rap culture are innovative *and* have helped to increase enrollment."

Before Lizzy could rebuke the compliment, she noticed a look on Dr. Darcy's face; a mix of surprise and disappointment.

"Hip. Hop," he said, slowly. "Are you that professor whose studies were featured in *Jet Magazine*?"

Lizzy set her plate down. She immediately recognized the sarcasm in his voice and prepared herself.

"Yes, I am," she replied. "Did you read it? The article?"

Dr. Darcy grimaced. "I'm afraid not. I only *heard* about the article. *Jet Magazine* isn't my usually reading material."

Lizzy waited. The next thing people typically said was that they either found her studies interesting and groundbreaking or, from the braver ones, misguided and destructive. She wondered where her new colleague landed. Before he could respond, Dr. Lucas spoke up. "It was a tough sell at first, and most of the older faculty were against it, but given the Bennet's dedication and history with Delany, we all thought we'd give it a chance." He winked at Darcy. "Especially if it brings the freshmen."

The shift in Darcy's expression stopped Dr. Lucas' chuckling.

"I don't see how enticing young Black minds to forgo serious study is funny," Dr. Darcy said, his face tight and serious. "Institutions such as this need to make sure they attract the best and brightest, but for the *right* reasons."

"Right reasons?" Elizabeth said. "And what reasons would those be, Dr. Darcy?"

"Studies that can guarantee a solid future; even better if it's one that can help others up the economic ladder."

"Do you have any idea how many young, creative, and intelligent young Black men *and* women have been able to rise from poverty through the music industry?" she asked.

Darcy met her gaze. "And are *you* aware of how many of these so-called talented men end up right back where they started because of drugs, crime, and an overall lack of discipline?"

Dr. Lucas stepped back a few steps, as if searching for a way to leave unnoticed. Although a near-perfect North Carolina late summer day, the tension in the air brought a sudden chill to the scene. Professors and staff tried to look, but without looking.

"Are you kidding me?" Lizzy gasped. "Whose side are you on?"

"I'm not on anyone's side," he said. "Unless common sense has a side," he added.

It was Lizzy's turn to take a step back. But she wasn't looking for a way out; she was steadying her stance while preparing to strike back. But before that, Dr. Wright came in from the left, slipped her arm around Lizzy's waist, and gently guided her away, saying: "Dr. Tennyson wants to see us about the travel budget. Now."

Lizzy immediately recognized the ploy and attempted to turn back, but then she caught sight of her mother and two younger sisters coming toward her. "Oh great," she said. "First Doctor Know-It-All, and now my mother, Mrs. Why-Aren't-You-Married-Yet." She gave her friend a wry smile. "It's turning out to be another great convocation!"

Before Dr. Wright could respond, Mrs. Bennet was upon them. "Was that Dr. Darcy I saw you talking to?" she whispered. Before Lizzy could answer, her mother continued, raining questions on her: "What's he like? Did he say anything about how he likes Delany? Maybe something about wanting to stay longer, or permanent? Did he mention that Bingley fellow? Is he here?" She stopped to crane her neck and survey the crowd.

"Mother," Lizzy began. "The only question I can answer is the first one. He's a jerk."

"Oh, hush! You say that about any man. What? Did he say something negative about your precious hip-hop?"

"Mother!" Lizzy said, looking embarrassed.

"Oh Lizzy," her mother responded. "You know I think you're the smartest professor on this campus, and I support you one hundred percent—in your studies. But when it comes to the opposite sex, well, even you would have to admit that ..." her voice trailed off, but her raised eyebrows and sad smile completed the sentiment.

Dr. Wright suppressed a laugh. She and the other female professors often teased their younger colleague about her lack of game and hustle with dating and romance.

Lizzy turned to glare at her friend. "Et tu, Brute?"

Lydia interrupted Dr. Wright's defense. "Brute? I thought your first name was Laura?"

Kitty shook her head. "It's from Shakespeare, Lydia." Before she could explain more, which really wouldn't have helped anyway, they were joined by Mr. Bennet.

"What's so funny?" he said, walking up to his wife's side. "Oh, never mind," he adding quickly, cutting Kitty off before she could offer an answer. Lizzy was the only one to notice the flash of disappointment on her sister's face.

Mr. Bennet turned to Lizzy. "I saw you talking to that Darcy prof," he winked. "He's something, isn't he?"

Mrs. Bennet's eyes widened. "Oh, husband. If you're going to say anything, talk to her about the importance of first impressions. Especially with men like him."

Mr. Bennet sighed. "First of all, this isn't the 18th century. Women don't need to worry about things like that anymore. And second, our daughter is here to teach young minds, not chase after rich Black men."

"Oh, for goodness' sake," his wife said, laying a hand on her forehead. "No one said anything about chasing."

For the second time, Lizzy felt many eyes upon her. She knew from experience that her mother was on the verge of one of her rants, so to avoid any more embarrassment, she intervened. "That's enough." She reached for her mother's elbow. "Let's go over to the dessert tent and see if there's anything left."

Her father stepped aside, a conspiratorial smile on his face, as Lizzy guided her mother past him. She tried to return his look with a stern stare, but her smiling eyes gave her away.

"That man is going to be the death of me," Mrs. Bennet said, grabbing a plate and reaching for the last of the mini chocolate eclairs.

"I know, Mother. I know," Lizzy said, looking around.

"He left," Dr. Wright said. Lizzy hadn't noticed her following them back to the dessert tent.

"Who cares?" Lizzy said, stuffing a plump red grape in her mouth.

CHAPTER 7

Darcy pulled into Netherfield's circular driveway and turned off the ignition. "You have some explaining to do, my friend," Darcy said into the evening air as he walked towards the massive home. After leaving the luncheon, he headed to his office to get some work done. He welcomed the silence and alone time but found it hard to concentrate. *Why did she have to be* that *professor?*

"Oh, William. You're home." He looked up to see a hurried and distressed Caroline walking towards him. His annoyance disappeared. "What is it?" he said, walking towards her.

"Charles," she began, in a voice that caused him to be even more concerned.

"He had a horrible accident this afternoon. I got the call just as I was heading out to the university," Caroline continued with a rush of breath. "How was that, by the way?"

"What accident? And why didn't you call me?" Darcy asked, getting impatient.

"At some third-world-like clinic downtown," she said, hand to her chest and clutching a string of imaginary pearls. "And, as you know, the cellphone reception is horrible. Those expensive devices are no better than paperweights out here." She sighed. "But no worries, all the phone lines will be in next week."

Darcy apologized for his curtness. "But where is he? Is he all right?"

"Upstairs," she said. "Resting."

Darcy turned around and made a direct line toward the stairs. He took them two at a time, turned left at the first landing, and continued up.

"Charles?" he said, opening the bedroom door. He entered the dark room and walked towards the bed. There he saw his oldest and dearest friend, sound asleep. He could see a large bandage on his upper left arm. On the nightstand was a glass of water and a prescription bottle. Painkillers or antibiotics, he assumed. There was enough moonlight for Darcy to see his friend's face, but what he saw surprised him. He bent down for a closer look. Charles was indeed asleep, his mouth pulled up in a gentle and sweet smile. Like a child dreaming of Christmas morning. So much for a terrible accident, Darcy thought, leaving the room.

Instead of going downstairs and conversing again with Caroline, he went to his bedroom. Getting undressed, he decided he could wait until tomorrow to get the details, and besides, Bingley didn't look traumatized. Just the opposite.

In the shower, his mind turned to the convocation and Professor Elizabeth Bennet. He remembered the nickname Dr. Lucas had uttered. "Lizzy," he whispered into the stream of hot water. He smiled. He saw her dark brown eyes, framed by long lashes. Her face was made up perfectly to his taste, light and with an accent on the eyes that reminded him of the ancient queens of Egypt. Suddenly, he saw himself lying next to her, gazing into those eyes, her soft lips inches away, so close and waiting.

A sudden rush of cold water snapped him from his daydream. "Arggg!!" He groped for the knobs and turned off the water. Grabbing a towel, he blamed the pulsating heat in his nether regions on his recent celibacy and not that Lizzy woman. "Don't be ridiculous," he muttered, walking towards his bed.

. . .

Lizzy, Mary, Lydia, Kitty, and the parents entered their home to find their eldest daughter and sister sitting at the kitchen table in front of a bowl of rocky road ice cream.

"There you are," said Lizzy. She stepped out of her shoes and moved to join her sister, stopping by the kitchen counter to grab a spoon.

"You all right, there?" Mr. Bennet asked from the doorway. Jane had been at the clinic for almost four years, and when the stress of it got to be too much, she turned to ice cream, her calming agent.

"Oh, goodness, Jane. If you don't catch some deadly disease from that place, you'll probably develop diabetes from all that ice cream," Mrs. Bennet said. She turned the fire on under the kettle. "At least have some peppermint tea along with it." Peppermint tea was Mrs. Bennet's cure-all.

Lizzy dipped her spoon into the bowl, clinking with her sister's spoon as she scooped out a portion for herself. They smiled at each other. "I'm all right, Mother. The shift wasn't as bad as it was long. We had a very … unusual patient come in towards the end of my shift."

"Is that why you missed the convo?" Lizzy asked.

Jane nodded. "How was it?"

Before anyone could answer, Mrs. Bennet launched into a retelling that skimmed over the speeches and luncheon and landed right on Dr. Darcy. "And guess who had him as a captive audience?"

"I—" Jane began.

"Lizzy! Why, they spent almost a half hour together!"

Lizzy choked on the spoonful of rocky road sliding down her throat. "It wasn't a half-hour, mother. More like 5 minutes." She set the spoon on the table. "Five *awful* minutes," she added with a grimace.

"Awful?" Mrs. Bennet asked. "What could be awful about talking to a rich, single, Black man like him?"

Both sisters glared at their mother. She swished away the condemnation with a wave of her hand. "All I'm saying is that you missed an opportunity to make a good impression on him."

"And why do I need to make a 'good impression' with him or anyone else, for that matter?" Lizzy asked. She placed a gentle hand on her middle section. The ice cream was making her queasy.

The kettle whistled, and Lizzy watched as her mother took mugs from the cabinet and prepared the tea. She talked as she worked, reminding her daughters of how it wasn't a crime to seek male companionship. "You two like to talk all proud and huffy about how you 'don't need a man.' Well, guess what? No woman does." She set the mugs of steaming tea in front of her two eldest. Lizzy's nostrils filled with the scent of peppermint, and she immediately felt her tummy ache melting away.

Mrs. Bennet turned to leave the kitchen. "But mark my words. One day soon, both of you will find yourself *wanting* a man." She winked. "Come talk to me then," she said with a thick layer of sarcasm.

Lizzy wrapped her hands around the warm mug and took a sip. She was curious who Jane's unusual patient was, but the two would talk about that later.

Jane finished her ice cream and took the bowl and spoons to the sink. "So, how was he?" she asked, while placing the dishes in the dishwasher.

"Who?" Lizzy said.

Jane turned to face her. A sly smile appeared on her face. "You know who, Lizzy. You try to play all cool around our mother, but come on, even you must be a *little* curious about him."

Lizzy leaned back in her chair and tilted her face toward the ceiling. Dr. Darcy appeared before her eyes and the first thing she noticed was his condescending smirk. "I *was* curious, but then I met him, and all that curiosity washed away." She lifted her arm and mimicked waves floating over the sea. Jane rejoined her at the table. "Tell me." she said.

Although Lizzy had just reminded her mother that her encounter with Dr. Darcy was less than five minutes, it took her almost 10 minutes to relate to Jane how awful it was.

"Common sense," Lizzy scoffed. "How about common courtesy?"

"Maybe he was nervous," Jane offered. "He was meeting everyone for the first time."

Lizzy got up and took their empty mugs to the sink. "People like him don't get nervous, Jane. They make it their business to make *others* nervous, but not them."

Jane cocked her head to the side. "And were you? Nervous?"

A short laugh burst past Lizzy's lips. "No! Why would I be? It wasn't *my* first day." She folded her arms and laid them across her chest.

Jane looked at her but didn't respond. Instead, she got up and stretched. "Well, that's it for me. I'm beat."

Walking up the stairs, Lizzy reminded Jane about her unusual last-minute patient, but Jane shrugged it off. "I'll tell you later," she said, entering her bedroom. "I'm about to collapse."

Lizzy blew her sister a goodnight kiss and headed toward her room. She passed Lydia and Kitty's and peeked in. They were sitting together, heads bent, looking at the small screen of a pager. Lizzy walked in. "Where did you get that?" she asked, startling them both.

A look of fear flashed on Kitty's face. "Don't tell Dad," she pleaded.

"He specifically told you not to get one of these." She reached out and snatched the small device from Lydia's hand. "Give it back!" Lydia yelled, groping for her sister's hand.

"Beepers are for drug dealers and certain types of ladies," Lizzy told them, repeating the reasons their father had forbidden the device.

"And doctors," Lydia said with a pout.

"Okay. As soon as you get your medical degree, you can have one."

"It's not funny! Mom said I could keep it, so hand it back!" Lydia held out her hand, palm up.

This new information momentarily shocked Lizzy. Their mother was forever spoiling Lydia, even going against her husband's wishes. Even though she believed Lydia, she was still hesitant to hand it back. During the past year, Lydia has displayed an incredible lack of good judgment. Her obsession with boys, clothes, and her social life took precedence over everything else, including school and family harmony. Like this beeper. She had to have known that eliciting her mother's support would cause an uproar, but she did it anyway. Lizzy imagined her whining to their mother about how she had to have one, and if she didn't, she would just die!

"You had no business going behind our father's back to get this," Lizzy said. "It's time you grow up, Lydia. Have you even looked at your class schedule yet?"

Lydia threw her head back and groaned. "Oh god! School! School! School! That's all you think about. Well, if you haven't noticed, there's more to life than school."

Before Lizzy could respond, she felt the beeper vibrate, signaling a new message. Lizzy read *411* on the small screen before Lydia snatched it back. The grin on Lydia's face as she read the message caused Lizzy to worry more. "I don't know what you two are up to, but you better start rearranging your priorities." She turned to leave. "Those beeper boys you mess with will not pay your rent or put food on your table."

Lydia tossed her beeper on the bed and turned her head with an elaborate flip of braids. "They will for me, Miss Lizzy-girl. Just you wait and see."

CHAPTER 8

Martin Delany University campus takes up about 250 acres, spread out over hills and a flat section. The section on the hillside, upper campus, is to the south; the lower campus, the flat section, is located to the north. They built lower campus first, so it holds the older, history-filled buildings and archives. The Bennet's home is also on the north-east side of lower campus, close to the athletic fields and the dance and music centers. A short walk from Longbourne is the liberal arts building where Lizzy works. The trek from lower to upper campus is steep, and an escalator went in about 20 years ago to help ease the walk. On lower campus, Determination Drive is about a quarter mile from Longbourne to the west. It is also where the frat and sorority houses live.

Delany's sororities and fraternities have proven to be a blessing and a curse. It was a blessing when one of the first houses organized a massive fundraiser that built the campus' first auditorium. Other houses have had members become successful business leaders and politicians, elevating Delany's stature and reputation. On the negative side, the administration had to come down heavy for a few years because of overzealous hazing rituals, eventually expelling one house because of under-age drinking and sexual harassment allegations.

In the fall of 1999, Determination Drive was all a buzz with the turning of the century and the party that had to go along with it. Dr. Lucas sent out letters warning fraternities and sororities that Y2K was not an excuse to disregard rules, civility, and more importantly, Delany pride. Of course, that stopped no one.

Fraternity row was removed from the Bennet family, both physically and socially. The first houses, in a misguided attempt to reverse negative stereotypes and labels, instituted their own form of discrimination and cast the Bennets (along with other working-class Blacks) to the lower rungs of society and treated them not much better than post-civil war whites. Generations passed and the divide slowly dissolved, particularly during the Civil Rights Movement. Now, in the year 1999, students, staff, and the community recognize and appreciate the history and dedication the Bennets bring to Martin Delany University. But like most things, the stings from the past linger beneath the surface, which is why Mr. and Mrs. Bennet still warn their children not to trust those frat boys.

Kitty conveniently forgot those warnings a few weeks before the opening convocation when a new, fresh-faced frat boy walked into the yogurt shop where she worked part time. Kitty graduated high school the year before and began at Delany, exactly like every other Bennet. But unlike most of the Bennets before her, college life was a difficult transition. Too difficult, and at the advice of her counselors, she left after the first semester, enrolled in junior college, and started working part time. For the first time, Kitty was spending more time away from the house and her younger sister. She was making new friends, saving her money, and feeling proud of her accomplishments, even if they weren't academic. The afternoon when the young, charismatic Darren, of the newly formed Mashujaa Fraternity, walked into the yogurt shop, the instant connection surprised her. Pretty soon, he became a regular.

Kitty had entertainment that did not include her younger sister, and she wanted to keep it that way. Which she did. For a while. It ended when Lydia discovered the young lovers one night when she surprised her sister at work. Kitty's shift was just about over, and Darren was waiting to walk her home. Being Lydia, she used this discovery to her full advantage. For years she had been eager to get to know frat life, and now she finally had a way. Using the threat of telling their parents, Lydia got Kitty and Darren to introduce her to his frat brothers and even to the house on frat row. Her sister's obsession embarrassed Kitty; Darren thought it was cute. "She reminds me of my kid sister," he told Kitty one afternoon. Getting into an argument over Lydia was the last thing she wanted, so she let it drop. She was beginning to worry about Lydia. Her boy-craziness was over the top sometimes.

Mashujaa Fraternity received their preliminary charter two years ago, but the house was still unsure of which direction it would take. One side pushed the house to stand up to its namesake, the Swahili word for heroes, and focus on cultivating brave men willing to fight for freedom and equality through education and scholarship.

The other side did not completely object to that idea, but they also pushed for the party-house label, claiming they could be both. This side was behind the over-the-top Y2K celebration and one brother, Taylor, was the reason Lydia owned a beeper. He gave it to her, saying that he needed someone with "inside information" on Delany. "Your pops knows everything about that campus," he had told her with a wink and a grin. "You can be our spy."

A week before the opening convocation and after Lydia bullied her way into going, the two sisters walked to the Mashujaa Frat House.

"Well, well, well. The lovely Bennet sisters are once again gracing us with their presence." Taylor stepped aside with a bow and waved the two inside. Female guests were allowed on the first floor, between the hours of 10AM and midnight. Lydia giggled as she walked through the door and into the large living room. "Why thank you, Taylor. Glad to see some men still have manners."

Kitty followed, trying to hide the flush of embarrassment as she took in the rest of the young men strewn about the living, or hang out room as they liked to call it. She didn't see Darren anywhere. "He's not here," Taylor said, closing the door and answering the question Kitty was too shy to ask. Taylor winked as he walked past. "But he'll be back soon."

"Where did he go?" Lydia said with a slight pout. Then turning to her sister. "Didn't you tell him we were coming?"

Kitty's breath stopped at the rebuke. Not here two minutes and Lydia was already crossing a line by trying her hardest to appear the older, more responsible sister. Kitty sucked in her breath and, once again, regretted letting Lydia blackmail herself into this part of her life. Lydia shouldn't even *be* in this house, let alone have a beeper given to her by a frat boy.

"Don't sweat it, Kit," Taylor told her. "He'll be back soon."

"We sent him on a very special mission." That was Douglas, a senior and the house vice president. He entered the hang-out room, holding a bowl of cereal in one hand and a spoon in the other. He sauntered over to a recliner tucked in a corner and plopped down. Douglas was a local boy and was well acquainted with the Bennets. He knew Lydia was only 17 and her frequent visits to the house were a recipe for disaster, but his girlfriend, an acquaintance of Lydia's, had convinced him to stay quiet. He did, however, warn his men to be careful around her. "We do not want to give them any excuses to expel us," he told them.

Douglas slurped down his cereal, ignoring the visitors, and Taylor waved for the two girls to join him in the back room.

"Did you get my message?" he asked, once they were out of sight of Douglas and the others. Lydia nodded and took the beeper out of her bag. "I don't know if I can get my dad to give me the key to the labyrinth gardens," she said. "He's pretty protective of that area."

Taylor's lips spread into a sly grin as he moved closer to Lydia. He placed a hand on her waist. "Oh, com'on, Lydia. My girl! Don't let me—us—down."

The garden and key demands were new to Kitty. She asked what the two were talking about.

Taylor and Lydia blurted out something about planning a community event for Y2K. "Frat row is going crazy trying to outdo each other," Taylor said. He winked at Lydia before continuing. "But Mashujaa is the only house with help from the lovely Bennet sisters."

Lydia let loose one of her signature giggles, complete with a hair flip.

Kitty grabbed her by the arm and pulled her away. "Are you crazy, Lydia?" she hissed. "Father will never let them use his garden!"

Lydia pulled away. "It's not *his* garden, Kitty. It belongs to the school and the Shujaas are students, so, technically, the garden is more theirs than Dad's." A smug smile spread across Lydia's face; her reasoning impressed her.

Before anyone could respond, Darren walked in. "There you are," he said, walking towards Kitty. "What's wrong?" The tension in the air didn't go unnoticed. Before Kitty could say anything, Taylor stepped forward. "Nothing, man. Did you get him?"

"Oh, yeah," Darren answered. "He's in there talking to Douglas."

"Sweet!"

They returned to the hang out room to see the same group of brothers, and an addition.

As Lydia and Kitty walked into the room, the stranger turned towards the group. His eyebrows raised at the sight of the two girls. "You didn't tell me this was a co-ed house," he said to no one in particular.

Douglas stood up. "It isn't, and the ladies were just leaving." He nodded his head towards the door, a sign to Darren and Taylor to escort them out.

Lydia stopped them at the door. "But don't we even get an introduction?" she asked with a pout so fake and exaggerated it embarrassed Kitty. The newcomer, however, didn't seem to mind. He stepped forward, hand outstretched. "Of course," he crooned. "Wickham. George Thaddeus Wickham, at your service."

Wickham was another one of Taylor's great ideas. He had heard from a friend of a friend that George Wickham could teach them a step routine sure to win. He flew out from Los Angeles and all he required were travel expenses and a percentage of the winnings. "I don't win unless Mashujaa wins," he told them. Leadership agreed, figuring that all they had to lose was the price of a plane ticket.

As the sisters walked back to Longbourne, Kitty tried to get Lydia to tell her more about what Mashujaa wanted with the garden. "You got to know Dad will not let them stomp, perform, or do anything in that garden. Even *you* know that much."

"No one's talking about doing the routine in the garden, Kitty. Don't be stupid. That Wickham sure was fine, didn't you think? Probably not." She laughed. "The only guy you notice these days is your precious Darren."

CHAPTER 9

Campus was open with fully staffed offices on the Saturday before the start of the semester, so Lizzy headed out early. She left everyone sleeping, except her father and Jane, who had also headed off to work. Walking through the quad, she decided against telling her father about the beeper. Partly because she couldn't see how the device could cause any actual trouble for her sisters. She also didn't want to do anything that could add more tension to the house. Especially between her parents. They loved and cared for each other, but lately, it seemed like their disagreements came more frequently. The other night, her mother accused her husband of ignoring her. Again. "You're always staring off into space," she said. "Did you even hear what I just said?" He hadn't. In the past, when this happened, he would divert with a sly smile and quick apology. But now, he seemed to get agitated more easily. Lizzy could tell something was wrong, and as she left the house the next morning, she decided she would go by his office later that day and see what she could find out.

"I hope you have a syllabus in there." Midge Jackson, one of the liberal arts secretaries, stood up from behind her desk to greet Professor Bennet as she walked into the office. She smiled, patted her bag, and nodded. "All done." She reached inside and handed her the folder. "Not too late, I hope."

Midge took the folder and chuckled. "Not too early either."

Lizzy walked past her to her office. "Thank you," she whispered in a sing-song voice. This was her third year, and she had gained the reputation of being the last one to turn her syllabus in for copying. Paperwork was the least favorite part of her job. She loved meeting the students, lecturing on the history of rap and hip hop, and introducing new ways of thinking. As she unlocked the door to her office, Midge returned the sing-song voice as she reminded the professor of another responsibility. "And don't forget to sign up for a committeeeeee!"

Although she couldn't see, Professor Bennet knew a devilish grin accompanied the reminder. Besides being notoriously late with paperwork, the hip-hop professor's reputation for avoiding committee work was also well known. Most were a waste of time; she'd much rather prep for classes or drive to the city to check out a new artist. But no, as part of their contract, each faculty member was required to serve on at least one campus committee a semester. Dr. Lucas had warned her at the convocation to not try to "shirk her responsibility" this semester, so she closed her office door and walked down the hall to the bulletin board that held the committee sign-up list. As expected, all the slightly interesting or low-stress ones filled quickly. She scanned the list and found two with open slots: Campus Beautification and one for developing and coordinating Y2K activities. *Committee members and student representatives will oversee the production and execution of the Y2K celebration.* Sounds like three months of arguing, she thought. The appealing aspect was that the committee would have student representatives. She enjoyed working with students and thought of herself as a staunch ally. And besides, nothing was interesting about the Beautification Committee. Her father and his crew kept the campus beautiful enough for her. Reaching for the pen that dangled from the black piece of yarn, she inked her name into the last slot under Y2K Committee. She let the pen drop and wondered who else from other departments had signed up. Her mind immediately fell on Dr. Darcy, but just as quickly, dismissed it. She doubted the precious professor was even required to do committee work. "The only committee he'd be successful at would be a committee of one," she mumbled as she headed back to her office. She had less than one week before classes began. No time to waste wondering about Dr. Darcy.

She spent the next few hours organizing her lecture notes and updating her PowerPoint slides. She was beginning to think about lunch when her phone rang. The person on the other end surprised her. "Father?" Before she could panic, thinking some emergency had occurred, he asked her to join him for lunch. "If you're not too busy," he added.

Her eyes scrunched together. "Lunch?"

He chuckled. "Yeah. You know that meal in between breakfast and dinner?"

"I know; I'm just surprised by the invitation. Tell me when and where."

Thirty minutes later, Lizzy and her father sat down on a bench in the Ancestors Garden. Since none of the dining facilities were open, Mr. Bennet drove to a nearby sandwich shop and returned with turkey sandwiches, chips, and sodas. "And for dessert," he said with a grin before presenting her with a giant chocolate cookie.

"Is this a cookie or a plate?" Lizzy laughed, holding the enormous treat with both hands.

He sat down next to her and began unwrapping his lunch. "Let's not tell your mother, ok?"

They spent the next few minutes in benign back-and-forth chatter. Father asked how her pre-semester plans were going; daughter asked about his new hires and shared which professors were returning, which were not, and so on.

About 15 minutes in, Lizzy suspected her father had something else on his mind. He kept pausing his meal to gaze around the garden. "The Japanese Andromeda looks good. Should have a lot of blossoms soon. The cuttings on the east side are doing well too," he said.

Lizzy turned to look at her father. "You don't sound too happy about that." His pause before answering caused her heart to skip a beat. Her dad rewrapped his half-eaten sandwich and laid it on the spot between them on the bench. He took a deep breath. "I've got to tell you something, Lizzy, but you need to promise me you'll keep it to yourself. Well, between you and Jane, of course. I know better than to think you could keep something from her."

Lizzy leaned forward. "You're worrying me, Dad. What is it?"

Mr. Bennet took a deep breath and, on the exhale, relayed his conversation with Dr. Lucas. He told her how he felt betrayed and helpless. "After all these years. Generations! They're just gonna end it all like it was nothing."

Lizzy waited for more. Surely her father wasn't telling her that Delany was getting rid of him? She shook her head. "Tell me again what Dr. Lucas said. Surely you heard him wrong?"

He swore, something he rarely did, telling Lizzy he had not heard wrong.

"When do they expect you to leave?" she asked, hardly believing the words coming out of her mouth. Bennet and Delany were practically synonymous. They were the Delany Bennets, after all.

He looked at his watch before answering. "This will be my last year here, Lizzy."

She wanted to ask, *and then what,* but remained quiet. She could hear that he was holding back tears. Her poor father. She stood up. "This doesn't have to be the end of it," she said, turning to fight mode. "Let me ask around and see what's up." She crossed her arms and squinted her eyes as she looked over the garden like she was trying to see the tiny insects that crawl among the leaves and branches. Mr. Bennet stood up, too. "Don't do that," he told her. "Dr. Lucas said he had already tried to dissuade the board. It's over." His shoulders slumped for a second, but then he straightened back up and looked at his daughter. "I didn't tell you this so you could fight for me, Lizzy. I'm telling you because I want you to be careful. Look out for yourself now. This new board doesn't give a damn about tradition or respect. All they care about is the bottom line. So, you be careful, Lizzy."

"Careful? Did Dr. Lucas say anything about me?"

Her father took his daughter's hand in his own. He knew her classes were popular with the students and that the other faculty liked her. But he also knew that her area of study was always under scrutiny. His second eldest had a hard pride streak that caused her to be less than cordial whenever someone questioned her. Now wasn't the time to ruffle feathers. "No one has said anything, sweetheart. All I'm saying is that it wouldn't hurt you to be a bit more ... patient when others question your classes." Before she could offer a defense, he raised his hand to stop her. "I saw how you reacted to that Darcy at the convo, Lizzy. All he was doing was stating his opinion. The University put out a lot to get him here, and I am sure they don't appreciate him being attacked by one of their own."

"I didn't attack—"

"He's a nice enough fellow. And so is his friend, Charles Bingley."

Lizzy crossed her arms and took a step back. "Father, what are you up to? You didn't just go out to Netherfield because of Mother, did you?"

Mr. Bennet suppressed the urge to tell her that his wife never made him do anything. Instead, he explained how he went out as a welcoming and neighborly gesture and that he approves of Dr. Darcy.

"Approve of him for *what*?"

He looked at his daughter. She really was beautiful. And smart. Sometimes too smart for her own good. He shrugged. "For whatever."

CHAPTER 10

Darcy's eyes blinked open before the alarm could wake him up. He had a restless night. Worrying about his friend, beginning classes, researching at a new university, and a certain professor. He threw back his bedcovers, swung his legs to the side, and sat up. He reached for his day planner, that he always kept on his nightstand, and flipped it open. Thankfully, the only thing he had scheduled was a committee meeting in the afternoon. He had intentionally left the day open. Grad students had to apply to get into his program, and they impressed him with the quality of the writing, calculations, and insights, making him feel he would have to up his game. His great-aunt, Catherine Deburge, chastised him when he had mentioned this to her.

"You have too much of your Father in you," she said. "He never gave Black colleges any credit for all the good they do."

Darcy closed his planner and stood up to get dressed. If his father were here, there was no way Darcy would be at Delany, at least not without a lot of grief. Mr. Darcy was a proud man, who worked his way up from humble beginnings, all the while fighting against racist stereotypes, even the ones that were more a product of his imagination than reality. He had told his teenage son to not even think about going to an HBCU. "I didn't spend money on private schools and tutors so you can flush it all down the toilet by going to a subpar college."

Young Darcy just nodded, knowing it was useless to fight his father.

Dressed and ready for the day, he headed down to breakfast, but had stopped by Bingley's room, only to find it empty. He hoped nothing bad had happened during the night.

"Charles! Hold still!"

He entered the breakfast room to find Caroline hovering over her brother with a thermometer.

"For the last time, I do not have a fever." Charles pushed her hand away from his mouth. "Oh, there you are Darce. Sleep well?"

Darcy took a seat, and looked around for the coffee.

"Breakfast will be a bit late," Caroline sighed. She slid the unused thermometer back into its case and sat down. "Corrine is getting in late because she had to take her child to the clinic. For his shots. If she wasn't helping us out on a Saturday, I would have—"

"Darius?" Darcy asked.

"Who?"

"Her son, Darius. He's about two, so I guess that means time for booster shots," Darcy replied matter-of-factly.

Caroline lifted her eyebrows. "Well, aren't we getting chatty with the hired help? So unlike you, Darcy."

He shook his head. "Not really. Just a bit of polite chit-chat." He turned to Bingley, hoping to end any further speculation from her. Caroline liked to take ownership over his personal life. "No, I did not sleep well, but we can talk about that later. How are you feeling?"

Bingley muttered that he was fine, but was more interested in what his sister had said earlier. "Did she say what clinic?" he asked his sister.

"What?" Caroline said, clearly confused.

Charles leaned forward, looking impatient. "Corrine, the helper you hired. Did she happen to mention the name of the clinic?"

"Charles, really," Darcy said. "Sit down and stop waving that arm around. You'll tear those stitches or something worse."

"What does that have to do with anything right now?" Caroline said. She gave both men a strange look. "You two are starting to bother me with your obsession over the staff."

The room erupted into a splattering of voices, each trying to get their point across. Darcy insisted he was just being polite, "as anyone would be," to Corrine and that Caroline was "rude" by calling her "that girl."

Caroline attempted to defend herself with claims of being "too busy" to get to know every hired hand who traipsed through the house. And all Bingley wanted to know was the name of that clinic. The sound of the front door opening and closing put a halt to the conversation. A few seconds later, Corrine entered the breakfast room. She was slightly out of breath and her forehead revealed a sheen of perspiration.

"Sorry, I'm late. I set up everything last night, so it shouldn't take long." She walked past them with a nod and entered the kitchen.

Caroline began massaging her temples. "Remind me to *remind her* about the back entrance," she sighed. "And don't look at me like that. You both were thinking the same thing."

Before either of the men could respond, Corrine re-entered, carrying a tray with glasses and a carafe of orange juice. "How is Darius?" Darcy asked.

"Oh, he's fine. He *finally* stopped crying after like, *forever*." The smile on her face let them know she was more amused than upset with her young son.

Bingley cleared his throat. "Tell me, Corrine, the clinic …"

"Good old Westside. The only free clinic we have for 50 miles." She finished filling the glasses and set the carafe down. "Everyone was talking about you being there yesterday and how Jane was your nurse."

Charles's eyes widened. "You know that nurse. Jane?"

A dinging noise from the kitchen caused Corrine to turn to leave. "Of course," she answered before going through the swinging doors. "Like I told you yesterday. *Everyone* knows the Bennets."

Caroline's mouth fell open. "*That* was the famous Jane Bennet?"

Her brother nodded. "So, the rumors are true." He turned to Darcy. "She's beautiful and kind, and—"

"Oh, stop it, Charles. She was okay. And as for being 'kind,' I suspect she was just doing her job."

Darcy sipped his orange juice and hoped the coffee would come soon. The effects of his restless night were creeping in. "Well, that makes two of the famous Bennet Daughters now known. I had the … pleasure of meeting Professor Elizabeth Bennet yesterday at the luncheon."

Darcy didn't try to hide his disappointment at discovering her area of study. "No serious academic would even consider rap music a scholarly study," he concluded. "The mother looked like a piece of work, too." Corrine arrived with the coffee and they waited until she had departed to continue.

"Don't be so quick to judge, Darce," Charles offered. "Especially coming from someone who wouldn't know Ice Cube from MC Hammer."

"For your information, I know of—and have listened to—both of them, which only confirms my original objections."

Charles dismissed the comment. "Whatever Mr. Posh Professor." He turned to Caroline. "I need you to take me back to the clinic after breakfast."

Darcy sighed as brother and sister morphed, once again, into an argument. A wave of fatigue came, and he abruptly stood up, causing the siblings to pause and stare up at him. "As interesting as this discussion is, I need to get to the university." He dropped his napkin on the table and left, mumbling a simple goodbye.

"What about breakfast?" Caroline said to his retreating back.

He didn't answer, having suddenly lost his appetite.

Their bickering, though constant, always held love and respect and he knew either would do anything for the other, unquestionably. Times like these brought feelings of annoyance and a tinge of jealousy toward his companions, reminding him that he and Charles would always be *like* brothers, and he would always be an only child.

After Darcy left, Caroline and Charles continued bickering until Corrine returned with their breakfast. She apologized, but Charles cut her off. "No worries. Glad you could get your son taken care of. Tell me, was Nurse Jane there?"

Corrine nodded. "Oh yeah. Seems like every time I go, she's there. She must like nursing." Corrine set a plate down in front of Caroline. "I almost became a nurse. Finished a year and then got pregnant with Darius and, well, things got kinda complicated after that," she finished with a shrug.

Caroline looked over her plate of poached eggs and wheat toast. "Well, it's never too late. I'm sure we could find a scholarship for you if you ever decide to go back."

Corrine paused what she was doing and looked down at her employer, her face a mixture of curiosity and gratefulness. "You all are turning out to be the nicest rich Black folks I know."

Caroline's eyebrows rose. "And do you know many 'rich Black folks'?"

"Oh, not as rich as you all, but some professors at Delany have a few bucks, if you know what I mean."

Charles was busy scooping his bacon and cheese omelet into his mouth. The sight and aroma of the food reminded him of how little he had eaten yesterday. "So, back to the clinic," he said in between bites.

"They were packed, but Saturdays are like that. People must have been partying like it's 1999 last night!" She laughed at her joke.

"Too busy for visitors, I assume," Caroline said, eyeing her brother.

.   .   .

Jane walked into the Westside Clinic's breakroom to find it empty. Not surprising, she thought, heading for the refrigerator to retrieve her lunch. It had been a busy morning. So far, she had assisted in three stitch-ups, one broken arm, two diabetic emergencies, and right before her break, a stabbing victim, who had to be transferred to the Raleigh hospital. His injuries were more than the small clinic could handle.

As she lowered her body into one of the hard plastic chairs, she let out a soft sigh. Opening her yogurt, she reminded herself of how she had wanted to do nursing where she could make a difference. Many of her nursing school colleagues turned their newly graduated noses up at the prospect of working in a "ghetto clinic." But for Jane, it was the only place she had felt drawn to. Westside, or maybe working overseas with a relief organization. She grinned, imagining what her mother would say when she told her she was off to Africa to work in some remote village. Her mother already disapproved of the clinic job, but only partly because of the clientele. "You'll never meet a decent man at that place," she often remarked.

Well, you were wrong about that mother, she thinks, scraping the last bit of peach yogurt from the container. I'd say that the Bingley fellow was a very decent man. Right after the thought left her mind, the door opened. Expecting another co-worker, Jane turned with a smile towards the door, but seeing Mrs. Griff, the clinic's director, surprised her. She rarely visited the clinic, let alone the break room, and especially on a Saturday.

"There you are, Jane," she said, coming in and taking a seat. "I've been looking for you ever since I heard."

"Heard what?" Jane asked, a little taken aback by her abrupt entry. Mrs. Griff was part of the interview process, but after that, Jane rarely saw her. Not unless you count the yearly fundraising dinners.

Mrs. Griff leaned forward and grinned as if she was about to share a juicy secret with her best friend. "About Charles Bingley. Of the Bingley Wineries, among other things."

"Oh, him," Jane said.

"Yes, him. I heard you two had a friendly exchange." She grinned. "A *moment,* if you will."

"He came in with a pretty nasty cut that required stitches. If you want to call that a 'moment', then …"

A look of impatience flashed over Mrs. Griff's face. "You know what I mean, and don't tell me that you haven't thought about him since. It isn't every day that the Westside Clinic gets a visit from someone so prominent."

"Of course I've thought about him. Much like I do with my other patients," Jane answered.

Mrs. Griff leaned back in her chair, the girlfriend talk demeanor gone, replaced with *I'm your boss mode.* "Look, Jane, one reason we hired you was because of your connections to Delany and the community. We thought you would be good for fundraising and bringing some positive attention to the center. And—this is strictly off the record—we also found your … charm to be a valuable asset, too."

Jane didn't bother to hide her astonishment.

"Oh, don't look so surprised. Yes, you are an *excellent* nurse, one of the few with an MSN, and the clinic is a better place with you here, blah, blah, blah, and all that. But, *as you know*, it doesn't hurt to have someone with connections and … a bit more on our side."

More? Jane sat back and felt the yogurt churning in her stomach. What more could they possibly want? She worked almost as much overtime as everyone else. She always volunteered for weekend vaccination clinics, and she rarely, if ever, complained. And why would she? She loved her job, but something about this administrator's demeanor made her nervous.

She got up to throw her empty yogurt cup away. Her break was almost over, and she did not want to spend the rest of it trying to decipher Mrs. Griff's cryptic messages. "Well, it's been nice talking to you, but—"

"Look, Jane, I'll be blunt. If that Bingley fellow gets back in touch with you—and I bet he will—we'd all appreciate it if you could talk the clinic up. Talk about how hard everyone works and how important we are to the community."

Jane rinsed her spoon and placed it in the drainer. "I believe he knows that already. He was here long enough to see how things are."

Mrs. Griff clapped her hands together and grinned. "Perfect! Now all you'll need to do is get him to take out that wallet and write a nice big check."

Mrs. Griff's message was now crystal clear. Jane turned towards her and said, "You hired me as a nurse, not a fundraising ... floozy." She walked past her and to the door. "Now, if you'll excuse me, I have to get back to my patients." She headed for the breakroom door, but the ringing phone stopped her. "Hello, Nurse Jane speaking," she said into the receiver. Her eyes widened when the person on the other end identified himself. Her cheeks burned, and she resisted the impulse to ask him if his ears were burning. The bewildered look on her face caught Mrs. Griff's attention. "It's him, isn't it?" she whispered, getting up to stand next to Jane.

The rest of the interaction unfolded in a way that confounded and confused Nurse Jane Bennet, making her wonder later if it was all a dream.

.   .   .

Dr. Darcy parked at the university in his designated parking spot. Before going up to his office, his stomach reminded him of his missed breakfast. He took a quick detour and walked to the only coffee shop open on Saturday, praying they would have something decent to eat.

Upon entering, he had to admit that it was a nice little shop, reminding him of the places that lined University Ave. in Berkeley. His mouth watered at the selection of pastries and muffins. Even the smell of freshly brewed coffee piqued his interest.

A young man smiled at him from across the counter. "Good morning, Professor. What can I get you this fine morning?" Darcy pointed to a banana muffin and asked for a large coffee. "With half and half, please."

The bell jingled, announcing more customers. On seeing them, the counter server broke into a big smile. "Well, there he is! The man of the hour, day, and new century." The chuckle that came from this pseudo-celebrity pierced Darcy's ear. His body grew rigid as he felt his stomach tightening. Before he could turn to confirm his suspicion, the man in question sauntered up next to him, hand lifted to offer a high-five to the barista. Before any of that happened, he caught sight of Darcy and stepped back and away, as if he had just seen a rattlesnake.

The barista laughed. "Wooo, not cool, man! How you gonna do a brother like that?"

Neither Wickham nor Darcy heard this rebuke. They were too busy staring at each other, one in disbelief, the other in disgust. Although now full-gown adults, the two men had met before either could form full sentences. Darcy's father hired Wickham's dad as a junior accountant in his new firm. Both men were newly widowed, and a bond formed between them which included taking the boys to the park, swapping babysitting favors, joining the same pee wee sports teams, and other activities designed to keep the youngsters entertained and give the fathers some peace of mind. When the boys were ready for kindergarten, Mr. Wickham began to take advantage of the arrangement, leaving his son at the Darcy's for overnights, then weekends. Mr. Darcy was hesitant to say anything because he saw how much his own son enjoyed the company. Young William was a shy boy who would spend hours in a corner entertaining himself.

As the years passed, Mr. Darcy came to realize that his employee and friend possessed many talents. He was a spectacular accountant—when he did any accounting work. He was great at networking and bringing in new clients, but Mr. Darcy learned early to double-check the terms. Mr. Wickham tended to exaggerate the firm's assets or make deals that left a very thin profit margin. Finally, Mr. Darcy forbid him from going out and representing the company. The boys were almost teenagers by then and still remember the argument. Mr. Wickham left angry and, in line with another bad habit, drunk. He tried to take Young Wickham with him, but Mr. Darcy wouldn't let him. "Leave him with me," he said. "You're in no state to drive, let alone take a child with you."

The police officer who wrote up the accident called Mr. Wickham a "lucky drunk." The only property damage was to his car, and his injuries were minor. When Mr. Darcy took George back to his father, he pleaded with him to get help. He didn't and about two years later, his luck ran out.

He died without a will, so the court gave George Wickham to the only relative they could locate—a great-aunt he barely knew. Mr. Darcy took pity on both and told the aunt that he would pay for the boy to attend the same boarding school his son would attend the following school year. This arrangement excited William because he was secretly terrified of being shipped off to a new school. The great-aunt agreed and looked forward to receiving Social Security survivor benefits she could spend on herself. There was no life insurance.

Chadwick Preparatory turned out to be William Darcy's catalyst to greatness. It was there that he met Bingley and now, out from under his father's critical gaze, he grew into his own man— proud, proper, and pragmatic.

Wickham's prep school experience was drastically different. While there, he learned the skill of testing boundaries and bending rules, and each infraction brought him closer to that proverbial line, but much to William's astonishment, Wickham never crossed it. Expulsion hovered around Wickham like a cloud, dark and full of rain, but never falling. "Guess I'm just lucky. Like my dad," he told William after he almost got caught sneaking out past curfew. Again.

As the two young men prepped for their final year at Chadwick, tragedy struck. Mr. Darcy was traveling for business when a heart attack took his life. The school gave both William and George two weeks' leave. After the funeral, they learned that Mr. Darcy had provided for George in his will. He had a fund setup for college tuition and expenses, and Mr. King, the elder Darcy's longtime personal assistant and friend, took over handling Wickham's affairs. King didn't have to and no one would have faulted him if he had simply walked away. He knew, more than anyone else, about the troubles the Wickham men caused, but his loyalty to Mr. Darcy, and now his son, overruled that issue. It would be a decision he would regret.

When George turned 21, he decided that college life wasn't for him. He had the option to withdraw up to 50% of the funds and do with it as he pleased, but forfeit the remaining balance. The idea of a huge payout now instead of a college degree in the future was too big a temptation for George Wickham. He took the money and literally ran. Neither Darcy, Mr. King, or anyone else from his former life had heard from him for several years.

As an undergrad, Darcy realized that the corporate world wasn't for him. He became a silent partner in the firm and got a doctorate in finance, with a specialty in micro-loans. He only got involved in the company when his research headed toward conflict-of-interest territory, which wasn't often. Darcy Finance and Consulting dealt with multi-million-dollar businesses. They weren't interested in dolling out two or three-thousand dollars loans so someone could buy a stove and set up a home-based business selling cakes and pies at local farmers markets. After Darcy began his teaching and research career, Wickham's name popped up now and then, but never in a good way.

The trance between the two men broke when Lydia entered the shop. "There you are, Wickham!" she said, her forehead covered in a sheen of perspiration as if she had been running, which she had. "I thought that was you! I was just walking up to Mashujaa when I saw you come from behind the gym, and I thought, is that him? So, I turned around and what do you know, it was, I mean is you!" Words tumbled out of the youngest Bennet's mouth like marbles, spilling to the floor before anyone could catch their meaning. Wickham, who was used to her babbling by then, laid a playful arm around her shoulders. "Yes, it's me. Can't get anything past you, can I?" He winked. She giggled.

Darcy rolled his eyes. *Still playing with the young ones*, he thought. Behind him, he heard the barista call his name. He turned to see his coffee and muffin, bagged and ready to go. "That'll be $5.65," he said. A momentary fluster passed through Darcy as he tried to bring himself back to the present moment.

Wickham removed his arm from Lydia's shoulders. "Allow me," he said, reaching for his wallet.

Darcy swallowed hard, and for the second time that morning, his appetite vanished. "I changed my mind," he told the barista. He left, ignoring the attendant's bewildered look and the stares of the other patrons. As the door closed behind him, he heard two things: someone calling him a snob, which he dismissed. But he also heard a name that caused him to pause. "Well Miss Lydia Bennet, looks like it's banana muffins for breakfast."

That girl—that child—was a Bennet? And what was she doing with him?

CHAPTER 11

The evening after the opening convocation, Charlotte Lucas paid a visit to the Bennet family. Her father, Dr. Lucas, has served as college president for almost 20 years, so although not as long on the campus as the Bennets, the Lucases also called Delany home. The president's estate was located off campus, but still within a reasonable walking distance of Longbourne.

"Oh, there you are Charlotte," Mrs. Bennet said after opening the front door. "What brings you here on a Saturday evening?"

"Hello, Mrs. Bennet," Charlotte replied, entering the small hall. "I had to get here as soon as I could to talk to Lizzy about her … encounter with Dr. Darcy."

Mrs. Bennet winced. "Oh that. I tell you, Charlotte, I just don't know what to do about that girl. I *am* proud of her and all, but is it so wrong for a mother to want her daughter to have it all? A career *and* a husband?"

Charlotte grinned. "And a rich husband at that!"

Right after Charlotte spoke, Lizzy walked down the stairs. She had entered the house about 15 minutes before her friend and came back downstairs after changing into a pair of comfy sweats and an oversized T-shirt she got at a Prince concert. Mrs. Bennet shook her head at the tattered and faded clothing. "Really, Lizzy. Isn't it time to throw those out?"

The conversation halted again, this time by the front door opening and Jane coming in. Seeing her mom, sister, and their friend in the entryway of her home startled her. She was trying to make sense of the scene when Charlotte grabbed her by the arm. "Your timing is perfect," Charlotte said. "Have I got news for you two!"

Before Mrs. Bennet could object, the three young ladies scurried upstairs, leaving the mother alone to wonder what the fuss was about.

They entered Jane's bedroom. Jane walked into the adjoining bathroom to undress, but she left the door open.

Lizzy sat on the bed while Charlotte sat across from her in Jane's desk chair. Lizzy smoothed the bedcovers before sitting and asked Charlotte to spill the gossip.

Jane agreed. "Don't worry about me. I can hear you," she said from the bathroom. Besides, Charlotte was mainly there for her sister. She surprised herself by being slightly annoyed at Charlotte's presence. As she bent over the sink to wash her face, she reasoned it was because she was eager to share her own news.

Charlotte leaned forward. "So, I saw you with Dr. William Darcy. How did it go?"

"Oh, not you too, Charlotte!" Lizzy exclaimed. "The semester hasn't even started, and I am sick of hearing about that man."

Charlotte's eyebrows arched in surprise. "What's with the hate? It isn't every day that our little community has someone like *him* here."

"What are you talking about? Delany has some very prominent professors already. There's Dr. Mays from the Biology department, whose work they featured in *Nature Magazine* a few years ago; Dr. James from the theater department, his Tony nomination, and you can't forget—"

Charlotte held up her hand. "Yes, I know about *all* of them, Lizzy. My dad's the president, remember? But they're all either married, so-so looking or broke. This Dr. Darcy checks all the boxes, and then some."

"You forgot arrogant, self-righteous, snobby." Lizzy ticked off each offense with her fingers. "I'd rather listen to 24 hours of the Macarena song than have to deal with him again."

Charlotte crossed her arms and shook her head. "Your mother is right about you. You're so in love with those rappers you teach about you can't even tell when a real, decent man is right in front of you."

"Charlotte, you know that's not right," Jane said, entering the room. She had changed from her uniform into a cotton housedress. "Have *you* met this Dr. Darcy yet?"

"Yes, I have," Charlotte answered, then to Lizzy. "And he's no better—or worse—than all those other snotty doctor-professors up there. Except you, my friend. And you know I don't mean anything by that. It's just that I have never met someone so fine *and* rich before." Her eyes widen. "And I'm forgetting the best part!"

Lizzy laughed. "That he's single too?"

"No, girl. That he did not come alone. Or rather, he is with an equally rich and fine brother. Apparently, the two are close. Have been for years."

Lizzy nodded. "My dad mentioned something about that. Some guy named Bigley?" She grinned. "Probably *not* related to that Biggie."

Jane peered at Charlotte and asked, "You don't mean *Bing*ley, do you? Charles Bingley?"

Lizzy and Charlotte were curious about how she knew about this gentleman. "You weren't here when the parents brought him up," Lizzy said.

Jane's head reeled over the coincidences as she relayed what had happened to him on the day of the convocation. She paused and inhaled deeply before continuing. "He called me today at work and now I—and Mrs. Griff—are going to have lunch with him and his sister at Netherfield tomorrow!"

"Yes!" Charlotte clapped her hands and pointed at Jane. "Now that's what I'm talking about! Sister didn't waste *any* time!"

Jane's back stiffened as she told Charlotte that she had behaved professionally with her patient. "I treated him just like everyone else," she said. "No better or no worse."

"Of course you did," Charlotte said with a wink, which Jane ignored.

"Lunch?" Lizzy asked. "At Netherfield? You, Charles Bingley, and his sister, and … Mrs. Griff?" She shook her head. "Girl, you've got some explaining to do."

Jane passed over sharing Mrs. Griff's offensive behavior before the phone call and jumped to the outright absurd part. "She practically took the phone from me and put him on speaker!" she said. "The next thing I knew, I had a Sunday lunch engagement with her tagging along."

Charlotte shook her head. "That Griff woman is a trip! My mom told me that folks have stopped taking her phone calls 'cause she's always asking for donations. So now she's turned her sights on the Bingley fortune," Charlotte added with a smirk. "She sure didn't waste any time."

All the while Charlotte was talking, Lizzy was gazing curiously at her sister. "Jane?" she began, "do you *want* to go? Mrs. Griff didn't—"

"No, nothing like that, Lizzy. I know you think I don't know how to stand up for myself, but I would like to go. If just to see Netherfield. I heard they've put a ton of money into fixing it up."

Lizzy nodded. "Well, be careful, okay? If this Charles really is close friends with Dr. Darcy, I can only imagine what kind of dude he really is."

Charlotte waved away the concern. "Don't listen to her, Jane. She's already got it in for poor Dr. Darcy. Just go with an open mind and wear something … nice."

Charlotte stayed for a bit more and Lizzy did her best to steer the conversation away from any Jane and Charles talk. But her friend seemed to have a one-track mind that evening. One of her last comments was on how Jane should be a bit conniving in her pursuits. "After all, this is what we call a once-in-a-lifetime opportunity."

Lizzy had heard enough. "Okay, Miss Charlotte. I am sure Jane knows how to conduct herself with members of the opposite sex." She stood up and moved towards the bedroom door. Charlotte took the hint and followed, leaving Jane sitting on the side of her bed.

At the doorway, Lizzy stopped when she saw Lydia coming down the hall. Charlotte took advantage of the distraction to add one more piece of unsolicited advice. "Jane, God didn't give you good looks and charm for nothing, you know. And Lizzy, you need to chill and give Dr. Darcy a chance."

"Dr. Darcy!" Lydia halted. A look of disgust on her face. "We saw him this morning at The Brew. What a snob! Wickham tried to talk to him, and he just walked away! And didn't pay!"

"What were you doing on campus?" Lizzy asked.

"And with George Wickham? A grown man?" Charlotte asked.

Lydia grimaced. "There's no rule against me being on your precious campus, Miss Lizzy." she turned to Charlotte. "*And* there is nothing wrong with who I was with, either. I'm old enough to pick my own companions, thank you very much."

Charlotte shook her head. "Be careful, Lydia. Wickham is with the Mashujaa boys and they're on thin ice this year. All they need is another scandal—"

Lydia brushed away the concern with a sweep of her hand. "Scandal-schmandel. If anyone is to be avoided, it's that stuck-up Darcy dude. Wickham has been nothing but a gentleman." She left before either could reply. Jane had gotten up to see what all the fuss was about.

Charlotte and Lizzy watched Lydia saunter to her room. She entered and closed the door with a slam. Kitty's loud protest leaked down the hall, causing the two sisters to shake their heads. "I swear, that girl is a trip!" Charlotte said.

Both Lizzy and Jane felt their sisterly protection mechanism click, but words in defense of their youngest escaped them. After a brief pause, Charlotte told them she had to get going. "See you tomorrow at church," she waved before heading down the stairs.

"That Charlotte!" Lizzy said, returning to Jane's bedroom. "Girl doesn't know when to stop."

Jane sighed and looked down at her hands. "She started to sound like Mrs. Griff. Almost makes me want to cancel tomorrow."

Lizzy shook her head. "Don't do that. Meet him and decide *for yourself* if he is worth pursuing. And if he is, well, you'll know what do to."

Jane nodded. "I hope so …"

Lizzy offered a reassuring smile and patted Jane's hand. "You will. Besides, God didn't give you all that common sense for nothing."

.   .   .

Caroline and Charles entered the large downstairs library to find Darcy sitting in an oversized brown leather chair and staring at an empty fireplace. In his hand were the remains of an amber liquid, Darcy's 15-year-old Bourbon. At $2500 a bottle, it only came out on special occasions, or when something had gone wrong. Bingley could tell it was the latter. Caroline breezed by them both and made a beeline for the newly installed wine rack. She uncorked a bottle of the family's Merlot, poured herself a glass, and sat down. After a long sip, she began. "It isn't enough that I've been out of my mind getting this 18th-century relic up to snuff, but now I have to plan a luncheon because someone has a crush! I blame you," she said, pointing her finger at Darcy. "You and those micro-loans and searching for research and more research. We're millionaires, darling. When it comes to money, the word 'micro' should never even pass your lips." She gulped another mouthful of the dark red liquid before continuing. "And what's the first thing my brother does? He almost loses his arm in front of the dirtiest, lowliest, and … yickiest clinic in the entire state." She shivered. "And then calls that nurse, gushing like a schoolboy. So embarrassing!"

The wine finished, she got up to pour another glass.

Darcy watched her. He was tired from his day and had wanted to discuss seeing Wickham with Bingley, but the mention of Charles and Jane Bennet intrigued him. He got another crystal tumbler from the cabinet under the bar and poured his friend a drink. "A crush, eh? And on Jane Bennet?" he said, handing him the class.

Charles grinned. "She's an angel, Darce, and the best part is that you'll get to meet her, too."

Caroline finished her second glass of Merlot and left them, claiming a headache and that she could not stand to listen one more time to the story.

After hearing Charles' side, Darcy suggested he might be moving too fast.

"I'm not," Charles said, shaking his head. "Look, it may seem like I'm rushing, but it felt like the right thing to do, so I did it. And she said yes!"

"And this, Mrs. Griff?" Darcy asked. "Is she to act like her chaperone or something?"

Charles shrugged. "She was a bit on the pushy side. It seemed easier to invite her, too. But who cares? She's coming!"

Darcy finished his drink. "Are you sure you're not overreacting? You met her just once. And not under the best circumstances."

Charles' face grew serious. "Overreacting? I'll claim that if it means finally meeting the woman of my dreams and not some stuck-up socialite more concerned with country clubs and jet-setting than what's going on in the real world."

Darcy noted the earnestness in his voice, something he had not heard recently.

"I'm serious, Darcy. I'm not going to say she's the one or that I've fallen head over heels for her, but there is something about her—"

"Her beauty?"

"Yes, there's that, but something more, and all I'm asking for is the chance to explore that 'something'."

"But is that fair? I haven't met her, but considering her circumstances, she's bound to fall for you. Or at least convince herself she has. You are, after all, quite the catch, as they say."

"You sound like Caroline. I had to stop her from labeling her a gold digger."

"I wouldn't go that far, but men like us have to be careful." He shook his head. "I hate saying it, you know that, but it's true."

Charles waved away the concern. "It's not even a date. It's lunch. Why is everyone acting like I asked her to marry me?" He gulped down the last bit of bourbon. "Besides, she has a job that she seems to love and is good at. I doubt she's in the market for a sugar daddy or something." His eyes widen. "And her sister is a professor. Sounds like the Bennet women are pretty independent."

Darcy sighed and nodded. "Well, I'll give you that. Professor Bennet seems quite independent herself." And beautiful, he mused.

As the two walked up the stairway to their rooms, Charles remembered to ask about what had caused Darcy to dip into his precious Bourbon.

Darcy shook his head. "Nothing that can't wait," he said. "Off to bed with you so you can dream about your lovely Jane."

CHAPTER 12

Lizzy's eyes blinked open. It took her a few seconds to figure out what day it was. She stifled a yawn, threw back the bedcovers, and sat up. Sundays in the Bennet home typically meant a family breakfast prepared by their mother, followed by church, and then home to spend the rest of the day relaxing and mindless activities. In a few weeks, Lizzy's Sundays would include grading and prepping for classes. She always had to suppress a groan when she heard the tenures complaining about their measly three classes. "Wimps," she murmured as she walked down the hall to the bathroom she shared with Jane. Mary, Kitty, and Lydia shared a small bathroom at the other end of the hallway and her parents had their own downstairs in their bedroom. When they were younger, the house always seemed cramped, chaotic, and loud. Sometimes suffocating, and Lizzy was always trying to get out and away. With four of the five siblings now adults and gone most of the time, she viewed her home as a refuge, rather than something to escape. Gazing at her reflection, she tried to imagine the Bennets not at Longbourne House. Her father had told her that under the new terms, he could stay until his death. But what would happen if he left first?

Walking back to her bedroom, she almost collided with Kitty and Lydia. From the look on their faces, she could tell that an argument was coming. She shook her head. One day they'll grow up, she hoped.

"Mom!" Kitty and Lydia skipped down the stairs and into the kitchen. The pair rushed in where they found their mother getting breakfast ready. A stack of pancakes was on the counter and the sound of bacon sizzled from the stove. Mrs. Bennet turned and frowned. "You two better get dressed, or there will be no breakfast for you."

"Who cares about breakfast," Lydia said. "Besides, I need to lose five pounds before school starts." She grabbed an apple from the bowl on the table and took a bite. "At least," she said.

"Mom," Kitty said, "Lydia wants to invite some guys from Mashujaa over after church, but it was my idea first and she shouldn't even be hanging with them since she's still in high school and they're all college boys."

Lydia set her half-eaten apple on the table. "Oh, shut up, Kitty! It wasn't *your* idea; it was mine and you're just mad because *I* thought of it first."

Before their mother could respond, Kitty and Lydia began hurling insults at each other. Either they were best and inseparable friends sharing secrets and giggles, or they behaved like lions fighting over the last zebra in the savanna.

"Oh, for heaven's sake! Girls! Stop this now!" Mrs. Bennet grabbed Kitty by her pajama shirt collar and forced her to sit down.

"She started it!"

"Well, I'm ending it." Mr. Bennet entered the kitchen and motioned for Lydia to join her sister. "Now, what's this all about?" he asked, taking his place at the head of the table.

The sisters glanced at each other, both knowing that their father would not allow a bunch of frat boys inside the house, let alone feed them.

"Mashujaa boys? That new fraternity?" Mrs. Bennet asked. She was back at the stove, tending to the sizzling bacon. "Is that what's been keeping you girls occupied all summer?"

"Not me," Kitty said. "*I* have a job."

Lydia scoffed. "*And* a secret place to meet your boyfriend."

Their parents exchanged looks while Lydia told them about inviting Darren over after church.

As soon as she was done, Mr. Bennet told Lydia that she could put her luncheon idea out of her head. "There will be no frat boys passing through my threshold," he told her before sending her to her room to get dressed for church. "And, yes, you have to go."

After she left, Kitty lowered her head and told them about Darren. She said that yes, he comes to the yogurt shop sometimes, but not always. "He walks me home," she said. "I knew it was time for you to meet him, so I invited him to lunch next Saturday. But then Lydia heard, and she wanted to turn it into a 'luncheon party' and invited some of his frat brothers. I just want it to be him, Mom."

The boyfriend was not news to her parents. Someone on Mr. Bennet's crew had seen the young couple one night and told his boss about it the next day. Mr. Bennet shared the news with his wife, but both waited until Kitty was ready to tell them. He reached out and laid his hand on top of Kitty's. "Yes, we, uh, heard about your new friend, but waited until you were ready to tell us." He glanced at his wife. "Is it getting … serious?"

Kitty lifted her shoulders and let them drop. "I don't know Dad. I just know that I like him; he's easy to talk to."

Mrs. Bennet removed her apron and joined them at the table. "Well, that's important. Your father used to be easy to talk to, but—"

"That's enough." He turned to Kitty. "Today might not be a good time to meet this young man, Kitty," he smiled. "Maybe in a few weeks after school starts."

Mrs. Bennet eyed her husband. "Why isn't today a good day? I say meeting him sooner rather than later is best."

Mr. Bennet didn't answer right away. He had planned on telling her about his forced retirement after church. He knew he shouldn't put it off much longer. "They've just started seeing each other," he offered as an excuse. "Is the coffee ready?" he asked, hoping to change the subject.

Kitty, taking in the awkward exchange, mumbled that she had to finish getting ready for church and left. "We're not done," she heard her mother say as she approached the stairs. She shook her head. Dad's right, she thought. Today would *not* be a good day.

Fifteen minutes later, all five daughters filed into the kitchen and took their seats. "Not so fast, Lydia," Lizzy said. "You're on kitchen duty this week." Lydia huffed and gave her chair a jolt. "I can't wait to get out of this house," she hissed as she moved to help her mother bring the food to the table. *Be careful what you wish for* was on the tip of Lizzy's tongue, stopped only by a warning glance from her father. Lydia returned, dropped the platter of pancakes on the table and stuck her tongue out at Lizzy before going back for the bacon.

Jane had taken extra care getting ready for church, and it didn't take her mother long to notice. When Jane took a small scoop of scrambled eggs and fruit, Mrs. Bennet's curiosity got the better of her. "And what are you up to, Jane?" she asked with raised eyebrows.

Jane glanced at Lizzy, swallowed, and then updated her mother on the past day's events. Mrs. Bennet dropped her fork. "You're having lunch at Netherfield? *Today*?"

Jane nodded. "But it really isn't a big deal, Mother. They just want to thank me for taking care of Mr. Bingley."

Mrs. Bennet ignored the protest. "That's what thank-you notes are for! No. This means he likes you, Jane. Or is at least interested!" She clapped her hands together and grinned. "Good for you, Jane!"

Before Jane could respond, her mother told Lizzy to go with her. "That way you can work on that Dr. Darcy too."

"Mother!" both sisters exclaimed.

"Mrs. B…" her husband added with a look of warning.

Jane shook her head. "Lizzy can't come. Mrs. Griff already invited herself along, so it would look … tacky if I brought someone else too."

Mrs. Bennet looked shocked. "Mrs. Griff! Why on earth is she going? Did she help heal him too?"

Jane's face felt hot, and she worried she would have to retouch her makeup before leaving for church. Thankfully, Lizzy spoke first. "Mrs. Griff is going as a representative of the clinic, Mother. This is not a social affair, but more of a … business thing."

"Are they paying you?" Mary asked.

"They better," added Lydia. "Double."

"At least," Kitty said.

"That's enough everybody," Mr. Bennet said, picking up on Jane's discomfort. "Sunday is supposed to be a day of rest. Not a day of inquisitions." He encouraged his family to finish eating so they could leave for church. "Lydia, you can clean up the kitchen when we get back."

.   ▪   ▪

"Good morning, Darcy." Charles walked into the morning room to find his best friend alone at the large table, with what looked and smelled like a marvelous breakfast. Charles took the seat opposite. He was still in his pajamas with a robe barely tied around his waist. "Looks fantastic," he said. "Is this Corrine's handiwork?"

Darcy shook his head. "Apparently, your sister found some weekend help through a local agency. She's in there now, making sure that all is running smooth and orderly."

"Who's in where?" Charles asked.

Darcy nodded his head towards the kitchen. "Caroline and the woman she hired. A Miss Sarah." Darcy continued eating. "I'm not sure about her other abilities, but she's a fantastic cook."

"Oh, there you are, Charles." Caroline entered the room, followed by a woman carrying a tray with what he hoped was his breakfast. "This is Sarah Mackay. She'll be helping us out on the weekends."

Miss Sarah smiled. She was short, barely five feet, medium build, and had a small round head, covered in short, black and gray hair. She wore gold-rim glasses over dark brown eyes. She was older than all of them, which accounted for the "Miss" Darcy had used. Charles was glad that he at least remembered that courtesy. Charles stood up. "Very nice to meet you. Now at the risk of sounding rude, I hope that plate is for me."

Miss Sarah let out a hearty laugh, which contradicted her petite stature. "It sure is," she said. "And this is gonna be a nice little job for me. I love cooking for big, healthy men like you two. I just have daughters who are always on this or that diet." She walked over to Charles and set a plate of grits, sausage, eggs scrambled with fresh spinach and tomatoes, and a big fluffy biscuit. Caroline must have told her about his arm because she cut his sausage into bite-size pieces. "Looks delicious," he said.

Miss Sarah smiled, revealing two gold front teeth. "You just let me know if you need anything else," she said before leaving.

Caroline sat at the head of the table and sighed as if she had spent the morning slaving over a hot stove.

"You look pretty proud of yourself," Darcy said. He removed the linen napkin from his lap and wiped his mouth.

"Well, I am now that you mention it. I had to up the pay a bit and convince her to begin right away, but this one looks like she'll be worth it. Too bad she can't work during the week. She watches her grandchildren."

Darcy nodded. "Childcare is often an immense burden on low-income families. Her family is lucky to have her help."

"Oh William, we can always count on you to have more sympathy for the 'low-income' than you do for me, or anyone else making a decent living."

Darcy frowned. "You misunderstand me. I neither have sympathy for them nor none for you. It's a simple fact of their living situation."

Sensing that he was going to launch into one of his long and boring economic explanations, Caroline waved away his last comment, but the reappearance of Miss Sarah saved her from his lecture.

"Is that all you're having?" Charles asked.

"That's what she told me she wanted," Miss Sarah said as she collected Darcy's empty plate.

Caroline cleared her throat. "Not everyone can eat like you two," she said, looking down at her plate of poached eggs, fruit, and whole wheat toast.

Darcy stood up. "Well, you're right about that. Good thing she is only here on the weekends." He looked at Charles. "Come see me when you're done. There's something I need to speak with you about."

Charles nodded, and he and Caroline watched him leave. "What's that all about?"

Charles went back to his meal. "No idea."

"Do you think he's regretting coming here?"

Charles didn't answer. After almost 20 years of friendship, he still didn't have the words to explain the bond between them. Even if Darcy had regrets (which Charles was sure he didn't) he wouldn't say anything to him about it. Besides, what was there to regret, anyway? "I'm sure it's nothing. Probably has some financial advice for me or something."

It wasn't financial advice.

Charles sat and stared at his friend, trying to digest what he had said. "You mean he just walked in, like he … he … belonged there?"

"Well, the server seemed to know him well enough. And so did the young lady he was with." Darcy decided not to mention the Bennet connection. Mainly because he wouldn't know what to say. Darcy typically only spoke when he knew exactly what he wanted to say. With Lizzy Bennet, he found himself in the uncomfortable position of being at a loss for words.

Charles stood up and paced in front of the empty fireplace. They were in the room Darcy was using as his home office. "Do you think he followed you here? But why would he do that?" He shook his head. "Wickham is smart, but it's the worst kind of smart. The kind that makes a man do all sorts of crazy, stupid shit, believing that their smarts will help them get away with it."

"That's what I wanted to ask you. I have to be on campus for most of tomorrow and with the time difference, it will be hard to catch people on the west coast. Can you call around and see if you can find anything about what he's been up to these last few months?"

"Of course. I'll start with the attorney. We should have never let him talk us out of pursuing civil charges."

Darcy leaned back in his chair and stared at the tables they set up next to the empty bookcases that lined the wall. He had laid out all his drafts, notes, and files on one table and the other had his computers. Today was supposed to be dedicated to research and review, but he realized his mind would have a hard time focusing. More than hating George Wickham for what he did to his family, Darcy hated how he let him take up so much of his mental space. He needed a distraction.

"Not much we can do about it today." He stood up. "What time are your guests expected?"

"About one," Charles answered. "You will join us, won't you?"

Darcy lifted his eyebrows. "Do you need me there? I thought this was a chance for you to get to know Jane Bennet."

"It is, but it would be awkward if you didn't join us. You live here too, you know."

Darcy picked up one of his files and looked through it. "And who is coming with her? With Jane."

"A Mrs. Griff. The clinic's director." He shrugged. "Must be a Southern thing, this chaperone business."

Darcy dropped the file back on the table. "I'll be there," he said, not sure Lizzy Bennet's absence disappointed him or not. He walked to the window and peeked at the newly finished pool house and landscaping. "Maybe I'll take a swim later to work off some of that breakfast."

"Good idea!" Charles said. "But, ummm … can you help me get dressed first?"

•   •   •

Jane looked back at her family and waved as Mrs. Griff drove out of the church parking lot. Mrs. Griff had grabbed her as soon as the service was over with a, "We need to go." Jane suppressed a grimace at the veiled order, turned to tell her family goodbye, and followed her to her car. Mrs. Griff glanced in the rearview mirror and saw the remaining Bennets watching them drive away. She grinned. "They act like you're going away on a Peace Corps mission or something. You did tell them it was just lunch, didn't you?"

Jane sighed and gazed out the window. "Yes," she replied, but inside she wondered, is it just lunch?

When Mrs. Griff's Mercedes was out of sight, Mrs. Bennet turned to her family and said it was time to go home. "Nothing more to do here," she said as the family began their short walk back to Longbourne. As she walked, Lizzy's mind turned to her school to-do list and what she could get done today. Not much, and going to her office wasn't an option since Delany is locked up tight on Sundays. She was just about to offer Lydia her help in the kitchen when a shout from Kitty stopped her. "Darren!" Like a flock of starlings, the Bennets turned to see the object of Kitty's attention.

A young Black man, dressed in tan khakis and a dark blue polo shirt, waved and made his way towards the family. Kitty smiled and stepped away to greet him. "That must be him," their mother whispered. The young couple exchanged a few words, then made their way to the family.

"Mother, Father, this is Darren."

Darren extended his hand to Mr. Bennet. "Nice to meet you, sir," he said. "Ma'am," he added with a nod to Mrs. Bennet.

Lizzy joined her mother in giving Darren the once over. He was as tall as Kitty, with a round face and a pleasant smile. He reminded her a bit of Carlton from the *Fresh Prince*. He looked good standing next to her sister.

He was skilled at making small talk and had her father smiling and nodding along at whatever he was saying. Thinking the four could use a little privacy, Lizzy turned to tell her sisters they should continue walking home. Mary nodded, but she had to give Lydia a little shove to get her moving. They were a few steps away when Lydia stopped, waved her hands above her head, and called out: "Wickham!" Across the street, a tall, slim Black man, dressed in gray sweats, turned and waved back at her. Lydia was about to dash into the street and oncoming traffic, but Mary grabbed her by the arm to stop her. "You trying to kill yourself, Lydia?!"

Mr. Bennet stepped towards his daughters. "What's going on?" he demanded. Lydia's eyes stayed on the man on the other side of the street, and everyone watched as he waited for a break in traffic to cross. Lydia stepped towards him with outstretched arms which he almost entered, but then, getting a glimpse of the parents, artfully avoided. Lydia was able to hook her arm with his, turned, and introduced him to her family.

"Oh my," flushed Mrs. Bennet. "This is turning out to be an interesting Sunday! First, our oldest is dining at Netherfield with CHARLES BINGLEY, and now we have two nice looking gentlemen escorting our daughters."

Mr. Bennet raised his eyebrows and stared at Wickham. "Escorting?" he said. It was almost a hiss.

Wickham untangled his arm from Lydia (who immediately pouted at the move) and shook his head. "No, sir. Nothing like that. I am here at this magnificent institute of higher learning through a special invitation from the Mashujaa Fraternity." He pressed a hand to his chest. "I'm here to help them with their performance."

Mrs. Bennet wanted to know more, but her husband put a stop to any further discussion. He pointed behind him. "Fraternity row is that way," he said. "Come along, girls; time we got home." He was about three steps away before he noticed his wife hadn't moved. He turned to find her chatting with the two men, her face glowing. He groaned at the plans he knew her mind was spinning. She finished, waved goodbye, and caught up with her family. "Come, come!" Mrs. Bennet said. "Lots to do. Lots to do."

About thirty minutes after the Bennets arrived home, Mr. Bennet opened his front door to Darren Parker and George Wickham, who had changed into black jeans and white polo shirt. Mr. Bennet gave both men a curt nod before inviting them in. His wife emerged from the kitchen, holding a tray of sandwiches. "You made it!" she beamed. "Mr. B, show our guests to the living room, please."

Kitty had changed into a yellow summer dress and greeted Darren with a shy grin. The pair sat on the loveseat as the rest of the family filled the room. The windows faced west, and the afternoon sun streamed in through the sheer curtains. On the opposite wall, the built-in bookcases held texts from the past and present. Family photos spaced throughout, showcasing the Bennet family through the years. Lizzy watched as George Wickham glanced around the space. He smiled when he saw her watching. "A lot of history in this room," he said. "Seems like a nice place to call home."

"That it is," Mrs. Bennet said, bringing in a tray with a pitcher of lemonade and glasses. Wickham dashed forward to retrieve the tray. "Allow me," he said. Lydia followed her mother with cookies and cut fruit.

Behind his newspaper, Mr. Bennet let out a short cough, which Lizzy took as her cue to change the subject. It was a bad time to start reminiscing about their home. She turned to Wickham. "Tell us about this performance you're helping with."

Before answering, he took the glass of lemonade Mrs. Bennet offered. Through a huge smile, Wickham shared his background in music and dance and what brought him to Delany. "I hope to help these young brothers make their mark this year," he said.

Mrs. Bennet clapped her hands and beamed. "Did you hear that, Lizzy? He's in the same line of business as you are! What a marvelous coincidence!"

Wickham smiled. "Oh, it's no coincidence, Mrs. Bennet. I have long wanted to meet the famous hip-hop professor."

Lizzy felt her cheeks burn and thanked her dark complexion for hiding her blush. She hated to admit it, but George Wickham was pretty good looking. She swallowed and prayed her voice came out steady. "Wanting to meet me?" she asked. "Whatever for?"

Wickham threw back his head and laughed. "You're kidding, right? Why, your work is legendary on the West Coast. Especially after that article in Jet Magazine came out. Rappers quote you all the time out there."

"They do?" Kitty said.

"They certainly do," Wickham answered.

It turns out that George Wickham had alternative plans when he had agreed to come and help them in the stomp competition. He had read about Professor Bennet's studies and wanted to ask her to endorse a new group he was working with. If not her endorsement, then at least some constructive feedback. He was a fast talker and after five minutes of him going on and on, Lizzy held up a hand to stop him. "Now's not the time to get into all that." She glanced at Kitty and Darren, feeling a little guilty for hijacking the afternoon.

He laid a hand across his heart and asked for forgiveness. "I get carried away, but as you said in that article: 'this music has a way to transport us to a different space and time.'"

Lizzy tried to stay objective, but his flattery and good looks proved to be a tough barrier to objectivity. She tried to figure out how she could use him to learn what Lydia was up to and, maybe, get to know him a little better, too.

Mr. Bennet stood up and walked to the fireplace mantel to retrieve his pipe. "Well, as you say Lizzy, now is not the time for this." He turned to Kitty and Darren. "Now, young man. Tell us a bit about yourself."

.   .   .

Mrs. Griff let out a soft whistle at the sight of Netherfield. "I knew they were doing some work out here, but this …" Living in the south, she and Jane had seen their share of Antebellum homes, but knowing that Netherfield was now in the hands of a Black family brought a different kind of awe. "You know, the Bingleys may own Netherfield," Mrs. Griff said before getting out of the car, "but it belongs to all of us now. 'Bout time."

The lingering smell of fresh paint greeted them as they made their way up the huge wooden steps. Jane tilted her head back to take in the newly polished mahogany door and brass doorknob and knocker shaped like a lion's head. Jane's thoughts went to her ancestors, enslaved men and women tasked with creating and installing this door, along with the rest of the enormous house. Taking a deep breath, she reached for the knocker, but the door swung open, causing her hand to drop.

"There you are!" said a smiling Charles Bingley. His dark brown eyes lingered on Jane for a few seconds before he stepped aside to let the pair inside. "Come in," he said. "And welcome to Netherfield."

The last time Jane had been on the property was during a 5th grade field trip. Everything was covered in dust, and the floorboards creaked and moaned as they walked through. Some spots in the old mansion were so bad, everyone joked, or worried, about falling through the floor. The remaining furniture was practically falling apart, and the teachers and guides shouted warnings not to touch anything, or worse, sit down.

Mary's class had been the last school visit. The city had little interest and no funds to take on the repairs and upkeep of another Southern relic, so the task fell to local volunteers. A few months ago, a newspaper article announced the sale, stating that at just $850,000, the property was a steal. The new owners were not known until recently.

Jane and Mrs. Griff stepped into the wide entry hall, where an oval mahogany table with a marble top and an empty crystal vase stood in the center. Above, a sparkling crystal chandelier twinkled in the afternoon sunlight. Behind the entryway table and directly opposite the front doors, a wide mahogany staircase led to the first landing, then split into two smaller flights up to the second floor.

As the guests stepped further into the mansion, their heels clicked on the marble flooring, causing both women to pause and look down. Mrs. Griff gasped. "Is this Italian?" she asked.

Jane winced at the question and was just about to offer their host an apology when Caroline appeared. "Yes, it is." She walked forward with a small, slightly fake-looking smile. Jane, remembering their brief encounter at the clinic, was instantly on her guard.

"It's beautiful," Jane said. "And thank you so much for inviting us."

Caroline offered a limp handshake, which Jane awkwardly took. "Well, I really didn't have a—"

"You are *always* welcome," Charles interjected, his eyes on Jane. He lifted his good arm to move them into the smaller parlor. "Please come in and make yourselves comfortable."

Jane and Mrs. Griff followed him, walking past the wide staircase. It too had polished, dark mahogany rails, with wrought iron spindles. Down the middle of the stairs, a dark red carpet ran from top to bottom.

"We had to have food brought in," Caroline said after everyone settled into the library. "I hope you don't mind." She poured two glasses of lemonade, added a sprig of mint, and handed them to her guests, who had taken seats on the suede sofa. A marble-topped coffee table separated them from Caroline and Charles, who sat in two of three wingback chairs covered in the same dark brown suede.

Mrs. Griff shook her head. "Oh, please do not worry, Miss Bingley. We are just so honored to be invited."

Charles leaned forward. "It's the least we could do after …" He lifted his injured arm as much as the sling would allow, grimacing slightly.

Jane leaned forward. "Are you all right? Is the pain still bothering you?"

"Not at all," Charles answered quickly. And then, "I mean, the pain is not bad, and I am all right. Better than all right, actually."

Caroline set her drink on the table. "Well, he may be fine, but I'm getting tired of playing nursemaid. You wouldn't happen to know of any nurse-type person we could hire to come to help a bit? Do you?"

Jane and Mrs. Griff glanced at each other, both wondering how to respond. Neither of them noticed the annoyed look Charles shot at his sister.

"Well," Mrs. Griff offered. "There *may* be an aide at the clinic who could come by occasionally." She stopped as issues of liability, overtime pay, and other obstacles came to mind.

"He just needs to keep the wound clean and dry," Jane said with a smile. "Westside can remove the stitches in a few days, or you can call your private physician."

Before his sister could respond, and to Charles' relief, Darcy entered the room. Jane tried her best to suppress a gasp at the sight of him. The way he entered the room reminded her of the overly confident and impatient surgeons she had encountered during her nursing school days.

Darcy stepped forward to greet them. Mrs. Griff stood up and extended her hand so hurriedly she almost bumped into the coffee table. Jane noticed Dr. Darcy's startled look, which also held a hint of annoyance. He took the outstretched hand, gave it a quick shake, and then turned dark brown eyes on Jane. Charles stood up and moved to be next to his friend. "Darce," he said with a triumphant smile. "This is Miss Jane Bennet. Jane, meet my good friend, William Darcy."

Jane stood up and felt her face warm as Darcy's gaze took her in, making her feel as if she were five years old and meeting her kindergarten teacher on the first day. She nodded, but kept her hands by her side, afraid they would be damp with sweat. "Hello, Dr. Darcy. Welcome to Delany University."

Darcy tilted his head in silent acknowledgment, then turned and took a seat next to Caroline. She offered him a drink, but he shook his head in refusal. After everyone sat back down, an awkward silence filled the room. Jane took advantage of the break to take in the newly redecorated space. Gone were the tacky, archaic, and offensive murals of the so-called Southern lifestyle; elaborately dressed ladies and gentlemen, frolicking in a field, surrounded by flowers, wildlife, and off in the distance, smiling Black people, usually bent over doing fieldwork. A sanitized and fictional version of the south's peculiar institution, known to the rest of the world as slavery. Whether Caroline had it stripped off or painted over, she couldn't tell, but the artwork that had replaced it was stunning. A larger piece in between the bay windows caught her eye, and she stood up and walked towards it, as if under its spell.

"Is this a Jacob Lawrence?" she asked as she stood before it.

Caroline join her. "Why, yes. It is. Are you familiar with his work?"

"Of course," Jane nodded. "The last time Lizzy and I were in New York we saw his *Migration Series* at the Museum of Modern Art."

Caroline glanced over at Jane. "Now that's something I wouldn't mind adding to my collection." she shrugged. "But, alas, MOMA got it first."

"It is so nice that you are filling the walls with African American art," Jane said, taking in the few other paintings and wondered if their other properties boasted Black art too. Behind her, she heard Mrs. Griff join them.

"Merryton boasts quite a few established and upcoming artists. Perhaps we can arrange a showing or something."

Caroline looked skeptical. "That could be ... interesting," she replied.

"I can't speak for paintings," Darcy said, causing everyone to turn toward him. "But the sculptures I've seen around campus are very nice."

Jane's eyes widened. "You mean in the Ancestors Garden? My father and his crew work hard to keep it up. It's his pride and joy."

Charles grinned. "Along with his daughters, I'm sure."

Jane offered a brief smile before lowering her head in embarrassment.

"Speaking of daughters," Caroline said. "Your father was here a few days ago and says that there are ... five of you in all. And that your sister is a professor? At Delany?"

Glad for the change in subject, Jane told them about Lizzy's studies and position at Delany. "She loves her job," Jane added. "We are all very proud of her." Remembering what Lizzy had said about Dr. Darcy at the opening convo, Jane stole a glance to gauge his reaction, but all she saw was a blank face. A few minutes later, Miss Sarah came in to tell them lunch was ready. Jane recognized her from the clinic and the neighborhood. Jane glanced at Mrs. Griff, who was busy chatting up Caroline. She sighed. With Miss Sarah taking in the afternoon, Jane feared that every aspect of the afternoon would be known to half of Merryton by the time she got to work tomorrow.

Miss Sarah served lunch on the back patio and afterward, Charles teased Jane away with a suggestion to take her to see the new pool area. Darcy excused himself and went upstairs to work, despite Caroline chastising him about Sundays being a day of rest.

"You've known me long enough to know that the beginning of the semester is always like this," he said before walking up the wide staircase.

Caroline groaned inwardly as she watched Darcy's escape. During lunch, she had recognized Mrs. Griff's hints and side comments, all designed to elicit a donation for that clinic. She had no idea how long her brother would be with Jane, so she decided to tackle the issue head-on, knowing that it may ruffle some feathers. Something she's grown accustomed to doing.

After Miss Sarah placed the coffee service and exited the porch, Caroline cleared her throat. "As I am sure you are aware, the Bingley Winery Foundation has a *very* generous philanthropy program, but I am afraid that we have allocated all funds for this fiscal year. If the Westside Clinic is interested, they can apply for a small grant next February."

Mrs. Griff took a sip of coffee before responding. "Oh, you bet I know all about your foundation, Miss Bingley. As board president, it is my job to know where the money is." She smiled. "And yes, I know about the grant application, but grants are not what I had in mind."

"Oh?" Caroline answered, her curiosity piqued.

Mrs. Griff paused for a few seconds before continuing.

"What do you say to a ball, Miss Bingley? A charitable ball, here at the beautifully restored *and* Black-owned Netherfield Mansion. You've worked so hard, and your talent is on full display here. It would be a shame *not* to show it off to the community."

CHAPTER 13

Lizzy looked over what remained of her mother's little get-together and smiled, thinking that Kitty got her family luncheon with Darren after all. Between herself and her mother, they put together sandwiches, salad, and some cookies for their guests. Mrs. Bennet kept apologizing over the meager offerings, but Darren insisted it was nice to have homemade food again. It had not taken Lizzy long to warm up to the young man. He spoke of his family back in San Antonio with love, pride, and longing, showing the Bennet family that he had been raised right. Her father seemed to like him, too.

George Wickham gave off an entirely different vibe. He oozed sincerity and charm that came off as being just about 75% sincere. He was good looking, although in a bad-boy sort of way. Tall, with light brown skin, and freckles across his nose. His brownish-gray eyes possessed a child-like twinkle. and Lizzy imagined he had grown the thin mustache and goatee to counter the adolescent appearance. Plus, that hair! She was a sucker for men with curly hair, just like her own. What gave her pause was that most of his stories centered on his past; tales full of woe and misfortune with him the perpetual victim. When Lydia tried to probe him about William Darcy, he sidestepped with a the-past-is-the-past comment.

Mr. Bennet eyed him over his glasses. "Well, most rich people are guilty of at least one or two infractions against their fellow man. But if he is at Delany, it must have not been too serious."

Wickham smiled and tilted his head. "As you say, sir. Delany would never let someone of ill repute get close to their students."

Lydia snorted a laugh and gave Wickham a playful slap on the arm. "You talk so funny sometimes! Trying to sound all fancy and old school. Like *really* old school."

Lizzy noticed a flash of annoyance on Wickham's face before he stood up and turned to her parents. "Thank you so much for your hospitality," he said. And then to Darren, "We should be leaving now."

It was Darren's turn to appear annoyed, but he also stood up and thanked everyone for the lunch. Kitty wanted to accompany Darren back to the frat house, but she was sure her father wouldn't let her go alone. Mary was the first to volunteer to accompany her. "Some of my traps are along the way so I can check them, too. For a Polyphemus moth, although I'm also hoping for—"

"Me too!" Lydia shouted.

"Not you, Lydia. You're on kitchen duty, remember?" her father answered.

"Oh god," Kitty groaned before turning to Lizzy, her eyes begging for an intervention.

"I don't mind," Lizzy said. "A walk will do me some good."

Darren and Kitty walked ahead of Lizzy, Mary, and Wickham, who nodded politely as Mary rattled on about moths, traps, and her research. "There's been a lot of concern about how some pesticides are affecting the population," she said before rattling on about statistics, breeding grounds, and intervention strategies.

Wickham smiled. "You are quite an unusual girl, Mary. All the Bennet ladies seem to be . . . unique."

Before Lizzy could ask him to elaborate, Mary held up her net and told them she was going to check on her traps. "I'll find my way home," she said, wandering off into the landscape.

"*Will* she be all right?" Wickham asked.

"Oh, yeah. Mary never met a bug she didn't like. While the rest of us ran from the room screaming from a spider, she would be down on the floor trying to scoop it up."

Instead of laughing at her joke, Wickham became serious. "Sounds like a fun house to grow up in."

An uneasy silence followed, causing Lizzy to feel a bit awkward. She glanced ahead and saw Darren and Kitty walking hand in hand. Young love. She crossed her arms. "You mentioned something about a new rap group you're working with ..."

He nodded.

"I'd like to give them a listen. Can you bring me their CD tomorrow?"

He jumped at the chance. "Just tell me when and where."

Lizzy explained how she would be in and out of her office most of the day. "I can meet you at the quad around two. There's a big meeting and luncheon there to kick off the different committees." She laughed. "Admin likes to bribe us all with free food and drink. Otherwise, no one would come."

Wickham nodded in agreement. "It's a date."

.   .   .

After Mrs. Griff dropped Jane off, she went straight up to her room, avoiding her mother's prying eyes and questions. "Just let me change," Jane begged. Lizzy joined her and shared the afternoon at Longbourne while Jane changed.

"So," Jane asked after Lizzy finished, "What did *you* think of this Wickham character?"

Lizzy shook her head. "Too soon to tell," she answered. "He charmed our mother, though, but I still can't tell if he's sincere or not."

"And with Lydia?"

Lizzy drew her eyebrows together. "You know, it didn't seem like there was anything going on between them, and I did notice him trying to put her off once or twice." She shrugged. "Let's hope it wasn't an act for the parents."

"Our Lydia is not a very good actress," Jane said, shaking her head.

Before Lizzy could agree, their mother started pounding on the door. "Jane? Lizzy? Are you two talking about what happened at Netherfield? Without me?"

After they began working full time, Jane and Lizzy started paying their father a modest rent, although they both knew that he put it aside and had plans to gift it to them when they eventually moved out. Since then, both parents agreed to not enter their bedrooms without permission. It still surprises everyone that their mother keeps to the agreement.

Lizzy got up and opened the door. "I was just telling Jane about our afternoon here, Mother. We *did not* talk about Netherfield."

"Well, good. Now come downstairs. Everyone is waiting."

By everyone, her mother meant Mary, who had returned to her corner and her scientific journals, and Kitty. Lydia was probably up in her room and their father had retired to his den.

"A ball?!" Mrs. Bennet moved to the edge of her chair, placed her hands on her knees, and craned her neck forward. She peppered her eldest with question after question, and Lizzy could tell that Jane was being selective in her answers. Lizzy couldn't blame her. Their mother was the queen of exaggeration, especially when it came to her daughter's romantic life. "Details, Jane. Details," their mother implored.

Jane shrugged. "I know little, Mother. Except that Mrs. Griff talked Caroline into hosting a charity ball for the clinic. I think it will be before Thanksgiving break."

This time, Jane was telling the whole truth. Charles had taken her to see the grounds and away from Caroline and Mrs. Griff. They had wandered around, admiring the landscaping, and ended up at the new pool area where they sat on lounge chairs and talked. When they came back to the house, Mrs. Griff was beaming with the news. She rattled on about it on the drive back, but Jane's mind had been elsewhere.

Mrs. Bennet became unusually silent as she drummed her fingers on her knee. This was her scheming mode, and everyone knew to sit and wait. It didn't take long. "November. That gives us just enough time. I'll ask your father to let us into the Christmas fund early. You girls need new gowns, shoes, the works." She turned to Lizzy. "And *you*. Make sure you are at least civil to that Dr. Darcy. That ball could be the perfect place to … well, you know."

Two minutes later, their parents' raised voices floated in from Mr. Bennet's den. Their bickering had notched up a level, and Lizzy was the only one who had a suspicion as to why. With the prospect of not having full-time income next year, her father would have a much shorter fuse than usual.

From her corner, Mary lifted her head and stared in the direction of their father's den. "Sometimes I wonder why he even puts up a fight," she said. "Everyone knows Mother *always* gets her way."

A rebuke was on the tip of Lizzy's tongue, but she held it in. Mary was correct, and this was yet another example of their fly-on-the-wall sister letting them know she does, in fact, pay attention.

Lizzy turned to see Jane trying to get her attention. She mouthed upstairs and the two of them left before their mother could return.

They plopped down on Jane's bed. "Well, I, for one, do not need a new gown. That one I wore to Mariah's debutante is perfectly fine. Plus, the Bingleys haven't seen it, so it'll be new to them."

Jane was right, of course, but since Lizzy had been one of Mariah's attendees, her gown from that night was a rose-pink satin affair that screamed bride's maid dress. "Well, it's a little early to think about that. Anyway, I may just skip it."

Jane became serious. "Oh no, Lizzy, don't say that. You have to come."

"Why? To hob knob with a bunch of folks I see every day. And *some of them* I have no intention of seeing outside of work."

Jane bit her lower lip. "About that …" She took a deep breath and told her about agreeing to a dinner date with Charles, but on a double date. "He suggested it first, I swear, Lizzy. I guess he wanted to make me feel more comfortable. I don't know, but I agreed and so now you have to—"

"When?"

"Tomorrow."

"Jane! You know how busy I am at the beginning of the semester. Any free time I have, I use for more prepping or just chillin'. Spending an evening with Dr. Darcy is *not* my idea of chillin'."

CHAPTER 14

Both Darcy and Lizzy spent Monday morning in their offices prepping for classes, answering students' panicked emails and messages, and hoping the committee work would magically disappear. Professor Bennet knew it was a waste of time to even think about getting out of the obligation, and even if she could, she wouldn't because the blowback from her fellow teachers would be harsh. Darcy wondered why he had even agreed to it. Dr. Lucas told him he did not have to, but that it would be a plus if he would. "It will help you appear as part of the Delany family and not some outsider."

A sandwich shop near Jane's clinic catered for lunch. Everyone lined up to grab their food and then set out to find their committee's table. The scene resembled a colony of Emperor penguins searching for their mates after months of being away at sea.

Out of the corner of her eye, Lizzy spotted Dr. Darcy coming towards the quad. Surely, he wasn't on a committee, she thought. Very few tenured profs bothered with the obligation and although not tenured at Delany, his stature would excuse him from the duty. But when he reached the food table and began serving himself, she realized that the opposite must be true. Good for him, she thought. And then she grinned. *I wonder who is going to be stuck with him for the entire semester.*

The Twig Book Shop

306 Pearl Parkway, Ste. 106
San Antonio, TX 78215
(210) 826-6411
Customer name: Customer

Transaction #:0000272248
Station:Station2, 2 Clerk:STATION2
Tuesday, October 24 2023   5:11 PM

SALES:
1@ 18.99 9780063275904		18.99
Best American Short Stories 2023		
1@ 24.95 9781685132897		24.95
Delany Bennets		
1@ 27.99 9781250282521		27.99
Maame		
SUBTOTAL		71.93

TAX:
Sales Tax	@8.2500%	5.93
TOTAL TAX		5.93
GRAND TOTAL		77.86

TENDER:
Bankcard	77.86
TOTAL TENDER	77.86

CHANGE $0.00

Please visit us at https://www.thetwig.com/

00272248

The Twig Book Shop

306 Pearl Parkway, Ste. 106
San Antonio, TX 78215
(210) 826-6411
Customer name: Customer

Transaction #:0000272248
Station:Station2, 2 Clerk:STATION2
Tuesday, October 24 2023   5:11 PM

SALES:
1 ⑪	18.99 9780063279504	18.99
	Best American Short Stories 2023	
1 ⑪	24.95 9781685132897	24.95
	Delany Bennett	
1 ⑪	27.99 9781250528521	27.99
	Maame	
SUBTOTAL		71.93

TAX:
Sales Tax	@8.2500%	5.93
TOTAL TAX		5.93
GRAND TOTAL		77.86

TENDER:
Bankcard	77.86
TOTAL TENDER	77.86

CHANGE	$0.00

Please visit us at https://www.thewig.com/

0072248

She was.

Coach Nelson, the girls' basketball coach, stood up and gave her whistle a quick blow. "Sorry to toot at you like that, but it's the best way to get you all's attention."

"Try something else next time," someone said. "I'd rather *not* be whistled at."

"Okay, okay," Coach Nelson said. "Message received. Now let me just say that I am very excited about this committee. When the clubs and the houses started asking about what we were planning for Y2K, I knew we needed to have some sort of formal organization set up to oversee it all." Like the Bennets, Coach Nelson's family had a long history with Delany. Her ancestors were early graduates, and many alums had served on the board, along with being generous financial supporters.

Although most of what Coach explained was in the yellow committee notebooks each member had before them, Coach Nelson continued to speak on basic matters. Lizzy opened hers and read the different tabs: Minutes, Roles, Applications, Vendors, and Committee Roster. She turned to that one and ran her finger down the list until she came to his name. *Dr. William Darcy, Economics.*

"Questions?"

Lizzy looked up to see their leader smiling down on her new committee. At over 6 feet, she had an impressive presence. Someone raised their hand and asked the one question that really mattered. "How often are we planning to meet?"

Coach Nelson's smile widened. "Great question and thanks for asking!" She reached into her binder and pulled out a handful of neon blue sheets of paper. "Now, I've served on a lot of committees (as I am sure you all have too) and I know we can all agree that the one thing that frustrates is wasting time in endless meetings." She paused as the nods, mmm-hmms, and an Amen! erupted around the table. "So," she continued, "I've taken the liberty of dividing us up into sub-committees, each with a list of specific duties." She began handing out the blue sheets of paper that held the subcommittee lists. "It will be up to each sub to decide on their meeting frequency; once a week, bi-weekly, or not at all if you can figure out how to meet the expectations via email, phone calls, or … whatever." She gave everyone a minute to look over the list. Lizzy kept hers turned down. Coach was proud of her arrangement, and Lizzy didn't want to spoil it by being one of the first to ask to be switched if what she feared came true. She looked around the tables and saw how others seemed pleased with the arrangement. Working and coordinating with smaller groups was always easier—fewer opportunities for friction and confusion.

Coach Nelson then asked the subs to gather to plan their first steps and choose a contact person. "As for all of us meeting again, I'll keep you posted, but I will check in periodically with your contact person, or CP."

Professors and students stood up and began searching for their group.

"I'm vendors. You?"

"Legal? Who's in legal?"

"What the heck is community liaison, anyway?"

When Lizzy finally looked at the assignments, she noticed each sub had from 3 to 5 members. She was in a 4-member group called Auditions. Two professors and two students.

"Looks like we'll be working together."

She turned around to see Dr. Darcy standing behind her.

Of course, she thought as she slipped the blue paper into her notebook. This semester keeps getting more and more interesting. "Looks that way," she said. Behind him, she saw two students walking towards them. One she recognized. "And here come the others." A young man and woman were making their way toward them. Lizzy knew one of them from when he was in her class last semester. The other one she wasn't familiar with, but she assumed she was a grad student.

"Hello, Nate," she said. "Good to see you again."

"Yo! Professor B! Great to see you too!" He reached out and gave her a quick hug, followed by a fist bump. Both broke out laughing.

"How was your summer?"

"Ahhhh, you know. Just kicking it with fam and stuff like that. But yo! I tried real hard to get me some action going at Death Row, but they just wasn't havin' it."

Lizzy had more questions, but she noticed the other student looking uncomfortable. "Hi. I'm Professor Bennet."

The student moved her notebook to her other arm before offering her hand. "Nice to meet you. I'm Charmaine."

Lizzy nodded. "Right. So, we have Nate, a sophomore, and you are ... ?"

"A junior," Charmaine said, looking amused. "I get that a lot, seeing how I am obviously *not* in my 20s." She laughed. "And white."

"Yo! Thanks for clearing that up," Nate said. "I was beginning to think you were from social services or something."

"Why would you think that?" Dr. Darcy asked, turning to Nate, his tone in full professorial mode. "There are plenty of returning students on campus, and Delany is not an exclusive African American college."

Nate's face took on that deer-in-the-headlights look, and he mumbled an apology. "I was just joking around. Didn't mean nothin' by it."

"Well, if you didn't mean *anything* by it, then perhaps you should—"

"Okaaaaay, that's enough for introductions," Lizzy said, hoping to bring an end to the exchange. She suppressed a groan and asked Nate and Charmaine to find a place where they could all sit. "We'll be right along." After they walked away, she turned to Darcy. "Does everything have to be an argument with you?" They were standing about two feet apart and she had to tilt her head up to see him. At the convo, she hadn't noticed how much taller he was.

"I wasn't arguing," he said. "I was simply pointing out the facts. His assumption was absurd."

"It was a joke. You know what a joke is, don't you?"

Darcy continued as if he hadn't heard her. "And he shouldn't be speaking to you that way; so informally."

"Nate was in my class last semester. Trust me, he knows how to behave. And in case you didn't know, it's called code-switching."

Darcy looked down and met her eyes. "I know what it's called and when it's called for. He's a student, you're a professor, and this is an institute of higher learning; not some street corner."

Lizzy opened her mouth to tell him he needed to relax but changed her mind. Nate and Charmaine were waiting, and the way he was looking at her made her uncomfortable. "Let's just drop it, okay? We're here to get started on this committee work, not debate dialects."

He nodded in agreement, then motioned for her to lead the way.

Turns out the Audition Subcommittee would receive, review, and approve applications from student groups that wanted to be part of the entertainment. It was, as Nate put it, "a big fucking deal."

"We need to make sure we remain objective," Charmaine said. "I'm sure there will be lots of competition and people trying to bribe us." The two professors glanced at her. "Not you two, of course," she said, stumbling over her words.

Darcy smiled. And for the first time, Lizzy noticed. "No, you don't have to worry about us," he said. "But you bring up a good point." He suggested they should develop some sort of rubric to grade or rate the different entries.

"What a great idea," Charmaine said. "We could have things like originality and how it relates to the theme. We used something like that for my daughter's school talent show. I was on the PTA committee."

Everyone agreed it was a good first step and Charmaine volunteered to write the first draft and email a copy to everyone within a week. They spent the next few minutes discussing deadlines, what should go on the application, and who would receive them.

"I'm no good at making forms, but I can be the first contact person," Nate offered.

"I'll put something together," Lizzy said.

Darcy, who had no intention of getting involved in any paperwork, added, "I can set up a private online message board we can use to share documents and notes." He removed a blank piece of paper from his folder. "I'll need your emails," he handed the paper to Charmaine who was on his right. Lizzy noted a faint smile and blush as Charmaine took the paper. She imagined he was on the receiving end of a lot of attention from the female student body and wondered how he handled that. Relationships like these have happened, but she's never heard of one that turned out well. There were always casualties on both sides. But, if anyone could get away with it, it would be the famous and rich Dr. William Darcy. People like him were always getting away with something. She felt her eyes draw together and narrow in on him when Nate nudged her. "Here ya go," he said, handing her the paper.

"Now all we need to do is decide who Coach's contact person or CP will be."

Darcy and Lizzy glanced at each other, feeling it would most likely be one of them, the professors, but to everyone's surprise, Charmaine volunteered. "I have a light semester," she said.

Nate slapped his notebook closed. "Sounds great to me. Hey, Professor Bennet, if you have a spare minute, I'd like to talk with you about something."

Lizzy glanced at her watch. Between this new set of obligations and worrying about Dr. Darcy jumping on Nate again, she had almost forgotten about Wickham. "Umm, can it wait?" She stood up, thinking she would have a quick word with Darcy about tonight, then off to meet Wickham, but he was walking away with Charmaine. Dr. Darcy said something that caused Charmaine to throw her head back and laugh. Lizzy wondered if she was seeing things. That man and laughter just didn't seem to go together.

She caught up with them. "Dr. Darcy," she said, causing them to stop and turn around. The uncomfortable feeling of being the third wheel crept up, and she swallowed before asking him if he had a minute to talk. He gave a quick nod, followed by, "Of course."

The quad area had thinned out, and she waited until Charmaine had stepped away before speaking. "I wanted to make sure you were okay with tonight. The dinner with Jane and Charles?"

"Yes. Why wouldn't I be?" He crossed his arms, causing the sleeves of his light gray dress shirt to tighten against his biceps. Not monogrammed, Lizzy noticed.

"Well, it was a bit presumptuous of him to just assume we were free and …"

"He asked me first and probably assumed your sister knew your availability. Are you saying you can't come?"

"No. Not at all. I wanted to make sure that you know it's just us going as …"

"Chaperones?" he offered, causing Lizzy to blink in surprise.

"Does Charles Bingley need chaperoning?"

Darcy chuckled. "No. I wouldn't think so, but perhaps he is worried your sister will take things more serious than they should be and invited us along as a sort of … buffer."

Lizzy's head snapped back; a movement that would have served as a warning to anyone else. "Serious? Buffer?"

He nodded. "Yes. Charles and I are just passing through. We wouldn't want anyone to get the wrong idea."

"Wrong idea?"

"Yes. Why do you keep repeating me like that? It's annoying."

Lizzy planted her feet into fighting mode, lifted her free hand to point a finger at his chest, and was just about to let loose when she caught sight of George Wickham over his shoulder. She took a calming inhale and lowered her hand. "While I would *love* to continue our conversation, I need to go see someone else now." Someone a lot more pleasant than you, she wanted to add. Darcy turned to follow her gaze. Wickham's steps slowed when he noticed Darcy staring at him.

"What's he doing here?"

Lizzy slipped the Y2K binder into her bag and slung it over her shoulder. "He's here to see me," she said. "See you tonight."

Wickham had stopped walking towards her and stood waiting next to a bench on the concrete path that surrounded the quad. As she got closer, she noticed a look of confusion on his face, so unlike the air of confidence he had yesterday in their sitting room.

"Hi! I hope I didn't keep you waiting."

He brushed away her concern with a wave of his hand. "Not a problem. You all looked pretty involved, so I just waited."

She smiled and looked at what remained of the Y2K folks. "Just another extra duty they expect us to do. And lucky me, Dr. Darcy and I are on the same committee!"

He nodded, but she got the impression that he wasn't listening, since his eyes looked past her. She followed his gaze and discovered that it rested on none other than Dr. Darcy. "So you two will be working together?" he sked.

"Unfortunately!" she laughed and then regretted the outburst. Despite her feelings, she knew she shouldn't talk negatively about a colleague. "It's not a big deal," she added. "Did you bring the CD?" But Wickham was not paying attention to her.

They were far apart, but the two men faced each other like bulls preparing to charge. The tension was palpable. Dr. Darcy took a step forward, then stopped.

"What happened between you two?" Lizzy asked.

Wickham turned to face her. "May I walk you home?" he asked, all smiles and charm. She glanced behind her. Dr. Darcy had vanished.

"Normally, I wouldn't say anything about the past—sleeping dogs and all that—but since you'll be working closely with him, I feel I must tell you what sort of man he really is," Wickham said.

"I'm listening," she replied.

CHAPTER 15

Lizzy was almost an hour late getting home. She rushed upstairs to find Jane pacing in the hallway. Before Jane could speak, Lizzy held up a hand. "Don't start. It's been a crazy day." A look of panic crossed Jane's face. "Don't worry, I'm still coming. Give me 15 minutes to dress and catch my breath." Jane nodded, but wanted an explanation. Lizzy placed her hands on Jane's shoulders. Already dressed for the evening, she wore a simple white sleeveless, knee-length dress and light makeup. "Just the typical pre-semester chaos."

In her bedroom and away from Jane's anxious gaze, Lizzy tried to focus on getting ready, but her mind wouldn't let her. What Wickham had shared was too disturbing, so she bypassed Longbourne and went to see Charlotte.

"He said *what* about Dr. Darcy?!" They were in her bedroom and with a house as big as the President's Mansion, there was no chance of being heard, but Lizzy asked her to keep her voice down, just in case.

"Wickham practically called him a thief. Said that after Darcy's father passed away, Darcy completely ignored the will. Overnight, Wickham lost his home *and* the money he was counting on to continue his education."

"Did he say why? Dr. Darcy doesn't seem like the sort to do something so devious. At least not without a good reason."

"When I asked him about that, Wickham wouldn't say, exactly. Mentioned something about jealousy and how Darcy may have resented all the attention he got from his father. Apparently, Wickham had a bright future in front of him. He mentioned something about board members of Darcy Finance hinting that *he* should get the leadership position and *not* Darcy."

Charlotte's face got serious. "Do you believe him? And don't let your prejudice of Dr. Darcy sway you."

"What do you mean, prejudice? I don't have a prejudiced bone in my body."

Charlotte crossed her arms, tilted her head to the side, and looked at her friend. "You do with him, admit it. Which is something I wanted to ask you about. Others have dismissed or talked down about your work; why does what he says or thinks matter so much to you?"

She had wondered the same thing, but with no answer, she used the urgency of the day to get out of responding. "Oh, no time to get into all that now. If I'm any later, Jane will kill me."

.　　.　　.

Lizzy stood in front of her bedroom mirror and smiled at her quick transformation. No time to iron, so she opted for her gathered skirt with a pink and blue floral pattern and soft blue short-sleeve top. She laid a hand across her middle to quiet her stomach. Ever since she had agreed to accompany Jane, her emotions ran from annoyance to anxiousness. Annoyance from the fact that she would much rather stay home and review Missy Elliott's latest album. It was on the syllabus, and she needed to study it before classes started. Her anxiousness was because she didn't want to let her sister down. Jane has had her fair share of interest from the opposite sex. The last was an intern at the clinic. When the internship was over, he left Jane and Merryton for Chicago. Everyone expected her to be upset with his absence, since they had dated steadily for several months. When asked, she would simply shrug her shoulders and say that she thought Chicago suited him well. "He'll be happy there."

Lizzy closed her eyes, took a deep breath, and exhaled slowly. It was something she did to quiet her mind and focus. Tonight is all about Jane, she told herself. And not about that back-stabbing, hoity-toity snob called—she stopped, refusing to even let his name enter her thoughts. She grabbed her purse and walked into the hallway. "I'm ready," she sang out. "Let's do this!"

Jane drove their 1990 Saturn into the restaurant's crowded parking lot. Lizzy hadn't been to the Medford Grille in several months. The last time was for a liberal arts faculty happy hour. The Grille, as the locals called it, was one of the city's oldest restaurants and a local favorite. No reservations, and diners could have up to an hour's wait. She doubted Charles Bingley or Dr. William Darcy had ever had to experience such an inconvenience.

"Do you think they're here yet?" Jane asked, as they made their way to the entrance. "I should have called ahead and asked Uncle James to save us a table." James, their uncle from their mother's side, started at the Grille back in high school as a dishwasher and busboy, rose to manager and is now co-owner.

"I'm sure it will be all right," Lizzy answered. "We can always kill time in the bar." She turned her head around the crowded parking lot, searching for an extraordinarily rich-looking vehicle. She didn't know what they drove, but was sure it would stick out like a sore thumb. A golden sore thumb.

They entered the packed restaurant. Couples and families crowded into the waiting area, looking impatient and hungry. Lizzy walked to the hostess to get their names on the list. "We are expecting two more," she shouted over the noise. Before the young hostess could write their names down, her Uncle James appeared. "There you are," he said with a hug and peck on the cheek. "Your father called and told me to expect you." He winked at the hostess, whose name tag said Sheila. "I've got this." He grabbed two menus and motioned for his nieces to follow him.

"Our father called?" Lizzy asked as they snaked through the dining room.

Jane told Lizzy she wanted to let at least one of their parents know. "He said it would be just between us. For now, at least."

James led them to the other side of the restaurant, and a corner table. He handed them the menus. "I'll direct your dates to the table as soon as they get here."

.   .   .

"Are you sure this is the place?" Darcy stared at the establishment in front of him. Medford Grille glowed in neon blue lights attached to what looked like a thatched roof. The red brick building was two stories, the second floor looking more like a residence than a restaurant. The bottom half was more commercial, with a bank of windows, a small courtyard, and benches. Rose bushes and other florals spilled out of oversized containers sprinkled throughout. A few people sat on the benches, waiting for what he couldn't tell.

"Looks ... interesting," he said. "I can't wait to see the wine list."

Charles walked around the car to join him. He had wanted to take them to a place called the Mustard Seed, the only Michelin-rated restaurant within 20 miles. But Jane had insisted on this place, saying it was a local favorite. He agreed, thinking that he would take her to the other place on their next date. If his friend did not blow this one. He loved him like a brother, but he could be trying sometimes. Bingley wiggled his shoulders, trying to adjust the strap of his sling. "Come on, old man, it will be fun. Something different. Just be ..."

"Myself?" Darcy supplied.

"No! I mean, yourself is fine for the lecture hall and academic debates, but this is a date, a social and casual affair, so please Darcy, I'm begging you." Charles took a deep breath. It had been a stressful day. He spent the afternoon trying to find out what George Wickham was up to and why he was here, in North Carolina of all places. His investigation yielded little, but he was still waiting on a few return phone calls that might shed some light. Darcy, it appears, also had a trying day. When he finally made it home, it was hard to get anything out of him, except for some mumblings about committees, Y2K hysteria, and Wickham.

"Did you see him? On Campus?" Charles had asked.

Darcy answered yes but left out whom he had seen him with. Having the sisters of the woman Charles was interested in involved with George Wickham was a train of thought he did not want to go down or tell Charles about. "He was just hanging around doing nothing. Like always.

Charles suggested that maybe, for whatever reason, Wickham had come to Delany to spy on them, but Darcy cut him off. "That man is the last person who should be on your mind right now," he said.

Darcy slipped his car keys into his pocket. "Don't worry about me, Charles. I know how important this is to you." He laid his right hand on his heart. "My best behavior. I promise."

Bingley smiled. "That's the spirit. And who knows, you may end up enjoying yourself!" He clapped him on the back, then glanced down at his friend's clothing choice for the evening. White pants with an off-white belt, a white polo shirt, and light beige canvas sneakers. The only spot of color on him was the small, dark blue Ralph Lauren logo. "What *are* you wearing, by the way?"

Darcy stopped and adjusted his belt. "It's from Ralph Lauren's summer collection. They say white down here is a big deal. In the summer, that is."

The only white on Bingley were his socks, which you couldn't see. He was wearing dark blue jeans and a coral-colored button-up shirt. One of the many custom-made shirts he owned, and it fit him perfectly, both in size and hue. "Well, I asked Corrine what the style was here, and she said this was fine."

Darcy chuckled. "Taking fashion advice from the cook, now?"

About five minutes after Uncle James seated Jane and Lizzy, he returned with their dates. Bingley came into view first with a big smile on his face. He looked like a kid coming down the stairs on Christmas morning. Lizzy blinked at the figure who followed him and suppressed a gasp when she realized it was Dr. Darcy. Without the dark blue suit and tie, he looked different. On anyone else, the abundance of white would look silly, but on him, just the opposite seemed to be the effect. The arms of the polo shirt hugged firm, muscular biceps, making the contrast between his dark brown skin and the bright white of the shirt very appealing. And sexy. She gulped.

"Hello there," Charles said as he pulled out the seat next to Jane. "You look beautiful."

Lizzy saw her sister's shoulders curl forward as if to shield herself from the compliment. "Yes, she does," Lizzy said, her voice strong and sincere. Charles pulled his eyes away from Jane, and smiled, looking slightly embarrassed, at Lizzy.

"Oh," said Jane, "forgive me. This is my sister, Elizabeth. We all call her Lizzy."

Charles extended a hand. "Nice to meet you, and thanks so much for coming." He turned to Darcy. "And I believe you already know Darce."

"Darce?" Lizzy asked, repeating the one-syllable pronunciation.

"Charles is the only one who calls me that. I prefer William," he said, taking the seat next to her.

Lizzy nodded.

"And you?" Darcy prompted.

Lizzy shook the cloth napkin and laid it across her lap. "Elizabeth is fine."

Miss Shannon, their waitress, came and greeted the Bennets like they were old friends, which they were. Miss Shannon was one of the older staff members. She was short, round, and tended to call her customers honey or babe. She had a plump, welcoming face and wore a pair of half-rimmed reading glasses perched on the tip of her nose. "Nice to see you ladies again," she said. "And your ... dates." Even though Lizzy knew full well that Miss Shannon, along with everyone else in the place, knew who their "dates" were, she provided introductions. Miss Shannon nodded her approval. "Now, what would you all like to drink?"

After she left, Bingley provided a brief retelling of how he and Darcy had met and their years-long friendship.

"It's really not that unusual a story," Darcy said after Charles finished. "Two very young and terrified boys, thrown into an unusual and often hostile situation."

"Hostile?" Lizzy asked.

"The school was full of ancient, blue-blood families; children born with a silver spoon and bored with life, so they picked on anyone different or appeared vulnerable." He nodded towards Charles, who was now quietly chatting with Jane. The two had morphed into their own little world. "We watched each other's backs as they say, and from that, our friendship evolved."

Lizzy thought about Wickham's story which, if true, would make his acquaintance with Darcy almost a decade longer. "So, you two are dear, old friends," she said.

"Like brothers," Darcy nodded.

Shannon returned with their drinks. "Y'all ready to order?" she asked. She took out her pen and pad and began writing. "The usual for the Bennet sisters?"

"Of course," Lizzy said. She and Jane always split the Grille's famous chicken fried steak with mashed potatoes, smothered in white sausage gravy. It came with green beans, cooked with smoked pork, and a brick-sized piece of honeyed cornbread.

Across the table, Jane nodded. "Lizzy and I always get this. Kinda a tradition. I hope you don't mind."

Charles picked up a menu. "Not at all." He peered over at Darcy, who was also looking over the menu. "Looks like the type of cooking our Miss Sarah would be good at."

"Miss Sarah?" Lizzy asked.

Before answering, they gave Miss Shannon their order. She scribbled it on her pad. "Sounds good."

"Miss Sarah is the new cook and housekeeper Caroline hired. She'll be there on Corrine's off days," Charles explained.

"*Two* household servants," Lizzy said. "Must be nice."

Darcy and Charles glanced at each other. They had become used to these snide responses whenever their ability to hire domestic help came up. Disbelief and questions from white people; sarcasm tinted with jealousy from everyone else. "It *is* nice," Darcy said. "Thank you."

"And necessary," Charles added. "Two bachelors like us would have that lovely mansion all in shambles if left on our own."

"At the risk of sounding sexist, you have a sister, don't you?" Lizzy asked.

"Caroline? Oh, good god no!" Charles said with a burst of laughter. "Her expertise is decorating. And spending money."

Jane nodded. "And she is very good at it. Decorating, I mean. Lizzy, you should see Netherfield! It's simply beautiful now, not at all like the mess it was when we saw it on that field trip back in the 4th grade."

"Fifth," Lizzy said. "And it was for Black History Month. But that was before it fell into private hands."

"Really?" Charles asked, looking surprised. "I wonder if we can bring that back? If all goes according to plan, Netherfield could welcome students by next school year." He looked at Jane. "I'd love to play tour guide."

"I thought you were heading to Cape Town in the spring. To check on the new wineries?" Darcy asked him.

"Cape Town?" Jane asked. "South Africa?"

Charles nodded. "Yes. We started a winery there a few years ago. Took over one, actually. From a colonizer." He grinned as his fingers made quotation marks around the label. "Some white family that was scared the Blacks were dead set on getting revenge for all those years of apartheid." He picked up his drink and took a sip. "So, Bingley Wineries grabbed it up, and now the place is run by the people who should have been running it all these years."

Lizzy laughed. "You sure are good at taking things back from white folks. A plantation and a winery."

He accepted the compliment. "I am, aren't I?" He continued to explain how his parents had instilled in him and his sister a duty to give back. "Caroline can seem a little … snobbish sometimes, but she and I share the same philosophy. At least when it comes to the business."

Lizzy noticed Darcy shifting in his seat. "And what's your family's business philosophy, Dr. Darcy?" she asked.

"To work hard and never make excuses," he said, sounding like a robot.

Three blank faces turned and stared at him, but before anyone could respond, Miss Shannon returned. A young man, dressed in black pants and a crisp white shirt, accompanied her, carrying a huge round tray with their dinners on it. "Here we are now," she said as she moved the plates from the tray to their table. She set the last plate, straightened up, and looked over the table. "Y'all need anything else?" Lizzy saw Charles's eyes widen as he took in Jane's meal. "Yes," Jane said before he could ask. "That's *half* the serving."

Talk quieted down as everyone's attention turned to their meal. The Grille wasn't fancy, but no one would deny the quality and taste of their food. Jane nodded towards Charles' dish. "That's my father's favorite," she told him.

Charles took a spoonful of his shrimp and grits. "It's delicious," he said. "I ordered it because I thought it would be a dish my one good arm could handle. Next time, I am having what you're having." In between bites, he glanced across the table. "How's yours, Darcy?"

"It's all right. The salmon is a bit dry, and it's farmed rather than—"

"Okaaaay," Charles said, cutting off the critique. "Next time, get what I'm having. You will not be disappointed."

"I'm so glad you like it," Jane said. Then to Darcy. "Sorry, you didn't like the fish."

Darcy shrugged. "It's my fault for trying to order something healthy." He looked around at the other tables and saw plates filled with deep fried foods and covered in gravy. Vegetables were mostly absent or prepared in a way that obliterated any nutritional value. "Tell me, as a health care professional, do you worry about places like this exacerbating the health problems in the Black community?"

Next to him, Lizzy stiffened. He really stepped into it now, she thought.

Jane set her fork down. "No, I do not." She waved a hand around the crowded dining room. "The people in my community are hardworking and honest, doing the best they can with what they have. Many have suffered *and* survived tragedies and setbacks that you can only imagine. The Medford Grille is one of the few places left in the community where people like them—like us—can go to relax and forget about our troubles." She took a deep inhale. "If you want to identify problems in the community, start with something else like predatory lending, police misconduct, or the under-funded education systems."

To Lizzy's surprise, he didn't bite back, but looked almost pleased with her comeback. "Well said, Miss Bennet. Thank you for educating me on that point."

Across the table, Jane smiled. She rarely spoke with such conviction, but she had very little patience for anyone who would criticize her beloved community. "You're welcome," she said. "We didn't get to talk much yesterday, but I am interested in your area of study. My father said it was something to do with financing in poor communities."

"Micro-loans," Darcy said. He glanced at Charles and decided to surprise him by not taking the bait and launching into an economics lecture—his favorite subject. "But tonight's not the time for that discussion. Tell us more about your family. Five sisters?"

Both Jane and Lizzy laughed before Jane introduced the other Bennet sisters to him and Charles. "And then there's Lydia," Jane ended with a sigh. "She's young, impulsive, and—"

"Silly," Lizzy interjected. "As our lovely father likes to say. Sometimes we think she believes all the Y2K hype about the world falling apart, so she's having as much fun as she can before the end arrives."

Darcy thought about the girl he saw with Wickham and decided that this description of her fit perfectly.

"It is crazy, isn't it?" Charles said. "Darcy and I know a few families who believe all hell is going to break loose and are stockpiling supplies *and* weapons. One or two have even built bunkers out in the desert."

"Our freshman class is a little low this year and Dr. Lucas and enrollment think it has something to do with all the hysteria."

They spent the next few minutes talking about the pending disaster. Jane told them about the patients wanting everything from extra meds to microchip implants. "The things people believe," she said, shaking her head.

Charles agreed. "Darcy tells me that all will be well. And I trust his judgment more than anyone else's."

Lizzy took one more bite of her chicken fried steak before surrendering. Even a half serving was too much. " And what makes you so sure, Dr. Darcy?"

He shrugged. "Practical common sense, mainly. The financial industry has been preparing for this for years. It's new to everyone *but* them."

"And Prince," Charles said.

"Excuse me?" Lizzy said.

"You know the song. *1999,* by Prince. He had to have known it would blow up when the year finally came."

"And when did he write it?" Darcy asked.

"1982," Charles said, surprising everyone.

Lizzy smiled. "Correct, but he wrote it wanting to give people hope for the future, despite how apocalyptic everything seemed."

"Did he?" Charles asked. "Ah yes, of course. You would know all about that. Your studies must be very interesting, *and* a lot of fun, I bet."

Lizzy bristled. "Yes, it is fun, but there's a significant and culturally relevant side to the genre that I try to focus on in my courses."

"And how are misogyny, sexism, and glorifying violence culturally relevant?" Darcy smirked.

Lizzy turned to face him. "And it's because of *people like you* that I designed the course. Those quick to judge based on racist stereotypes and irrational fears."

Darcy opened his mouth to fire back, but Charles' wide-eyed stare stopped him. He also noticed Jane looking uncomfortable. He swallowed his rebuke and turned back to his meal.

"Well," Charles said into the awkward silence. "I hope you and I can discuss it further … next time."

Darcy took one more bite of his salmon, set his fork down, removed his napkin from his lap, and placed it on the table next to his plate. Lizzy glanced at him, but his eyes were pointed toward Charles. Something passed between them, reminding her of how she and Jane could communicate with just a simple look.

Lizzy folded her arms and leaned back in her chair. "Sure," she said. "Next time."

Miss Shannon appeared, saving them from any more awkwardness. "Who's ready for dessert? I saved y'all some peach cobbler."

Everyone passed on the cobbler. Charles paid the bill, including a generous tip, and the foursome made their way to the parking lot. Jane and Charles lingered behind the two professors, who walked silently, side by side. During dinner, Lizzy had listened for an opportunity to bring up Wickham, but the time never came. Overall, the evening turned out better than she had expected, at least until that last bit. Well, she did learn that the bond between these two men was close and sincere. One regret Wickham had shared with her was being cut off from Charles. "He's a good one, that Bingley," Wickham told her.

She turned to see her sister and the good one deep in conversation. Dr. Darcy was looking at them, too. "It must be nice being so close to your family," he said. "Always having someone to talk to and do things with."

"People from small families say that," she said. "But *we're* always thinking about how nice it would be to be an only child or have half the number of siblings."

He lowered his eyes and stared at the pavement for a few seconds. "Yes, being an only child has its advantages. But then we go out and find our own siblings. We latch on to the first fellow who doesn't tease or bully you and hope for dear life that he's a keeper."

"Like you and Charles," she said.

He nodded. "Exactly."

Throughout dinner, Lizzy tried to pick up on Jane's feelings, but her sister was good at guarding herself. Charles, on the other hand, seemed to be the type to wear his heart on his sleeve. His admiration was on full display that night. And his best friend confirmed it. "Charles is quite ... taken with your sister," Darcy said to fill in the silence.

Lizzy agreed. "Is he usually 'quite taken' with women?"

His face stiffened. "If you're asking me if he's a player, then the answer is no. A definite no."

Lizzy didn't know what had compelled her to ask that. She got a pleasant feeling from this Charles Bingley, and she was eager to get home so she and Jane could debrief. A feeling of relief came when she saw Jane and Charles walking towards them. "I didn't mean to insinuate anything negative," she said. "I know a good fellow when I see one." When the pair were a few feet away, she offered her hand. "Well, goodnight then. I guess I'll see you on campus. Maybe."

Before he could respond, Charles and Jane were upon them. They had a favor to ask.

CHAPTER 16

Jane wanted to take Charles for a drive around Merryton's historic downtown. Darcy could take Lizzy home, couldn't he? Jane pulled Lizzy to the side. "Please, Lizzy. I know I've already asked a lot of you, but …?"

"Of course," Lizzy agreed. She patted her sister's arm. "Take your time," she said. "I'm sure William and I can manage for a few more minutes." Jane and Charles practically skipped to the Saturn. Despite this final inconvenience, Lizzy was happy for her. Stress from Jane's work at the clinic was showing, so it was nice to see her relaxed and happy.

"I parked my car over here," Darcy said, turning Lizzy's attention away from the happy couple. She followed him and despite trying not to, she couldn't help noticing and admiring the way his backside looked in those white pants, which were tighter than the suits he wore on campus. Physically, Dr. Darcy ticked all her boxes, except for the hair. She always preferred longer curlier hair, loose enough to run her fingers through. Like Wickham's. Darcy sported a short, faded style.

He led her to a silver Lexus RX, which surprised her. She imagined him driving a sporty Porsche or Beemer, not this mini-SUV, what she would classify as a family car. The Lexus chirped. "Allow me," he said, opening the passenger side. Lizzy slid in and inhaled that new car smell. The Saturn that she and Jane shared was hitting the 10-year mark. It ran well, but getting a new car was on her 2000 to-do list. Maybe I'll get one of these, she thought with a laugh.

Darcy was taking more time than necessary, and she was just about to turn her head to look for him when he finally joined her.

"Got lost?" she joked.

"What?" he said, his voice harsh, as if he was reprimanding a disobedient child.

"I was joking."

He sighed. "I apologize. I've been told that I sometimes appear … abrupt." His mouth parted into a small, child-like smile. "One of my many faults, as Bingley says." He turned his attention to driving out of the crowded parking lot. After he was on the street, he asked for directions to her house, but she didn't hear him. She had her head turned, gazing at the buildings and signs she had seen a thousand times before, debating whether it was worth it to revisit their rap music debate. But then what for? Dr. Darcy didn't sign her paychecks and as long as her students gained new understandings and enjoyed her classes, she had nothing to worry about. Something told her not to bring up George Wickham either. He broke into her thoughts, asking again for directions.

The drive to Longbourne took longer because of Lizzy's misdirection. "I'm sorry," she whispered after her mistake. "I must be tired."

He agreed. "It's been a long day. Besides prepping for classes, that committee—"

"About that. I wanted to ask why you are doing committee work. Surely, you're excused. Unlike the rest of us."

"You're right. It is not part of my contract."

"And?"

"And I am not here just as an instructor to lecture on micro-loans and economics. I'm also interested in getting to know the Delany faculty and community." He left the part out about Dr. Lucas suggesting he serve on a committee. The car slowed as they approached an intersection. "And besides, this one should be interesting." He shrugged. "Maybe I'll come to understand what all the hype is about."

"Well, I don't believe all that about planes falling from the sky or the banks failing. But I know people are going to be partying like—"

"It's 1999," he said, flashing a smile and taking Lizzy by surprise. She swallowed and felt her dinner churning inside her stomach. The to-go container sat awkwardly on her lap, making her wish she had just left it at the Grille.

"That was a joke," he said. "Not a very good one, obviously."

"Or original," she added, and to her surprise, he laughed.

"You're discovering all my faults this evening, Elizabeth."

"Lizzy. You can call me Lizzy if you like."

He pulled to a stop in front of her house. The downstairs lights shone through the sitting room curtains and she could see people moving about.

"I'd like to," he said, his voice almost a whisper.

The unfamiliar tone caused her to turn towards him. When their eyes met, what she saw surprised her. What a beautiful shade of dark brown, she thought. She cleared her throat, then turned away, muttering something about how using first names was okay, but only when they were not at work. Worried he would misunderstand her, she added that she "didn't think" they would see each other "too much" outside of school.

"We won't?" he asked.

"Didn't you see those two prancing away towards the car? They couldn't *wait* to be rid of us."

His face shifted. "I noticed that too."

"And does that bother you?" she asked.

He shook his head. "No. Charles knows what he's doing–"

"And so does Jane."

He was silent for a moment, staring out the front window. "And do you know what you're doing?"

"Oh god," she said, reaching for the car's door handle. "If this is about my work at Delany, then we can end this discussion right now. Dr. Lucas, the board, and my students have no—"

"Not about that. Wickham. What were you doing with him this afternoon?"

The streetlamp above the car flickered. "Oh yeah," she said. "I saw you spying on us."

"I wasn't spying. Wickham is the one that needs to be watched. At all times. I had the unfortunate experience of seeing him the other day, too." He glared at her. "On campus and with *your* sister."

"Lydia?"

"That one. And judging by the company she keeps and the apparent silliness—"

"*Excuse me,*" she said. "I know you're an only child, raised in a different environment, but even *you* should know that's crossing the line."

"What?" he responded. "Speaking the truth?"

"Disrespecting my sister and *right in front of my face!*"

"It wasn't disrespecting; it was a warning." He shook his head. "If you knew what I know about George Wickham you'd be thanking me."

"He said the same thing about you," she said.

Darcy's grip on the steering wheel tightened and twisted as if he was wringing out a wet rag. Or strangling somebody. Lizzy began to regret her last comment, but just as quickly she reproached herself for the knee-jerk need to apologize. She turned to look at her house and could see more movement behind the curtains. Hopefully, it wasn't her mother trying to get a peek at who was in front of her house. The porch lights flicked on, and Lizzy knew it was time to end this, whatever it was.

"Well, thanks for the ride," she said, unbuckling her seat belt. "I guess we'll see each other at the next committee meeting." When she reached for the door handle, Darcy placed his hand on her shoulder. "I don't know what Wickham told you—don't want to know—but you have to believe me when I say he is not one to be trusted. Or even befriended, for that matter."

Her mouth formed to answer back, but when the front door opened, she stopped. She sucked in her breath as she recognized the people coming out of the house. All family, except for one. The sight of him caused panic to rise. Darcy continued to speak, but all her attention was on the front porch. Like an animal sensing, but not yet seeing the danger, she knew the quicker he left, the better. She opened the car door. "Thanks again for taking me home." She stepped out of the car and while fumbling with the to-go bag, she misjudged the Lexus's height, and stumbled a bit. As she righted herself, she heard Darcy asking if she was okay. She kept her eyes on the front porch and told him she was fine. His eyes followed hers and when he saw what she saw, his plan to get out and help her evaporated. Then they both heard her mother. "Lizzy? Is that you?"

Mrs. Bennet pushed past Lydia and Wickham and headed towards the car. "It is you! I was hoping you would make it home before our guest left." Mrs. Bennet turned to beam at a startled Wickham who was standing in between Lydia and Kitty.

Lizzy adjusted her purse strap over her shoulder and silently cursed her awkwardness.

"Who is this, Lizzy?" Not waiting for an answer, she walked to the passenger window and bent down to see for herself. Mrs. Bennet could have hurt herself by the way she snapped back up, eyes wide and mouth hanging open. "Elizabeth Marsha Bennet," she said with a sly grin. "Why, you little devil."

Lizzy tried to pull her away from the Lexus. "It's not what you think. He was just driving me home."

Mrs. Bennet escaped her grip, bent back down, and tapped on the window. "Is that you, Professor Darcy?" She motioned for him to roll down the window. By then, the rest of the front porch party had joined them. Lizzy noticed Wickham hanging back, his eyes on the Lexus.

"Cool car," Lydia said. "Were you on a *date,* Lizzy?" she added with a giggle, which was immediately interrupted by the sound of the Lexus speeding off and a short outcry from their mother. "Why I never! Did you see that, girls? He practically ran me over!"

"Are you all right?" Kitty asked.

"How could he run you over, Mother?" Lydia said. "You're on the *sidewalk.* Duh."

Wickham stepped forward. "I'm sure it startled your mother, Lydia. After all, he just sped off like he was a wanted man or something." He stepped up to Mrs. Bennet and put a hand on her shoulder. "Are you okay, Mrs. Bennet? Can I get you anything?"

"Yes, yes. I'm fine. Just startled. In all my years here at Delany, I have *never* been treated with such disrespect." She turned to glare down the street. "Just goes to prove that money can't buy manners."

Wickham looked at Lizzy with an I-told-you-so-gaze. "You are certainly right about that, Mrs. Bennet. It seems like the years haven't improved his manners, but then he was never known for having good manners."

A combination of tiredness and confusion overcame Lizzy. "It's getting late," she said. "And he's gone and probably will never come back, so let's drop it for now."

The others protested, saying they needed to hear more from Wickham. "You can't drop a bomb like that and then just leave," Lydia said, pouting.

"Lydia, your sister is right. Why ruin a good evening talking about him?"

"Agreed," said Mrs. Bennet. "Lizzy, into the house. You have some explaining to do, and George, so very nice seeing you again."

Wickham bowed his head and tipped an imaginary hat. "Good night, ladies." He walked away with a smile and a wave.

The Bennet women went back into the house. Lizzy spied Mary peeking down on them from an upstairs window. She assumed their father was asleep, or at least hiding away in his study. Her mind turned to Jane, wondering where she and Charles had gone to. Mrs. Bennet continued to ramble on about how nice Wickham was compared to, "That Professor Darcy!"

Lizzy sighed. "It's *doctor*, not professor, Mother."

"Hmph! It could be *King* Darcy, for all I care. I forbid you to see him, Lizzy," she said, closing and locking the front door.

Before driving around the corner, Darcy used his rearview mirror to look back at the scene. As the tallest one present, Wickham was easy to pick out, still on the sidewalk and surrounded by Bennet women. Darcy revved the Lexus' engine and turned. Lizzy's house was across the street from Delany, so he knew the way back to Netherfield. He hoped, but doubted, that Bingley would be home by now. "Lucky bastard," Darcy muttered to himself as he made his way onto the two-lane highway.

.　　.　　.

"What do you mean you 'drove off'? Please tell me you said goodbye, see you later or, or something." Bingley looked at his friend with worried eyes. Jane had just dropped him off and he had intended to go straight to bed, holding on to the romantic high he was experiencing. But he took a detour to the library when he noticed the light on. Darcy was there, deep in thought, and his bourbon. After asking if everything was all right, Darcy relayed the evening's events, including his hasty exit.

He shook his head. "It was stupid of me, but it was leave quickly, or get out of the car and—"

"And what? Punch him in the face?" Bingley walked over to him. "Give me that," he said, snatching the crystal tumbler from his hand. "I need this more than you." He downed the brown liquid and then immediately went into a coughing fit.

Darcy sat down and lowered his face into his hands. "What the hell is going on with that family? Did Jane mention anything about him?"

Bingley placed the empty tumbler on the table before joining him on the leather sofa. "Of course not. We had ... other things to talk about. I know you want to make sense of all this—and so do I—but hitting the booze every time you run into Wickham is not doing you any good."

Darcy leaned back and stared at the ceiling. "One of my reasons for accepting a position in this god-forsaken part of the country was the idea of getting away from it all. I hadn't expected to run into anyone I knew, let alone that bastard." He shook his head. "And he seems to have two Bennets under his spell. Lizzy and that young one."

"Lizzy?" Bingley asked. "Sounds like you had a cozy little car ride."

Darcy let out a disapproving grunt before quickly standing up. "It was, but then ..."

Charles suppressed a yawn. "Well, just ask 'Lizzy' about it tomorrow. Jane and I have a lunch date, so I'll ask her too."

Darcy vetoed the idea. "I'm sure he's filled their heads with lies and half-truths by now, so let's first try to uncover more about why he's here."

Charles agreed. Walking up the stairs, he cursed Wickham. "That dude sure knows how to ruin a great evening."

CHAPTER 17

Despite yesterday's drama, Lizzy had made good progress prepping for classes. On today's schedule, she had a mandatory training session with library services to go over the new computer system and security training. Another Y2K precaution. By the time she woke up, Jane was already gone. She would have to wait to find out how the rest of her evening with Charles had been. She decided to tackle the Lydia issue instead.

She caught Lydia in the hallway just as she left the bathroom. "What was Wickham doing here last night?" she asked, getting straight to the point.

"Why do you ask like that?" Lydia responded. "Delany students have been here before."

"He's neither a Delany student nor a teenager," Lizzy said. "I hope you and—"

"He was here to see *you*, not me, Miss Know-it-All," Lydia said. "Little did he know you were out with someone else."

"See me? What for?"

Lydia shrugged. "Claimed he had something to 'discuss' with you." Lydia eyed her sister up and down before continuing. "We into juggling men now, are we?"

The self-satisfied look on Lydia's face annoyed Lizzy more than she liked. "I'm not juggling anything," she said. Lydia wore tight jeans and a bright pink crop top and overdone makeup. This time with bright pink lipstick, thick mascara, and dark blue eyeshadow. She was getting bolder. She usually dolled up after she left the house.

"And where was Jane last night?" Lydia pointed a finger at Lizzy. "You two have got some explaining to do. Do the parents know?"

"Know what?" Lizzy realized that her intended confrontation with Lydia was not going as she had planned. She decided to leave it and see what she could find out on her own. Once Lydia felt she had the upper hand, there was no stopping her.

Lizzy pushed her attitude up a notch. Crossing her arms, she took a small step toward her sister. "In case you have forgotten, Jane and I are full-grown adults with careers and autonomy. *You* are still a minor, so please do not compare our behavior to yours." She was just about to tell her to wash her face when a vibrating noise stopped her. Lydia's hand flew to her jeans' back pocket. She pulled out her beeper and checked the screen. Whatever she read caused a smile to spread. "Sorry to interrupt our ... chat, but I have to go now, Miss Lizzy." She waved the beeper in front of Lizzy's face. "Some of us have things to do today. Important things."

About 30 minutes later, Lizzy left the house and headed towards her office. After she reached the quad area, she heard someone from behind calling her name. She turned around to find George Wickham waving at her.

"I was hoping to catch you this morning," he said when he got closer. It was obvious he had been out for a morning run. He wore black Adidas running shorts and a black T-shirt with the arms and collar cut off. Or torn off, she couldn't tell. His hair was secured back with a dark blue bandana. Sweat from his run made the shirt cling to his skin, outlining a firm, muscular chest. She stopped herself from taking a peek at his lower region.

Lizzy shifted from one foot to the other. "If this is about the CD, I haven't had a chance to listen to it yet."

He shook his head. "No. Nothing like that." He hesitated a few seconds before continuing. "Look, I may be way out of line, but I was wondering if you would want to go to this show tonight. I'm sure you've heard of it, being the resident music expert and all." He explained how he had heard about an open mic, spoken word event at The Crash Pad and thought it would be nice to go with her. "You know, check out some local talent and get your opinions."

She knew of the place, just like everyone else at Delany. It was a favorite student hangout. Faculty and staff went too, but always with a lot of discretion, and being seen there with a student was not at all discreet.

"Of course," he continued, "if I were a student here, there's no way I would ask you, but since I'm not."

"No, you're not, are you?" She conjured up a scene with the two of them at one of the Crash's small tables in the back, heads together as they discussed the entertainment, the crowd, and each other. "When did you say this was?" she asked, stalling for time.

He reminded her of the date. "Of course, I'd like to get to know *you* a little better, too."

Ten minutes later, Professor Bennet walked into the elevator that would take her to the 3rd floor and her office. She shook her head in disbelief at what she had just agreed to. She blamed the hair. She was a sucker for men with hair close to her texture. Of all the sisters, she had the most relaxed curl pattern and began wearing it in its natural state a few years ago. In high school, she discovered her attraction to men with the same hair type when her hand accidentally landed in Troy Fitzgerald's wavy locks during a game of volleyball. "You sure took your time removing that hand from Troy's 'fro," Charlotte commented later in the locker room.

Lizzy sighed. "It was just so soft, and, and—"

"Sexy?" Charlotte finished with a wink. Soon, Lizzy and Troy became an official couple, her first (and only) serious boyfriend. They were together until he moved away during her second year at Delany. The breakup hit her hard, and she soothed herself by spending hours listening to a rap mixtape he had left behind. Pretty soon, she was watching *Yo! MTV Raps*, collecting CDs and tapes, and then became a little obsessive with hip hop online chats and message boards. After she got caught scrolling through one in the Delany Library computer lab, she escaped reprimand by claiming it was research for a class. She earned a B for her persuasive speech defending Public Enemy's controversial song, *By the Time I Get to Arizona.* The instructor disagreed with her premise but appreciated the bold stance and reasoning. "We need creative thinkers like you," he had commented.

The elevator door opened to her floor and as she walked out, she reasoned it was the Troy similarity that pushed her to accept Wickham's invitation. She wondered if Jane and Charles could join them, but knew that wouldn't work. If Dr. Darcy had ill feelings for Wickham, it was almost certain that his best friend would too.

In her office, she stopped and stared at the university wall calendar. The Fall 1999 semester began tomorrow, but it already felt like mid-term to her. Between new happenings at Longbourne, the Y2K stuff, William Darcy, her father's forced retirement, and now Wickham, she prayed that nothing else would come up. As she waited for her computer to boot, she hoped that with the students busy moving back and setting up their dorm rooms, the Crash Pad would have a light crowd. She hadn't been there in a while and if nothing else, she'd get to see what's going on locally in the rap and hip-hop world. Could make a good lecture, she thought as she turned to her work.

.   .   .

William Darcy knew enough about higher education to understand how the beginning of the semester was the wrong time to plan anything extra. Last night's resolution to look into Wickham's affairs got pushed aside as anxious undergrads filled his inbox with questions or concerns, and ready-to-impress grad students vied for his time and attention. The department secretary, Mrs. Hoffman, handed him a stack of phone messages as he entered his office. He had spent most of the day with Dr. Baei, putting the final touches on a grant application and interviewing fellowship candidates. He took the stack of messages and walked to his office, hearing a mumbled, "You're welcome," before moving behind his desk. I'll make it up to her, he told himself as he leafed through the stack.

Most were from students whom he had already responded to via email, but he stopped when he saw one from Charmaine. *Have the first draft of the rubric ready. Could you give it a look?*

She can't be serious, he thought, but the idea that she could be an excellent source of information dissolved any irritation. Yesterday, after the committee broke up, she shared with him that this was her fourth time returning to Delaney. The first was almost ten years ago. "I've gotten to know folks here pretty well," she had told him.

Let's see how well, he thought.

.   ▪   ▪

Charmaine suggested they meet about 4PM in the Ancestors Garden, the one to the north of the Economics building. When he walked past the gates and into the area, he immediately recognized it as the place he had seen Professor Bennet. Mr. Bennet had told them about this garden when he came to Netherfield. Gazing around the lush and unique landscaping, Darcy now fully appreciated the reverence and pride which Mr. Bennet had used to describe the garden. "It was my great-great-grandfather's idea, but every Bennet after him has treated it as their own special project," he shared. The area possessed the trick of appearing manicured and uncultivated at the same time. Bright greenery lined the paths and spots of color peeked out here and there. He heard, but could not see, water trickling and assumed a fountain was nearby. Charmaine hadn't said where to meet, so he sat at the first bench he came to.

A storage facility in San Francisco held a few of his father's garden sculptures; the ones his Aunt Catherine didn't want. He wondered if Delany would like them for this garden. Who could he see about that? Before his mind could go too far down this new idea, Charmaine appeared from the opposite side of the garden.

She smiled and waved. "I thought you might be on this side," she said when she got closer. "I was at the part where the labyrinth is."

"Labyrinth? The famous labyrinth?" he asked.

She nodded. "One and the same. In the early spring, I try to volunteer here to help get the area ready for all that fresh growth."

"I thought the campus had a grounds crew."

"Oh, they do, but Mr. Bennet likes to let students work in here—under his strict supervision, mind you. He says it helps to give us ownership of the place." She sighed and looked around. "And it certainly does that, I can tell you."

"You know Mr. Bennet, the lead groundskeeper?"

"Yes, I do, and he's more than that. He drives around campus in that golf cart, giving us students pep talks, and, if necessary, warnings. Mr. Bennet is one reason I'm back. He keeps telling me that there is no such thing as 'too old' to do something. 'You aren't dead yet. Until then, you have the time.' That's what he keeps telling me, so I keep coming back."

Dr. Darcy stared at a tree he recognized as a magnolia, thinking about what an unusual family the Bennets were turning out to be. Gardener and campus sage?

"Oh, well," Charmaine said, interrupting his thoughts. She handed him a piece of notebook paper. "Here's what I have so far. Forgive me for not emailing it. I'm still waiting for my student email account to reactivate."

He glanced at the paper. "This is all right," he said. "Besides, your handwriting is impeccable."

She laughed. "That's what 12 years of Catholic education will get you. That plus a few raps of with ruler!"

Dr. Darcy grimaced, then turned his attention to the list Charmaine had made. They chatted a few minutes about it and then he returned the rubric, saying he thought it was fine. "You seemed to have covered everything," he said.

"Thank you."

He hesitated, trying to decide if asking about the Bennets was a good idea. But he didn't need to ask.

"You know," Charmaine said as she slipped the paper into her binder. "I heard a rumor about Mr. Bennet that's been bothering me."

. . .

Ten minutes later, Dr. Darcy left Charmaine and the Ancestors Garden. The rumor she had shared with him pushed all thoughts of Wickham aside. He wondered if Lizzy had also heard. He sat in his car and used reason to talk himself out of caring or doing something about the issue. Besides, what could he do anyway?

Before agreeing to work at Delany, he researched the institution looking for red flags around finances and reputation; their endowment was small but adequate, and he found nothing suspicious or unethical. If anything, Delany's historical roots and the community's continued pride and support impressed him. But he had seen nothing about the Bennets.

In reviewing the board's history, he noticed steady change in leadership beginning about 10 years ago. A few names he recognized as those of new and upcoming African American families gaining prominence in the business community. These were strictly bottom-line people who would have little regard for the sanctity of the Delany Bennet legacy agreement. But wasn't he also one of those people? He groaned and decided that the best course of action would be to learn as much as he could about this century's old agreement. But how could he find time for that?

CHAPTER 18

Longbourne House was quiet that evening. After a family dinner, minus Jane and Kitty, Lizzy went to her room to finish organizing her papers for tomorrow. It wasn't long before she heard Jane coming up the stairs. The clock told her she had about a half hour before leaving for the Crash Pad. Hopefully, Jane would be in a talking mood, she thought, walking to her bedroom.

After knocking, she opened the door to find Jane halfway out of her uniform. "Oh good," Jane said, tossing her uniform top into the dirty clothes hamper. "Hand me my robe." Lizzy unhooked a faded blue house robe from the hook on the door. She passed it to Jane before sitting down. "I was on my way to see you, but you got to me first!" Jane said. Lizzy eyed a bouquet on the bed, a colorful bunch of summer flowers and greenery.

"You saw Charles again?" Lizzy asked. " When?"

Jane tied the robe around her waist and sat down. She picked up the bouquet and held it on her lap like she was cradling a baby. "Charles is just … so nice!" she said. "We talked and talked and talked last night, both of us super surprised about how much we had in common."

"Like what?"

Jane shrugged. "Like everything—well, not everything, but you know what I mean. He's so easy to talk to and he really listens to me, Lizzy." She stopped and gazed down at her bouquet. "We had lunch today, and he's taking me to dinner on Thursday."

"Well, that answers my first question," Lizzy said. She glanced at the bouquet. "Not a rose guy, huh?"

Jane pressed the flowers to her chest. "Roses are so cliché. And he knows better than to pop something so serious on me too early."

"Well, that must be it 'cause he certainly can afford them." She looked at Jane, who was in another world as she gazed at her gift. "When are you going to tell the parents that it's … progressing?"

Jane sighed and rolled her eyes. "I guess it will have to be soon. Mother saw the flowers and had nothing but questions. Everyone at the clinic knows I had lunch with him today, so it won't be long before she gets a whiff of it. She may already know!"

"Oh, I doubt that because if she did, she'd be up here right now, giving you all sorts of tips on how to reel him in."

The sisters laughed. "But seriously, Jane, I'm really glad it's working out for you. You deserve some happiness."

Jane nodded. "I'm just going to take it one day at a time. He did mention how he and Darcy weren't sure how long they'll be here, so … we'll see what happens."

"A lot can happen between now and then," Lizzy said with a sly grin. "Besides, with all that money they've poured into Netherfield, I am sure he'll be coming back. A lot. And not just to spend time in that mansion."

Jane set the flowers next to her before asking Lizzy about how it had gone with Dr. Darcy. "I was worried," she said.

Lizzy shrugged. "It was all right. I did learn that he can act like a regular guy when he wants to." Lizzy closed her eyes and released a heavy sigh before continuing. "But then we got home."

After explaining what had transpired, Jane's look of shock made Lizzy smile. "Mother was DONE with him after that," she said.

"I wonder what it is about Wickham that made him so upset?" Jane said.

"Did Charles mention anything about him?" Lizzy said.

Jane shook her head. "Do you think I should ask him? I mean, for Lydia's sake."

Lizzy shifted a bit in her chair. "About that," she said. "Ummmm, well, I ran into him this morning—George, I mean Wickham—and he sort of asked me to go with him to Crash tonight and I said I would."

"Lizzy! What about Lydia?"

"What about her? There is nothing like that going on between those two. George Wickham may be … suspicious, but he's not dumb enough to get involved with a minor."

Jane crossed her arms. "And you know that because …?"

Lizzy shook her head and waved away Jane's concern. "Forget him. *Lydia's* not dumb enough to try something like that. Besides, when I asked her about him this morning, she told me he was here last night to see *me*, not her."

"You?" Jane asked with raised eyebrows.

Lizzy quickly filled her in. "He's interested in my musical opinion, that's all. And don't look at me that way. What more could he want?"

"Does Dr. Darcy know?" Jane asked.

"No. And why should he? What I do on my own time is my business."

Jane looked down at her feet. "I know that; it's just that he and Charles are like brothers. I'd hate for either of them to think we were keeping things from them."

"Oh," Lizzy said. "I guess that does kinda complicate things." She told Jane that she had no problem with her sharing it with Charles. "But I don't plan on telling Dr. Darcy anything if that's okay with you."

A look of relief swept over Jane's face. "Of course," she said, then added a thank you. They spent the next few minutes catching each other up. Lizzy told Jane about the Y2K committee and how she would be working with Dr. Darcy. Jane shared Mrs. Griff's glee over the upcoming ball. "She met with Caroline to plan it all out. Invitations are coming soon."

Lizzy stood up, shaking her head. "That was fast. Wonder who's going to make the list?"

Jane shrugged. "The usual Delany crowd. Plus, Caroline is inviting people from New York and California. Mrs. Griff is over the moon about that."

Lizzy stood up to go. "I bet she is."

. . .

As she had predicted, The Crash Pad was about half empty. She recognized a splattering of 4th years or grad students. George Wickham had called right before she left, saying he would be about 15 minutes late. "I'll get us a table," she had told him. Before sitting down, she walked to the bar and ordered a glass of red wine. Covering the wall behind the bar were pictures, small sculptures, and art, all dedicated to the school's mascot, the rhinoceros. Back in the day, the Rhino Wall's only décor was a real rhinoceros' head, a gift from an alum who killed one while on a hunting trip in Africa. It came down in the 80s, replaced with artwork from local artists and students. Anything with a rhino theme was welcome, as long as real rhinos weren't injured or killed in the process. Somewhere on that wall was a small picture made by Mary, the only Bennet to contribute.

Wine in hand, Lizzy wove through the tables until she found one near the back, giving her a good view of the front door and the stage. She kept her eyes on both. Twenty minutes later, and no Wickham, she contemplated leaving. Just then, the house lights dimmed, and the MC walked onto the small stage. He did the usual welcome and then informed the crowd that sign-ups had been light. "But not to worry," he crooned into the microphone. "The few brothers and sisters we have tonight are fly! Lit!" He pointed to the tip basket, a rhino's foot made of blue and gold fabric, and asked the audience to be generous. "We split the take between all the entertainers," he said. "After The Crash takes their quarter percent, don't you know?" He wink-winked at the audience.

"Twenty-five percent?!"

Lizzy looked up to see George Wickham standing next to the table. "Man, these guys need an agent." He laughed at his joke and sat down. Gone were the sweaty running clothes, replaced with black slacks and a dark blue shirt. He wore a gold chain around his neck, and for the first time, she noticed a diamond stud in his left ear. "Sorry to keep you waiting, but Douglas kept me late. He had a bunch of questions about the routine."

"Douglas?"

He noticed her drink and asked her if she wanted another. She declined. "He's Mashujaa's VP and the one all up in arms about this Y2K routine," he told her before excusing himself to get his drink.

He returned with a glass of beer and a shot of whisky. "That hard a day?" she asked.

He downed the shot and nodded. "I keep telling him not to worry, but …"

"Well, seeing how you came all the way from California to help them, it must be worth it."

He took a sip of beer. "Traveling the country teaching stomp wasn't what I had in mind for a career," he smirked. "But as you know, my career path was … stolen from me."

She leaned forward to respond, but the MC returned to introduce the first act, someone going by the name of NC Rap. She had never heard of him and about two minutes into the routine, she hoped to never hear him again. The audience was generous with their applause, but she and Wickham gave each other a knowing-eye look. "Don't quit your day job," Wickham whispered before downing the last of his beer.

Lizzy laughed, "Be nice. It's hard getting up there."

After a few more sub-par acts, he leaned over to ask her if she wanted to leave. "You start classes tomorrow, too," he added as they made their way toward the door.

The warm night felt good after the chilling A/C. Somewhere, a night-blooming jasmine was filling the air with its heady scent. Wickham inhaled deeply and patted his chest. "So, this is North Carolina?" he said.

"Well, part of it," Lizzy said. "Your first time in these parts?"

He nodded. "Never had a reason to come before. Besides the boarding school in Massachusetts and some time in New York, this is the only other time I've been on the East Coast."

She suggested they walk around the corner to a 24-hour coffee shop. He looked down at her and smiled. "Sounds like a plan."

He ordered a patty melt and fries, and Lizzy opted for hot tea with lemon and honey. "To help me sleep," she told him and then wondered why she felt the need to explain.

"So, this boarding school was the one you went to with Dr. Darcy?"

His mouth twisted into a skeptical grin. "*Doctor* Darcy. Yeah, but back then he was known as *awkward* Darcy." He laughed at his joke.

She thought about Darcy's hasty exit and had no trouble picturing him as an awkward, geeky teenager. An image of him in high-water pants, mismatched socks, black-rimmed glasses, and a shirt with plastic pocket protectors came to mind. But instead of ridicule, she felt the urge to hug this fragile young man. Wickham rambled on about Darcy's many faults, and she wondered how to make him stop. She took a sip of her tea, now lukewarm. "You and he weren't always enemies," she said. "Do you have any ideas about what made him turn on you like that?"

He popped the last French fry into his mouth. "Like I said, jealousy. Little Darcy couldn't stand it when his father paid any attention to me."

Lizzy nodded, but she had trouble conjuring up a jealous William Darcy. It just didn't seem to fit his personality. What little she knew about it.

"Tell me more about this stomp routine and working with the Mashujaas."

"Ahh, that," he said, "is a secret. Those brothers *do not* mess around. They really want to win this competition or whatever, which explains why they would shell out the dough to pay for someone like me to train them. Travel *and* living expenses."

This impressed Lizzy. She'd had very few lecture gigs that covered travel and other expenses. It was her turn to feel jealous.

"You probably heard Mashujaa is skating on thin ice this year. No doubt they're hoping a win—or at least a good showing—will take off some of the pressure."

He nodded. "Those frat boys …"

"I understand my sisters have been spending time at that house. You know anything about that?"

He gazed at her from across the table and a few beats passed before he answered. "Kitty and Darren are an item, I hear."

"Yes. And so far, the parents approve."

"Of Darren?"

"Yeah. Why?

"No reason. He seems like a cool dude." He laughed. "The kind a girl would take home to meet the parents."

She leaned back in the booth and folded her arms. "And you, Mr. George Wickham? Are *you* the type of 'dude' a girl would take home to meet the parents?"

He reached for his wallet, pulled out a few bills, and tossed them on the table. Lizzy noticed it was more than enough to cover both of them. He stood up and offered his hand to help her out of the booth. She took it, but he pulled her up with a little too much force and she found herself standing almost directly under his chin. She tilted her head up and when their eyes met, a feeling of claustrophobia overcame her. Her foot tried to step back but found it had nowhere to go. He held her there for a few seconds before moving aside. "No. I am not that type of dude."

CHAPTER 19

The sun was setting when Darcy pulled up into Netherfield's circular driveway. Exiting his vehicle, he cringed at the layer of dust and splattering of insect carcasses that covered the exterior of his Lexus. His deluxe condominium in San Francisco, Pemberly Towers, had a full-service garage that took care of cleaning and routine maintenance. Another big-city perk he was missing.

Caroline greeted him in the foyer. "I was on my way to call Charles to dinner," she said. "Now you can," she added with a grin.

"Sure," Darcy said. "I need to talk with him first, anyway."

"Don't be too long," Caroline said. "Corrine leaves in an hour."

He gave her a mock salute before walking up the staircase. Despite her constant moaning and complaining, he knew she was secretly enjoying her role as head of the manor, and he was glad she was there to take care of those things. The idea of hiring help never set well with Darcy, so he lived in an upscale condo whose homeowner fees included housekeeping and concierge services. He also had access to private secretaries; one at the university and the other from Darcy Finance & Consulting. As for meals, he ate mostly from restaurants, but could cook himself a simple meal.

He knocked before entering. Charles was sitting up on his bed wearing a dressing gown over his undershirt and slacks. He had removed the sling and stretched his injured arm across the bed, supported by a pillow. His other arm held the phone, and he motioned for Darcy to come in.

"Mmmm hmmm," Charles said into the receiver. He mouthed, "Wickham" and Darcy received the information like a splash of cold water to the face, bringing back into focus another unsavory issue in his life. He sat down on the side of Charles' bed, shook his head, and scolded himself for getting caught up in other people's business—specifically Bennet family business. What was it to him if this so-called legacy agreement was ending? Wasn't it he who thought it a one-sided arrangement, anyway? Before he could scold himself further, Charles ended his phone call.

"Well," he said, placing the phone on the receiver. "Seems like our old chum is *not* mending his ways."

"Stomp routines?!" Darcy exclaimed after Charles shared what he had found out.

"What the hell does Wickham know about that?"

"It seems that after they released him—"

"God, I regret agreeing to that deal," Darcy said, his voice shaking with anger.

"We all do," Charles said. "Hindsight and all—"

"That DA should have been fired."

Charles nodded. "Yes, yes, you know I agree with you, but do you want to hear what I found out or not?"

Darcy suddenly stood up and paced the room. "No! Yes! I mean … oh shit! Classes start tomorrow, and the last thing I need is George Wickham in my head."

Charles frowned. "That's true, but you *did* ask me to look into it, and seeing that he has taken up with Jane's sister, I thought it a good idea, too."

Darcy stopped pacing and leaned his back against the wall. "Not just Lydia," he said. "It seems like he's enamored the whole family."

"Wickham is like that. At first. The lucky ones discover the conniving SOB hidden underneath before it's …"

"Too late," Darcy whispered, finishing the sentiment.

Darcy doubted anyone from the Bennet family would be stupid enough to fall for one of George Wickham's scams. But he had thought that before and with people he knew well. Charles was worried about Jane and he—he admitted to himself—was worried about Lizzy. Plus, with her father's forced retirement, having a Wickham issue on top of that was something he wouldn't wish on anyone.

He released a long exhale and asked Charles to tell him what else he had discovered.

From their old acquaintances, Wickham still had a few friends willing to help. One of them scrubbed a few incidents off his record and another took him under his wing at a west coast record company. "Mostly rap music," Charles said. He snapped his fingers. "I bet Professor Bennet has heard of them."

Darcy nodded in agreement and could see Wickham using the connection to his advantage. "Go on," he said.

"Well, one thing led to another and a fraternity," he consulted his notes. "Mashujaa House contacted Wickham to help them plan their Y2K stomp competition. Mashujaa means hero in Swahili, by the way, but I understand most refer to them as just Shujaa, which translates to warrior. The folks in ASI were very helpful."

"And that's why he's here?" Darcy asked. "Do you know how much they're paying him?"

Charles shook his head. "But from what I learned, he's being reimbursed for actual expenses and only gets paid if they win. A percentage of the prize money. It's that kind of deal. So at the least, he's getting a free vacation."

"I don't buy it. That man has traveled all over the world, and I can hardly see him being satisfied with spending time in Merryton, North Carolina, for goodness' sake." But then a thought came. "Did he know I was here?"

Charles frowned. "That's a good question, but how could he? You would think that after what happened, he would want to stay as far away from you as possible." He flipped his notebook closed and set it on the nightstand. Dialing a phone and taking notes with one arm was more of a challenge than he had anticipated. At lunch with Jane, she advised him to take it easy, but doing this favor for his friend was too important to put aside. "Well, whatever the reason, I think it's time we tell them what we know. We need to stay at least one step ahead of that bastard."

Darcy agreed and checked his watch. "Caroline is waiting for us downstairs."

Charles' sore arm could use another dose of pain meds, but he also needed to get some food in him first. Before leaving for the dining room, Darcy asked him to wait on sharing any Wickham news with Jane. "I'll just let him know we are watching him," Darcy said. "Maybe that will be enough."

.   .   .

It was close to midnight when Lizzy made it home, so seeing her mother and Jane sitting at the kitchen table surprised her. Lizzy dropped her purse on the small entry table before joining them. "What's wrong?" she asked, hoping it had nothing to do with their father. Jane greeted her with tired, but happy, eyes. "Nothing. Mother was just giving me some dating tips."

Lizzy suppressed a laugh before pulling out a chair to join them. "So, she knows it all, then?"

Their mother crossed her arms. "Yes, and I had to hear from— of all people—Mrs. Lucas!"

"Well, now that you know," Lizzy said, "aren't you happy?"

Their mother unfolded her arms and turned to gaze at her. "I know that's what you think of me, Lizzy. That all I care about is getting my daughters married off to rich men. But it most certainly is not." She placed a hand on her heart. "All I want is for my girls— all of my girls—to be happy."

"We are hap—"

"And secure!" Mrs. Bennet said before getting up. She pushed in her chair. "And," she said, looking down on her daughters, "I would hate to see you two wait so long that having children became an … issue." She clicked her tongue. "Those biological clocks are going to start ticking pretty soon." She ignored the shocked look on their faces and turned her attention to Lizzy. "And where were you, Miss Elizabeth Bennet? *And* on the night before classes start. Must have been important."

Lizzy sighed and explained that Wednesdays were her late days, so she could sleep in, hoping her mother would forget about the early morning first-day ritual with Father.

"And …" Mrs. Bennet prompted.

"I just went to the Crash Pad to listen to some local rappers," Lizzy shrugged.

Her mother's lips pressed into a thin line. "I know you're keeping something from me," she said. "But no worries. I'm sure *Mrs. Lucas* will fill me in."

About 15 minutes later, washed and ready for the night's sleep, Lizzy thought about how her evening of collecting intel on Lydia hadn't materialized. In her freshman literature classes, she reminds her students that sometimes what an author doesn't say about a character or situation can be just as, if not more, enlightening than what was said. She turned onto her side, recalling how Wickham had left out any mention of Lydia when the subject of the two sisters came up. So, he either had little to do with Lydia, or he had too much to do with her; two scenarios that could make him hold his tongue. What she learned was that he was—she hated to admit—a bit of a charmer. Not charming in the prince on a white horse way, more of the used car salesman way. She could understand how her mother and Lydia would fall for his allure. But for her, there was still something off. Although his smile oozed *trust me*, his eyes gave the opposite effect.

Dr. Darcy, on the other hand, was about as transparent as a person could be. Almost too much, and at dinner last night, she saw how Charles was good at reining him in at just the right moment. But, she suspected, that with or without his best friend there, Dr. Darcy would be less than forthcoming with whatever had happened between him and Wickham.

Lizzy rolled to her other side and groaned in frustration. She was starting to resent how these two men were taking up so much of her headspace. With Wickham, she had no actual cause to be worried. Plus, Lydia hadn't seemed like she was into him *that* way. Dr. Darcy was another matter. Between the Y2K committee and Jane falling for his best friend, their time together would only increase.

She got out of bed and walked to her satchel which was hanging on the closet doorknob to retrieve her new CD, *The Miseducation of Lauryn Hill*. Slipping it into the Bose CD player on her nightstand, Lizzy returned to bed. She'd much rather fall asleep with Lauryn Hill in her head than those two men.

CHAPTER 20

"Hello," Darcy groaned into the receiver.

"Did I wake you? Oh, dear, I'm sorry. I wanted to catch you before you left for the university. Today's the first day of class, isn't it?"

"Mrs. King?" Darcy said as he pushed himself to a sitting position. The bedside clock glowed 5:30, an hour and a half before the alarm. Half expecting a telemarketer, he had prepared a few choice words, but the speaker's accent stopped him. He only knew one person with that accent. "Is everything all right? Carlton?"

"Is fine, honey. Just fine. I was calling about something else."

Beatrice King was the widow of Terry King, the senior Darcy's longtime personal assistant and close friend. After Terry's passing, Beatrice returned to her home country, Saint Lucia. She had a rich deep accent that, although having lived most of her life in the States, never faded. Terry and Beatrice had one son, Carlton, who still lived in Northern California. Darcy saw him a few weeks before he left for Delany.

Now fully awake, he moved the phone to his other hand and switched on the bedside lamp. "Something else?" Darcy asked.

There was a five-second pause before she spoke. "A little bird told me that you are asking around about ... him."

Darcy's chest rose and fell with a deep inhale. Beatrice King was a woman he had a great deal of respect for and he immediately worried that he had done something wrong, or at least overstepped his bounds. The unspeakable tragedy that had transpired between their families and George Wickham was something both needed to move past. And they had. Mrs. King returned to her home country, where the only thing people knew about her husband was that he was a decent man and a good provider. Darcy excised all traces of Wickham from family and financial records, and the people around him were smart enough to know never to speak of him. But now, almost a year and three thousand miles away from the tragedy, he's back.

"Who told you?"

"Never you mind about that," she said. "I am safe and fine here on my little island home. But I wanted to make sure you weren't trying to get some sort of revenge or something."

Darcy stiffened. "Not revenge. Protection." He told her what he had learned from Charles (although she probably already knew) and how he was concerned about the Bennets. "He seems to have his hooks into the youngest sister," Darcy said. "And you and I both know that can't be good."

"And why does that concern you?" Mrs. King asked.

Darcy opened his mouth to answer, but nothing came out.

"Listen now to what I'm going to tell you," Mrs. King said into the silence. "*You* are not responsible for what happened to Terry, to me, or Carlton, and you certainly are not responsible for that George Wickham either. What's done is done; he paid his dues to the court and there is nothing more that can be done about it."

"This isn't about the past, Mrs. King. I consider it my duty to see that Wickham doesn't hurt anyone else."

"Ha!" Mrs. King blurted out. "Your 'duty'? No, son, your father would *not* want you to spend the best years of your life chasing after a man who is not worth two cents! And neither would Terry."

"I'm not chasing after anyone," Darcy said, feeling defensive. He and his father were too dismissive of Wickham's actions before, considering him to be a low-key and harmless hustler. After the tragedy, he couldn't help but believe that they were guilty of willful ignorance.

Mrs. King sighed into the receiver, causing Darcy to feel some guilt creep in. Then annoyance. Once again, George Wickham slithered into his otherwise happy and contented life.

Knowing he would not be going back to sleep, he reached over and turned off the alarm mode. "Mrs. King," he began. "I can't explain to you what is happening here, but I don't want you to worry about me. I'm fine. Really."

Mrs. King reluctantly accepted his plea, but added: "If you notice anything suspicious, promise me you'll go to the police right away and not get involved."

He promised.

.   .   .

Terry King was the youngest son of a Baptist minister who headed one of the larger congregations in the Bay Area. Terry's older brother followed in his father's footsteps, but Terry never felt drawn to the church, and he avoided it as much as he could. He started working for Darcy Financial as a junior clerk and after a few years, Mr. Darcy, impressed with his drive, took him under his wing and trained him to be his personal assistant. After Mrs. Darcy passed away, Mr. Darcy found the extra help to be very beneficial. Terry King, whom Mr. Darcy called King, did typical PA stuff, but then Mr. Darcy began trusting him with tasks closer to the family's financial and personal affairs. When Mr. Wickham died, Darcy's dad was more than happy to assign King any duties related to the Wickhams. After Darcy and Wickham went to boarding school, King was the one handling the payments, allowances, and school correspondence. It was Terry King dropping them off and greeting them at the airport, not Mr. Darcy. In between all of this, Terry King married Beatrice and five years later, had Carlton their only child. On the outside looking in, the marriage seemed happy in the best of times, and content in all others. Everyone would later learn how skilled Mr. King was at pretending. It was a trait he developed early in life, not long after fully realizing his father's, and by extension, the church's anti-gay stance. "Devils!" his father would preach.

When George Wickham took the payout from Mr. Darcy's estate instead of continuing his education, Mr. King handled the transfer of funds. Darcy assumed that was the end of the dealings between the two, but George kept in fairly constant contact with Mr. King. As an outsider himself, Mr. King took pity on young George Wickham. He even invited George over for Thanksgiving dinner one year. Mr. King tried to steer him away from risky investment deals, but Wickham always felt like he knew better. When his money ran out, he appealed to Mr. King to help him get more from the Darcy estate. Mr. King, still loyal to the Darcys, refused. He worked at the main office, but not just for the money. About five years prior, and unable to suppress his sexuality any longer, Mr. King began a relationship with a senior account executive who also worked for Delany Finance. The couple took lunches together, then business trips, all under the guise of work.

No one knows exactly how Wickham discovered the affair, but he did and began using it to blackmail Mr. King. At first, it was easy to just pay him off, but Wickham's demands grew in frequency and amount. After a while, his lover got sick of it all and ended the relationship, devastating Mr. King. When George showed up a while later, demanding more money, Mr. King snapped and told him he did not care who knew and that he had nothing more to lose. Not ready to end this gravy train, Wickham decided to tell Mr. King's father, believing that he would be just as eager to keep his son in the closet. But on the same day he scheduled to meet Reverend King, Terry King hanged himself, using his lover's silk necktie.

Terry left a note. In it, he confessed everything. Apologized to his wife and son and swore that he loved them both, despite being a gay man. He thanked them for loving him. He told his former lover that while with him, he had never been happier. He apologized to his father for being a disappointing son. He also included a list of all the money he had given to Wickham and his recordings to back them up.

William Darcy, by then Dr. Darcy, wanted Wickham prosecuted to the full extent of the law. He called in IOUs from city officials and hired his lawyers to see that no legal stone was left unturned. To his horror, Mrs. King and the Reverend wanted the entire matter to go away quickly and quietly. That meant no trial. The judge granted Wickham a lesser sentence for a guilty plea. He served less than three months, followed by a short probation.

For his part, Darcy made sure Darcy Financial had nothing more to do with Wickham. It wasn't hard, although there were a few from the give-the-brother-another-chance camp who pushed back. As Darcy got out of bed, he wondered if it was one of them who had helped Wickham with his entry into the music world.

Deciding he needed coffee before anything else, he pulled on his robe, opened his bedroom door, and headed towards the stairs. No one else would be up, but he figured he could tackle a cup of coffee on his own. Stepping down the hallway, he saw light coming from under Charles' bedroom door. He did not have to wonder for long why Charles was up so early because just as he approached the door, it opened, and someone stepped out.

It would be hard to say which figure was more embarrassed by this early morning run-in: Darcy dressed in a robe and slippers, or Jane Bennet, fully dressed but looking sleep deprived. "Good morning," both whispered into the dark hallway.

Charles came out of his room and hurried Jane away from the awkward encounter and downstairs. After she left, Charles sought Darcy out in the kitchen. "Since when do you wake up so early?" Charles glared at Darcy who was at the sink filling the coffee pot carafe with water.

"Since I get 5AM calls from Mrs. King." He poured the water into the reservoir and pushed the button. He gave Charles a quick summary of the conversation. "Any idea who this 'little bird' could be?"

Charles shook his head. "Unless it was Carlton," he mused. "Who knows who Wickham still talks to or has relations with?"

"That would be my first guess too," Darcy said, grabbing a coffee cup from the cabinet. His hand was on a second cup, but Charles stopped him. "None for me. I'm going back to bed." A yawn escaped, causing Darcy to flash him a devilish grin. "Busy night, huh?"

"Don't start," Charles said. He pointed his finger at Darcy. "I am going to tell you she came over to check on my arm and that will be the end, okay?"

Darcy grinned. "Anything you say, sir." Despite the play, a look of understanding passed between them, putting the conversation at an end. Charles nodded and walked towards the swinging door. He stopped before pushing it open. "Thank you, Darcy," he said. "This one is … different. I don't want to mess it up before we can even start." Charles pushed through the swinging door. The coffee pot chimed.

Walking back to his room with his coffee, Darcy agreed that different was the perfect word to describe the Bennet women.

.   .   .

The first few days of the semester seemed like an invasion as new and returning students, faculty, and staff swarmed the campus. Laughs, smiles, and hugs for the returners; looks of worry, fear, and confusion on the fresh-faced freshmen. Lizzy loved the scene. As per tradition, she arrived on campus hours before her first class and sought her father.

"There you are," Mr. Bennet said as she walked up to his side. It was a bright and warm day and the sun's rays turned the Ancestors Garden into an emerald wonderland. Her father was standing by the four-tiered fountain, holding the 3-foot-long water key he used to restart the flow. He and his crew had spent the last month repairing cracks, and jets, and cleaning it up. "There she blows," her father said as water sputtered out of the top tier. Lizzy and her father stood in silence as the water cascaded down the tiers and into the circular reservoir below.

"It shoots out higher," Lizzy observed, tilting her head back to get a good look.

"Mmmm hmmm. New pump."

Lizzy hooked her arm through his and leaned her head on his upper arm. "It's beautiful," she sighed. "And peaceful."

Mr. Bennet looked at his watch. "I wasn't expecting you until at least 11," he said, "seeing how your first class isn't until 1:30."

Lizzy removed her arm and walked around the fountain. The pool was almost full, and she watched her father step over to where the water shut-off valve was. She reached into her pocket and pulled out three silver dollars. One for her, one for her father, and one for Mary.

"The outstanding students of Delany tossed in almost $100 in coins last year," he said as he returned to her side. Lizzy handed him the coin. "You were right about using these silver dollars to salt the kitty. Hardly had any pennies this year."

Coming to the fountain on the first day of the school year was a tradition that began so many years ago that no one remembered who started it or why. The Bennet coins were the first ones in the pool, and the gardeners cleaned it out at the end of the school year. They donated the money to the student food bank. In years past, the amount collected was nothing to brag about; the haul being mostly pennies and nickels. But seeing a shiny silver dollar at the bottom of the pool inspired students to toss in their silver coins.

Her father took the coin. "Will Mary be joining us?" he asked.

"She has a 9AM class but should be here soon." Lizzy looked up at her father, who was gazing at the fountain. In years past, he would share how hard the crew had worked, his fears about this or that area of campus, and wonder how his new hires would turn out.

She could only guess what his thoughts were now. He lowered his eyelids and took a deep inhale. Lizzy watched, and it struck her how old he suddenly seemed. When did he get all that gray hair? she thought. And those wrinkles around his eyes?

She turned away as if she had seen something she shouldn't have.

"I'm going to tell Mrs. B tonight," he said in a way that made it seem like he was talking to himself.

Lizzy's right hand squeezed around the oversized coins. "Has Dr. Lucas said anything else? Did he try the board again?"

He shook his head. "I never had any hope for that. He wouldn't have said anything to me unless it was … settled."

"Can you wait …" she began, but he held up a hand to stop her.

"It's getting out, and the last thing I need is for your mother to hear it from someone else."

Lizzy couldn't disagree and wondered if Charlotte had been talking again.

"Then we'll have a family meeting so we can start planning."

An involuntary shiver ran through Lizzy's body. Her stable and predictable life was in for big changes. And soon. Knowing what was coming and all that would need to be done was overwhelming. "I still can't believe it," she said.

"Me neither, but it's happening, and I am going to leave with my head held high."

Lizzy wanted to ask him what his plans were, but she saw Mary making her way toward them. As always, she looked harried and anxious. "Dr. Jones piled on the assignments already," she said, reaching out her hand towards Lizzy, who dropped the third silver dollar into her palm. "I know what I'm wishing for this year!" Without waiting for the others, Mary whispered her wish, kissed the coin, and tossed it into the pool. She turned to her father. "Did you bring the basket?" she asked.

Lizzy and her dad chuckled, both glad for the change of subject. Mr. Bennet told Mary that everything was back at his office and that they would walk over after he and Lizzy tossed their coins. Once done, he gathered his few pieces of equipment, and the trio set off. Waiting for them in his office was a picnic basket with orange juice and pastries for the three of them. Another beginning-of-the-year tradition. They would spend about half an hour wondering what the semester would bring and musing over years past. Since Mary was the only student, she filled them in on her current classes—the last ones!—and her future educational plans.

"Whoa," her father said. "I know your grades are fine and all—"

"Four-point-o," Mary said while licking pastry frosting from her fingers.

"But what about looking for work?" her dad continued. "You said that there were plenty of jobs in your field that only required a master's degree."

Mary nodded. "But there's this doctoral program in Tanzania I'm interested in."

"Tanzania?!"

"Yes!" Mary said. She told them about a visiting professor looking for interns to travel back with him. "The actual school is Michigan State, but we spend about three months in Tanz."

Their dad set his coffee mug down and leaned back in his office chair. He regretted not paying more attention to Mary. Out of all his daughters, she probably possessed the most unabashed passion and talent for her chosen profession. He had no problem seeing her traipsing around the wilds of Africa, hunting for bugs and insects. "Well, if that's what you want, I support you … 100%." His voice wavered at the end, bringing looks of concern to his daughters' faces. He tilted his head down and covered his eyes with his hand. Lizzy stood, saying that it was time to go. "Hopefully, our mother will be just as supportive," she told Mary as they re-packed the uneaten food and drink back into the basket. Their dad walked them to the door, hugged and wished them both a successful school year.

"So, it must be true," Mary said when they were far enough away. Lizzy stopped and turned to her sister. She could have played dumb, but the look in Mary's eyes told her that the situation was past that. She placed a hand on Mary's arm and gave it a slight squeeze. "Our parents are going to need us now. Do you think planning this Tanzania thing is a good idea?"

Mary's eyes turned cold. "It's not a 'thing' Lizzy. It's my career and yes, I think now is the perfect time. Unlike you, I have no problem envisioning myself in a life away from Delany, Longbourne, or this town."

Lizzy dropped her hand and stepped back. She had no idea Mary thought of her this way. Putting her doctoral program search on hold had been a tough decision, based on reasons Mary could never understand since every other college on the planet has an Entomology graduate program. Lizzy's area of research was somewhat new and required creative convincing, which she had failed at. "Seems like you also don't have a problem abandoning your family, either," Lizzy said.

To her surprise, Mary snickered. "Like anyone would notice my absence," she said. The campus clock tower chimed, announcing the 11th hour. "See you at home," she said before turning away.

CHAPTER 21

Mary walked away and, for the first time, Lizzy noticed a certain determination and steadiness in her stride. Mary was always the one who rambled and flittered about, easily distracted by this bug or an interesting plant. Her love of insects began the summer when the family went to Philadelphia for vacation. Mary had just turned three that year. At the Insectarium, the other sisters avoided the creepy, crawly things, but they enthralled Mary. "What a super cool place!" Mary exclaimed. In her hand was a small plush toy scorpion she had used her vacation money to purchase. Almost 20 years later, she still had it.

Lizzy took her time walking to the lower campus and the Liberal Arts Buildings. She had ended the previous semester with a list of books and research she wanted to complete, which she had. Sitting on the hard drive of her home PC was a detailed outline of her research and drafts of scholarly articles she had yet to finish and send out for publication. Since she did not have a doctorate, getting published was not a career necessity, but it was something she thought would bring more legitimacy to her studies. Plus, Dr. Wright was always encouraging her to publish. "Don't make the mistake of thinking the old 'publish or perish' rule doesn't apply to you," she would tell Lizzy. "With just a masters, you need to do all you can to keep your position."

Just a masters? Lizzy had sweated blood during those two years in graduate school. It seemed that every professor had it in for her, resentful of her free ride as a Bennet, not knowing that she was racking up student loan debt like everyone else. The legacy only covered undergrad tuition. Her advisors rejected her master's thesis three times before Dr. Wright stepped in.

Lizzy was one of the few Bennets that had stayed on past undergrad years. Most either worked or sought other institutions to continue their studies. Jane, for example, got her MSN at New York University, and she has the student loan debt to show for it.

Sometimes she wondered why moving away never occurred to her. Her father often joked that she must have lived several past lives here, since it seemed as if she was born to live in Merryton, North Carolina. And what's wrong with that? she thinks as she walked into the lobby of her building. Mary accused her of being a homebody and too afraid to venture out. Lizzy scoffed at the idea, wondering when Mary got to be so mean.

She entered her small office, sat down at her desk, and sighed. She resented how the first day was unfolding, and she hadn't even taught her first class yet! Glancing at the clock, she found she had a good two hours to kill before her first class, Intro to African American Lit, began. There would be at least a dozen students hoping to get in, but she had a full roster. She hated turning them away, especially when after a few weeks, there would be plenty of space as the less-than-eager students dropped out.

She rubbed her tummy and wondered if she had had too much coffee with her father and Mary. The first-day ritual of meeting before classes, tossing a coin in the fountain, and sharing breakfast was usually filled with stories and laughter, but this year—their last one—was different. Mr. Bennet had tried to put on a brave face, and she hated how Mary had blurted out her, *I'm going to study in Africa* news as if she were announcing a trip to the grocery store. Her stomach churned again, so she began searching her desk drawers for some Tums, or an old Alka Seltzer packet. Reaching into the middle drawer, her fingers fumbled around the contents, hoping to discover something that felt like the medicine she needed. Instead, her fingers touched a thin packet of envelopes, secured with a rubber band. She pulled them out and let out a gasp when she saw what they were. No, she hadn't thrown them away.

Lizzy dropped the letters on her desk and stood up quickly, as if she had pulled out a hissing snake. Charlotte would call this a sign from above, but all Lizzy wanted to call it was a mistake. She sat back down and peered at the letters. In her mind, she clearly saw herself tossing them in the trash. That made sense because who keeps rejection letters? But no, she hadn't since here they were, almost 18 months later and in her office and on her desk. She slipped the rubber band off, remembering how she had slit the tops open with her silver letter opener, a graduation gift from her parents. Her thumb and forefinger pushed open an envelope, and she peeked in to see if the letter was still inside. No need to pull it out to read.

Dear Miss Bennet,

Thank you for your interest in X university's doctoral studies. After careful consideration, blah, blah, blah, we are unable to extend an offer of admission, Blah, blah, blah . . .

She had applied to three institutions. Two of the rejections were practically identical with their boilerplate rejections. But the last rejection claimed that the decision had more to do with an overabundance of applicants than her qualifications. They also encouraged her to re-apply next year. She hadn't, and by that time she had convinced Delany's liberal arts department to include a hip-hop studies class. As she predicted, the classes were very popular, and the demand ended up taking up both her time and her doctoral degree plans. Jane or Dr. Wright would occasionally ask, but she always had an excuse ready. After a while, they stopped asking. She re-wrapped the rubber band around the letters and stuck them back into the drawer. With her class load, the Y2K committee, and the end of the Bennet legacy, she doubted there would be time to think about doctoral programs, let alone apply.

Professor Bennet spent the next hour organizing paperwork and going over her first-day lectures in her head. She was recounting a stack of syllabi when the phone rang.

"Jane?" she said. "Is everything okay?" She tucked the phone between her ear and shoulder and went back to her counting.

"Everything's fine," Jane said. "Glad I caught you before you left for class. I wanted to tell you something before … well …"

"Jane! I'm kinda busy here," Lizzy said, but kept counting in her head, her fingers flicking through the pile.

Jane mumbled an apology and then: "I saw William this morning."

"Dr. Darcy? If you were on campus, why didn't you come to the—"

"At his house … I mean Netherfield … not at school … as I was leaving."

"Why would you leave school to go to Netherfield?"

Jane let out a frustrated sigh. "Lizzy! I went out to Netherfield last night, *not* this morning."

.   ∎   ∎

About five minutes later, the department secretaries watched Professor Bennet hurrying out of the office while muttering under her breath. Mrs. Jackson smiled and went back to her work. "She gonna be late," she whispered.

And she was, but not by much. "Sorry. Sorry!" she said as she made her way to the podium. Her waitlist students had tired of waiting and were now on the floor, their backs against the wall. Professor Bennet had to step over them to get to the front of the class. She dropped the syllabi on the first desk in the front row. "Hand these out," she said. She was breathing fast and could feel a layer of perspiration on her forehead. Before addressing the class, she went to the blackboard and wrote her name and the course section. She narrated as she wrote. "I am Professor Bennet, and this is Intro to African American Literature. Please make sure you are in the *right* class. If you have *not* taken—and passed—Freshman Comp, you *cannot* take this class. If you are a poetry major and need a level 3 lit class, this is NOT the right one. Yes, there is a lot of homework; yes, attendance *and* participation count toward your final grade. If you have any other questions related to your attendance, the textbook, or anything else that is NOT in the syllabus, come see me during office hours, which you will find in your syllabus." She dropped the piece of chalk on the tray, turned around, and faced her class. "Are we good?"

Despite the rocky start, the rest of the class went well. She took her time going over the syllabus and then an introduction to Zora Neal Hurston. After everyone left and she was packing up to head to her next class, Professor Bennet congratulated herself for staying focused on Hurston, and not on what her sister had to tell her an hour earlier.

"For some reason, I thought to give Charles a call before I went to sleep," Jane had told her. "He said he missed me and then we chatted for a while and the next thing I know, I'm dressed and in my car driving out to his house! I tried to kid myself and say it was only to check on his arm, but that was too stupid even for me!"

The stack of syllabi slipped from Lizzy's desk and onto the floor. "And you stayed there all night?"

"Yeah. But nothing happened! We had some tea in the kitchen and then we went to his room and … talked."

"Talked?" In the background, Lizzy could hear the commotion of the clinic. Someone was calling for Nurse Jane.

"Listen, Lizzy, I've got to go. But I wanted to let you know that I ran into Dr. Darcy as I was leaving, so if he says anything to you, you won't be surprised." Something crashed in the background.

"But—" Lizzy began.

"Can't talk. Got to go."

The next thing Lizzy heard was a dial tone.

CHAPTER 22

"Ta-da!" Caroline greeted Darcy as he walked into the breakfast room. She had the table set with a full breakfast, including French toast. "Nothing like a substantial breakfast to start your first full day of teaching," she said, handing him a linen napkin. After his predawn chat with Charles, he was hoping for a quick breakfast, followed by a quick exit. But what he saw before him altered his plans. Caroline sat down and motioned for him to join her. "Thanks," he muttered.

A little over an hour later, Darcy pulled his Lexus into his designated parking space in front of the Economics Building. He exited his car and noticed that the serene feel of the campus was gone, replaced with the buzz and energy of the newly arrived and returning students. The sight of so many black and brown faces startled him for a moment. He had seen nothing like it since his time touring Botswana with the Bingleys. He stopped to take in the scene. Deep in his core, he felt a stir of emotions, which his practical side dismissed as first-day anxiousness. Later, he would recognize what they truly were: pride and awe.

"There you are, Dr. Darcy."

He turned to see Dr. Baei. "I was hoping to catch you before your first lecture." He held up a binder, which Darcy recognized as the grant proposal they had been working on. He frowned. "Don't tell me. We missed something else?"

Dr. Baie smiled. "Yes, but not that bad." The two economists chatted as they made their way into the building. They parted at the entrance, with Dr. Baie saying that he needed to be on the other side of campus for a meeting. "Sorry to drop this on you."

Darcy nodded. "Not a problem. I can have it taken care of by the end of the day."

Dr. Baei gave a nod of thanks before hurrying off. Darcy slipped the stuffed binder under his arm and readjusted his bag's shoulder strap, all while trying to push through the glass doors into the Econ Building.

Seeing the crowd waiting for the elevator, he took the stairs to his office. By the third floor, an ache in his left leg told him he had been away from the gym too long. In his office closet was a packed gym bag he hadn't touched since he put it there. Need to remedy that, he thought as he reached the fourth floor.

Next to Mrs. Hoffman's desk sat one of his grad students, the anxious one, which was the only thing he remembered about him.

"Are you here to see me?" Darcy asked.

The young man stood up quickly. "Yes, sir. I wanted to talk to you about some research I found on Albanian banking." His arms held a stack of disorderly looking paperwork.

"What? And why? I don't recall asking you—or anyone—to investigate that."

The grad student followed Darcy to his office, his sheaf of papers clutched to his chest. "Yes, sir, I know, but I was thinking that there may be some … connections or at least … information from other areas we could use in our research into the Johannesburg project."

Darcy placed his bag and the notebook on his desk and sighed. He didn't have time for this. "Look … Ummm?"

"Johnson, sir. Michael."

"Michael. Let's just stick to the parameters we outlined and keep our meetings to the allotted times. If you have questions that need immediate answers, please email me."

Michael nodded. "Yes, sir. Sorry, sir, but I thought—"

Darcy held up his hand. "You don't have to call me sir."

"I don't?" Michael said, grinning.

"Doctor. Dr. Darcy."

The grin vanished. Michael held his precious paperwork close to his chest as if he were holding a winning poker hand. Darcy shook his head. Some people have too much time on their hands. *Time?*

Michael thanked him and turned to leave. "Hold on, Michael," Darcy said. "You seem to have time to spare. I wonder if you would like to do a bit of ... private research for me."

Michael's eager grin reappeared as he nodded a firm yes. "Of course, sir—I mean, Dr. Darcy."

Not entirely sure that this was proper or wise, Darcy asked what he knew of Mr. Bennet, the groundskeeper.

A confused look passed over Michael's face. "Nothing, but I'm new to the area. From New Jersey, actually. But I think I've seen him around campus."

Darcy nodded and told him about the agreement between Delany University and the Bennet family. "Agreements like these were fairly common back then, but it would be interesting to know if they would stand up to today's legal scrutiny. I understand the original documents are in the library's archive. Do you think you could—"

"Oh, of course, Dr. Darcy! I would be happy to."

"Good. I'll inform the librarians that you are there on my directions, so you shouldn't have any trouble with access."

"Yes. Yes," Michael answered as he fumbled with his papers. "I'll get right on it."

"Thank you. And Michael, let's keep this between us for now." Michael nodded and left. Darcy took a seat behind his desk, wondering if he would regret this later.

During his graduate studies, the benefit of becoming a tenured professor with a light class load was a factor that kept Darcy going. When it finally happened, he learned that the reality was not as nice as the dream. It took the absence of teaching to show him how much he enjoyed it, and his first day of lecturing at Delany reinforced this. In his first class, he was happy to see an almost equal number of men and women. He began with the typical first-day messaging, and then jumped right into the lecture. Notebooks flew open and for the next 45 minutes, students scribbled, asked questions, and a few even laughed at his jokes.

"Excuse me, Dr. Darcy?"

He looked up from re-packing his bag. "Yes, ahh…?"

"Chantell."

"Right. Forgive me," he replied. "It's going to take me a while to get names and faces straight."

Chantell leaned her head to the side. Her huge gold hoop earrings dangled about her neck. "You know, I never understood why we don't use nametags in college. I mean, they were good enough for our K through twelve education and there were way fewer students."

Darcy snapped his bag shut and looked at her. "Are you asking me to use nametags?"

Chantell shook her head quickly, causing her chunky, shoulder-length braids to dance around her round face. "Oh god no, I was just … you know, thinking out loud, which is something I've been told I do too much of."

Darcy pressed his lips together hoping the *I agree* on the tip of his tongue wouldn't come out.

Chantell took a deep breath. "Well, what I really wanted to talk to you about was if maybe you'd be interested in speaking at my church? We've had so many families get caught up in these payday loans and other high interest traps, so the church board thought it would be a good idea to have a few talks on financial literacy. And we were hoping you could maybe offer us some guidance?"

Dr. Darcy picked up his bag. "Well, from what I heard from you today in class, it seems like you are more than capable of providing guidance."

This brought a huge smile to her face, and Darcy started to leave before she could say anything else. His schedule had no time for speaking at some local church.

"I could, but we like to have people from the community come in too. Like Dr. Neal from Health and Sciences comes and gives nutrition lectures, and Mr. Bennet always gives talks about gardening and stuff."

He stopped at the door and looked back at her. "The Bennet family belongs to your church?"

•   •   •

"Good first day, Dr. Darcy?" Mrs. Hoffman asked.

"Not bad. I've had worse. Tell me, are you acquainted with the Bennet family?"

Mrs. Hoffman nodded. "Who isn't? We call them the Delany Bennets since their family has been here since the school's founding. Harold and I met in primary school."

"That long? Any other founding families around?"

Mrs. Hoffman thought for a moment. "Not that I know of. But Dr. Lucas could give you a better answer." He thanked her, but said he was only curious about the family and Delany. "It is a fascinating history."

"Mmmm hmmm," Mrs. Hoffman hummed, wondering about his real purpose. She knew enough about the famous professor to know that he was never just curious about anything.

At his desk, Darcy flipped through his calendar and frowned. He had done a "Let me check my calendar" dodge with Chantell. There were a few weekends that they had set aside to go exploring, but nothing that couldn't wait. Plus, with Charles beginning a relationship with Jane, Darcy doubted his friend would swap his time with her for a sightseeing trip.

The grant binder on his desk reminded him of one more task to complete. Turning his attention to it now annoyed him, but years of academic discipline have taught him that with deadlines, sooner was always better than later. Like his father, discipline and personal responsibility were also the principles of Chadwick Prep and after 13 years of his father's guidance and example, it was easy for young Darcy to adapt to the demanding boarding school culture. George Wickham was not that fortunate. The first year, Mr. Darcy made excuses for him and attributed his destructive behavior to the lack of a proper role model. Darcy soon tired of hearing his father and Mr. King's the-apple-doesn't-fall-from-the-tree reasoning for Wickham's misdeeds. After Mr. Darcy passed away, everyone believed—or hoped—that Wickham would change. And he did, but for the worse. Just how worse no one knew until it was too late.

Fortunately, everything Darcy needed for the grant update was on his hard drive, so it took him less than 30 minutes to complete. He printed the revised pages and added them to the binder. It was still early, so Darcy decided he would follow through on his promise to work out again. He grabbed his gym bag.

After changing in the faculty locker room, Darcy warmed up with 20 minutes on the treadmill. The familiar rush of endorphins felt good, but also made him realize how stressful these last few days had been.

Pumped from his run, he walked to the weight room. It was relatively empty, with only a few of the machines occupied. He was halfway through his second round on the leg press when a group of young men paraded through. Each had on khaki cargo pants, black boots, and red polo shirts. The black emblem embroidered on the front upper left appeared to be an African-type battle shield, crossed with two spears. Must be the Mashujaas, he thought, abandoning his workout to follow them. As they chatted, he picked up a few words, mostly about first-day classes and which professors were going to give them the most grief. They walked through a set of double doors and onto the basketball court. "You're late!" said a voice from the other side of the court. "We only have the place for an hour, so let's not waste any more time than we have to." The group snapped to attention. "Sir, yes, sir!"

Darcy moved into the court behind them, but froze when he heard another voice. "Now, Douglas, a few minutes won't hurt. Besides, we made fantastic progress last night."

Douglas glanced at Wickham, then folded his arms across his chest and turned his attention back to the men. "In formation! Now!"

The group scurried to form three lines of five on a thin pad that was spread across the court floor. Douglas walked up and down each line, like a drill sergeant inspecting his troops. Only when he seemed satisfied with each man's presentation did he turn back to Wickham. "When you're ready."

Even from this distance, Darcy recognized Wickham's annoyance. He had seen it many times before. Some things never change, it seems.

Wickham moved to the front of the group. "As I said earlier, you all are making good progress, but going over the tape of yesterday's practice, I see a few of you still need to work on the squat-kick and tap at the end of the first hop-turn. Now, on my count! Five-six-seven-eight!"

The sound of stomping boots, clapping hands, and warrior cries reverberated through the court.

His father used to say that the Wickham men were chameleons, possessing the rare quality of being able to fit into almost any situation. "Too bad they aren't using it for good," he would say. Wickham was proving his father's assessment. Thinking he had seen enough and wanting to leave before Wickham spied him, Darcy turned to leave.

"I'm here!" He stopped at the sound of the female voice and saw Lydia Bennet enter the gym through a door on the opposite end. She was carrying a medium black case. She rushed to Wickham's side, and he bent to tell her something. She nodded and walked to the side of the group.

Darcy had his eyes fixed on this new situation and didn't notice Douglas walking towards him until he was a few feet away. "Excuse me, sir, but this is a closed rehearsal. Can I help you with anything?"

Darcy pointed towards Lydia, who had now removed a small camcorder from her bag and was filming the group. "So, why is she here? And George Wickham for that matter; neither are students and one of them is a minor."

Douglas looked a bit amused at the unexpected confrontation. "I'm Douglas Jackson, vice president of Mashujaa Fraternity, and both Wickham and Lydia are here under my direction."

"Do you think that's wise?" Darcy responded.

"Excuse me?" said Douglas with a short, nervous laugh. "Who are you, exactly?"

"Dr. William Darcy of UC Berkeley," Wickham said, walking towards the two men. "*And* of the distinguished Darcy Financial Services located in New York, Los Angeles, London, and I believe ... Johannesburg?"

Wickham stopped a few feet directly in front of Darcy. Douglas took a step back, suddenly feeling like he was standing in the line of fire. "Do you two know each other?" he asked.

"Yes."

"From a very long time ago."

"Unfortunately."

"Agreed."

"All right, then," Douglas said, looking more confused than before.

"Why are you here?" Darcy asked.

Wickham turned and waved a hand at the men, "As you can see."

A skeptical grin spread across Darcy's face. "And this involves collaborating with minors." He shook his head. "As I recall, you tended to prefer them on the younger side."

"And as I recall," Wickham said, "your obsession with *my* business is still as active as ever. Why don't you go back to your precious, *tiny* loan business and leave us to ours."

Darcy felt his hands ball into tight fists. "What did you say?" he said, chest rising with a sharp inhale.

Douglas immediately recognized the volatile situation and stepped forward. "Gentlemen, let's all take a breath and calm down. Dr. Darcy, if you would like to talk to me about this, let's step outside." He turned to Wickham. "Get back to the men. Now."

By that time, the trio had attracted the attention of everyone else. Lydia had stopped recording, and the Mashujaa brothers stood gazing with questioning looks. Darcy recognized one or two from his class that morning. This wasn't good. He exhaled and forced himself to relax. "No need. I was just leaving." Darcy turned to exit the gym but then a sarcastic sounding "bye-bye now!" coming from Wickham snapped within him like a dry twig. He stopped, pivoted around, stepped forward, and let his right fist smash into Wickham's jaw.

"What the fuck?!" Douglas shouted. Lydia screamed, and the rest of the members streamed forward. Wickham steadied himself and prepared to return the punch, but two brothers restrained him.

It didn't take long for Darcy to regain his composure, and when he saw all eyes were on him, he mumbled an apology and left. Douglas tried to follow him back into the workout room, but Darcy was not in the mood to talk. "Just leave it, please," Darcy told him. "It won't happen again."

"Yes, sir," Douglas responded. "Hopefully, you two will work it out."

"I doubt that," Darcy said, leaving for the locker room.

Darcy cleaned up and changed back into his work suit. His hand was sore from the punch, making him curse his loss of temper even more. He thought about calling the Darcy Finance PR department to ask them about damage control, but decided against the idea. He would handle it himself, and the first person he wanted to let know was Professor Elizabeth Bennet. By this time tomorrow, the entire campus will know, and it bothered him that she would find out from the rumor mill rather than directly from him. He stopped in the gymnasium lobby and used the phone to call her office. She picked up on the first ring.

CHAPTER 23

By now, Dr. Darcy's behavior should not surprise her, but Lizzy hung up the phone, puzzled by the call. She had agreed to meet him, mostly out of curiosity. He used the words "urgent" and "private" making her think it had something to do with Jane. Lizzy sat at her desk, staring at the door, debating whether to contact Jane. Could something have happened at Netherfield that morning? Or perhaps he wanted to apologize—or explain—his behavior from Monday night? She gathered her papers and sighed. Only one way to find out. At the last minute, she shoved the Y2K folder into her bag, thinking that if their conversation veered into hostile territory, she could pivot into something neutral.

The other interesting thing about his call was that he suggested they meet in the Ancestors Garden. It surprised Lizzy he even knew about it.

He stood up as she approached, and she noticed a leather satchel on the bench and a gym bag on the ground. She assumed that he, like her, would head home afterward. As she got closer, she noticed the satchel was older and well-worn, like a child's cherished teddy bear.

"Thanks for meeting me on such short notice," Darcy said with a quick nod of his head. Lizzy, still unsure, nodded in return. "You caught me before heading home," she said. She sat down on the bench and placed her bag on her lap. He sat down next to her, his bag in between them.

"Home to Longbourne?" he asked.

Lizzy chuckled. "Yeah, that's the only home I have. Right now, at least."

He turned to her quickly. "Are you thinking about leaving, moving out soon?"

Lizzy blinked at the direct and personal nature of the question. "Maybe? Why, may I ask?"

Darcy shrugged. "It seems like that's a Southern thing; a family's grown daughters staying at home until ..."

"Marriage?" she laughed. "I don't know if it's a Southern thing, but the situation suits Jane and I just fine for now. Longbourne is big enough that we don't run all over each other. It's conveniently located plus ..."

"Plus what?"

"Plus, it suits us financially, if you must know." She was growing impatient. "Is that why you called to see me? To discuss my living arrangements?"

"No, I'm sorry." He rubbed the back of his head. "It's been a long day."

She agreed. "So, how was your first day of instruction? I hope you weren't disappointed."

"Of course not. Why would I be?"

Lizzy shrugged. "Oh, you know. Some people seem to harbor a below-average view of Black colleges."

He smiled. "Don't let my Aunt Catherine hear you say that. She graduated from Howard and is forever grateful to them and all the other HBCUs. Howard wasn't the only university willing to accept her, but she says it was the only one that treated her as a serious student. She's been loyal to them ever since." He nodded his head towards an abstract sculpture about 20 feet away. "In fact, I was thinking about talking to her about donating a piece from our family's collection to add to the sculpture garden here."

Lizzy looked at him. He was gazing out across the garden, giving her a good view of his profile. She swallowed. "If you wanted to talk about an art donation, I'm the wrong person." She waved a hand over the garden. "And my father is only responsible for the living aspects of the garden."

He turned his attention back to her. "Actually," he began, "I need to first apologize for my hasty departure that night." He shook his head. "George Wickham brings out the rudest parts of my behavior."

Lizzy grimaced. She would hardly call stealing someone's livelihood rude. More like abhorrent. "Well, the only one that was offended was my mother, and I doubt you'll be seeing—"

"Your mother?" he said, looking regretful. "I'll make sure to apologize the next time I see her."

Next time? Lizzy thought.

"Ummm, how long did Wickham end up staying?" he asked.

Why do you need to know was on the tip of her tongue, but something told her to take it easy on him. "Not long. I found out later that he came to see me, but he left before saying anything."

"You?" Darcy blurted out. "Not Lydia?"

Lizzy nodded. "Yeah. He's given me a CD of some rap group he's helping to promote and asked me to give it a listen."

"And have you?"

"I tried," she said, shaking her head. "They need a lot of work. I haven't given it back to him yet because, frankly, I don't want to hurt his feelings."

Darcy laughed. "No need to worry about that. George Wickham has no feelings." He stood up and turned to face her. "The real reason I asked to meet you was to warn you about him. I can't get into the details, but you must trust me when I say this. Take my advice and cut that man out of your life—especially your sister's."

Lizzy tilted her head back to look at him. "Like I said in the car that night, he gave *me* the same warning about *you*." She held up her hand to stop him from interrupting. "And between the two of you, I have to say that I know *him* a little better."

Darcy pointed a finger at himself. "No one here knows how … evil Wickham is better than me. Or Bingley. I've known him since we were kids, so don't tell *me* what kind of man George Wickham is!" He stopped, closed his eyes, and took a deep inhale. "Look, I didn't ask to meet you so we could argue. As a matter of fact, I just left him at the gym. We had a … confrontation."

"A what?"

"And your sister was there too. Filming the step practice. Did you know she was helping them like that? Shouldn't she be in school or something?"

Lizzy stood up. "Wait. What are you talking about with Lydia and a confrontation?"

"Not with your sister. With Wickham. One thing led to another and …"

"And what?"

He shrugged. "And I hit him."

Lizzy's hand flew to her mouth. "You didn't!" she gasped.

Darcy sighed. "Yes, and I am very ashamed of the way I behaved. Especially since some students witnessed the whole thing, and I am sure that by tomorrow it will be all around campus." He gazed at her. "But I wanted you to hear it from me first."

"Forget me!" Lizzy said, still trying to understand the situation. "I'm not sure how things are done at Berkeley, but instructors getting into fights in front of students is kinda a bad thing here."

"I am aware that there will be consequences, but I can handle that. What I can't handle is you thinking badly of me."

Their eyes met, and Lizzy wondered at the tenderness she saw. "Why me, Dr. Darcy? Why does what *I* think matter?" she whispered.

He took a step towards her. "I wish I knew why; it just does. Isn't that enough for now?"

Lizzy looked up at him, her face full of confusion. "Look, Dr. Darcy—"

"William," he whispered, stepping even closer.

She cleared her throat. "William, I don't know what—why are you smiling?"

"I like the way you say my name."

She stepped back and held up her hands. "Okay, let's just slow down, shall we?"

"Why?"

"What do you mean 'why'? Did Wickham hit you back and knock something loose? Because this," she gestured between them, "is *way* out of line."

He parted his lips to speak, but she got distracted by what she saw over his left shoulder. She groaned. "I think you should leave, Will—Dr. Darcy. My parents are heading this way and now is not a good time for a … meeting."

He turned and followed her gaze. Of course, she was right, and it was the last thing he wanted as well. He moved around her to pick up his belongings. "I hope we can continue this later," he said.

Lizzy sighed. "I'm the least of your worries right now. I hope Wickham doesn't press charges or something."

"I doubt that," he said. "Goodbye, Lizzy. I'll see you tomorrow."

Not if I can help it, she thought, watching him depart. *What the heck was that about?*

She turned to see her parents still heading in her direction. Mr. Bennet had his arm around his wife, but something was off about the way they moved. Lizzy squinted, trying to decipher the situation. She flinched when she realized that her father's arm and body were helping to keep her mother upright. She trotted towards them. "Mother! What happened?"

Mr. Bennet shook his head. "My fault for thinking here would be a good place to break the news to her."

"Oh, Lizzy! How could they do this to us? We'll all be ruined!"

Lizzy glanced around to make sure no one—especially Dr. Darcy—was in earshot. "Oh, Mother. It's not that bad. You both can stay at Longbourne until—"

"Until I'm a widow! And then I bet those Lucases will have us tossed out on the street before your father is cold in his grave!" She wiped her eyes with a white handkerchief. It was one she had embroidered with her initials.

Her father looked at Lizzy with imploring eyes. "Lizzy, can you please help your mother home? I'm expecting a delivery and can leave after that."

"Of course—"

"Oh, why bother!" Her mother interjected. "That's your problem. You—and all the other Bennets before you—just gave and gave to this place, getting nothing in return."

"Mother, you know that's not true. Every Bennet received a generous wage for their labor *and* given a place to live. We've been very fortunate."

Mrs. Bennet pulled away from her husband and stood up straight. She dabbed her face with her handkerchief before slipping it back into her handbag. "Well, all that's coming to an end." She grabbed Lizzy's hand. "You and I need to get home and start planning."

Lizzy let out a short laugh. "Planning what exactly, Mother? It'll be years before any changes will occur." She looked at her father, whose face revealed a mixture of sadness and annoyance. "Isn't that right, Father?"

Instead of answering, he looked at his watch and told them to head home. "You may tell the others, but we'll have a family meeting this weekend, too." He leaned forward and pecked his wife on the cheek. "I'll see you at home, dear. Get some rest."

Mrs. Bennet followed her daughter back to the bench, where she retrieved her bag. Her mother simply nodded when Lizzy asked if she was ready. Expecting her to be in full-on chatty mode, the silence that followed alarmed Lizzy. She hooked arms with her mother as they walked through the campus. Her mother sighed. "A scholarship offer was finally available to the Bennet spouses right before I married your father. I had plans to attend, wanted to study home economics, but then you girls started coming ... "

Lizzy felt this wasn't the time to give the it's-not-too-late talk and remained quiet.

"Your father and I were hoping for a son, but we got Lydia, and then we spoiled her rotten." She sighed. "I know you and her don't see eye-to-eye on most things, but promise me you'll look after her."

Lizzy stopped walking. "Really, Mother. Don't you think you're being a bit dramatic? If anyone needs our support and understanding right now, it's Father; *not* Lydia." She added an eye roll to that last bit.

Her mother continued as if she hadn't heard her. "Kitty is finally on the right track, and Mary, well, let's just hope she'll find some sort of insect business to keep her afloat. And you and Jane." She released another deep sigh. Anyone listening would think she was giving a deathbed confession. "I know I don't say it enough, but I am so very proud of you two. It comforts my heart to know that you both will be okay, no matter what."

Even without a husband? It was a premature thought.

"But," her mother continued, "it wouldn't hurt to have a little insurance."

Lizzy groaned at the scheming tone in her mother's voice. If they had arrived a minute earlier and witnessed the interaction with Dr. Darcy, she'd never hear the end of it.

Mrs. Bennet tugged on Lizzy's arm. "When we get home, let's have a chat with Jane and see about having Mr. Bingley over for dinner. And soon."

"Do you think that's even necessary, Mother? The ball is soon, and they are seeing each other pretty regularly, you know."

"Yes, but Jane needs to make sure she has him firmly under her arm before the ball. Who knows how many of Merryton's debutantes will be there, strutting and prancing about? No. Jane needs to have some … assurances."

Lizzy thought for a moment. "What about Dr. Darcy?"

"What about him? Wickham has told me all I need to know, and after he just ignored me that night, well I bless whoever gets him!"

Lizzy's mind worked, wondering how she could keep what happened between those two men away from her mother's prying ears. "Well, like they say. Every story has two sides, Mother."

Mrs. Bennet waved away the proverb. "And so does a man's heart, and we need to make sure our Jane lands on the right side of Charles Bingley's."

CHAPTER 24

By the time Mr. Bennet made it home, the house was in chaos. From the hallway, he heard the raised voices of his wife, Kitty, and Lydia. He peeked his head inside the kitchen to see Mary fiddling about. The Saturn was in the driveway, so Jane and Lizzy were home too, but upstairs, probably with heads together figuring out a plan, he imagined.

After a shower and a change of clothes, Mr. Bennet entered the living room. Mary greeted him. "Dinner's ready," she said. In response to his raised eyebrows, she added: "Yes, I prepared dinner. But don't worry, just leftovers."

The last time his family had been so quiet during dinner was the evening of his mother's funeral, about 15 years ago. His very young children had sensed the need for silence and behaved accordingly. Even Lydia. It saddened him to think that this occasion warranted the same reaction. He looked up from his plate to find his wife gazing at him from across the table. With a sigh, he put his fork down.

"Well, family," he began. "No sense in pretending anymore." He looked at each of his daughters while he shared the college board's decision and what Dr. Lucas had told him.

"We should get a lawyer and sue their asses off!" Lydia was the first to speak, sparking the others into action.

Mrs. Bennet cautioned Lydia about her language.

Jane insisted no one should take the change as a personal attack.

Kitty wondered which of her friends she should ask about renting an apartment with.

Mary shared her Tanzania plans with an "I'll be all right," declaration and a shoulder shrug.

Lizzy sat back, taking it all in, and when a break in the conversation finally came, she asked when a formal announcement would come.

Mary laughed. "Like that's really necessary," she said. "It's all over campus already."

Mr. Bennet looked surprised. "How can that be? Dr. Lucas said they did everything in strict confidence."

"Well, today was the first time *I've* heard about it," their mother said, full of irritation. She glared at Lizzy. "And when did you know? Hmmm?"

Instead of answering her mother, Lizzy turned to Jane. "I meant to tell you earlier, but with everything else going on ... Plus, I hoped the board would eventually change their mind." She shrugged. "Guess it's too late to wish for that." Tears pooled in her eyes, and Jane reached over to place her hand over Lizzy's. "It's okay. I understand."

Mr. Bennet had had enough. He slapped his hands on the table to get everyone's attention. "You all are acting like you're the ones losing a job. You aren't. *I am,* and that has absolutely nothing to do with your future. We can stay at Longbourne until I am sure all of you will be out and on your own. Your mother and I will be fine."

Mrs. Bennet's eyes widened. "Will we now?" she asked, her voice high and shrill. "You said they'd let you stay until your ... you know," she added, unable to say the rest. She pointed at herself. "And then what?"

"You are assuming a lot, my dear," he said. "For example, you could go before me," he added with a wink. He meant it as a joke, but his wife's icy stare told him he had miscalculated. Without taking her eyes off her husband, she told Kitty and Lydia to make up the couch. "Your father will spend the night there." She walked out without another word.

•   •   •

"Do you think Mother will ever get over this?" Jane sat down on Lizzy's bed. Thankfully, Mr. Bennet knew when to give his wife space, so he retreated to the sofa, despite his daughters telling him he needed to go apologize to their mother. "Leave it alone, girls," he had told them, his voice weary and slow.

"You know our Mother," Lizzy said. "She loves to put on a show."

Jane smiled and when Lizzy tried to apologize again for not telling her sooner, Jane cut her off. "I told you it's okay." She tilted her head and offered a sly smile. "Besides, I have had *other things* on my mind."

Lizzy's eyes widened. "That's right, girl! Tell me what happened last night. I didn't even hear you leave!"

Jane explained how she had woken up around midnight to go to the bathroom and noticed a voice message from Charles on her phone. "I was staring at the phone, wondering if I should call him back, when it rang again!" Jane said. She shook her head. "I don't know what came over me, Lizzy! The next thing I know, I'm dressed, in my car, and driving toward Netherfield. At 2 in the morning!"

Lizzy giggled. "When love calls, gu-rrrrl!"

Jane sighed. "But seriously, Lizzy. It was just so … sweet. We didn't *do* anything you know, except talk and sleep, a bit."

"And Dr. Darcy?" Lizzy asked. "When did you see him?"

"Oh god, Lizzy! I wanted the floor to open up and swallow me! Charles told me he never gets up that early, but there he was in the hallway when I left Charles' room. So embarrassing!" Jane shivered.

"Did he say anything?"

"No. Plus, Charles came out right behind me and took me downstairs. He said not to worry about Darcy, but I hate to think that he thinks . . ."

"Thinks, what?" Lizzy asked. "That you're a grown woman with her own mind? This isn't the 18th century."

Jane turned serious. "I like Charles, Lizzy, and he and Dr. Darcy are best friends—like brothers—but he is just so proud and formal. If he doesn't approve of me, then I am sure he will say something to Charles."

"And do you think Charles would listen to him?" Lizzy asked.

Jane took a deep breath before answering. "I really don't know."

Lizzy reached out and took her sister's hand. "Well, first of all, the only thing Dr. Darcy—or anyone else—could say about you is that you're perfect." She held up her hand to stop her sister's protest. "And second, Dr. William Darcy isn't as 'formal' as we first thought."

Jane eyed her sister. "And just how many times have you been with Dr. Darcy?"

All evening, Lizzy had been considering whether to tell Jane everything, but after the dinner drama and hearing her worries about the developing relationship with Charles, she held off.

Instead, Lizzy told her about the Y2K meeting and working with the students. "He didn't have to do committee work, you know."

Jane nodded. "That does say a lot." Both were quiet for a minute before Jane continued.

"Charles asked me about George Wickham. I told him I haven't seen him but know that he's here to help a fraternity. I didn't tell him about you or last night."

Lizzy nodded. "Good." She didn't want Dr. Darcy to find out about that. Especially now.

"Do you know what he told me, Lizzy? He also said that Wickham couldn't be trusted, and that he had done something horrible to Darcy's family. I asked him what it was, but Charles declined to say, telling me it was Darcy's story to tell, not his."

Lizzy thought for a moment before telling Jane what Wickham had told her about Darcy taking his inheritance. "He practically accused Darcy of stealing from him! When I first heard it, I had no trouble believing it, but now … "

"It can't be true," Jane interjected. "Someone is not being honest, and I seriously doubt it to be Charles or William Darcy." Lizzy gave her a skeptical look. "No, I am not just saying that because I have feelings for Charles." She nudged her sister. "Knowing what you know about them, can you *really* believe that one, William Darcy is a *thief*, and two, that Charles would be best friends with one?"

Lizzy sighed and admitted that it was a "no" on both counts. Considering them all, Wickham was the only one to raise the player-hustler vibe. His relationship with Lydia was definitely questionable, and after listening to that CD, he obviously knew very little about the music industry.

Lizzy yawned as the events of the day suddenly caught up with her. "Well, with all that is going on with our family, I think we have enough drama without adding whatever is going on between those two grown men."

Jane agreed. "Oh! I didn't even tell you about the ball plans!"

Lizzy held up her hand. "Not tonight. I'm beat and Thursdays are my full days. First class at 8:00 AM!" She winked at her sister. "And I am sure you need to catch up on your sleep too," she added with a grin.

"Oh, be quiet," Jane said.

.   .   .

"There you are," Charles said.

Darcy looked up to see Charles at the top of the stairs. "I was just thinking I would need to get dressed and go looking for you."

Darcy mumbled a "sorry" and started up the staircase. After he left Lizzy in the garden, he sat in his car and tried to make sense of the last few hours. He had no trouble admitting his attraction to

Elizabeth Bennet; she was beautiful, smart, and self-sufficient—all qualities he admired. The issue was that, for the first time, he didn't know what to do with it. The prospect of marriage and family had never been a priority for him; it would happen someday. But he had always assumed she would come from the same social circle as him. Someone he met traveling through Europe or from a mutual friend. Did that make him a snob? Or practical? Yes, it had to be the latter. Relationships are already challenging, but two people who are opposite in all aspects? He couldn't see how that would work. Plus, her area of study! He groaned and rolled his eyes. Eight years ago, Darcy Finance formalized a policy forbidding investment in organizations associated with violent rap music production or distribution. The more conservative board members pushed for it after that song, *Cop Killer*, made the headlines. It was one of the first significant and controversial votes he had cast as a board member.

And then there was Wickham. The last time he had hit someone was at Chadwick Prep after another student told him to stop crying over his "dead nigger father." Ironically, it had been Wickham who eventually stepped in and pulled Darcy off him. Fearing expulsion, Darcy went to the dean the next morning to explain what had happened. To his relief, he was told not to worry, and that they had been looking for an excuse to expel the other student. It was the first time Darcy had heard someone call a rich white family "bad blood." Darcy got off with detention and 20 hours of work duty. "Lucky you," Wickham had told him.

Walking up the stairs to Charles, he noticed he was in the same robe and pajamas. His hair was a mess, and he needed a shave. "Some of us have actual jobs to go to," Darcy said as he stepped into the hallway.

Bingley looked down at his clothes. "Oh, god," he said. "The day got away from me, and before you say anything, I was working. For you."

"Do tell," Darcy responded with raised eyebrows.

"Well, after you left, I began thinking about Mrs. King and wondering who her informant might be, so I did some poking around." He stopped to take a breath. "And it seems like Carlton has a guy on Wickham. A private detective," Bingley added in response to Darcy's blank look. "So, it must be *him* who is keeping his mother informed on all things Wickham."

"A private detective?" Darcy's first thought was that he hoped the Kings were not wasting money chasing after Wickham, but then he had no idea what their financial situation was. Bingley continued.

"And apparently, they followed him here, so of course, they saw you two together, and voila!"

The pair had made it to Bingley's bedroom and Darcy sat down on the bed while Bingley went to his bathroom to wash and change. He left the door open so the conversation could continue. "I got the name of the agency, but of course, they wouldn't give me any information, but I found out that Bingley Wineries also used the same company a few years ago—you know that liability case we had—and that their specialty is finding fraud and hidden assets."

One of the big mysteries of the whole King-Wickham affair was what Wickham did with all that money he extorted from Mr. King. Part of the settlement had him liquidate assets and turn the cash over to the court. So far, Mrs. King has received about 45% of the money back. The rest, Wickham claimed, was gone.

"So now we know why she needed to warn you off him," Bingley said. "Probably afraid you'd tip him off or something." Bingley emerged from his bathroom, washed, shaved, and partially dressed.

Darcy stood to help him button his shirt. "Does this mean that they believe he has a stash of cash somewhere? What makes them think that?"

As the pair walked down the stairs, Bingley shared more of his day-long investigation. Wickham, it seems, has turned his attention toward the music business. Specifically rap music. His short stint in prison netted him a few choice relations. "Behind bars, he met some so-called 'future super stars' and anointed himself their manager. Of course, once they found out about his background with you, going to that fancy school and all, they were hooked."

They entered the dining room, and they could hear Caroline in the kitchen with Corrine and another voice neither recognized. "Now, here's the most interesting part," Bingley said, taking a seat. "He came here—to Delany—with the specific intention of meeting the famous hip-hop professor."

Darcy turned to him as if someone had slapped him. "What?!"

"Yes," Bingley continued. "That whole 'teaching step routines' is an excuse to get himself inside Delany. You may not know this, but rap music is big business. Million-dollar big."

"And what does Elizabeth Bennet have to do with that? She's a professor, not a music producer."

Bingley looked at his friend, not bothering to hide the pity in his eyes. "You really should get away from your calculators and spreadsheets sometimes, you know." He did his best to explain how Professor Bennet's work and research into the new mainstream rap industry are pretty influential. "An endorsement from her can open doors."

Darcy stood up and started pacing. "And this new group he's discovered—"

"BINGO!" Charles said.

"What BINGO?" Caroline emerged from the kitchen. She rolled her eyes in response to Darcy and Bingley's exchanged looks. "Oh, why do I even bother," she said. "You two really should have worked for the CIA or FBI or something."

Darcy re-took his seat. "It's not that we don't *want* to tell you, Caroline. It's more because there is nothing *to* tell. Not yet, anyway."

She snickered. "Well, I should be grateful. Lord knows I've got my hands full with getting this place up and running and that ball."

"And what a fabulous job you've done, Sister!" Charles raised his glass. "And not too much over budget." Corrine entered the dining room with their dinner. "Is he still here?" Caroline asked

Corrine as she set a plate of roasted chicken and potatoes on the table.

She shook her head. "Just left, but said he would be back first thing tomorrow to 'catch the morning light,' whatever that means."

"Who and why?" Charles asked as he loaded his plate.

Caroline let her fork drop to the table. "For heaven's sake, Charles. Can't you remember anything? The photographer. From *North Carolina Magazine.* He's been here for hours, but you wouldn't know that since you've been up in your room all day."

"Ahh," Darcy interjected. "For the layout. When will it run?"

Caroline sighed. "After the charity ball. In between that photographer and the back-and-forth emails with Mrs. Griff, it's been a day. The woman acts like I know nothing about planning a charity event."

"She's probably just trying to be helpful," Darcy said.

Corrine snickered. "Not that one. She's known for being kinda bossy."

"That will be all, Corrine. We'll call you if we need anything," Caroline said.

Corrine blinked at the rebuke, pressed her lips together, and left the room.

"What?" Caroline said to Darcy and her brother's reproachful look. Both men shook their heads and continued eating. Caroline asked Darcy about his first day. "I hope you weren't disappointed," she added.

Darcy glared at her. "No! And why does everyone keep asking me that?" As soon as the words were out of his mouth, he regretted the outburst. The day's events were getting to him. "I'm sorry, Caroline. Guess I'm tired." He glanced at Charles. "Let's just say that as far as academics are concerned, everything is fine. Better than fine." He shared a bit about how his classes went and about Chantell's request.

"What a great idea, Darce," Charles said. "But make sure you go when the Bennets will be there. What a great chance to meet the whole family."

"Oh, you—we all—will meet them before that," Caroline said. "They, along with many, many others, are invited to the Westside Clinic Charity Ball hosted by the Bingleys of Netherfield Manor."

Darcy laughed. "That's a mouthful."

"Yes! It barely fit on the invitations. But that Mrs. Griff insisted, saying it's the Southern way. Whatever that means."

Corrine came in to collect the now empty plates, her lips still pressed firmly together as if she was afraid some more unsolicited input would pop out. Darcy decided to relieve her. "And what is the 'Southern way' Corrine? Enlighten us."

She grinned but glanced at Caroline, who gave a slight nod which Corrine took as the okay to answer. "Well, if I know that Mrs. Griff, she's probably thinking about a full-out cotillion-type affair. Ladies in fancy dresses, men in tuxes, servers walking around with silver platters of fancy food, and a small band or orchestra playing music that nobody can dance to." She shrugged. "Not sure how you can make any money, though."

"Sounds interesting," Darcy said. "And don't worry about the fundraising aspect. Our Caroline is a master at getting people to open their wallets for charity."

Charles nodded. "And that clinic seems like a much-needed community resource. How long has it been here, Corrine?"

She shrugged. "Long as I've been in elementary school. The first time I went there was for my vaccines. Dr. Chaffee took care of me during my pregnancy. She was great, but she left soon after to start a private practice."

"Have you talked with this Mrs. Griff about how they will use the funds?" Darcy asked.

Caroline sighed. "On my list, but I think I'll have someone in legal take over that part. The last thing I need with that woman is one more point of friction."

Charles lifted his wineglass. "I am sure God will reward you sister."

Darcy joined in the toast but was sure Caroline was already reveling in her self-made heaven. She truly loved planning these types of events. The bigger, the better. And she was good at it. Darcy Finance had consulted her several times for their events, each a tremendous success. Taking a sip of his wine, his mind wandered to Elizabeth Bennet. Would she come?

"Darce?"

Darcy looked up to see Charles staring at him. "I'm sorry, did you—"

"Oh, don't mind him," Caroline said. "He was just going on about how his Jane will be the, and I quote, 'belle of the ball'."

Darcy grinned. "I'm sure she will be, Bingley."

"Thanks, Darce. By the way, are you bringing anyone?"

"No. But it would be my pleasure to escort Caroline for the evening."

Caroline smiled. "Why thank you, Dr. Darcy. I'll be sure to wear my best 'fancy dress' for the occasion."

CHAPTER 25

It surprised Lizzy to see a light on in the kitchen. She entered, expecting to see her father at the table.

"Good morning, Miss Lizzy." Lydia sat at the kitchen table; her arms folded across her chest. She was still in her pajamas and the black silk cap she wore to keep her braids looking fresh.

"Good morning?" Lizzy whispered. "Don't tell me you got up early to send me off to classes." She walked to the fridge to retrieve something for her lunch. All the leftovers were last night's dinner, so she made a ham sandwich.

"You're half right, Sister. I got up extra early to inform you about what your precious Dr. Darcy did yesterday."

Lizzy sighed. She had almost forgotten that he told her Lydia was there. "You lost out on your beauty sleep for nothing, I'm afraid. Dr. Darcy told me everything yesterday."

This surprised her sister. "He did? When? Oh, never mind. This just means I can go back to bed sooner. What I *really* wanted to tell you is to tell *him* to keep his mouth shut about it." She glanced at Lizzy. "But I guess I'm too late. Who else do you think he's blabbed to by now?"

Lizzy finished her sandwich and slipped it into a Ziplock bag. "Does it matter? You can't think that something like this won't get around—"

"It won't. After Darcy left, Douglas warned everyone to keep quiet. He made the brothers—and me—take an oath. So, I need *you* to tell that Darcy to keep his mouth shut."

With Mashujaa House on the administration's watch list, it made sense that they would want to keep this quiet. She couldn't see Darcy lying about the situation, but with physical violence, someone always gets punished, and she, like the Mashujaa brothers, doubted it would be the prominent Dr. William Darcy.

She grabbed an apple to add to her lunch bag. "Why me? Besides, I have a full day of classes and doubt I'll even see him today." Hopefully, she thought.

Lydia stood up. "I told Douglas you would say that." She walked to the phone on the wall. Lizzy watched her finger rapidly punch a slew of numbers before hanging up. "And who were you paging?"

"Don't you worry about it," Lydia said, leaving the kitchen. She stopped at the door. "Oh, and have a nice daaaay!"

Lizzy left Longbourne a few minutes later, not bothering with breakfast since there would be coffee and pastries at the office, a gift from administration. She had no idea what Dr. Darcy planned to do about the incident, but knowing his proper, by-the-book self, he would probably report it to his Dean, or even Dr. Lucas. *Forgive me, Father, for I have sinned.* Lizzy chuckled at the image of him genuflecting in front of the board.

"Mind sharing the joke. I could use a good laugh this morning." Wickham came to a stop in front of her.

"You're out early. Is this the beginning, or end of your run?" Lizzy asked.

He wiped his brow with the back of his hand. "End. Got to get it done before the heat."

"Ahh," she said, nodding. "Good point." She continued walking, and he joined her. "Well, today's my early day too; back-to-back classes until lunch." She stole a glance at his face, wondering if the hit left any marks. His head was down, and he walked with a heaviness that was new to her. She stopped when they reached the spot where the paths intersected. "Well, I'm that way," she said, pointing.

He looked confused for a moment, as if he had forgotten she was there. "Yes," he said. "Well, it seems like my time at Delany will be ending soon."

"Oh?" she asked. "What about the step routine? And the competition?"

He waved away her concern. "Douglas thinks the guys are almost set, plus there's some urgent business back in California I need to get to."

"About that rap group?"

"Yes … I mean no, but yes, I need to check in with them, too."

"I should return your CD."

"What?"

"Your rap group—"

"Oh yeah, yeah. Don't worry about that. I have a few … some time left before I go. I'm sure we'll see each other before then." He nodded. "Goodbye for now."

Before she could offer her own goodbye, he turned and jogged off. The campus clocked tower rang. "Damn!" she muttered. "Late again!"

.　.　.

Mrs. Hoffman greeted Dr. Darcy as he entered the Economics Department. She told him that there were two gentlemen waiting to see him. He recognized one of them. They stood when they saw him. "I told them to come back during your office hours, but they insisted."

"It's all right," he told her. They followed him into his office, closing the door behind them. Darcy walked behind his desk but remained standing, wondering if he would need to get his lawyer involved. He did not know what the punishment was for assault, but also knew that George Wickham could be bought off. He had considered this last night, but decided he would rather do the time than give that man any more of his money.

"Good morning, Dr. Darcy," Douglas said. He nodded towards his companion. "This is Blake Harper, our chapter secretary."

"Good morning, gentlemen," Darcy responded. "If you're here about yesterday, which I assume you are, rest assured that I intend to take full responsibility for my—"

Douglas held up his hand. "Yes, we are here about that. We wanted to let you know that the Mashujaa Fraternity House would prefer it if we could all just move on from the situation."

"Move on?"

Douglas nodded. "Yes. We spoke to Wickham, and he explained that the … business between you two has nothing to do with Delany or current events. Mashujaa leadership," he motioned to Blake, "decided that the best way forward would be to forgive and forget, as they say."

"Excuse me, doesn't your fraternity have a president?" Darcy asked.

Douglas laughed. "Oh, yes, of course. But he's studying abroad this semester. Costa Rica."

"Ahh," Darcy said. He gazed at the two young men and wondered if there was an underlying motive. "I've always found it best to get incidents such as this resolved as soon as possible. Plus, you can't expect it to be kept a secret. Can you?"

"Yes sir, we can," Blake said. "The Mashujaa oath is sacred, you see, like the warriors we are."

Although never a member of any fraternity, Darcy knew enough to know that he spoke the truth. "Did Lydia Bennet take that oath too?" he asked.

The two men glanced at each other. "She did," Douglas said. "You don't need to worry about her."

"And Wickham?"

Another look passed between them. "George Wickham's time with us will come to an end soon," Blake said.

"You do not need to worry about him either," Douglas added.

Darcy sighed. "Well, it looks like you have it all taken care of." He felt his shoulders relax. He offered them his hand, and both shook it with a firm grip, sealing the agreement. "I appreciate your coming by," he said.

Blake and Douglas nodded, thanked him for his time, and left. He sat down, feeling an unexpected sense of relief. He had little time to settle into it since his group of research students were due in a few minutes. Pushing all other thoughts aside, he busied himself with getting things ready. Minutes later, Mrs. Hoffman buzzed with their arrival. Grabbing his papers, he left his office to meet them in the conference room. They filled the next 90 minutes with facts, charts, banking statistics, numbers, and more numbers. Dr. Darcy was, as Bingley likes to say, in his zone. To his surprise, Michael Johnson reminded him a bit of his grad-student self; unsure at times and always believing he needed to do more than the rest. For Darcy, being the sole Black student, followed by the inevitable (and incorrect) affirmative action label, had been the source of his uneasiness. He wondered what Michael's could be.

After two hours, the session ended with everyone having their next steps laid out and planned. "Thanks, everyone," Darcy said. "Good work."

Michael lingered behind and when they were alone, pulled an oversized envelope from his backpack. He handed it to Dr. Darcy. "Thanks for giving me this assignment. I did not know Delany's history was so rich."

"Oh?" Darcy said. "What made you come here, then?"

He shrugged. "It was one of only two places that accepted me. The other was too expensive, so ... "

"I see ..." Dr. Darcy's voiced trailed off, not knowing what else he could offer. Eight out of ten of his grad applications succeeded, and the words "too expensive" never factored into his final decision.

"But when I found out that *you* would be here," Michael continued, "I knew I made the best decision."

Feeling a bit embarrassed and eager to change the subject, Darcy asked him to share his findings.

"The ladies at the library were very helpful," Michael began. "And you were right about the archives; they had *all* the documents relating to the Bennet Legacy, as it's called." He explained what he learned about the original reasoning behind the agreement. He shrugged. "I guess they had good intentions, but it would have been better to give the following generations completely free tuition or something else that could have helped them move up." He told Darcy how the research librarians explained that most of the Bennet children have received scholarships, full or partial, and the ones who typically acquire debt are those who go on to grad school. "Money can be a great deterrent, you know."

Darcy nodded while he looked through the papers. He held up one, a copy of the original declaration, written in elaborate script, and signed with signatures he could not make out. Fortunately, there was a transcript. He slipped the papers back into the envelope, wondering what his next step could be. And why? "Well, it seems to have been a mutually beneficial arrangement for both sides and to sever it now seems harsh."

"That's what the librarian said. She referred to them as The Delany Bennets and said that everyone was pretty sad about the breakup."

Darcy didn't know about everyone, but he suspected Elizabeth Bennet would take it particularly hard. He would admit to not knowing too much about her, but he understood her pride in the university and her father's work.

He thanked Michael and told him he would see him next week.

"Are you thinking of giving them a micro-loan?" Michael asked, stopping Darcy at the door. "What? No, of course not."

"Oh," Michael said with questioning eyes. "I was just wondering."

So am I, thought Darcy. He had no answer to satisfy Michael's curiosity, so he just nodded and left.

Back in his office, he surveyed the university calendar, hardly believing that it was only the second day of classes. He sighed, wondering how he was going to make it through the year, let alone the fall semester.

CHAPTER 26

Professor Bennet's morning went by in a chaotic blur. Besides being hyped on sugar and caffeine from the apple fritter and coffee she had inhaled between her first and second classes, Enrollment had messed up half of the students' registration and her roll sheet was full of errors. She spent half the class trying to figure out who was—or was not—supposed to be there. At 12:15, she collapsed into a chair in the Language Arts breakroom. "You too," Dr. Wright said after she walked in and saw her harried co-worker almost passed out.

Lizzy placed her elbows on the table and rested her forehead in her hands. "Oh god," she groaned. "Worst first day ever!"

"Welcome to the club," Dr. Wright said, pulling out a chair to join her. "Did Enrollment mess up your sheets too? They're blaming it on the Y2K upgrades."

"Well, I don't care who's at fault as long as it's straightened out soon. The students were in a panic, and some said their loan disbursements were late or hadn't gone through at all."

Dr. Wright unwrapped the sandwich she had bought from the snack bar in the quad. "Like this year is any different," she said, taking a bite. "Wonder who they'll blame it on next year?"

Lizzy reached into her bag to pull out her lunch, although she didn't feel like eating. Tea, she decided. She walked to the counter, hoping there were some peppermint tea bags in one of the drawers. There were, and she took a mug, filled it with water, and set it into the microwave. Leaning against the counter, she folded her arms and asked Dr. Wright how things were otherwise.

She shrugged. "Same ole, same ole," she answered. "After my research trip to Africa, it's been hard for me to get back into lecture mode."

The microwave dinged. "Well, you are due for a sabbatical, aren't you?" Lizzy asked, taking her mug back to the table.

"I am, indeed," she mused. "Wonder if I could get a sweet deal like that Dr. Darcy?"

Lizzy took a sip of her tea. She had no idea how much Delany was paying Dr. Darcy, but knew they would not be happy with what happened yesterday. "Well, I'd pay you twice as much if I could."

"Why thank you," Dr. Wright said. She put down her half-eaten sandwich and peered at Lizzy. "Speaking of pay and Delany, I've been meaning to ask you about ..."

"Yes, it's true," Lizzy said with a sigh. "The Delany-Bennet legacy is ending."

Dr. Wright sat back in her chair. "Wow. That's some cold shit right there." She shook her head. "Are you going to stay on?"

Lizzy looked at her. "What? Leave Delany?"

"Well, there's nothing keeping you here now."

Mary's words in the garden came back to her. "I'm here because I like it and it's where I want to be," she said. "Same as you, I presume."

Dr. Wright shrugged. "Sure. If you say so." She leaned forward. "Look, all I'm suggesting is that with what they are doing to your father—your family—no one would be surprised if your *loyalty* to Delany waned." The two educators eyed each other for a few seconds before someone entering the break room broke the spell.

"There you are!" said Mrs. Jackson, the Liberal Arts secretary.

Dr. Wright popped up from her chair. "Oh crap! I forgot all about the meeting." She gathered the remains of her sandwich and tossed it into the trash. "We'll chat later, Lizzy, okay?"

Lizzy wrapped her hands around her mug as she watched Dr. Wright's hurried departure. *Leave Delany?* The thought pecked inside her like a chick escaping its shell. But then two concerns crept in: Why? And where?

.   .   .

When Douglas and Blake told Dr. Darcy that he didn't need to worry about Lydia Bennet, they said it with more hope than certainty. Both men knew that Lydia Bennet was far from discreet and would take advantage of every opportunity to advance her stature in the community. Having a juicy tidbit as this would surely earn her a few clicks up. She also had nothing nice to say about Dr. Darcy, but they blamed that on Wickham's influence. After telling him to keep the fight under wraps, Douglas warned him about Lydia. "Last thing Mashujaa House needs is being involved with some jail-bait scandal." Wickham assured them that nothing inappropriate was going on between them. "Besides," he told them. "It's the sister I am really interested in. Musically, that is."

Still not completely convinced, Douglas and Blake let him go, but asked Darren to keep his ears open and warn them if Lydia started blabbing. "Ask Kitty," they instructed. He nodded, knowing it was his only option. This was on his mind as he waited for Kitty in front of her junior college. They had agreed to meet so he could help her pick out textbooks for the next semester after he bragged about being an expert in finding near-perfect used editions. He saw her across the street, waved, and breathed a sigh of relief when he didn't see Lydia with her. After meeting her family, they became more open with the relationship, so he greeted her with a quick kiss. "Ready?" he said, taking her hand.

An hour later, the young couple sat opposite each other in the same diner that Wickham and Lizzy had visited a few days ago. After the waitress left, Kitty thanked him again for his help. "And," she began, looking a little shy, "for not making fun of me for being at a JC."

The comment surprised and disappointed Darren. "I wouldn't do that. And besides, why would anyone? There's nothing wrong with going to a junior college. I almost did."

Kitty gave a half-smile. "Some people do."

"Like Lydia?" Darren sneered.

"Why do you say it like that? I know Lydia can be … you know, but she's not *all* bad. We used to be really close …"

Darren reached across the table to take her hand. "I know, and I'm sorry. It's just that she tends to suck all the energy out of the room and keep it for herself."

Kitty pulled her hand away, making him immediately regret his words.

"I guess you don't understand what it's like to have a big family," she said. "Lydia's just trying to find her way, that's all."

"With Wickham?"

She shot him a look. "What does that mean? I know Lydia can be … wild sometimes, but it's mostly play."

The waitress returned with their orders, and both took advantage of the distraction to gather their thoughts.

"Has she said anything to you about him?" Darren asked as he shook the ketchup bottle over his fries.

"Wickham? Just the usual about how smart he is and how he's going to go far in the rap music business. That group—whatever they're called—is fantastic, according to her."

Darren chuckled. "I heard them, and they are far from fantastic." He set down the ketchup and gazed at Kitty. "Anything else?"

Kitty set her burger on the plate and leaned back in the booth. "Like what? You seem more interested in her than in—"

Darren held up his hand. "Don't go there, Katherine. Please." He took a deep breath. "This has to do with Mashujaa business and that's really all I can tell you, okay?"

Kitty's look turned to concern. "Is she in trouble, Darren? 'Cause if she is, you need to tell me."

Darren shook his head and gazed out the window. Over the treetops, he could see a few of the Delany University buildings. He had not been present at the gym, but Douglas and Blake had told him what had happened, and then swore him to secrecy. He hated secrets, and keeping one from Katherine was especially bothering him. "The only thing I can tell you is that if she ever is in trouble, I'll let you know right away. Promise."

The last thing Kitty wanted to do was mess up Darren's standing with his frat brothers. Being a neophyte was hard enough, and adding a pesky, uncooperative girlfriend to the mix would make things even harder. For him and her. "Okay, and thank you."

He smiled and nodded. "Good." They finished eating, chatting through the meal, but their already spoiled conversation struggled to recover. He walked her home, and they made plans to see each other in a few days. He placed his hands on her shoulders and looked down into her eyes. "I wish I could see you more right now, but with both of us starting classes, it's going to be—"

"Crazy," Kitty said, wrapping her arms around his waist. "Plus, I still have work."

He hugged her back. "Don't you worry Miss Katherine Bennet. We'll make it work."

·   ■   ■

"Well, didn't you two look all cozy-wozy," Lydia crooned when Kitty entered their bedroom a few minutes after saying goodbye to Darren.

"What are you doing here?" Kitty went to her closet to get her uniform. "Shouldn't you be out school shopping with Mom rather than spying on people?"

Lydia fumed. "Ha Ha! And shouldn't *you* be putting on that tacky uniform and going to work instead of smooching with your boyfriend on the street in front of everybody?"

Kitty's face burned and when their eyes met in the dresser's mirror, the daggers coming from each were unmistakable. Kitty grabbed her uniform and left to change in the bathroom.

As she walked to work, her mind wandered back to when she and Lydia were close. "Thick as thieves," their parents used to say. They were, and it had been fun. For both sisters. Getting into antics together was always more fun, and since Lydia was the youngest, the parents were usually easy on them. Lizzy once accused Kitty of using Lydia as a get-out-of-jail-free card. Had she? After Kitty's failed first semester at Delany, Lydia's unsupportive and almost mocking attitude surprised her. It would be years later before she understood that her younger sister had been afraid of losing her running buddy, but now Lydia's behavior really hurt Kitty.

She was early to the shop and walked in to find the manager hanging a *Help Wanted* sign on the window. "We lost Melissa *and* Tiffany," he said. "Both are back to school full time this semester. Know anyone who needs a job?"

CHAPTER 27

The following weeks were a whirlwind of classes and back to campus activities. Delany's Fighting Rhinos won their first two home games, adding an extra bit of jubilation to the beginning of the school year. The campus grounds filled with pep rally cheers, pounding drum lines, impassioned speeches, and panicked first years. Admissions eventually settled the enrollment fiasco, leaving a few students angry at being dropped from classes they had thought were secure. Professor Bennet even had one cry in front of the entire class. This was the part of education she hated, the bureaucracy and constant screw-ups. She promised to look into it. In between all of this, the board sent a mass email announcing the retirement of Mr. Harold Bennet; Our beloved groundskeeper.

They left out the word forced, she thought, re-reading the email. She printed it and tacked it to her bulletin board, giving her something to point to whenever anyone entered, asking her if she had seen the email. She did just that when Dr. Wright walked in waving a piece of paper. "Lord, oh lord!" she said. "Looks like I made the cut!" Dr. Wright followed Lizzy's finger to the printed email. "Not that, girl," she said, waving away the misdirection. "This!" She handed Lizzy the paper.

We request your presence at the
Westside Clinic Charity Ball
hosted by
the Bingleys of Netherfield Manor
Saturday, October 23, 1999
6-9pm

There was another card soliciting donations, announcing the silent auction and RSVP details. Lizzy handed it back to Dr. Wright. "Well, first, I thought it wasn't until *November,* and second, I never understood why people won't simply donate the money and skip all the ... fuss."

Dr. Wright slid the invitation back into its envelope. "November is too busy with Thanksgiving break and end of semester chaos. And this is how it's done, darling. Rich people *love* killing two birds with one stone: a way to show off their wealth *and* their generosity."

Lizzy shrugged. "I guess." She assumed an invitation was waiting for her at Longbourne and wondered if they would invite the whole family.

"I just hope they invited some people outside of Delany and Merryton. I don't want to get all dressed up to parade around a bunch of folks I already know. This could be a perfect networking opportunity, too."

Lizzy clicked her tongue. "It's a fundraiser, not a meet-and-greet. But Jane did tell me that Caroline invited some from her New York crowd, so ..."

Dr. Wright's eyes widened. "Jane? Caroline? What aren't you telling me, Professor Bennet? Sounds like you've gotten pretty cozy with these Bingleys."

Lizzy grimaced at her mistake before sharing as few details as possible about Jane and Charles. Dr. Wright's face moved from surprise to disbelief. "Promise me you won't say anything?"

"Of course not. Besides, I'm sure it will all be an open secret after this ball." She cocked her head to the side. "I hope it works out. This would be good security for you all now since ... you know."

Lizzy's face fell. "Oh god! You sound like my mother. Jane, like her sisters, is perfectly capable of taking care of herself. We all have—or will have—suitable careers, you know."

"I know that. But tell me the thought hadn't crossed your mind, so I can call you a liar."

Lizzy didn't answer, but busied herself with getting ready for her last class of the day. Dr. Wright took the hint and turned to leave. "Ummm," she said, pausing at the door. "Does he know about the ending of the legacy?"

"Who?" Lizzy asked, as she slung her bag over her shoulder.

"Charles Bingley. He must know, since that email came out. Dr. Darcy probably told him."

Lizzy's breath caught in her throat. "Does it matter?" she managed to say.

Dr. Wright shrugged. "It shouldn't."

Two minutes after Dr. Wright left her office, Lizzy followed. Today was the third week of her Hip Hop Studies class. Last week, with all the enrollment issues, she couldn't get through the material on West African oral recitation traditions, which she and many others believed is the backbone of today's rap. Hopefully, they can get through that, and then talk about final group projects. Walking across campus, Lizzy hoped to escape any more probing questions. *Yes, I've heard, and of course, I'm upset. But we'll be ok.* Jane had suggested she print cards with that on it and hand them out like flyers. "It'll die down soon," her father said. To the children's surprise, both he and Mrs. Bennet turned down the offer of a retirement party. "I will not pretend I am happy with any part of this," her mother said to Mrs. Lucas' request.

There was one person she hadn't seen or talked to. Over a week since the Ancestors Garden and no sign of him. Or Wickham. She entered her classroom and 35 anxious faces turned to greet her. "Good afternoon, class. Who can remind us of where we left off last week?"

. . .

Instead of going back to her office, Lizzy decided to go straight home. Jane should be home, and the two of them having a night out sounded like something she really needed right now. Longbourne came into sight, causing Lizzy to sigh. If Jane has plans with Charles (which she probably does) Lizzy told herself, she would try to do something with Charlotte. Ever since the announcement, her time with Charlotte had become tense, not that Lizzy blamed her, but she held a bit of resentment towards her father, Dr. Lucas.

"Oh good, you're home." Mrs. Bennet greeted Lizzy at the door. "I was just about to call Midge and tell her to shush you home."

Lizzy set her bag down. "That's not her job, Mother, and I can decide for myself when to come home."

Mrs. Bennet eyed her. "Don't tell me you forgot?"

Lizzy stared back with a blank face until Lydia's voice coming from the family room jolted her memory. Her shoulders slumped, and she rocked her head back. "Is that today?" she moaned, staring at the ceiling.

"Yes," Mrs. Bennet said. "And the last one, thank God."

Lizzy set her bag on the entry table and followed her mother. "What did she decide to do?"

Tomorrow was the first day of Lydia Bennet's last year of high school. As was tradition, the daughter entering the oldest grade got to choose how the family spent the evening before school starts. Within limits, of course, usually consisting of getting to choose what to have for dinner and a family activity afterwards. Lizzy remembered how angry Kitty and Lydia would get when she chose family reading night for her activity. "You'll be reading all year!" Lydia had complained. "What a waste!"

Lizzy and Mrs. Bennet walked into the living room. "Dad! Please!" Lydia reached down to wrap her arms around her father as he sat in his chair. "I'm the last one. After this year, you'll never have to treat us all out like this again."

Mr. Bennet chuckled. "What do you mean, young lady? I'll have *five* weddings to pay for, you know."

Lydia scoffed. "Not five, maybe three, since I'm not *ever* getting married and Mary, well …"

"Hey!" Mary squeaked.

"Lydia …" Mr. Bennet warned.

Lydia turned to Mary. "Sorrrrry. But I really want to go to The Grille tonight. And that's it. No *family activity*. Yuck." She shivered.

Lizzy stepped into the sitting room. "You're not really helping your case, Lydia."

"No, you are not," Mrs. Bennet said. "Anything The Grille can make, I can make here, and for a lot less. With your father losing—"

"All right, Lydia," Mr. Bennet said, standing up. "You win." He checked his watch. "Everyone be ready in 45 minutes or we're leaving without you."

Mrs. Bennet watched her husband leave the room and head to his study. "Well, I guess that's that. Lizzy, make sure Jane knows. I think she's in her room."

Lizzy told her she would and then wondered if her mother had just played a clever trick of reverse psychology on her husband. Whichever was the case, Lizzy made her way upstairs, wishing her father had not fallen for it. Dining at Merryton's most popular restaurant and being seen by half the town was the opposite of how she had wanted to spend the evening.

She entered Jane's room, threw herself face down on the bed, and screamed into the pillow. "Oh god," Jane said. She was sitting at her desk with her checkbook and a small stack of bills. "What did Lydia decide?"

"Is that all?" Jane asked after Lizzy told her. "I know we were just there, but—"

"It's not that," Lizzy said. "It was bad enough being gawked at when we were there with two rich guys. Now everyone will look at us with pity and wanting to get into our business."

Jane licked and sealed an envelope. "No one's going to pity us, Lizzy, because there is nothing to feel pity about. And as far as all the questions, well, like Father said, that'll die down soon."

Lizzy sat up, sighed, and gazed across the room. She watched Jane, who had opened another bill and was writing another check. Jane was meticulous with her money and kept track of her balances and bills in a way that would impress any accountant. Lizzy, not so much, and had received her fair share of overdraft notices. I bet Dr. Darcy or Charles Bingley has never had to deal with those, she thought. And if things progressed with Charles, neither will Jane. Lizzy felt dizzy thinking about how different Jane's life would be if she were to become Mrs. Charles Bingley.

"Oh shoot," Jane said, waking Lizzy up from her daydreams. "I can't find my stamps."

"Do you think I'm afraid of change?"

Jane stopped her stamp searching. "What? Where did *that* come from?"

Lizzy looked down at her hands and told Jane what Kitty had said to her in the garden and then Dr. Wright. "Everyone thinks I'm trapped here or something, unable to move because of … fear."

"Do you think that, Lizzy? Because that's all that really matters and *not* what other people say."

Lizzy lifted her shoulders and let them drop. Two weeks ago, she would have called her life stable, satisfying, and happy. She opened her mouth to answer but stopped after seeing the time on Jane's desk clock. "No time for any life reflections, I'm afraid. Maybe later."

"Lizzy?" Jane stopped her at the door. "Are you all right?"

Lizzy smiled. "That's an excellent question, sister."

.   .   .

"No Jane Bennet tonight?" Darcy pulled out a dining room chair and sat down. Caroline sat at the head and Charles opposite. Both had glasses of Cabernet and he picked up his empty red wine glass and passed it to Caroline. "Really?" she said with raised eyebrows. "Don't tell me the Fighting Rhinos are getting to you already."

Charles laughed. "The *what*?"

Darcy took a long sip. "The rhinoceros is the school's mascot, colloquially called the fighting rhinos." He looked at Caroline. "I'm surprise you know that."

She finished her wine and poured another glass. "Corrine. A number one fan, as she says."

"Football?" Charles said. "Wonder if Jane would like to go to a game sometime?"

"Probably," Darcy said. "Although she doesn't seem like the sports type to me. By the way, not seeing her tonight?"

Charles shook his head. "Nope. Some family obligation. Something to do with Lydia, the youngest, and her first day of school."

Darcy rotated his wineglass in a small circle and watched the red liquid swirl along the sides. With Lydia back in school, she'll have less time to waste with those fraternity boys and Wickham.

"Have we met Lydia?" Caroline asked.

Charles shook his head. "Jane mentions her now and then, but she mostly talks about Lizzy. They're very close."

Darcy had decided not to share his run-in with Wickham. Enough time had passed without it coming up, so he had to assume that the Mashujaa oath was indeed, sacred. He suspected Lizzy would be just as keen to keep it quiet since her youngest sister was also involved. "I haven't met her but have seen her around campus." He glanced at Charles, wondering if he remembered the mention of Lydia with Wickham that day in the campus coffee shop. Charles was focused on his dinner, so Darcy assumed he did not. "Tell us, Caroline, how goes the ball plans? Everyone on campus met your invitations with great excitement ."

Caroline grinned. "Surprisingly well, Darcy. With Merryton being such a small town, there are not too many choices, so deciding is relatively easy." She listed caterers, florists, and party suppliers whose names meant nothing to either man. "Oh, and that Mrs. Griff, I'll have to give it to her. She's a whizz at getting special offers and extras. The silent auction should bring in quite a lot. And she even convinced a fraternity to act as valets and wait staff."

This got both men's attention.

"From Delany?"

"Is that a good idea?"

"Which one?"

Caroline blinked at the sudden interest. "One of the Divine Nine, of course. Phi Beta Sigma."

The men exhaled. "Oh. That's good."

Caroline looked from one to the other and shook her head. "More secrets, huh?" Before either could respond, the phone rang, and she excused herself.

"Whew!" Charles said after his sister left. "We need to let her know what's going on, Darce. With her getting more involved in the town and Delany, she's bound to come across something."

Darcy agreed. "But only that Wickham is here and if that frat name—Mashujaa—comes up, she needs to avoid it, them, I mean."

Charles nodded. "Ok. I'll do it tomorrow after you leave. That way, you can avoid all the hysterics. She hates Wickham probably more than you do."

"I doubt that," Darcy said.

Caroline rejoined them, looking concerned. She sat down and replaced her napkin on her lap. "That was your Aunt Catherine," she announced. "She's coming next week *and* staying to at least the ball."

"Ahh ..." Charles said.

"I didn't know she knew about it," Darcy said.

Caroline shrugged. "Well, you know how these things tend to get around. She also chided me for *not* inviting her."

"As if she needs inviting," Charles said. "And staying … here, you say?"

"Yes, Charles. Where else would she stay? The Merryton Holiday Inn?"

Aunt Catherine Deburge was Darcy's great aunt, from his father's side. One of a few remaining relatives. She was instrumental in helping his father with his early financial success, being one of his first, and largest, initial investors. She and her husband were physicians and retired comfortably. They had no children. A widow now for almost ten years, she spends her time doing philanthropy work and bugging her nephew to get married and carry on the Darcy name. "Before I die," she teases him.

Darcy looked over at Caroline's worried expression. "I'm sure it will be okay, Caroline. Aunt Catherine isn't that much trouble. Let me know what I can do to help. And thank you."

Caroline smiled. "I know. It's just that she can be so … critical. Thank god we got the grounds done, but I'll definitely have to get the guest room in order … " Her voice drifted off and the two men knew she was back in home improvement mode. They exchanged knowing looks before returning to the meal.

CHAPTER 28

After the drinks were served, Mrs. Bennet gazed around The Grille's dining room and sighed. "As much as I prayed for this day, it's sad to have it finally here." They were not the only family commemorating back-to-school night. "There are the Baileys, and the Washington family," she said with a sigh. "Everybody's growing up so fast." She looked at her husband. "Well Mr. B, are you ready to send our youngest out into the big, bad world?"

He laughed. "You should be asking Lydia that question, not me."

All eyes turned to the youngest Bennet, who was busy trying to stab the maraschino cherry in her Shirley Temple with a straw. Mrs. Bennet groaned and cast her eyes to the ceiling. "Oh, Lydia."

During the meal, Lydia kept them entertained with summer gossip, and the teachers and classes she was not looking forward to. "I hope I don't get Mr. Brooke for biology. He's soooo boring."

"Science isn't supposed to entertain Lydia; it's supposed to *inform*," Mary said from across the table.

"Whatever it's supposed to do," Lizzy said, "just make sure you get higher than a C. You need all the help with your GPA."

Lydia shrugged. "It doesn't matter." She paused. "I'm not going to Delany or any university."

Mr. Bennet eyed his daughter. "I think we have already established that, Lydia. You'll be starting at Merryton Community first, then Delany, or wherever else you choose to attend."

Lydia set her fork down and pushed her plate away. She set her hands in her lap and took a deep breath, piquing her family's interest. "What's going on, Lydia?" her mother asked.

"Well, I was going to wait to tell you, but … I've decided *not* to go to college—Delany or MC."

Six pairs of eyes stared blankly, except for Mary's, whose eyes held the twinkle of vindication. "I knew it!" she said. "Lydia Bennet, college student! Talk about an oxymoron!"

"Be quiet, Mary! You're the biggest Bennet moron—"

"Enough!" Mr. Bennet glanced around the dining area and caught a few curious looks. He waved for the waitress and signaled for the check.

"But what about dessert?" Lydia whined.

"Well, I, for one, couldn't eat another bite," Mrs. Bennet said. "Lydia, dearest, I do not know where you got such an idea, but—"

"Wickham says that students in Europe do it all the time. It's called a skipped year, or something."

"Gap year," Lizzy said. "So you mean to take a year off, then? *One* year?"

Lydia shrugged. "Maybe."

"And just what do you plan to do during this 'gap year'?" Mrs. Bennet asked.

Another shrug. "I don't know … yet," Lydia mumbled.

"The yogurt shop is hiring," Kitty offered. "You could start part-time and then, when school's over, full time."

A look of disgust twisted across Lydia's face, but before she could spew words to match, Mr. Bennet instructed his family to wait for him outside while he paid the check. "No need to spread *all* our family business tonight," he said, handing Lizzy the keys to the family minivan. "Wait for me in the car."

The drive back to Longbourne was quiet. After Mr. Bennet pulled into the driveway, Lizzy asked him if she could borrow the car. "To take Lydia to get her dessert," she said. "*All* of us," she added, motioning to her sisters.

It was times like these that Mr. Bennet truly appreciated his second eldest. He handed her the keys and followed his wife into the house. Both sides needed alone time right now.

Lizzy got into the driver's seat. "Where to, Lydia?"

Mabel's Sweet Shop in downtown Merryton had the best banana pudding, Lydia's favorite dessert. The five Bennet sisters entered the small shop and slipped into a corner booth by the window. Jane went to the counter to order. "I got us an extra-large tray with five plates. We can bring the leftovers home," she said, returning to the table. She slid in next to Lydia.

"Thank you, Jane," Lydia crooned.

From across the table, Lizzy watched Lydia with curiosity. During the drive, Lydia had babbled on as usual about her hair, wardrobe, the Shujaas, and dreading school, but conveniently left off any mention of her post-high school plans.

"You seem to spend a lot of time with Wickham," Lizzy said after everyone was served.

"Jealous?" Lydia asked with a grin.

Lizzy shook her head. "No, but curious. *Very* curious, actually. Especially since he's putting gap year ideas into your head."

Lydia glanced around the table at her sisters. "I know you all think I'm stupid—"

"No one thinks that Lydia," Jane said. "We just want you to succeed."

"A college degree isn't the only way to succeed, you know." She pointed a finger at Lizzy. "Tell them how many rappers have become famous—and rich—*without* a college degree."

"You want to become a rapper?" Lizzy said. "Since when?"

"Not a rapper, but my *point* is that people can be fine without college. Dad never went."

"Dad has an associate degree, Lydia. Even *you* could get that if you tried." Mary said.

"Mary," Jane warned. "Now is not the time, okay? We need to do what we can to support each other, especially now since Father will be ... retired."

"And how does my wasting time doing something I don't want to *or* need to do showing support? As long as I'm out of their hair, they should be happy." Lydia's voice trembled, and she raised a hand to brush away a small tear. She cast her head down when she saw her sisters' faces. "Don't look at me like that. You all know it's true."

Jane sighed. "Oh Lydia, where do you get such ideas?"

Everyone's appetite for sweets vanished, so Mary and Kitty secured the leftovers and cleaned the table. When they left to throw away the trash and get a bag for the leftover pudding, Lizzy turned to Lydia. "Promise me you'll put this no-college business on the shelf for now. You have at least six months before any firm decisions need to be made anyway, and we could use a break from any more family drama."

Lydia folded her arms across her chest, then nodded her agreement.

"Thank you," Lizzy said. "And you need to stay away from Wickham *and* those guys from Mashujaa House." She held up her hand to stop Lydia's protest. "This is for you *and* them. You're a minor Lydia, and nothing good can come from you associating with those grown men who ought to know better, anyway."

"You're kidding, right?" Lydia said. "You do remember that it was DR. DARCY who punched Wickham, and for no good reason. Ha! He's the one you should be telling to stay away. Not me."

"What?" Jane said. "Who punched who? Lizzy?"

Lizzy glared at Lydia. "We were sworn to secrecy, Jane, but this just proves my point. Who else did you tell Lydia?"

"Tell who what?" Kitty asked.

Lizzy grabbed her purse. "Nothing and no one. Time to go home."

Longbourne was dark and quiet. The sisters mumbled goodnights and went to their respective rooms. Lizzy hoped Lydia and Kitty wouldn't get into a screaming match. She was climbing into bed when she heard the knock on her door. "Come in," she said, and then, "Oh, it's you." when Mary entered, wearing blue pajamas with colorful dragonflies sprinkled throughout; a Christmas gift from the parents. Mary entered and closed the door behind her. "I want to apologize for what I said the other day. About you being afraid to leave and everything."

Lizzy sat down on the side of her bed. "You don't have to apologize. In fact, I think your words did me a favor. Made me think about things I haven't—or wouldn't—think about in a long time."

Mary smiled. "Change isn't bad, Lizzy. Caterpillars do it all the time and look how beautiful they turn out!"

Lizzy laughed. "You're right, of course."

"Yeah. Well … good night then …"

"Is there something else?" Lizzy asked.

Their eyes met. "You know what Lydia said about being out of everybody's hair? That's how *I've* always felt. I never knew she had the same thoughts as me."

Mary pulled open the door and left, leaving Lizzy wondering what was happening to her sisters.

CHAPTER 29

Mr. and Mrs. Bennet decided that the best way to deal with Lydia's proclamation was to ignore it. The next day at breakfast, they wished her well and sent her off to school. "It's your last year of high school, Lydia. Focus on that, be yourself, and have fun," her mother said with a kiss and hug.

"Okaaaay. Don't worry about me. I know what to do." As per tradition, the family came out to wave goodbye and watched her until she turned the corner. It was a 15-minute walk to the high school, and she would meet up with some friends along the way. Over the years, the ratio of walkers to wavers shifted, and, for a few magical years, the parents were the only ones doing the waving. This was Lydia's second year leaving by herself.

To Lizzy's surprise, and probably everyone else's, the following weeks passed without incident. At Longbourne and Delany. Mr. Bennet carried on with work while Mrs. Bennet turned her energy to preparing her family for the charity ball. They addressed the invitation to The Bennets of Longbourne, which Mrs. Bennet took to mean *all* the Bennets. Mr. Bennet chuckled. "I hope they know what they're in for."

Of course, her father had been right. The questions and looks about the Bennet Legacy died down, pushing it out of Lizzy's mind and leaving her free to concentrate on her students and lectures. The Y2K committee was almost ready to preview the acts, and then the commitment would be over. Another committee oversaw rehearsals and the final production.

That first meeting in the quad was the only one Dr. Darcy had attended. A few days before the next meeting, he called her office and asked to see her. "It's about the committee," he said after her hesitation.

She agreed and suggested they meet at the café in the quad. Meeting him again in the Ancestors Garden didn't seem like a good idea to her.

"Thanks for taking the time to see me," he said as he took a seat across from her at the small outside table. "Can I get you anything? Coffee?"

"I'm good," she said, folding her arms. "So, what's this about? You didn't ..." She grinned and held up a fist in a mock punch. His flash of embarrassment made her regret the attempted joke.

"No, but I wanted to meet you about that." He took a deep breath. "Considering what transpired between myself and Wickham, it would be better if I was not involved with the decision making. He is associated with one of the acts, after all."

Lizzy nodded slowly. "I hadn't thought of that, but yes, I would have to agree." She felt a hint of disappointment rise. "So, you're out then? Do you want me to tell Coach—"

"Not out, completely," he said. "I made a commitment and still want to help as much as I can, but shouldn't be involved with the decision-making aspect of the committee."

"Help?"

"Yes. I've already set up the message board and can keep in the loop that way."

Lizzy agreed, although she wasn't sure if a message board was necessary. "Well, whatever you want to do, Dr. Darcy. We appreciate any help you can offer."

"Good," he said.

A silence followed, and Lizzy cast her eyes around the campus as she wondered how to make a graceful exit. "Well, I'll let Charmaine and Nate know—"

"How are your classes going? So far?" he asked.

Lizzy's eyebrows drew together. "My classes? Just fine. And yours?"

"Fine, actually. The students have interesting questions and insights, some I've never heard or thought of before. I'm enjoying getting to know them."

"You sound surprised."

He nodded. "I am. The students, white and Black, at Berkeley are great and well prepared, but they can be a bit too serious, as if they're afraid to let their guard down."

Lizzy placed her arms on the table and leaned forward, as if she were getting ready to share a secret. "Some students tell me that being at an HBCU gives them a feeling of freedom. Something they have never felt before. Some even call it magical."

Darcy thought for a moment. "Yes, I can see that." He met her eyes. "Is that why you stay here?"

Lizzy groaned, sat back, and shook her head. "Why does everyone keep asking me that? Do they know something I don't?"

"What do you mean?" Darcy asked. "I was just—"

"Oh, never mind. If you must know, I am seriously thinking about picking up my doctoral program search again." She took a deep breath. "I think it's time."

Looking skeptical and a bit amused, Dr. Darcy asked, "A doctorate in hip hop studies?"

She waved off his assumption. "No. Besides, hip hop studies aren't as revolutionary as they were when I first started. By the year 2005, every other university will offer some version of the subject." She pursed her lips and stared out across the quad area. "Besides, my original intentions are getting away from me. These days, all students are interested in is how to make quick money in the business or, even worse, endless debates on the Tupac-

Makaveli conspiracy." She shook her head. "There's so much more …" Lost in thought, she sighed.

Darcy, mesmerized by her countenance, was reluctant to interrupt her thoughts, but then the clock tower rang and brought her back. Her eyelids fluttered, and she turned towards him. She pressed her hands to the sides of her face. "Oh god, I'm sorry. Guess I got lost in my own little world."

Darcy, also lost in his own little world, cleared his throat. "Well, yes. I've kept you too long."

Lizzy stood up. "Sorry to bore you. It's just that I've had a lot on my mind lately."

He stood up, too. "You didn't bore me. I enjoy getting to know you."

Their eyes met. Lizzy's breath caught in her throat when she recognized the same soft and tender look he had shown in the Ancestors Garden. Her pulse quickened as she tried to make sense of the moment.

"Did I say something wrong?" he asked after a moment of silence.

"Yes. No!" She took a deep breath. "Look, I'll let the others know about your change with the committee, without telling them everything, of course. I mean, I wouldn't do that. I'm not stupid or anything ."

He smiled. "No, you most certainly are not."

The need to get away overcame her, but when she tried to step away from the table, she ended up almost tripping over the chair's leg. He reached out to steady her, but physical contact at this moment would not be a good idea. She held up a hand to halt his movements. "I'm fine," she whispered. She straightened up and nodded. "Well, goodbye then." She turned and walked away, but felt his eyes watching her back.

Walking, but not knowing where she was going, Lizzy began chastising herself for being so open with him. It's none of his business what I do, she thought as she remembered his sarcastic grin at the mention of her PhD plans. But then those eyes. And he said he enjoyed getting to know her better? Not the smoothest line, and if the man standing before her had been anyone but Dr. William Darcy, she would have no problem interpreting the situation. Sighing, she realized she had no way of knowing how he felt and that she wasn't ready to contemplate her feelings either. Not now, at least. "This won't do," she whispered as she headed back to her office.

. ■ ■

A few days later, Nate and Charmaine joined Lizzy in the Liberal Arts' conference room. On the agenda was the final review of applications and sending out invitations to the groups they selected for tryouts. Lizzy explained Dr. Darcy's absence with the, *he is really busy right now* excuse. "But he'll still be maintaining our message board and helping in other ways," she added.

"That's cool," Nate said. "To tell you the truth, I couldn't see him judging the acts. Probably into opera, ballet, and hoity-toity boring shit like that."

"He would have been all right," Charmaine said. "He helped me with the rubric, too."

"He did?" Lizzy asked. "When was this ...?"

"Right before I sent it to you guys. We met in the Ancestors Garden, and he looked it over and gave me some feedback."

A sly grin spread across Nate's face. "Ahhhh, look at you! Getting all cozy with the sexy Black professor! *Meeting* in the garden uh?" He waved air quotes around meeting and gave her an exaggerated wink.

Charmaine's cheeks glowed red, and Lizzy told Nate to stop messing around. "You're embarrassing Charmaine *and* being very inappropriate."

Nate mumbled an apology, and they got down business. Nate left right after, but Charmaine lingered behind. "I saw Dr. Darcy earlier, and he told me he wouldn't be coming anymore. He also asked me to pass on any paperwork to him, along with our meeting notes, so he can put them on the message board."

"Oh?" Lizzy had placed everything in her bag, assuming she would be the one keeping him updated. She handed Charmaine the meeting notes, who thanked her. "See you at the tryouts," Charmaine said, leaving the conference room.

After she left, Lizzy wondered if he had contacted Charmaine before, or after, he saw her at the café? Was he avoiding her? Had she embarrassed herself that day? She shrugged off the thoughts and contemplated what she needed to do before calling it a day. Only one thing came to mind.

George Wickham was no longer residing at Mashujaa House. That's all she got from the young man who opened the door. She didn't have a straightforward way to contact him, so she went to the only place she thought he could be, or at least get a clue where to find him. Retreating down the walkway, she wondered if Kitty's Darren would know more. As soon as the thought came, she looked up to see him heading up the walkway. "Hello, Professor Bennet," Darren said. "Can I help you with something?"

She held up the CD. "I was looking for Wickham, but they told me he isn't staying here anymore. Where can I find him? Is he still in Merryton?"

Darren looked over her shoulder at the house, and then motioned for her to follow him. When they were on the sidewalk and a house away, he stopped. "After what happened in the gym with Dr. Darcy, Darren told him he couldn't stay at the house and to keep off campus. They practice at the downtown Y now."

"Do you know where he's staying?"

He hesitated before answering, then held out his hand. "I see him from time to time. I can pass the CD on to him."

"I don't just need to return it. He asked me for feedback on the group," she told him. His sudden uneasiness didn't go unnoticed. "Do you have a number where I can reach him?"

"I can page him and let him know you want to see him. Will that work?"

Lizzy took a step back and folded her arms. "Well, if that's the best you can do. Ask him to call me at Longbourne. If you don't mind."

He told her he would get right on it.

"Thank you," she said.

With nothing else to do but head home, she turned towards Longbourne. Darren was definitely not telling her everything, but she had become so suspicious of all things related to that house, perhaps she was overreacting. As far as she could tell, Lydia had been following their agreements. No more not-going-to-college talk, and she hadn't mentioned, or been seen with, Wickham. But that meant nothing. "Oh, Lydia," she whispered. "Please be good."

.   .   .

Caroline Bingley and Mrs. Griff sat at the dining room table, poring over floor plans and seating charts. The current discussion was where to place the Delany table. "Dr. Lucas would love to get into the ear of our big donors," Mrs. Griff said. "So, let's put them on opposite sides."

Caroline picked up the small white card with *Delany Board* printed on one side. "That won't do, I'm afraid. Dr. Darcy and I will be at that table." She moved the card to a table near the podium.

"Oh? I assumed he would sit with the family."

"I did too, but he insisted on sitting with Dr. Lucas and the others. Something about wanting to get to know them better." She looked over the RSVP list. "We'll have at least three more tables with people representing the university. We can spread those others around."

"Good idea," Mrs. Griff said, looking at the partially finished seating chart. "I see you placed our two lovebirds together," she said with a sly smile.

"What?" Caroline looked to where Mrs. Griff was pointing. "My brother Charles and Jane Bennet? I'd hardly call them lovebirds," she scoffed.

Mrs. Griff's self-satisfied smile remained. "Well, from what I hear ..."

Caroline stood up abruptly and looked coldly at Mrs. Griff. "I think we've done all we can for today. I will complete the seating arrangements after the remaining RSVPs come in."

Before Mrs. Griff could reply, Corrine entered with a message for Caroline.

"Excuse me, but they're some men at the backdoor needing to talk with you, Miss Caroline."

Caroline's shoulders relaxed. "I hope it's the furniture delivery, or we'll be needing sleeping bags for our guests! Corrine, please see Mrs. Griff out," she said, walking past her and through the dining room's back door.

Mrs. Griff smirked and began collecting her things. "Is she worried I'm gonna steal the family silver or something?"

"No," Corrine responded flatly. "I think she was just being polite."

"Yeah, and she just *politely* told me she doesn't approve of her brother seeing Jane Bennet." Mrs. Griff looked slyly at Corrine. "Have you ... heard anything about that ... maybe?"

Corrine smiled. "Why Mrs. Griff, I know you are not asking me to divulge my employer's private business, are you? Because *that* would be wrong, as I am sure you know."

Mrs. Griff's face warmed with embarrassment. She hastily finished gathering her papers into her briefcase and turned to leave. "I can see myself out, thank you." Corrine followed her anyway. A commotion coming from the back of the mansion announced the furniture delivery.

"What's all that racket?" Charles asked as he came downstairs, dressed in swim trunks and a short-sleeved shirt. His wound was almost completely healed, and covered in what looked like Saran

Wrap. Caroline entered the large hall, followed by three men maneuvering a large dolly with an even larger oak and brass chest of drawers.

"Please be careful of the floor!" The workers grunted a, "Yes, Ma'am," and continued towards the stairs.

"Charles, move out of the way, please," Caroline said. "The back stairs aren't wide enough. Oh! You're still here," she said to Mrs. Griff, who then pointed towards the front door. "Just leaving now."

"I'll join you," Charles said, skirting around the moving furniture. He followed Mrs. Griff out onto the front porch.

"Off for a swim?" she said. "Make sure to keep that wound dry. I'd hate for it to get infected."

Charles smiled. "Don't worry, Jane says it will be perfectly fine. She's joining me. She should be here any minute. Ah! Here she comes!" She turned to see a dark blue Saturn come to a stop. Jane got out, looking lovely in a loose-fitting pink summer dress that swayed when she walked. Charles waved enthusiastically, started down the steps, but then stopped to turn back to Mrs. Griff. "Ummm …?"

Mrs. Griff waved him on. "Oh, don't mind me. You two lovebirds have fun."

"Thanks!" Charles said, grinning like a five-year-old.

.   .   .

Darcy came home a little while later. The sun was setting, but the heat of the day barely waned. He was entering the house when he saw Corrine returning from the pool area carrying an empty tray. "Is Charles out there?" he asked her.

"Yes. With Jane Bennet."

"Oh," Darcy replied, dropping his idea to take an evening swim before dinner. He had no desire to be the third wheel.

He entered the mansion. The entryway floor was littered with discarded boxes and packing material. "Looks like a lot has been happening today. Where's Caroline?"

Corrine pointed to the upstairs. "In one of the guest rooms. *All* the guestroom furniture came today, and she made the movers stay until she has everything right where she wants it. Plus, someone from Dillards is here to measure for new curtains because she didn't like how the old ones went with the new furniture."

"Typical, Caroline," Darcy said, smiling and shaking his head. He went upstairs, entered his office, and got a surprise when he saw Caroline standing by the balcony window. "Well, hello. I thought you were busy measuring curtains and ordering movers around."

"What?" Caroline said, not turning away from the window.

He joined her. "What has your attention?" He followed her gaze to the pool. "Oh."

"They've been out there for over an hour now," Caroline said.

"I heard. I hope you haven't been watching them that whole time," he said with a smile.

"Don't be ridiculous. But ... it may be time for me to get to know this Jane Bennet a little better, don't you think?"

Darcy took one more glance before turning away. "I don't think so, actually. Charles is just being Charles." He shrugged. "Besides, you don't think he can be serious about her, do you?"

A soft tap-tap from the office door interrupted her response. "Yes?" Caroline said to the sales rep.

"I've finished the measurements. Is there anything else before I put in the order?"

Caroline glanced at Darcy with a look that meant their conversation wasn't over. "Let me check those swatches one last time," she said, leaving his office. Darcy watched them depart, then went back to the window. Jane and Charles were relaxing on lounge chairs and holding hands in the space between. He certainly looked serious with Jane Bennet, but he didn't know if he should feel glad or worried. Two burly and tired looking workers interrupted his focus when they passed by the open door. "That woman's a trip," one of them said. "Yeah," said the other, "rich folks be like that."

CHAPTER 30

Darren was true to his word, and Wickham called Lizzy at Longbourne one morning a few days later. "Hello," he said. "Excuse me for being MIA. Plans changed."

"Are you still leaving soon?" Lizzy asked.

"I've left the Delany campus, but I'm still in the area," he said. "Staying with a friend of a friend."

"Oh," she answered, wondering who that could be. "So, where would be a good place to meet?"

Wickham thought for a moment, then suggested the diner they had gone to before.

She agreed. "See you then," she said, hanging up the phone.

"What was that about?" her mother asked, emerging from the kitchen.

"Nothing. I just need to give him his CD back. He asked me for feedback on a rap group he's working with back in Los Angeles."

"Interesting," her mother nodded. "You should have asked him to Longbourne, Lizzy," she said, ticking her tongue in disapproval. "Poor Wickham."

"Why do you say that?"

"Mrs. Lucas told me he's not at that fraternity anymore and practically banned from campus."

"Did she say why?" Lizzy asked, wondering if Dr. Darcy had anything to do with that.

Her mother frowned and shook her head. "You know how she is, always telling *part* of the story, never the *whole* story." She turned to leave. "If you find out anything, don't keep it to yourself."

Lizzy caught her reflection in the entryway mirror and sighed. They had agreed to meet after her classes and office hours, and she hoped this would be the last time they needed to see each other. Based on what he had shared about his past with Dr. Darcy, it would have been natural for him to demand some sort of justice after the unprovoked assault. Instead, Wickham seems to have faded into the background, as if hiding from something. Or someone. The situation didn't smell right, but she reminded herself that it had nothing to do with her.

She had three student visits during her office hours, which was a record. One needed clarification on the Hurston essay assignment, and the other two were lodging complaints about their work groups. She had to stress the individual grading aspect and that switching groups wasn't allowed. "College is a good time to practice getting along with difficult people," she told them with a smile. "Because in the real world, you'll run into them all the time." Both students left unsatisfied.

Heading out to meet Wickham, it occurred to her how she would see a lot less of her own difficult person. With Charmaine as his Y2K contact, Lizzy had no reason to see him, at least not intentionally. If things progressed with Jane and Charles, then naturally their paths would cross. *And how did she feel about that?* she asked herself. Since that afternoon at the café, she had done a good job of avoiding thinking about him, except when others brought him up, which they seemed to do often. It annoyed her how he was occupying so much of the Delany chatter this semester. Was she the only one who realized that he'd be gone soon, back to his snooty west coast life? He'd probably never think about Delany again. Or her.

She made it to the diner at 4:30. Wickham was in a booth near the back. She joined him, declined any food from the waitress but asked for a glass of water. She pulled the CD in its clear plastic case from her bag and slid it across the table. "Does this group have a name?"

Wickham finished the rest of his Coke before answering. Before him was a plate with a few French fries scattered about. "Sunset Rap," he said. "After the infamous street in LA. That's where most of the guys are from."

She nodded. "That could work."

He picked up the CD. "So, what did you think? We hope to debut soon."

Lizzy inhaled and then exhaled through pursed lips. "Well, they certainly are ... loud. Lots of screaming, too." She clasped her hands together, placed them on the table, and leaned forward. "I don't think they're ready. There are a lot of things going on in their music, but the main issue seems to be a lack of originality."

"What do you mean?"

"It sounds like they are trying to imitate others like Big Pun or—"

"It's called sampling," he said with a smirk. "You know what that is, right?"

"Of course I do, but what I heard isn't sampling, but more like plagiarism. Do *you* know what that is?"

He waved away her question. "Ok, well, that can be fixed. What else did you think?"

All thoughts of taking it easy on him faded. "Well, the lyrics are lame, laced with obscenities that add nothing except annoyance; the rappers always lag behind the beat *and* sound like they're having difficulty breathing. Maybe get them to lay off the Marlboros?"

"Wow. Wasn't expecting *all that*. Not one for encouragement, are you?"

Lizzy paused. "Well, you asked me for my honest opinion. Better to hear it now before it's too late." After he didn't respond, she continued. "Since you read the *Jet* article about me, you should know that one of my objectives is to bring more attention to rap's socially conscious and uplifting side. Songs with authentic lyrics that entertain but also shine a light on America's century's old issues with racism, poverty, and police brutality, to name a few." She shrugged. "More Tupac's *Changes* or Public Enemy's *He Got Game* than—" His sudden smirk stopped her. "What?"

He shook his head. "Look, all I need is for you to write something nice and positive. Not a lecture. These niggas been working their asses off and we just need a little help, that's all. Something to make us stand out."

She looked at him, wondering if he had even listened to her. "Well, have them work on their sound and lyrics, and I'll give them another listen. That's the best I can do for now."

He held the clear plastic CD case between his thumb and forefinger and tapped it on the table like a judge's gavel, his eyes on Lizzy. The child-like playfulness was gone and cold, dark brown pupils stared back at her. "Lydia was right about you," he said. "You're nothin' but a dream killer."

Her mouth fell open, and she snapped back into the booth's seat as if someone had shoved her. "*Excuse* me?"

"You heard me," he said, getting up. He was walking out of the diner's front door before she realized what was happening. She got up to follow him. "Excuse me, miss." She turned to see the waitress handing her the bill.

"*Are you kidding me?*" She snatched the slip of paper from the startled server's outstretched hand.

By the time Lizzy made it outside, Wickham was nowhere to be found. She paced up and down the sidewalk, fuming. "Wow! Just wow!" was all she could manage. He owed her seven dollars, but she knew she could kiss that money goodbye. She headed home.

It was another rare evening with the entire Bennet family home for dinner. Their mother droned on about the ball and Lydia filled them in on high school gossip. Jane was silent and picked at her food. Lizzy volunteered for kitchen duty and asked Jane to help her.

Lizzy washed; Jane dried. "So," Lizzy asked, handing Jane a dripping wet pot. "How are things at the clinic and with you-know-who?"

Jane focused her attention on drying the large pot that their mother had used to boil the potatoes for dinner. She sighed. "I thought things were going well, but then ..." Jane lowered her voice and moved closer. "Charles doesn't want to take it ... further." She looked shyly at Lizzy, whose questioning face dissolved after a few seconds. "Why? What happened?" Lizzy asked.

Jane closed her eyes and sighed. "I've never been more embarrassed in my life. We were in the poolroom and things got ... you know, and I thought he was going to ask me up to his room or go to a hotel or something, but then he pushes me away and starts apologizing and babbling how it isn't the right time, or *thing* to do, and ..." She covered her face with her hands. "It was awful!"

"Well, maybe he thought it wasn't the right time. You guys were in the poolroom?"

Jane nodded. "Yeah, but this wasn't the first time it's happened. When I suggested a weekend trip to Elizabeth City, he said that it wasn't a good idea. I can't tell if he's being respectful, super cautious or doesn't want me ... that way."

"And the only way to know for sure is the one way you won't do. Ask him."

Jane groaned. "Oh god no. I couldn't! But you could."

"What? I love you, sis, but—"

"Not Charles. William, Dr. Darcy. See if you can get him to share anything about what Charles may be thinking."

"That won't work either. Our paths hardly cross now, Dr. Darcy and I."

"Oh god!" Lydia said, entering the kitchen. "Dr. Darcy this and Dr. Darcy that! They should have kicked him out of Delany after he punched Wickham." She opened the refrigerator, took out a juice box, and exited.

They both watched her leave, Lizzy's face full of frustration, Jane's all confusion. "What did she say? Is this what she was talking about when we were at Mabel's?"

Lizzy grabbed a dish towel from the counter, dried her hands, and gave Jane an apologetic glance. "I'll fill you in later," she said and left the kitchen.

"Hey!" Lydia said. "Don't you know how to knock?" She pulled off her earphones and frowned at Lizzy. She was sitting up on her bed, back against the headboard, legs splayed out in front. Next to her on the floor sat a pile of schoolbooks and papers. Kitty was at the desk, studying. Lizzy walked in and closed the door behind her. She faced Lydia, hands on her hips. "I saw Wickham today," she began.

"Oh," Lydia replied, jutting her chin forward. "Good for you."

"And apparently, you and he have had some interesting conversations," Lizzy said.

"What? Is there a law against me having 'interesting conversations' now?"

Lizzy's hands fell to her side, and she took a small step towards Lydia. "You promised to not see—"

"And I have *not* seen him," she said, standing up. The two sisters faced each other. Lizzy eyed her youngest sister, knowing that she was most likely lying, but had no way to know for sure. "And what about this Mashujaa oath you took? The whole campus probably knows by now."

Lydia folded her arms and huffed with an eye roll. "You sure are concerned about the Shujaas all of a sudden."

"She hasn't seen him," Kitty said from her desk. "Darren would have told me."

"What?" Lydia said, turning accusing eyes on Kitty. "Is he *spying* on me?"

Kitty shook her head. "Not you, but Mashujaa's VP asked him to keep an eye out on Wickham." she shrugged. "That's all I know."

Kitty cringed. "You and your *precious* boyfriend."

The exchange was brief, but Lizzy gleaned much from it. Her stance towards Lydia softened. "I—we—just want to make sure you're all right and doing your best. You do know that Lydia, don't you?"

She plopped back down on her bed. "Yeah, yeah, yeah. Everybody wants what is best for me, but, surprise, surprise, no one ever asks *me* what I want."

"Well, what do you want, Lydia?" Kitty asked.

"*Not* to work at that stupid yogurt shop!"

Kitty's face fell, and she opened her mouth to respond, but Lizzy spoke first. "Well, it's time you think about, and focus on, what you *do* want to do, Lydia. You're almost an adult, you know."

"Yes! And I can't wait. Then I can do what I want, and no one can stop me!"

Lizzy exhaled a frustrated sigh. "I'd advise you to consider options that won't cause people to *need* to stop you."

Lizzy went back to the kitchen to find it clean and empty of Jane. She walked back upstairs, intending to go to Jane's room and fill her in, but a sudden wave of fatigue and frustration overcame her, so she walked past Jane's door and into her own bedroom. It's gonna have to wait, she told herself.

.　　.　　.

Professor Bennet walked into the multipurpose room in the Alumni Center. She was the last one to arrive. "Sorry," she said. "But," she continued looking around, "seems like you guys set everything up and are ready to go." Charmaine smiled and nodded; Nate clapped his hand together. "Let's start the show!" Lizzy agreed. She was looking forward to the end of this commitment. They took their seats behind a long table that faced a small stage area. Nate and Charmaine had laid out copies of the applications with one of Charmaine's rubrics attached to each. Lizzy picked up the first application. She had vetoed Nate and Charmaine's suggestion to spread the review process over two days. Looking over the stack of applications, she wondered if that had been a mistake. They had 12 acts to see and only seven could perform in the final show and contest. "So, how should we do this? Just call them in?"

Nate turned around and motioned for a young man, who Lizzy had not noticed earlier, to come forward. "I thought we could use an extra hand since Dr. Darcy isn't here, so I asked one of my brothers to come." Nate introduced him. "Telford can be the one to bring the acts in and make sure everyone gets seen and stuff."

"Good idea, Nate. And thank you, Telford." He glanced at Nate, who gave him a quick head nod and then responded, "My pleasure to be of assistance, Ma'am." He turned, looking more like a soldier than a college student, and walked to the door.

"Let me guess," Lizzy said with a grin. "A pledge?"

"You know it!" Nate replied.

The first three acts ranged from just okay to so-so. All three scored low on the rubric and the judges passed worried looks, hoping this wouldn't be the norm. A sigh of relief came after the next act; a small band with a great vocalist who reminded Lizzy of Dinah Washington. "Well, they're a definite yes," Nate whispered as Mark helped them off the stage.

"We need to see them all," Charmaine cautioned. "Who knows, the next eight could be just as good."

Nate checked the list to see who was next. "The Mashujaas. I doubt that." He smirked. "Warriors my ass."

Lizzy and Charmaine looked at him with questioning eyes. "It seems like you have already made up your mind," Lizzy said.

"We need to appear objective," Charmaine said. "Dr. Darcy says that's what's most important."

Lizzy pressed her lips together and wondered just how much time he and Charmaine were spending together. She hadn't heard from him, but it looked as if he was in constant contact with Charmaine. A student. She turned her attention back to scoring the last rubric. "We know how to be objective, Charmaine. Even Nate." "Send in the next act," she told Telford.

A dozen men, dressed in cargo pants, tight fitting black T-shirts and black combat boots, marched on stage, stood in formation, and waited. The front man started a call and response. *Who are we?! Mashujaa! What's coming? Y2K! What?! Two-thousand-unnn!* This continued for about a minute, and then they moved into the routine.

It wasn't bad, per se, but not as vibrant and polished as it could have been. Lizzy searched for the right words, but then Nate summed it up after the group exited the stage area. "Well, that was pretty lame."

Charmaine shot him a look of warning.

"It wasn't that bad," Lizzy said. "And besides, there's still about a month before the show. Maybe they can pump it up a little."

"Yeah, now that the shyster Wickham is gone, they can't get any worse."

Lizzy glanced around the room, half expecting to see Wickham lurking in a corner. He was their trainer, after all. "Let's keep it civil." Lizzy said. "Just score them, and we'll figure out who made the cut, and who didn't *after* we see all the acts. Okay?"

She did her best to focus on the following acts, but found her mind wandering, and then gave higher marks more out of guilt over her inattention than actual merit. Forty-five minutes later, they were done. Charmaine collected the rubrics. "I can sort these and tabulate the results, put them in a spreadsheet so we can compare more easily."

"Ahhh," Nate said. "I don't think we need to get that serious about it. I mean, spreadsheets? Really?"

Charmaine looked hurt. "We need to keep clear records. Besides, I talked to Dr. Darcy, and he said he would help."

"I bet he did," Nate replied with a knowing look and a twisted smile.

"Oh, you two. Really?" Lizzy said. She held out her hand to Charmaine. "I'll take those."

"But—" Charmaine began.

Lizzy fished a rubber band from her bag and used it to secure the rubrics. "Nate is right. We can wrap this up in a few days and it's better if I—a faculty member—hold on to these."

Charmaine did little to hide her disappointment, which irritated Lizzy even more.

Telford returned to Nate, who took pleasure in ordering him to break down the tables and stack the chairs. Charmaine remained silent as she gathered her things. Lizzy stared at her movements, wondering if she was going to report back to Dr. Darcy. Was she his spy? And what would she say? *Professor Bennet was mean and snatched the results from me.* Probably put on a great damsel in distress act, too. And how would he respond? Her mind spun into various scenarios, making her feel as if her thumping heart was stuck in her throat.

"Professor Bennet?"

She blinked to readjust her vision and saw Charmaine looking directly at her. Lizzy shook her head, willing the images to float away. "Yes?"

Everyone agreed to send their next available meeting dates and times via email and before Charmaine could mention Dr. Darcy again, Lizzy said, "*I'll* contact Dr. Darcy and give him an update. Since he didn't actually see the acts, he shouldn't be involved in the final decisions."

CHAPTER 31

Lizzy left the alumni building and walked east on Delany Drive, past the student dorms and health center. She was intending to take the escalator to upper campus, but her body took a turn north in the direction of the econ building. Since it was Friday, there was a good chance he wouldn't be there, which was even better, because then she could leave a note for him. What it would say, she would figure out later, but offering a warning about Charmaine was in order. He already had one altercation with a, well, not a student, but someone on campus. All he needed now was a misunderstanding between him and Charmaine. Some Southern ladies (especially older ones) tend to misinterpret cues from members of the opposite sex. West Coast William Darcy probably wasn't aware of how his constant communications with her could lead to an awkward moment between the two. These are the thoughts Professor Elizabeth Bennet conjured up as she made her way to Dr. William Darcy's fourth-floor office. I'm doing *him* a favor, she told herself as she pushed through the department's door.

He was in, Mrs. Hoffman informed her, and would see her right away. Mrs. Hoffman grinned at Lizzy's departing back.

The first thing she noticed was that his office was considerably larger than her own. He was standing behind his desk, an open file folder and papers scattered about. His light blue dress shirt was partially rolled up at the sleeves, his suit jacket on the back of his chair. She felt that same throbbing heart-in-my-throat sensation return. "I hope I'm not disturbing you," she said, stepping inside and closing the door behind her.

"Not at all. I'm just surprised to see you here," he said. "How can I help?"

Lizzy shifted her bag to her other shoulder. "Well, we finished with the auditions, and I thought you might like a ... report?"

"Report?" he said, looking confused.

She nodded while glancing around his office. An oil painting of Delany was on the wall to his left, next to the coat of arms and a copy of the original college declaration. On the opposite wall hung the university calendar. She didn't see any personal photos or mementos. "Yeah ... well, to let you know everything went well, and we should make our final decisions by the middle of next week."

He looked at her for a few seconds before responding. "Yes, I just had a call from Charmaine, and she told me—"

"Do you think it's a good idea for you to be in *direct* contact with her so much? I mean, she *is* a student, older but still ..." His eyes narrowed as her voice trailed off. She took a deep inhale.

"Professor Bennet, I can assure you I know how to conduct myself with students, male and female."

"Do you?" she shot back, causing him to flinch. She held her hand up and waved her palm, attempting to wipe away the rebuke. "Not that," she said, "But ..."

He moved from around the desk and stood in front of her. "Is that why you came here? To make sure I don't offend Charmaine?"

"Well, from what she says, you two have been seeing each other."

He laughed. "'Seeing each other'? I'd hardly call it that. No, she's just my point person for the committee. I told you I would still contribute. *All* of our communications have been—and will continue to be— professional."

A small voice inside her asked, *why not me?* but thankfully, she kept it in. Although what he said next would have her wondering if he had read her mind.

"I know how busy you are with classes, your PhD plans, and family matters, so I thought it best not to burden you with an extra task."

She looked up, meeting his eyes in an intense gaze. "It wouldn't have been a burden," she whispered.

"It most certainly wouldn't," he whispered back while closing the small distance between them. He placed his hands on her shoulders. "It isn't Charmaine that I am worried about behaving inappropriately with, Lizzy." His hands slid down her arms before she felt them encircle her waist and gently pull her forward, completely closing the gap. Her arms stayed frozen at her side, and she willed her eyes to fixate on his shoulder. She heard her breath escape her body, right before he tilted her head back and pressed his lips against hers. Both moaned softly, releasing a swell of passion that brought surprise to one, relief to the other.

If not for the Delany clock tower ringing the four o'clock hour, Lizzy had no doubt she would have stayed in his arms forever. Instead, the familiar gong broke the spell, and she pushed away, bringing the back of her hand to her mouth. Moving her head slowly from side to side, she stepped back until she felt the office door behind her back. Darcy's face filled with worried. "Please," he said. "Don't go. Not yet."

Lizzy lowered her hand. "I see no reason for me to stay. I told you all I came to say."

"Did you?" he replied with a lopsided grin that annoyed her. "You aren't going to deny what just happened, are you?"

"Not deny it," she said. "Consider it, maybe, and then brush it off as a ... mistake." She opened the door. "Goodbye, Dr. Darcy."

She hurried out of his office, thankful that the administrative staff had left. Desiring a quick escape, she bypassed the elevators and took the stairs. Being a Friday, the campus was fairly empty, which she was also thankful for. Once outside the building, she stood for a moment, trying to decide where to go. Jane had taken the Saturn to work, so driving somewhere was out of the question. The Ancestors Garden used to be her place of refuge, but going there would only remind her of William Darcy. She needed a distraction. After a moment, she knew exactly who to seek.

"Well, well, well," Charlotte said, coming down the stairs to greet Lizzy. "Long time, Professor Bennet."

Lizzy thanked their housekeeper for letting her in before going to join her friend. "Well, you know how the beginning semesters are, Charlotte. Being the president's daughter and all." The two old friends laughed and embraced.

"Well, your timing couldn't be more perfect," Charlotte said. "I was just thinking about going for a swim. Let me grab another suit and you can join me."

Lizzy agreed with a grateful sigh. Her body was screaming for some sort of physical release and a swim would do just that.

An hour later, two wet and tired bodies pulled themselves out of the deep end and collapsed on lounge chairs. "Oh god! I needed that!" Lizzy said, turning her face to the setting sun.

Charlotte dropped a towel onto Lizzy's lap. "You were going at it like an Olympic swimmer," she said, removing her white swim cap. Her shoulder length hair tumbled out, and she ran her fingers through it, checking for moisture. "I need to go natural, like you, girl. Must be nice not having to worry about getting your hair wet."

Droplets of pool water sprinkled about as Lizzy shook her natural curls and smiled. "It is, and I wish I had done it earlier."

"Well, not all of us can look great going natural," Charlotte said with a laugh. "Remember our junior year when I tried to grow locs! What a mess! My head looked like an upside-down spider!"

"It wasn't that bad," Lizzy said. "You should give it another try."

Charlotte finished drying and wrapped the oversized towel around her waist. "Well, maybe when I'm old and married." She performed an exaggerated hair flip. "But I need to keep *this* until I land a man!" After the laughter stopped, Charlotte relaxed into the lounge chair, and the two friends slipped into a comfortable silence. Lizzy closed her eyes against the warm sun, glad that she had come.

Some minutes later, they both heard Dr. Lucas's car enter the driveway. Lizzy reluctantly sat up. "Well, I guess I should head home."

Charlotte nodded. "Yeah, because I am sure Daddy will want to bring up the Bennet Legacy mess and I am also sure you *do not* want to talk about it."

Lizzy reached out and squeezed her arm. "Thank you, Charlotte."

They went back to Charlotte's bedroom to change. Lizzy was smoothing lotion on her arms when Charlotte brought up another touchy subject. "So, this Wickham dude. Have you heard or seen much of him lately?"

"Yeah," she said before explaining about the awful Sunset Rap group and the awkward meeting at the café. "At least this could mean I won't see him again," she said. "Niggas who owe money tend to stay outta sight."

Charlotte's eyes widened in mock shock. "Gu-rrrrl, he must have really ticked you off seeing how you've slipped into that gangsta talk!" Charlotte laughed. "Don't let Daddy catch you!"

Lizzy grinned, but remained silent. After she received approval for her hip hop classes, the board told her to keep the language civil. "I *do not* want to walk into your classroom and hear that street talk," her chair had warned. It seemed a silly stipulation, but she had eagerly agreed.

"But seriously, Lizzy," Charlotte continued. "*This* Negro is different, and I could see how he could make you lose your shit that way."

"What does that mean?"

Charlotte took a deep inhale. "You know all that talk about Mashujaa fraternity being on thin ice and all? Well, that's just BS. Ain't nothing gonna happen to them. Mashujaa's president is a nephew of a new board member; a *very* influential board member," she added, rubbing her thumb against the other fingers, the universal sign of money changing hands. "Anyway, this nephew— who's studying abroad in Costa Rica this semester—got wind of Wickham and some trouble Wickham's caused, and he asked his uncle to look into it." Charlotte shook her head. "That dude's an ex- con, Lizzy."

"Wickham? For what?" Lizzy asked, not sure if the news surprised her.

"Don't know, but it must have something to do with Dr. Darcy too, because he came by the house before school to warn Daddy about Wickham."

"And did *he* say why Wickham was imprisoned? He must know."

"No, only something about how he's known Wickham for years … a big disappointment, blah, blah, and that he shouldn't be trusted. Daddy tried to explain to him how HBCs are known for giving second chances and being nonjudgmental, but Dr. Darcy wasn't having it, especially since Wickham isn't even a student! After Daddy found out about the prison thing, he wished he had heeded the warning." Charlotte shrugged. "But better late than never. George Wickham is now banned from stepping foot on Delany."

"Wow," Lizzy whispered. She turned a questioning face at Charlotte. "But why are you telling me this now? Is there something else …"

"Lydia," Charlotte said, confirming Lizzy's worst fears. Charlotte held up a hand to calm her. "Nothing's happened, that I know of, but you should really keep an eye on her. People have been seeing them together around Merryton."

"Recently? Not since her school started, I hope." She stopped short of sharing Lydia's promise.

"Nooo," she said slowly through pursed lips. "But Mariah says that Lydia has missed some days at school." Mariah is Charlotte's younger sister, same age as Lydia.

The tension that Lizzy had drowned in the pool returned. She stood up to leave. "Thanks, Charlotte. I appreciate you telling me."

Charlotte looked up at her from her seat on the bedside. "I'm sure everything will be okay, Lizzy. Besides, the charity ball is next week! Let's focus on that. What are you and Jane wearing?"

"Oh, god," Lizzy groaned. "That's tomorrow; shopping with our mother! I almost forgot."

Charlotte told her to have fun and that whatever she wears will be fine. "And Jane could wear a gunny sack, but I'm sure Charles Bingley wouldn't mind!" Lizzy agreed.

They hugged and said their goodbyes. For the second time that day, Lizzy hoped for a swift and unnoticeable exit from a building. She was beginning to feel like a thief. Back on the sidewalk, she breathed in the evening air and headed to Longbourne.

.   ■   .

Darcy entered Netherfield to see a slew of overall clad workers hanging garlands, moving furniture, and rolling in banquet tables. Caroline and Mrs. Griff stood to the side, overseeing it all. "Isn't it a bit early for this?" Darcy said, walking across to stand beside the two women.

"It is," Mrs. Griff said. "But with heavy rains in the forecast, we needed to get everything in here now, rather than later."

He glanced at Caroline, who only nodded in agreement. Someone dropped something, and she turned towards the noise. "Oh god," she groaned. "William," she began moving towards a pair of workers standing over a broken mirror. "I hope you ate already.

Corrine has the evening off and with all of this, I haven't had time to think about anything else."

He welcomed this since he was in no mood to sit around the dining room table and make small talk. Two hours earlier, he was sharing an intimate moment with Lizzy Bennet, causing him to have a hard time focusing on anything else. Walking up the staircase, he wondered if she was experiencing the same. Darcy had just removed his shirt and tie when Charles knocked and opened the door. Charles entered without words and plopped down on an oversized chair next to the dresser. He exhaled an exaggerated sigh. Darcy grinned. "Yes? What's wrong now?"

Charles raised the sleeve on his left arm, revealing his newly healed gash. "I got an all clear for the wound today."

"And that's a good thing, isn't it?" Darcy said. He took a dark blue polo shirt from his closet and slipped it over his head. "Who did it? Did Caroline find another doctor for you to go to?"

Charles sat up straight. "That's just it. I insisted on going back to the clinic. It wasn't entirely necessary, but I wanted to see Jane, which I did, but she ignored me!"

"Ignored you? Are you sure?"

"Yes! Well, she saw us come in and said hello and all, but then she told another nurse to take care of me and that was that. She left!"

"You do know that she was at work? What did you expect?"

"Yes, I know that, but it still felt off. We were supposed to have dinner tonight, but she canceled. Again." He sighed. "Oh well, women, huh?"

Yes, Darcy thought as he finished changing out of his suit. Women. Well, for him, one woman. He wasn't ready to share this with Charles and besides, he wouldn't know what to share.

They decided to find a nice restaurant for dinner and to toast Charles' healed arm. They left Caroline and Mrs. Griff to handle the party business and Darcy, craving a bit of an adventure and distraction, took Highway 1 to Raleigh. "Welcome to the capital of

North Carolina," Darcy said about an hour later, driving through the streets of downtown Raleigh. After driving around for a few minutes, they settled on what seemed like a decent enough restaurant. The boisterous crowd at the bar reminded Darcy that it was Friday, and he decided right then to partake in the pre-weekend celebration. Two stools opened at the bar, and he took that as divine approval of his plan. Charles followed. "Two shots. Don Julio, if you have it."

The bartender nodded and smiled at the request. He knew a big tipper when he saw one. "Salt and lime, gentlemen?"

"Sure, why not?" Darcy answered.

Three hours later, and slightly inebriated, Charles and Darcy sauntered out of the restaurant. The cab the hostess called for pulled up and drove them to the nearest Embassy Suites hotel. "Caroline is going to be as mad as a wet hen," Charles said as they rode the elevator to their room. Darcy erupted in laughter. "Man, you've been spending way too much time with the locals!"

Charles leaned against the elevator walls. "Not enough time with one local, though." He closed his eyes and took a deep inhale. "I haven't slept with her, you know. Although she has let me know she is more than ready." He opened his eyes to gaze at Darcy.

"And ...?"

Charles placed a hand on his chest. "And I, Charles Gregory Bingley, the party boy, turned her away, mumbling on about how it wasn't time or something like that." After a burst of sarcastic laughter, he continued. "Which is completely *insane* because it was 'the time' about 10 minutes after I met her." The elevator doors opened, they exited and walked silently down the hall to their room. Inside, each picked a queen-size bed to collapse on.

After a few minutes of silence, Darcy sat up. Charles was quiet, but awake, lying on his back and staring at the ceiling. "Maybe, after getting to know her, you discovered that you aren't attracted to her ... that way." As the words came out, he realized that this had been his own wish involving Lizzy Bennet. Of course, just the opposite had occurred.

Charles rolled to his side and stared at the window, his back to Darcy. "I *hurt* women, Darcy. That's what I do, and the thought of hurting Jane Bennet is just so … *un*bearable. I imagine the angels would weep. And it would be all my fault."

CHAPTER 32

Mrs. Bennet woke up with a migraine, so Lizzy and Jane would go dress shopping on their own. Lizzy wanted to go to Raleigh to shop at Dillards, but Jane convinced her to stay in town. "That dress shop next to Mabel's has some good stuff," she said. She turned to look at the passing landscape as Lizzy drove. "Besides, it doesn't matter what I wear."

"Oh, Jane. You know that's not true. Anyone can tell how much Charles is into you."

"Did you see William? Did he say anything?"

Lizzy turned her focus to driving. She had a restless night filled with questions, and something else she was afraid to acknowledge. After Troy, her next longest relationship was with a music professor from NC State. After six months of sporadic dating, the relationship died a natural death, with each going their own way. The next time she saw him was at the Crash Pad, and he was with someone else; a waitress she recognized from The Grille. "Some men—most—can't handle a strong and independent Black woman," Dr. Wright had told Lizzy after she shared the sighting. "He may be a professor, but that doesn't make him smart or confident enough to handle a woman like you." She's heard that phrase a lot: *a woman like you.* But what kind of woman was she, exactly? Did William Darcy know? She suppressed a frustrating groan. What she did know was that he disapproved of her hip hop studies, a subject she was passionate about and had no intention of abandoning. Not for him, anyway.

"Well?" Jane said, interrupting her thoughts.

Lizzy shook her head. "No. I forgot to tell you he left the Y2K committee." She inhaled and gave as quick a recap as possible, beginning with Darcy's altercation with Wickham. She pulled the Saturn into the dress shop's parking lot, turned off the ignition and faced Jane. "And on another topic, Charlotte told me yesterday that Wickham has done some time in prison. In California."

Jane's mouth fell open.

"But no one knows why. No one except Dr. William Darcy, I assume."

"Oh, god," Jane gasped. "I hope it wasn't for anything violent."

Lizzy thought for a moment. "I doubt it. Wickham seems more like a white-collar criminal." She laughed. "Which is lucky, because he would have beat the crap out of Dr. Darcy!"

"That's not funny, Lizzy." Jane opened the car door and stepped out.

"Why do you hate him so much?" Jane asked as they walked towards the shop doors. Lizzy's pace slowed. "I never hated him, but I don't … understand him. I can never tell what he's thinking."

Jane grinned. "And why do *you* need to know what he's thinking?"

Lizzy gave Jane a playful slap on the arm. "Oh, be quiet!" The giggling sisters entered the shop. Jane's laughter came to a stop after seeing who had also decided to go shopping that morning.

Caroline Bingley turned from the counter, an exasperated look on her face. Jane composed herself and stepped towards the counter. "Hello, Caroline. I'm surprised to see you here."

Caroline frowned. "Not as surprised as I am at being here, but I was told they do seamstress work, and I need a seamstress."

"We have alteration and mending services, but you need to bring in the garment." Jane recognized the saleswomen behind the counter.

"Yes, I heard you," Caroline said. "What I need to know is if there I someone who could come to Netherfield."

The salesclerk repeated that there was not. "But you can leave your name and number, and I'll ask around."

"*Ask around?*" Caroline said, lifting an eyebrow.

"There's probably someone at the university who could help. From the fashion design department," Lizzy offered.

Caroline considered the suggestion. She nodded. "Yes, that could work. And William would certainly approve." Her eyes roamed over Lizzy before turning them to Jane. "And this is …?"

"Oh, that's right. You haven't met," Jane said. "This is my sister, Lizzy, or Professor Elizabeth Bennet."

Caroline's lips curled up into a thin smile. "Oh yes, William has mentioned you. You teach … music?"

Lizzy stared back at her, instantly recognizing the same disdain Dr. Darcy had displayed at their first meeting. "No, not music. I'm a literature professor but also teach rap and hip hop studies."

Caroline acknowledged the information with a single "Oh," then turned to Jane. "I am surprised to see you this morning, too. I assumed you were with Charles. He didn't come home last night."

Jane's eyes grew wide. "No, we haven't seen each other for a few days now."

Caroline's face shifted to shock, fooling no one. "*Really?* That's interesting." She shrugged. "Well, you'll see him at the ball, I'm sure." She turned to thank the salesgirl, then walked towards the front door. "I'll ask William to follow up on your suggestion, Professor Bennet. I will leave you two ladies to your shopping."

"Well, that was interesting," Lizzy began, but stopped when she saw the worried look on Jane's face. "He and William probably just went out exploring or something," she said. "I'm sure it's nothing to worry about."

Jane sighed. "I don't know what to think, Lizzy."

Lizzy placed her arm around Jane. "It'll be all right, you'll see." She would wait to talk about that sister. "Come on. The perfect dress is here, I know it!"

Lizzy moved to the display of ballerina style dresses. She preferred mid-length rather than floor, since her legs were one of her better features, so she'd been told. She was hoping to find a stylish, off-the-shoulder number. Worn with her hair up and the right makeup touches, she could pull off a simple, yet elegant appearance. She selected three and went to the dressing room. Jane sat in the upholstered chair and waited.

"They're pretty much the same," Jane said after Lizzy modeled her third choice. "But this one fits you the best. Plus, the white with black accents look really nice." Lizzy turned and twirled in front of the dressing room's full-length mirror. She agreed. "This one then." She returned to the dressing room. "Your turn," she said, coming out and handing her chosen dress to the saleslady.

Jane also gravitated towards her go-to style. Vintage styled gowns made of organza fabrics with flowing skirts and a modest neckline. Lizzy fell in love with the first dress Jane tried. A lavender chiffon strapless gown with a gathered waist embellished with a crystal band. "You look like a princess!" she exclaimed.

Jane nodded, staring at herself. "A perfect, sweet princess. That's what Charles calls me all the time. *Sweet*. I hate it."

"Jane," Lizzy said cautiously. "Don't go there, please. I know you really like him, but if he's messing with your head like this—"

"It's not him, Lizzy. It's me." She took one more look at herself in the mirror. "I'll take this one," she said. "Not that it will make any difference."

. . .

Sunday at Longbourne passed with no upsets. Lizzy noticed that Mary's jabs at Lydia lessened, and Lydia, without a sparring partner, was on the quiet side. Darren came by after church and took Kitty on what everyone considered her first proper date. "What a nice young man," Mrs. Bennet said as she watched them drive away. "I agree," Mr. Bennet said. "Let's hope it lasts." He looked at Jane, who was sitting on the settee, reading. He opened his mouth to say something, but a warning look from Lizzy stopped him. Oh well, he thought. The less he knew about his daughter's dating life, the better.

Mrs. Bennet had the opposite opinion. "Jane?" she asked. "It's been a while since you've seen Charles. Is everything okay?"

Jane kept her face in her book. "Yes. He's just busy right now."

"Oh," her mother replied as she picked up her needlepoint. "Well, I will ask him to dinner after the ball. When he sees how beautiful you are in that gown, I'm sure he'll be hooked!" She smiled at her conclusion. "Mrs. Jane Bingley. I like the way that sounds!"

Jane slammed her book closed and stood up. "He isn't the only man on the planet, Mother!" she said before storming out.

Mrs. Bennet looked flustered. "Why ... what did I say? Mr. B, what's going on with our sweet Jane?"

Mr. Bennet reached over to pat his wife's arm. "Leave it alone, dear. Jane knows what she is doing and doesn't need any help, or input, from you or me." He held up a hand to stop her protest. "Leave it. Please."

Lizzy got up to leave, knowing everyone assumed she would go to Jane. She would have gone to comfort her sister, but her mind was constantly turning to William Darcy. Their kiss, and a longing for more. "This won't do," she whispered, entering her bedroom and straight to the stack of essays on her desk, grateful for the distraction.

.   .   .

With the Economics and Liberal Arts Buildings in different parts of the campus, the chances of Darcy and Lizzy running into each other were slim. In her office Tuesday morning, she replayed the conversation and worried if she had said the wrong thing? Did it matter? She drafted an email in her head. *Not a mistake* would be the subject line, laughing at the idea. But then doubt crept in, making her wonder if he now thought it had been a mistake and was avoiding her? She threw her head back and groaned but snapped it back to the screen when the email notification chimed.

NOT from Dr. Darcy, but Charmaine, CC'd to Nate. *Can we get together on Wednesday at 4?* Lizzy clicked reply all: *Fine, but make it 5:30. My office.* Send. She was ready to leave the Y2K committee behind.

One more class to go, she sighed, logging off. Through her office window, she saw dark clouds rolling in from the south, casting shadows on the campus grounds. She left, hoping the rain would hold off until she got home.

The rain held off, and she hurried down the path, along with everyone else. As her grandmother would say, *Looks like we're in for a real frog choker!*

She was walking by the library when she saw her father outside with a few of his crew. They were in the beds, shovels in hand, waiting. Mr. Bennet stood to the side, having what looked like a heated discussion with the head librarian, Mr. Blake. In the past, Lizzy would have kept walking. She and her father had an unwritten agreement to keep out of each other's Delany business. But that was before Delany decided to give him the boot.

"Hello, Father," she said, interrupting Mr. Blake, his hands propped on his hips and a look of annoyed dissatisfaction on his face. "Everything okay?"

"*Excuse me,*" Mr. Blake said, his eyebrows high.

"Everything is fine, Lizzy—Professor Bennet," her father began. "Nothing for you to concern yourself with."

Mr. Blake stepped out of the flower bed as if he were maneuvering through a river of crocodiles. "Everything is *not* fine," he said. "Tell him, Professor Bennet—as a fellow educator—why he shouldn't be doing this now."

"And why shouldn't he, Mr. Blake?" Lizzy asked. "It's his job, you know."

Mr. Blake's back stiffened. "Yes, I know that. And I also know that he's had *all summer* to take care of this issue. Digging up the grounds *and* shutting off our water *in the middle of the school day* is hardly appropriate."

Her father turned glaring eyes on Mr. Blake. "Like I told you, the part came in a few days ago, so we couldn't do it earlier. Now, if you would just leave us be, we need to get on it before the sky cracks open." Mr. Bennet returned to his workers.

"Why I never!"

Mr. Blake turned to Lizzy. "I know what this is all about." He pointed an accusing finger at Mr. Bennet's back. "This is payback."

Mr. Blake was on the advisory board and no doubt provided input into the discussion to end the Bennet legacy. He had been someone Lizzy meant to talk to, but judging from his behavior, she didn't have to guess which side of the decision he landed.

"My father is not like that, and you know it. He's just doing his job." Students and staff walked by, a few slowing down to take in the scene. She gazed at her father as he supervised the repair. He used to tell her how he was the luckiest man on earth because he got paid for doing something he loved and was good at. "Out all day, working with nature. What's not to love?" he would say. Tears welled and the last thing she wanted was for Mr. Blake (or her father) to see her crying. She lowered her head, mumbled a good day, and turned to leave. Mr. Blake's extra-loud *humph*! whooshed past her as she hurried towards the Liberal Arts Building and her office.

She was in no mood to talk, so with head down and quick, determined steps, she weaved through the passageway mumbling an occasional, "Excuse me." A drop fell on the sidewalk, but she couldn't tell if it was hers, or from the sky above.

"Professor Bennet? Are you all right?"

She lifted her head to see Dr. Darcy's dark brown eyes peering into hers, his face full of concern. The next thing she felt were hot tears streaming down her cheeks. She shook her head and whispered, "No."

She offered no resistance as he took her arm and maneuvered her into an empty classroom. He brought her to a chair and lowered her body into the hard seat. When he held out a bottle of water, she took it from his hand and brought it to her waiting mouth. The cool water calmed the throbbing in her chest and dampened the simmering fire inside her. Darcy took a seat opposite and waited. She took another sip and glanced around the classroom. It was one of the smaller lecture halls and the last time she had been in it was during her freshman year. She smirked. "I had statistics in this room and swore I would never come back. Only C I ever got, and I was praying for at least that much."

Dr. Darcy nodded. "Yes, I hear that a lot. But that's not why you're upset, is it? Did something, or someone, hurt you?"

"Yes—no—I mean, I am more angry than hurt. My family has given so much to Delany and now it feels like everyone is turning their back on us!" She stood up, stepped onto the lecture stage, and began pacing. "And not only my father and his dad, and his dad, and all the way back to when this place was just a shack in the woods. Me!" She pointed a finger at herself. "I don't have to be here, you know. After that *Jet* article came out, I was getting offers from NYU, Howard, and UCLA. But did I take them? No! And why? Because of some messed up sense of loyalty I had to this place!"

"And to your family, I suppose," Darcy offered.

"Yes. That too, of course," she said. "But now, after this school year ... "

"I heard about the upcoming termination of the Bennet Legacy from ... someone. I reviewed the original documents to see if anything could be done, but so far, no luck."

"Why?" She glared down at him. "Looking for a way to get us out of here quicker?"

Darcy stood up. "Of course not! I may have had issues with the original terms, but anyone can see that to just terminate it so quickly seems heartless and could even be illegal. I thought it was worth looking into."

Lizzy closed her eyes and willed her pulse to slow down. "That was unfair. I'm sorry." She paused. "I don't think that about you ... anymore."

He grinned. "I get that a lot. Sometimes my first impressions are lacking."

She laughed. "I'd say." Another thought came to her. "Does Charles know about the Delany Bennet legacy ending? Is he worried about Jane?"

He shook his head. "As far as I know, he doesn't."

She gazed past him, wondering if this could be why Charles had been cold towards Jane; worried he'd end up supporting her and the family. Dr. Wright had implied that it could make a difference. Perhaps she's right. "Make sure he knows he doesn't have to worry about the Bennet Family. We'll be just fine, with or without Delany University."

"I think he knows that," he said, stepping onto the stage. He stopped about six feet from her. "As do I."

Outside, the sky finally cracked open with a flash of lightning, followed by rolling thunder that rattled the hall's small windows. They turned to the sound of rain crashing against the building. She crossed her arms together and shivered.

"Are you cold?" he asked, moving closer.

"No. Of course not. This isn't like California, you know, where it gets cold when it rains. For most of the year when it rains here, all we get is wet and hot."

"Really?" he replied, lowering his voice to a soft caress.

She held up her hand. "Okay, I know how that sounds, but it was *not* a … come-on. Just an innocent comment about Southern weather."

"Well, that's a disappointment." He kept his place on the stage and waited until their eyes met before continuing. "Tell me how to convince you that what happened before was not a mistake."

The next flash of lightning was fainter, telling her that the storm was passing. She barely heard the following clap of thunder. "Why would I do that, Dr. Darcy? I thought it over and cannot see how anything good could come from us—"

"You don't?" he whispered, stepping closer. Was that hurt she saw in his eyes?

He lowered his head towards hers, placing his hands on the sides of her face. She reached up and wrapped her fingers around his wrist, intending to pull him away, but found herself leaning forward, overcome with the need to breathe him inside herself. An invisible force tilted her face up to his waiting mouth. His kiss was slow at first, but when her lips parted in welcome, any reserve he was holding on to vanished. The Doctor of Economics and the Hip Hop Professor melded into one, each kiss pushing them deeper into the passionate moment. When he moved his lips from her mouth to her hair, she pressed her palms into his back, needing to keep him close. "I knew you felt the same way," he whispered.

She froze. *Did she?* Her hands slid slowly down his back and rested on his waist. She closed her eyes and inhaled deeply, pulling all the reasons this needed to stop to the surface. She stepped back, shaking her head. "I should go." She said, moving around him. He reached out and stayed her with his hand on her arm. "Go where? You're done for the day. And so am I."

She removed his hand. "Like I said before, I can't …"

"Can't, or won't?"

She paused, not knowing how to answer. "I wasn't expecting this."

"Neither was I," he answered, causing her to chuckle. "What's so funny?"

"I think this is the first time we've agreed on something."

He smiled and nodded. "Yeah, how does it feel?"

She folded her arms and gazed about the lecture hall. The rain had subsided. "I'm not sure, but it complicates things. With Jane trying to figure out what's going on with Charles, my father getting dumped by Delany, and me trying to figure out what's next in my life, this adds a whole 'nother level of complication." She looked at him. "Plus, you're just here temporarily, correct?"

He gazed at her for a moment. "We're two adults who are obviously attracted to each other; something that has happened since time immemorial. Does it have to be that complicated?" He lifted a shoulder as if the decision was as trivial as choosing Chinese or Mexican for dinner.

The slight movement brought the reality of their different world views back to light. She gave him one more look before turning to walk down to the seating area. "I'll see you at the ball," she said, reaching for her bag and umbrella. "Probably not before, as I'm busy with committee work and teaching."

"Is that it? Don't you think I deserve more of an explanation?"

"No, I do not, actually."

CHAPTER 33

Dr. Darcy fought the urge to follow her. He mumbled with frustration, pacing the stage. If somewhere private, he had no doubt things would have progressed to the obvious conclusion. He fluctuated between gratitude and frustration. Never had a woman captured his desire so swiftly, and all without her doing a damn thing. Just being Lizzy. Another groan formed to escape but stopped when the lecture room door opened. A few students walked in, looking startled when they saw him at the lectern. "Umm, is this Religious Studies?" one of them asked. "Where's Professor Bentley?"

"On his way, I presume," Darcy said, leaving the stage and walking past them to the door. He escaped into the humid late afternoon. The rain had stopped, but a quick glance upward warned of more to come. He noticed that Mr. Bennet and his crew had abandoned their work by placing a tarp over a mound of dirt. Bright orange cones warned walkers to step carefully. He had left his office earlier to venture down to lower campus intending to get something to eat, and then back to his office to work on some Delany Finance business. His appetite vanished and the idea of pouring over financial records annoyed him. For the first time since coming to Delany, he was glad of the distance between his office and the café area. He needed to expel some energy.

The escalators were turned off, probably because of the rain, so he took the longer way around the quad area. Hands in his pockets and head down, he only looked up when the Econ Building came into view. The rain hadn't returned, and he found himself drawn to the Ancestors Garden. He followed the path to the bench they had met at a few weeks ago and realized he had seen little else of the space. He continued along the wet pavement, glancing left and right at the various shrubs, plants, and flowers. With fall on the horizon, flowers were losing their vibrancy, and the rain had forced a few trees to drop their leaves. He imagined the upkeep was a never-ending project; one that Mr. Bennet would no longer have to deal with. He walked on and soon saw the fountain. It was running, with water spewing from the top and cascading to the pool below. He thought to walk around it, then head to his office. A small sign attached to a wooden stake caught his attention.

Make a wish and toss a coin!
We donate all monies collected to the
MDU Student Emergency Resources Fund.

He peeked into the reservoir and saw a splattering of coins, mostly silver, including three silver dollars. He didn't have one of those, but he reached into his pocket and pulled out a handful of change. *Make a wish.* He curled his fingers around the coins and laughed at himself. That woman has got me doing all kinds of crazy stuff, he thought before gently releasing his silver. After the coins settled to the bottom, he turned to retrace his steps out of the garden, grateful no one had witnessed his moment of silliness.

A few steps away from the fountain, he heard giggling. Turning towards the sound, he thought it was a voice he had heard before. "St-ooop. Not here!" Followed by another giggle spasm. Frisky co-eds, he assumed. He continued walking until the sound of rustling leaves and stomping feet caused him to turn around just in time to see two bodies emerge from the brush. "I'm covered in muck!" the female said as she wiped wet leaves and bits of mud from her bare arms. The young man grinned and moved his hands to her backside. "Let me help you," he said, grabbing her behind. She let out a playful yelp, followed by an unconvincing, "Stop it!" She looked up to see Dr. Darcy. Her hand flew to her mouth. "Oh, shoot." Dr. Darcy's eyes widened with recognition. Both were at the Mashujaa stomp practice that day in the gym. He waited until they both saw him, then turned to leave, wondering if the Bennet family was aware of what their youngest was up to.

.　.　.

Dinner was over and Caroline, Charles, and Darcy gathered in the sitting room enjoying an after-dinner cocktail. Caroline shared news of the final ball plans. "Mrs. Griff swears by this gentleman she secured to act as MC, but I would prefer to see him in action first." She frowned. "Especially since your Aunt Catherine will be present."

"She's not that bad, Caroline. Besides, as a retired physician, she will be nothing but supportive," Darcy said.

"That reminds me," Caroline said, "she would like to take a tour of the clinic. Perhaps Jane could help with that?"

"Jane?" Darcy asked. "Not Mrs. Griff?"

Caroline shivered. "Oh god, no. Your aunt can spot a charlatan a mile away. No, Jane—despite my *other* reservations—is truly sincere in her reverence for the Westside Clinic and the community. She would be a much better representative."

Darcy eyed Charles, who had been unusually quiet that evening. "*Other* reservations?"

Charles stood up from the leather sofa, walked to the large bay window, and stared out into the darkness. "She means that Miss Jane Bennet is *not* a suitable ... partner for me, the soon to be CEO of Bingley Wineries." He slid his hands into his pants pocket. "And she is right." He turned around to face them. "Which is why I've decided to take a break from Netherfield and will leave after the ball."

"Leaving?!" Darcy sat up in his seat and placed his hands on his knees. "Where and for how long?" He glared at Caroline. "Did you know about this?"

She lifted her chin. "Yes, I did, and think it is an excellent idea." She tried to explain how Charles should become more visible in the day-to-day operations and taking an end-of-the-year tour through their various enterprises was a good place to start. "I'll be going with him, of course."

This last bit made Darcy come to his feet. "Oh, great! Am I to stay here in this enormous mansion all by myself now? Plus, don't you think this is an extreme and expensive way to ditch a girl?"

"I'm not ditching her, Darce," Charles replied, his voice tinted with anger.

"Everyone, calm down, okay? William, we know about her father losing his job and the family their home. Don't you realize the awkward position this could put Charles in?" She took a breath. "Not just financial, but the whole family is … off. And you know it too," she continued, pointing an accusing finger at him. "Otherwise, you wouldn't have kept secret the fact that Lydia Bennet, a *high schooler*, is cavorting around town with that George Wickham." She shivered. "Talk about shameful. I just hope Aunt Catherine doesn't hear of it."

Darcy glared at Charles, who held up his hands. "Don't look at me," he said.

He turned back to Caroline. "Let me guess. Mrs. Griff? Or Corrine?"

Caroline had the decency to lower her eyes. "Does it matter?" And then with a bit more confidence. "But why are you so concerned about the Bennets? You don't even like that professor one."

He swallowed. It was his turn to stare out the large bay window. His dark reflection stared back at him. "You're right, of course. I don't."

CHAPTER 34

"Oh, good. You're home." Jane greeted Lizzy in the entry hall. She took her bag and set it on the floor. "Come with me, Lizzy," Jane said, taking her hand and leading her into the family room.

Her mother and father sat in their chairs, but Mary had abandoned her place by the window and sat by Kitty on the sofa. Lydia was absent. Mrs. Bennet released a sob and used her handkerchief to dry her face. Mr. Bennet's face held an angry expression that frightened Lizzy. "What's wrong?" she said, moving towards her parents. Mrs. Bennet cried louder, and Lizzy saw her father's grip tighten on the chair's arms, as if he feared sliding out. "Mary?" Lizzy turned to her sister with questioning eyes.

Mary glanced at her father before speaking. "Mrs. Dole called today and told Mother that Lydia has been ditching school and is failing her classes."

"Including PE!" Mrs. Bennet exclaimed. "How can *anyone* fail PE?"

Mrs. Dole was the school's counselor and had seen all the other Bennet daughters through high school. Her previous calls to Longbourne were to inform the parents of a perfect attendance, good citizenship, or scholarship award. Truthfully, no one had expected the same type of correspondence from Lydia's time at school. But a call like this? Even more unthought of.

Jane sighed. "She's failing PE for not going to class, Mother."

"Ditching is the fastest way to fail anything," Lizzy said. She moved to stand in front of her parents. "Where is she now?"

Kitty pointed to the ceiling. "In our room. I tried to talk to her, but she was just so angry. Kept screaming how it wasn't fair."

"Father won't let Lydia go to the ball," Jane said, answering Lizzy's questioning look.

"And?" Lizzy said, knowing the punishment had to be greater than just that.

"And," her father said, breaking his silence. "grounded until *after* Christmas break. At least." He moved his hands to his lap, lacing his fingers together. Gazing around at his family, he continued. "I'm afraid I've—we've—let our Lydia go on like this for too long. I blame myself." he said nodding slowly.

Lizzy's mouth became dry as her mind floated back to last week's conversation with Charlotte. She had completely forgotten the mention of Lydia and her missing classes.

Mr. Bennet looked at his two eldest. "Jane, Lizzy, I hate to impose on you, but the three of us will have to figure out a drop off and pick up schedule for Lydia. I don't trust her to walk to school by herself." Mr. Bennet's voice broke.

"I can help too," Mary said, surprising everyone. "I mean, not with driving, but I can walk with her on some days." She thought for a moment. "Thursdays are good! My first class isn't until 10."

"Thank you, Mary. Much appreciated," Mr. Bennet said, his mouth forming a small smile. He, Jane, and Lizzy talked about the remaining days and after they set schedules, Mrs. Bennet released an enormous sigh. "Can one of you see to your father's dinner? I'm just too upset to even *think* about cooking."

"Don't worry about me, Mrs. B. You go to our room and lie down. I don't feel like eating, anyway." He nodded to his daughters before leaving them.

Mary and Kitty went to the kitchen to see what they could do for dinner, while Lizzy followed Jane upstairs. Jane peeked in on Lydia before going into her room. "Looks like she fell asleep," Jane said. "Did you ever think about ditching school?" She pulled out her desk chair and sat down, facing her sister.

Lizzy laughed. "No. I actually enjoyed school. Especially high school."

Jane nodded. "Well, I couldn't say that I liked school, but ditching never entered my mind. Even though some of my friends did it pretty regularly. They called me goody-two-shoes for not coming along."

"Sounds like something Lydia would do. I wonder who her ditching gang is?" Lizzy thought for a few seconds, then turned worried eyes towards Jane. "Oh god, I hope she wasn't ditching to meet him! Wickham!"

A soft knock on the door halted Jane's response. "Yes?"

Kitty came in carrying a plate with a nearly burned grilled cheese sandwich on top. "I tried to give this to Lydia, but she doesn't want it." She offered the sandwich to her sisters. Lizzy declined, but Jane took it and set in on her desk. "And how are you in all this, Kitty?" Jane asked.

Kitty shrugged. "I don't know, plus I hardly see Lydia outside of home anymore. Classes, work, and Darren keep me pretty busy."

Jane glanced at Lizzy, expecting her to say something. When she didn't, Jane continued. "Has Darren said anything about Wickham?"

Kitty shook her head. "No, he hasn't, which is a good thing because he told me that if he found out anything was happening between Lydia and Wickham, he'd tell me."

"Hmmm," Jane said. "I guess no news is good news, then."

Kitty smiled. "Yeah, funny, huh?"

"It won't be funny if Lydia can't graduate," Lizzy said. The harshness in her tone startled Jane and Kitty.

"Oh, Lizzy," Jane said. "I am sure it's not that bad. And we can all help her get caught up on her assignments."

Kitty placed her hand on the doorknob. "You two and Mary will have to help with the homework issue. I doubt Lydia will even listen to me now."

After she left, Jane took a bite from the cold sandwich and frowned. "Who puts mustard on a grilled cheese?"

Lizzy laughed. "Our Mary, I believe." Her chest lifted in a heavy sigh as Mary's confession to her on Lydia's back-to-school night returned. She once prided herself on being close to her family and knowing them—especially her sisters—like one knows the back of their hand. These last few weeks had her doubting that belief.

"What's bothering you, Lizzy?" Jane said, breaking into her thoughts. "You're not blaming yourself for this, are you?"

She laid her hands on the top of her thighs and slid them back and forth as if trying to warm herself. "Noooo," she said. "But there are some things I've been meaning to tell you." Her hands froze, and she released another sigh before continuing. "After Charlotte told me how Wickham is more of an ex-con than a dance instructor, she said that Mariah had mentioned how Lydia has been missing classes at school." Lizzy shook her head. "I had planned to talk to Lydia about that, but my mind is filled with other things these days."

Jane cocked her head to the side. "What 'other things'? Not your classes?"

"No. Not teaching."

.   .   .

"You can close your mouth now," Lizzy said after relating the two romantic encounters. "And I am just as shocked as you are."

"In the lecture hall? Lizzy! You didn't?"

This made Lizzy laugh. "The room was empty, Jane!"

"Well, that's good—"

"Yep! Because if we had been someplace private, who knows what could have happened!" Thinking about the possibilities brought a flush of warmth to her body. She raised a hand to fan herself. "Lord, have mercy! That man is fine and sooo sexy! Wonder why it took me so long to notice?"

Jane offered her a cynical smile. "You know why, Lizzy. But what I really want to know is how long do you think *he* has felt that way about you?"

Their first encounters ran through Lizzy's mind, but she decided it couldn't have been as far back as that. "He's always been so … curt with me, and not afraid to dismiss my studies," she said. "Besides, *when* he started to feel that way isn't as important as *how long* it would last. I'm not interested in becoming just another notch on the famous Dr. William Darcy's bedpost!"

Jane blinked and stiffened, looking suddenly uncomfortable in her chair. Lizzy reached out a hand to her. "Do *not* compare this to you and Charles, Jane. Charles wears his heart on his sleeve, and what you see is what you get with him, which is a good thing in this case."

Jane looked down at her hands as they rested in her lap. "That was true at the beginning, but now, he just seems so distant." She attempted a smile. "But he said that he needed to talk to me about something. Maybe he'll do it at the ball."

Lizzy smiled. "I'll bet you a hundred bucks it's a good thing. Maybe he's changed his mind about going away for the weekend with you. Or …" She lifted her left hand and pointed at her ring finger. "Wink, wink!"

.   .   .

Lizzy had volunteered to take Lydia to school on Wednesdays, her late day. She woke up early, dressed, and went to knock on Lydia's bedroom door. "Be ready in 45 minutes, Lydia!"

Mr. Bennet had stayed around and was sitting at the kitchen table when Lizzy entered. They exchanged good mornings while she busied herself with fixing her toast and coffee. Mrs. Bennet hurried in a few minutes later. "You should have woken me up. Are you hungry? Probably, since you didn't eat last night." She went to the refrigerator.

He smiled and nodded. "Why, thank you, Mrs. B. I appreciate that."

Lizzy smiled too, loving how her parents had always called each other, even though her friends thought it was weird. When she giggled, thinking about how Mr. D and Mrs. D would sound, her mother wanted to know what was so funny, "This early in the morning?"

"Leave her alone," her father interjected. "We need some laughter in this house right now."

Lizzy took her coffee and toast and joined her father at the table. "Lydia will straighten out," she said. "It's been hard on her with all of us off doing our own things now, especially Kitty."

Mr. Bennet reached over to pat her hand. "I know, and don't you concern yourself with it too much. You're Lydia's *sister*. Her parents will take care of her; you just take care of yourself, okay?"

Mrs. Bennet put a plate of scrambled eggs and toast in front of her husband. "Speaking of which, is that girl up yet?"

Mary and Lydia entered, answering Mrs. Bennet's question. Lydia plopped down with a huff. "Why does Lizzy have to take me to school? I'm not a baby."

Mrs. Bennet used her spatula to point at Lydia. "You need to count your blessings, young lady. Back in the day, you would have been taken out back and givin' a good whopping for what you did."

"As if!" Lydia said. She jumped up, planted a fist on her hip, and held her other hand to the side of her face in a mock phone call. "Hello 9-1-1. I'd like to report some child abuse!" She was the only one laughing as the small kitchen fell silent. Mr. Bennet got up so fast his chair tipped backwards. Mary gasped at the rage she saw in his face. In the next moment, he was in front of Lydia, his hand raised when Mrs. Bennet shouted, "Harold! Please!" His open palm froze about five inches from Lydia's cheek. He curled his fingers into a tight ball before lowering his hand. The sound of his heavy breathing filled the kitchen. Lydia's shocked eyes looked back at her father's. "Go to work, dear," Mrs. Bennet said, moving towards him. "Walk with him, Lizzy. *Please.*"

Mary, Lydia, and their mother stayed in the kitchen, and after they heard Lizzy and their father leave, Mrs. Bennet turned to Lydia. "Just so you know, I stopped him for *his* sake, not yours. Laying his hands on one of his children—his *precious* daughters— would have surely killed him." She paused to let the revelation sink in. "Mary, go to the school later today and see if you can collect Lydia's assignments. I'll call Mrs. Dole to tell her Lydia won't be attending today. Go to your room, Lydia."

CHAPTER 35

Lizzy and her father parted at the entrance to the Ancestors Garden. It had been a silent walk. With heavy footsteps, they moved through the campus as they had many times before. The sun was already warming the grounds, vanishing any evidence of yesterday's rain. On mornings like this, she usually loved to escape to a hidden seating area inside the Ancestors Garden where she would grade papers or read while listening to the sounds of the students' comings and goings. But today didn't seem like the time for that. Plus, the apprehension of running into Dr. Darcy outweighed the call of the outdoors. She glanced around, sighed, and continued her walk to upper campus and her office.

At the end of her teaching day, she sat at her desk preparing to go home. Her door opened. "Hey, Professor B! Ready to start cutting?" Nate strutted in and sat down in the chair in front of her desk. He glanced around. "This a small office," he said.

Lizzy mumbled an apology while searching for the performance rubrics. Did I leave them at home? she thought with a panic. Charmaine entered the office a moment before Lizzy found the rubrics under a stack of College Composition journals. "Wa-la!" she said, pulling them out.

"Did you get a chance to score them?" Charmaine asked.

Lizzy's face warmed. "No, I did not, but if we split them up, it shouldn't take long." She divided the rubrics into three stacks, dealing them out like a deck of cards. "We can use the conference room, if you like," she said, handing Nate and Charmaine their share.

Charmaine frowned. "I could have done this last night, so we wouldn't need to take time doing it now," she said.

Lizzy ignored the rebuke and focused on her first rubric. Nate started too, and after a few more grumbles, Charmaine followed.

Forty-five minutes later, Charmaine read the list of accepted acts, including Mashujaa's stomp routine. Nate objected. "I say cut the *shoe-jaas* and go with that singing group from Delta Sigma."

"We already have two singers," Charmaine said. "And Delta Sigma has another group performing."

Lizzy agreed with Charmaine. "Variety is important, Nate. But why are you so set on not having Mashujaa perform?"

Nate shook his head. "You just don't know, Professor B. Those guys are messed up and will ruin things for all the houses. Not just theirs."

"By performing at the Y2K celebration?" Charmaine asked.

Nate rolled his eyes. "No. I mean in general. We shouldn't do anything to encourage those guys."

"Well, it's kinda our policy to encourage our students, Nate," Lizzy said, but she sensed his objections were over something else, and it would be useless to ask. Fraternities keep secrets better than the FBI.

Charmaine raised her hand. "Maybe we should ask Dr. Darcy to chime in on this? He can be objective, plus since he's new to Delany, he wouldn't be prejudiced against the Mashujaas."

"Prejudiced?!" Nate said. "What do *you* know about prejudice?"

"That's enough!" Lizzy said. She was tired of playing the referee between these two. "Charmaine, we do not need Dr. Darcy's input, and Nate, Mashujaa is on the program." She opened the email on her desktop. "I will email Coach with our final list right now."

The two students sat back in their chairs and watched Professor Bennet compose the email. "Yours truly, Professor

Bennet, Nate Thompson, and Charmaine Barnes," she said before hitting send. "Done!"

Charmaine stood up and gathered her things. "Well, thanks. I guess I'll see you all at the show."

Lizzy stood up and held out her hand. "Yes, you will. And thank you. I know these committees can be an extra burden on top of all your studies."

Charmaine took her hand and gave it a firm shake. "I don't mind," she said. "It's fun meeting new students and professors." She turned and winked at Nate. "Even you."

"You shouldn't have been so hard on her," Professor Bennet told Nate after Charmaine left.

Nate scoffed. "She knew what she was getting into when she decided to go to a Black college. Heck, I came here to get away from folks like her."

Lizzy crossed her arms. "This is America, Nate. You will never get away from 'folks like her', and the sooner you learn how to deal with them, the better."

"That's what my dad says. But enough about her. Looks like I'll see *you* at the Netherfield Ball on Saturday."

"Oh? Is Phi Beta sponsoring a table?"

"No, nothing like that. My brothers and I are volunteering, acting as valets, servers, and such. The clinic's giving us volunteer hours for the gig, plus a special mention in their newsletter."

The Netherfield Ball was finally happening with all the Bennets in attendance, except Lydia, of course. "Well, that's good for you all. I, for one, will be happy when it's over."

Nate laughed. "Yeah, me too. I hope someone drives up in a Rolls though. Would love to get behind the wheel of one of those!"

Lizzy couldn't think of anyone in or around Merryton that owned a car like that, but with the company the Bingleys must keep, one was bound to show up. She was looking forward to her sister getting insight into her relationship with Charles. And she and William Darcy? Getting through the evening without breaking into a fight, or something else, would satisfy her.

.   .   .

"Is that my nephew?"

Darcy smiled at the sound of the familiar voice. He set his bag on the entry table and walked to the sitting room. "Yes, it is, Aunt Catherine." The two embraced before she held him at arm's length. "Let me get a good look at you," she said with a huge grin as her eyes roamed up and down his frame. She patted his middle. "Putting on a few pounds, I see. Watch out for that Southern cooking. Everything is deep fried or covered in gravy or sugar."

"Oh, not here, Aunt," Caroline said. "I gave our cooks strict instructions on—"

"Never mind that," she said. "Come, William, sit and tell me all about Martin Delany University."

Aunt Catherine was Darcy's closest living relative. He had a few distant cousins, but he rarely saw them. He held her hand in his as he told her about the research with Dr. Baei, his grad students, and Delany. "You know, there is definitely a strong sense of community, history, and pride here, Aunt. It's nice."

Aunt Catherine gave his arm a playful slap. "What were you expecting? Bedlam?"

He laughed. "No, nothing like that." He reflected for a moment before continuing. "I'm ashamed to admit it, but I let ... others plant a negative bias in me."

His aunt knew who these others were. She laid her hand on his cheek. "We all do and say what we think is best, dear. Your father included."

He nodded. "I know." Caroline sat opposite them, observing. "So, how was your day, Caroline? Ready for the big event?"

Caroline set her glass of wine on the small side table. "Yes. Quite frankly, I can't wait until it's over. Oh, and thank you for reaching out to the theater department. Someone will be out tomorrow morning."

"Good." Darcy explained her search for a seamstress. "Clever idea you had to reach out to Delany's theater department, Caroline."

She tilted her head to the side. "It wasn't my idea, actually. I didn't mention it? I ran into Jane and her sister, the rap music professor, at the dress shop in Merryton on Saturday. *She* suggested the theater department."

"Lizzy Bennet?"

Caroline's eyebrows lifted at the informal address. "Yes, they were there to purchase dresses for the ball, I assume. Although lord knows what they could find there," she added.

"Rap music professor?" Aunt Catherine asked. "At Delany?"

Darcy nodded. "Yes. Professor Elizabeth Bennet. They call her the hip hop professor. Her courses are very popular, it seems."

Aunt Catherine's hand flew to her chest. "What in God's name is there to *teach* about that vile music? Just a bunch of screaming, cursing, and misogynistic nonsense as far as I'm concerned. And at Delany University? Makes me want to reconsider my plans to donate to their endowment."

"Well," Caroline said, "it seems like the Bennets have a long history with Martin Delany University." She tried to explain the Bennet Legacy agreement. "And," Caroline added with a flourish, "the Delany Board has decided to end the legacy this school year. Looks like the turn of the century will bring an end to the Delany-Bennet relationship." She shrugged. "Maybe they'll cut ties with Professor Bennet too."

"Stop speculating, Caroline," Darcy said, his voice full of irritation. "I doubt Delany will do any such thing. Professor Bennet is a competent and well-respected member of the faculty. They'd be crazy to get rid of her."

Caroline's mouth fell open at the swift rebuke, leaving her speechless.

Aunt Catherine noted her nephew's response. "It sounds like you know this professor quite well," she said, turning to Darcy.

"We were on a committee together," Darcy told her. "Something to do with organizing a Y2K event on campus."

"Oh?" Caroline said, finding her voice. "You never mentioned that."

"Didn't I?" Darcy said mockingly. He was tired of this game.

"Well, whatever it was," she said, picking up her wineglass, "she must have made a good impression on you."

"Very good," he answered, looking directly at her.

Caroline swallowed and turned away. Aunt Catherine sighed and stood up. "As much as I'd like to continue this discussion, I need to lie down before dinner. Will you see me to my room, William?"

.　　.　　.

Aunt Catherine was still asleep when Darcy went to call her to dinner, so he let her rest. He asked Corrine to prepare a tray for her. "Set it up," he said, taking a seat. "I can take it to her later." Darcy was quiet during dinner, and excused himself directly after, saying he had work to catch up on, which he did, but turning his mind to it would be virtually impossible.

Twenty minutes later, Charles knocked. "There are you." Charles entered his office, closing the door behind him.

Darcy kept his eyes on the computer's screen. "I said I needed to work,"

Charles sat down in the chair next to Darcy's desk. "I know that's what you *said*, but I assumed it was a little fib. You looked like you had a lot on your mind. And not work."

Darcy sat back in his chair and rubbed his eyes. "And are you still planning on leaving?"

Charles looked down at his hands. "I know you think I'm being a chicken shit for running away." he shrugged and offered a half-smile. "But that's what I do."

Darcy thought for a moment. Would now be a good time to tell him? *Well, it just so happens that* I'm *very interested in her sister. Stay and we'll pursue them together.* No, that wouldn't work. Elizabeth Bennet had already told him she was not interested, and the possibility of another rejection was something he'd rather not risk. He rubbed the back of his neck, surprised at how tense it felt. "Look, Charles, I would be the first one to tell you that a relationship between yourself and Jane Bennet could prove challenging." He looked his friend in the eye. "And if you don't feel it's worth it, then …"

"I do love Jane, you know." Charles said. He tilted his head to the side. "Do you think it's possible to love someone too much, Darce?"

"What do you mean?"

Charles stood up and paced the room. "Caroline is wrong about her. Jane Bennet neither wants nor needs my money, fame, or glamourous lifestyle." He scoffed. "Which, my dear friend, is too bad for me since that is all I have to offer her." His light tone was a direct contrast to the pain in his eyes.

"Charles, I had no idea you felt this way, but you couldn't be more wrong. Where do you get these crazy ideas about yourself?"

Charles turned his palms up and shrugged. "Everything I have has been given to me, handed on the proverbial silver platter. I listen to Jane's stories about her work at the clinic, how challenging nursing school was, and all the good she's doing, and I almost feel … ashamed." He shook his head. "She's too good for *me*, Darce, and the only good thing I can do for her is to get out of her way and let her find someone more deserving."

It was true that Charles Bingley was an open book with his emotions, but this revelation shocked and saddened Darcy. He had never seen his friend so torn up over a woman. He was experiencing his own type of female torment, but for entirely different reasons. Realizing this made him wish they had never come to Merryton, North Carolina. He stood up and patted Charles on the shoulder. "Whatever you need from me, you got it."

Charles exhaled loudly. "Thank you."

After a few moments, Charles thanked him again. "Sorry to bother you, but …"

Darcy waved away the apology. "Don't worry. And I'm glad you confided in me."

Charles stopped at the open doorway. "Why don't you leave with me? After the semester? No one expects you to stay the entire school year, do they?"

Darcy thought for a moment, unsure of how to respond. "Do you plan to never return to Netherfield, then? After everything you put into it?"

Charles gazed around the room and shrugged. "It's just a house," he said. "We can lease it, or turn it over to our management department to … I don't know, rent it out for weddings, parties, galas, that sort of thing."

"*Just* a house?"

"Yeah. Just a house."

CHAPTER 36

Dr. Wright caught Lizzy before she left for the day. "Got a minute? It's important." Lizzy followed her into her office. Dr. Wright sat down on the small, worn brown leather sofa and motioned for Lizzy to take a seat on one of the small chairs. "Do you know a Taylor Armstrong? He's a sophomore this year."

Lizzy blinked at the directness of the question which meant something serious was brewing. She shook her head. "Name doesn't ring a bell, although he could have been in one of my freshman comp classes. They're so huge, you know."

Dr. Wright nodded while picking up a paper from the glass top coffee table. Lizzy recognized it to be a student's essay, but with a large red *Plagiarized* scrawled over the text. Dr. Wright handed it to her, shaking her head. "He turned this in for my Romanticism class. These students must think we're stupid. Or don't read their work."

"Is he requesting a hearing?" Lizzy asked, glancing over the pages.

"Yes, and that's why I wanted to talk to you." Dr. Wright leaned forward and looked pointedly at Lizzy. "He claims to be 'tight' with the Bennets and that we shouldn't 'mess with him.' His words."

Lizzy's mouth fell open. "He said that? To you?"

"Mmmm hmmm. But you say you don't know him?"

"No. And even if I did, it wouldn't give him cause to say something like that!"

Dr. Wright held up her hand. "I know, I know. But you also know I had to ask, no matter how outlandish it is."

Lizzy took a deep breath. "Yes, of course. I'm sorry, it's just that with this semester, it's been one thing after another." She took one more look at the essay before tossing it on the coffee table. "I have no idea why he would say—" Her face froze.

"What's wrong, Lizzy? Have you remembered something?"

Lizzy's head dropped into her open palm, and she let out a small groan. "Please tell me he is NOT with Mashujaa House."

"Why, yes, I think he is? Does that matter?"

Lizzy's mind worked fast as she tried to decide how little she could share without incriminating herself or her sisters. "My younger sisters are ... acquainted with a few Mashujaa brothers, but I never heard this Taylor guy mentioned."

Dr. Wright stayed silent a few seconds before responding. "Well, I suggest you look into these acquaintances soon." She stood up. "I have a solid case against this young man and plan to recommend expulsion."

This shocked Lizzy. "Is this his first offense?"

Dr. Wright walked behind her desk. "Probably not, judging by the cockiness of him."

"Well, if I find out anything, I'll let you know."

Dr. Wright's eyes softened. "Thank you, Lizzy. And I'm sorry to drag you into this, but ..."

"I understand," Lizzy said, turning to leave.

"Will you be in tomorrow?" Dr. Wright asked, stopping Lizzy at the office door.

"No. Jane and I will be busy prepping for the big event," she said with a sarcastic smirk.

"Ahh, yes." Dr. Wright smiled. "I just hope there's an open bar! And I will be taking a cab!"

On the way home, Lizzy took a detour to her father's office. The work by the library was completed, and she hadn't seen him anywhere else on campus. Although going through the Ancestors Garden is the shorter route, she walked around it on the path in between the Econ building and the Campus police. Her father's workroom and office came into view at the same time she heard his motorized cart behind her. "Coming to see me?" he said with a grin, pulling up beside her. "Hop in." They rode in silence. At the storage facility, Lizzy stood to the side and watched him unload the cart and talk with a few of his men. "I won't be in tomorrow, so do the normal rounds and make sure to check the stage equipment. I think we're missing some planks for the flooring. Start a list and I'll put in the order next week." She followed him into his office. "If you're here about what happened yesterday morning, no need." He sat down behind his desk. It was covered with papers, small garden tools, and bits of dirt.

"Just came by to see if you wanted to walk home together."

He laughed. "Oh really? No need to worry about me. I'm sure things will get back to normal soon. Well, as normal as they can with Lydia."

"I know but—"

He pointed a finger at her and smiled. "You four spoiled us. Never gave us a spot of trouble, leaving your mother and I thinking how *easy* parenting is, but then here comes our Lydia and Bam! Not so easy." He shook his head. "I'm taking tomorrow off, and your mother and I are going to the school to meet with her teachers."

Lizzy nodded. "That's a good idea."

"I'm glad you approve," he answered with a chuckle.

"Father," Lydia pleaded. "I'm just worried, that's all. Besides, what Lydia does can affect all of us, you know."

Mr. Bennet lowered his chin to peer at her over his glasses. "Really? How so?"

She sighed. "Delany is small. Merryton is small. People … talk."

"Lizzy, I think you're overreacting. Lydia's behavior has nothing to do with you, or Jane, Mary, even Kitty. Besides, she's just testing the boundaries, something all teenagers do. After a few weeks, she'll straighten out." He smiled. "Trust me."

Lizzy left a few minutes later, without her father, who still had work to do. "I'll see you at home," he said.

Of course, her father would be optimistic, as any father would. She needed to adopt a little of this optimism. Besides, yesterday's events could prove to be a big enough shock to jolt Lydia into acting more sensibly. And this Taylor business could turn out to be related to Kitty and Darren, not Lydia. Whatever it was, Lizzy decided she wouldn't bring it up until after the ball. Dr. Wright wouldn't expect to hear back before then, anyway. Plus, she just did not want to deal with it. In the next few days, she'd receive an email listing her preliminary spring classes, along with the option to decline them all. She could afford to take a semester off and dive back into her PhD search. Maybe she would.

. . .

Lizzy woke to the sound of light tapping on her bedroom door. Her eyelids blinked open, then closed tightly, not ready to take in the morning sun. Her mind played the *what-day-is-it?* game as she rolled onto her back. Another light tapping. Her eyes opened. "Yes?" she groaned. Lydia walked in, still dressed in PJs. Must be Saturday, she realized. "What time is it?"

Lydia entered and sat on the bedside. "About 7. Sorry to wake you."

Was that a sincere apology? Lizzy maneuvered her body to a sitting position, resting her back against the bed's headboard. "What is it, Lydia?"

Lydia's eyes glanced over her sister. Lizzy's washed and conditioned hair was tucked into a pink satin head covering. Newly manicured hands rested at her sides. "These are pretty," Lydia said, inspecting the French manicure. "Who did it? Leticia?"

Lizzy nodded. "Yeah. Glad you like it." She tilted her head to the side. "I'm sorry you won't be joining us tonight."

Lydia dropped Lizzy's hand. "Oh," she shrugged, "that's no big deal." A fake smile spread. "Besides, I'll have all that time to catch up on schoolwork! Lucky me!" She released a humorless laugh. "So," Lydia continued, "tell me, how is your semester going so far?"

It was too early to play games. "What do you want, Lydia?"

A flash of innocence crossed her face. "What?! Can't I even ask how you are? Geeze!"

"You're right," Lizzy said, remembering Thursday's vow. "And I'm sorry." She clasped her hands together on her lap. "The semester has been … interesting."

"Oh?"

"Yes, it has. Especially with all the Y2K hysteria going on. So many—"

"And Dr. Wright?" Lydia said suddenly, throwing cold water on Lizzy's pledge of optimism.

"What about Dr. Wright, Lydia?" Lizzy asked cautiously. "Is there something you need to tell me?"

Lydia jumped up. "No! Nothing to *tell.* Just say hello for me. She'll be at the ball too, right?"

Lizzy threw back her bedcovers and swung her legs to the floor. "Yes, along with many other Delany faculty. As I'm sure you know."

Lydia crossed her arms and Lizzy recognized the confused and slightly panicked look. She reached for her robe, knowing that asking her anything would only elicit half-truths or lies. "I will be sure to share your greetings. Is there anything else?"

Another fake smile. "No, and thanks for the chat!" She slipped out of the room.

Returning from the bathroom. Lizzy pulled her blackout curtains shut and returned to bed. She and Jane had spent much of yesterday at the hair and nails salons, and shopping for accessories, but this morning she felt like she had run a marathon instead. Who knew beauty could be this tiring? She pushed Lydia's early morning visit to the back of her mind, telling herself that her own world needed some serious looking into. After a few more hours of sleep, she intended to go to the Delany Library to research and outline a plan for her PhD search. A few days ago, she reread her old proposals and applications and cringed at the badly worded and desperate sounding tone. "Do better," she whispered into her pillow before closing her eyes.

.   .   .

The only thing Caroline wanted from her brother and William was for them to stay out of her way. "And keep Aunt Catherine busy too." After a bit of discussion, they decided that Darcy would take them on a tour of Delany, followed by a lite lunch at the Medford Grille. "I'd like to try something local," she added.

"I can't believe I haven't seen the campus yet," Charles said from the backseat of Darcy's Lexus.

"Oh? What has been occupying your time, Charles?" Aunt Catherine asked. "I can't imagine you helping your sister with the decorating."

Charles laughed. "Nothing like that, I can assure you." He looked out the window. "No, just researching things for the business and ... thinking about the future."

She nodded. "I hope to go to Johannesburg next year. I'll be sure to visit the winery, too."

"Well, we'll probably run into each other then. We're starting on the new resort next spring." He sighed. "Going to be a lot of ... work."

Aunt Catherine chuckled. "You don't sound so happy about that."

When Charles didn't respond, Darcy glanced at him in the rearview mirror. He seemed to be in another world, staring out at the passing landscape.

"Breaking ground, especially in foreign country, is always a tiresome affair," Darcy said. The car rounded a bend in the road, and he pointed through the front windshield. "You can see the university clock tower ahead, just over the trees."

"Very nice," Catherine mumbled.

Tour guide wasn't one of Darcy's strengths, so the three of them wandered around campus while he tried to answer his aunt's questions, who had many. "I tell you what," he finally told her. "You can meet Dr. Lucas tonight, and I am sure he has more than enough information to satisfy you."

His aunt paused and looked around. "It is a beautiful campus," she said. "Especially the landscaping."

"Yes," Darcy agreed. "Now there is one place you really need to see."

"Ahh, the famous Ancestors Garden," Charles said after Darcy lead them through the gate. "Jane talks about this a lot. Says it's her father's pride and joy."

"Jane?" Catherine asked. "Is this the same Jane Caroline mentioned before?"

Darcy and Charles exchanged looks, each waiting for the other to respond. After Charles mumbled an "Mmmm hmmm," and stepped away, Darcy filled in his aunt. "Mr. Bennet, the lead groundskeeper, is Jane's father. Their family has been involved with Delany since the beginning."

"And Charles knows this Jane Bennet how?" She raised questioning eyebrows at Darcy.

"How do you think, Aunt Catherine?" he answered, trying to sound light. "They met. Jane's an attractive woman, and Charles is … Charles."

Charles had continued up the path and was nearing the fountain. Catherine and Darcy began walking again. She was feeling tired, and her steps slowed considerably. "Do you think that's wise?" she asked. "The young ladies here are, well … let's just say that I'd rather *not* have to return for a shotgun wedding."

Darcy's jaw clenched. His aunt's assumption was as inappropriate as it was absurd. "Calm your fears, Aunt," he said. "Charles is leaving next week. Never to return, most likely."

She murmured her approval. "That's good, isn't it?"

Darcy did not know if leaving was a good thing or not. He only hoped that this escape would give his friend some peace. He'd deal with finding his own peace later. "Yes," Darcy finally answered. "A very good thing."

The trio left a few minutes later. The garden had more people coming and going than he had ever noticed before. Lizzy's place of solitude was no more, he thought as they headed back to his car. Of course, he was mistaken.

Tucked behind rows of foliage including Eastern blue stars, azaleas, ferns, and Japanese maples, a bench and table sat, hidden from view. Desiring a hideaway spot, gardeners of the past created the secluded space to use for smoke breaks and other frowned upon activities. The person sitting there that afternoon was neither smoking nor goofing off. She stared down at the papers she had printed at the library. The words blurred as tears welled. "God damn him," she hissed.

.   .   .

Lizzy stayed in the garden until the sun's beginning descent told her it was time to head home. She ran scenario after scenario through her mind, trying to decide what to do. There was no way she would tell Jane. Maybe she could find a way to speak to Charles, but say what? And then perhaps she wasn't giving her sister enough credit? Jane isn't new to the world of love, loss, and heartbreak. After what happened with that intern, she'd grown more resilient. Pushing her way through the dark branches and taking care not to step on any plants, Lizzy emerged onto a back path and glanced around to make sure no one had seen her.

By the time she reached Longbourne, she only knew one thing. She was going to make Dr. William Darcy regret he had ever met her.

CHAPTER 37

Heads turned as the Bennet family entered the Netherfield ballroom. Mr. and Mrs. Bennet walked arm in arm, followed by three of their five daughters. Delany folk grinned at the sight of their groundskeeper, who looked like a different man dressed in a navy suit and a silver silk necktie. His wife's dress possessed a sparkling bodice, three-quarter sleeves, and a flowing A-line skirt. The color matched her husband's necktie. Jane followed, a shy princess in her lavender chiffon. Kitty and Mary were too busy gazing around the ballroom to notice anyone else, both dressed simply, yet fit for the occasion. Charles was the first to greet them, his eyes fully on Jane. "You came," he whispered, taking her hand.

She smiled. "Of course we did."

Behind them, Mrs. Bennet cleared her throat. Charles turned to greet them. "Hello, Mr. Bennet. Nice to see you again." Mr. Bennet extended his hand. "You also," he said. "Let me introduce my wife, Mrs. Bennet." Mrs. Bennet's smile spread so wide it practically covered the bottom half of her face. She presented her hand, palm down, causing Charles to grab awkwardly at her dangling fingers. "So very nice to meet you, Mr. Bingley. Jane has told us so much about you!"

"Please, call me Charles. And it is nice to finally meet you, too." He lowered his head. "Forgive me for not coming by sooner."

Mrs. Bennet brushed away his admonishment. "Oh, never mind about that. Besides, I am sure we will see a lot more of you in the future."

Charles looked up to see his sister coming forward. "Welcome to Netherfield," she said, moving to stand next to her brother, placing herself between Charles and Jane. "I'm Caroline Bingley. Your hostess for the evening and Charles' younger sister."

"Hello, Caroline," Jane said. "May I introduce my mother, father, and these are my younger sisters, Katherine and Mary."

Caroline greeted them with silent acknowledgement. "But where is your other sister, the … teacher?"

Mr. Bennet's eyes narrowed at the slight, but his wife remained oblivious. "Oh, you mean Lizzy—Elizabeth—our second oldest. I believe she needed to stop by the powder room." Mrs. Bennet craned her neck and looked back towards the large entryway. "Oh! There she is!" Mrs. Bennet exclaimed, pointing towards an entering Elizabeth Bennet.

She had indeed required a visit to the powder room before making an entrance. Her nerves were causing her palms—and other areas—to perspire. After freshening up, she gazed at her reflection. Soft curls, glowing like black onyx, framed her face, thanks to Friday's 30-minute hot oil treatment and trim. The back section was pulled up and secured with a pearl head comb. The style showed off her slender neck, also adorned with a pearl pendant necklace, her grandmother's. Needing to get the look just right, she had asked Lydia's help with her eye makeup. Examining her lids, she smiled with satisfaction. Smoky, sophisticated, and sexy. The hint of gold lining the lower lash line added the perfect amount of drama, although it took some convincing from Lydia. Burgundy matte lipstick completed the look. She took a step back. The push-up bra didn't hurt either. She took a deep, calming breath before leaving to rejoin her family. She paused at the entryway to the ballroom. Caroline and Charles were standing near the center of things, along with her family. She could see her mother's huge, giddy smile, but it was Charles' eyes on Jane that captured her attention. She stood observing, only moving when she saw her mother pointing in her direction.

"Hello, Caroline. Charles," Lizzy said to the siblings when she got closer. A brief but noticeable hush fell over the ballroom. Caroline opened her mouth to speak, but Lizzy cut her off. "Where have you placed us, Caroline?"

Caroline tilted her head up to gaze down at Lizzy. She smiled sweetly. "The Bennet family is over there," she said, pointing to a table near the back. She turned to Jane. "I hope you don't mind, but Charles will be at the VIP table near the front. There are some people from Bingley Wineries he needs to associate with."

This affront did not pass by Mrs. Bennet, who was on the verge of objecting, when her husband spoke first. "Thank you," he said to Caroline. "Come along, family. Let's take our seats so Charles and Caroline can get back to their business."

Caroline attempted to pull Charles away, but he broke from her to speak quietly with Jane. He tilted his head down to whisper. Jane smiled and nodded before he rejoined his sister. "Everything okay?" Mrs. Bennet asked as they took their places. "Yes," Jane answered, keeping a straight face. "Why wouldn't it be?"

There were not as many attendees as Lizzy had assumed there would, but the $200 per table suggested donation could be the reason. She looked around and nodded at people she recognized and saw the Lucases heading their way.

"Hello, Bennets!" Dr. and Mrs. Lucas smiled down at the family. "Isn't this lovely!" Mrs. Lucas said, clasping her hands. She looked around the table. "But where is Lydia?"

Mr. Bennet stood up to shake Dr. Lucas's hand. "Lydia is taking the evening off," he said.

"Really?" Mrs. Lucas asked. "By herself? At home?"

Mrs. Bennet scoffed. "And why not? Lydia is almost 18, you know."

"Well …" Mrs. Lucas smiled awkwardly. She knew, of course, and this infuriated Mrs. Bennet.

"I assume you're at the VIP table, Dr. Lucas," Mr. Bennet said.

"Why yes, you know. Got to rub elbows with the hob-knobs every once in a while," he attempted a chuckle.

"Don't let us keep you then," Mrs. Bennet said.

"Mother, that was rude," Jane scolded after the Lucases left.

"What's rude," her mother said, taking a flute of champagne from the waiter, "is them not sitting you with Charles. *You're* the VIP."

"This is for Westside, Mrs. B. Or have you forgotten?"

Mrs. Bennet took a dainty sip. "I know, and our Jane works at Westside, which gives her *even more* VIP status, if you ask me." She set her flute down and peered across the table. "And what about you, Miss Lizzy? I'm sure you didn't get all dolled up just to sit back here, next to nobody."

Lizzy gazed around the small ballroom. "It really doesn't matter to me where we sit, Mother, and besides, I'm sitting with my family. The most important people here, as far as I'm concerned."

Mr. Bennet smiled. "Well said, Lizzy."

The waiter came to her side, a silver tray perched on one hand. She reached for a champagne flute. "Thank you." He nodded, smiled, and then winked, causing her to flinch. He was in her African American Lit class. She took a gulp. This is going to be a long evening. Jane sat quietly beside her. "What did Charles say?" Lizzy asked.

"He apologized for us not sitting together but said he would break away as soon as he could."

"Good." Lizzy had noticed that the puppy-love exuberance Charles had displayed during their date at the Grille was gone, replaced with a sort of loving awe. Lizzy reminded herself that she had only heard Darcy's feelings, not Charles', and if he says he doesn't love Jane, she'll call him a liar.

The room quieted when Caroline and Mrs. Griff walked to the mic that was on a small platform. Caroline began by welcoming everyone and introducing her brother, who stood and waved. She talked about the Netherfield renovations and how happy and proud she was to bring it back to life. "And," she added with a huge smile, "owned by an African American corporation!" This brought a hearty round of applause.

After the applause died down, Caroline continued. "One of our first encounters within your community was the Westside Community Health Clinic, and Charles and I, along with Dr. William Darcy, are looking forward to a very enjoyable *and* successful evening!" She stepped down from the platform, leaving Mrs. Griff to take over. She began by thanking the Bingleys, and then launched into a brief history of Westside. Lizzy, along with everyone else at the table, knew the story, so she used the time to fully take in the room and the people. Dr. Wright was sitting three tables over and with a few people Lizzy couldn't place. She looked around some more, surprised by the high number of unrecognizable faces.

The Phi Beta men looked distinguished in their black suits and gloves. They stood to the side, waiting for the talks to end. Also lined up next to the wall near the silent auction tables were large easels, each displaying a blown-up photograph from different areas of the clinic. A nice touch, she thought. A light round of applause pulled her attention back to the speaker's platform. Mrs. Griff highlighted a few auction items and then pointed out the donation envelopes on the tables. "Every little bit helps," she said. She stepped down and the music started, from where Lizzy could not tell, but she knew it wasn't live.

"I heard there's a macaroni and cheese bar," Mary said, standing up. "Let's check it out, Kitty." The serving stations were set up in an adjacent room, and Mary and Kitty made their way there, along with a few others. "We can wait," Jane said. "Charles told me there's a ton of food."

Lizzy agreed, although eating was the last thing she thought she could do that evening. When she was offered another flute of champagne, she took it, even though a little voice advised against it.

.   .   .

Caroline took her seat next to Darcy and gazed around the room. "Well," she said, "so far, so good."

Darcy agreed. "Yes, very nice." He nodded towards the table next to theirs. "I wasn't expecting to see so many New York and Napa people here."

Caroline followed his gaze. "Yes, but I just had to have some of my people here or else you and Charles would be stuck talking with me all evening!"

Darcy chuckled. "That's true." Although he would have rather not had Archie and Eldon Lange present. Both were from his Chadwick days and even though they had become friends, there would always be that distance old money families are good at preserving. Archie brought his wife; Eldon, recently divorced, was without a partner.

"By the way," Caroline said, recapturing his attention. "Have you seen … Lizzy yet?"

"No. Why?" he asked.

Caroline shrugged. "No reason."

Dr. and Mrs. Lucas returned to the table after visiting the serving stations. "Everything looks so good! And I got to meet the chef from The Mustard Seed!" Mrs. Lucas declared.

After taking a few bites, Dr. Lucas asked Darcy how things were going. "Dr. Baei has nothing but positive things to say," he said.

Darcy nodded. "Yes, it's been a very productive few weeks."

"You mean months!" Dr. Lucas laughed. "You must be enjoying your stay, seeing how time has gotten away from you."

Enjoying would be one way to put it, Darcy thought. "I've been meaning to talk with you about—"

Dr. Lucas held up his hand. "If it's about that business you mentioned before school started, no need. That person is no longer associated with the university."

Darcy had forgotten about Wickham, if that's possible. "Yes, I know. Thankfully. But what I wanted to ask you about was another matter. The Bennet Legacy business."

"Oh?" Dr. Lucas asked with raised eyebrows.

Mrs. Lucas set her fork down. "Are you asking because of your friend? Him and Jane?"

Darcy looked confused. "No, of course not. I was wondering how firm the board's decision is."

"Very," Dr. Lucas said. "In fact, it's a done deal. With no Bennet heir ready to step into the position, now seemed like the perfect time. And, if you—or your friend—are worried about the Bennet's future, don't be. Harold is a smart man, and he knows how to provide for his family, with or without the Delany-Bennet Legacy."

"So, it's true," Mrs. Lucas whispered. "Jane *is* a beauty. And smart! Such a sweet girl." She thought for a moment. "Everyone always says how Jane got the beauty and Elizabeth the brains, but I always thought Lizzy possessed a certain, unique beauty."

Dr. Lucas wiped his mouth with his napkin. "I'd say. Especially tonight. If she doesn't land a man by the end of the evening, I'll swear all the young, single brothers here must be blind!" He noticed Darcy's shocked look. "You'll have to excuse me, Dr. Darcy, but the Bennets and our family go way back. Why, my Charlotte and Lizzy are best friends. Outside of work, we are basically family."

"I see," Darcy said.

Caroline, who had been taking in the conversation, asked, "So, what kind of family are the Bennets?"

"Extremely close," Dr. Lucas replied. "As thick as fleas on a farm dog, as we say."

"How … interesting," Caroline said. She looked over at her brother, who was busy talking to Chet, one of the company's CPAs. Lately, he's shown a greater interest in the family business, which was a good thing, but she struggled to feel good about it.

"I think I'll get some food," Darcy said. "Caroline, can I bring you anything?" She told him she would have whatever he was having, which meant that she wouldn't be eating.

.   .   .

After Lizzy's third glass of champagne, she decided to walk around and mingle to help clear her head. Jane and her parents had visited the serving stations and returned raving about the fancy food and semi-celebrity chefs. "Do you think they'll offer doggie bags?" her mother asked. Lizzy hoped she was joking.

At the silent auction tables, she read over the offerings, not seeing anything she needed, wanted, or could afford. Her donation limit was $100, which severely limited her options.

"Well, hello there. I was thinking about that one myself," a man said, pointing to the sheet where she was about to list her bid. She looked up to see another unfamiliar face, white and very good looking. "Oh," she said, grinning. "And you are in need of …" she turned back to the sheet and read, "a $100 gift certificate from Mabel's Sweet Shop?"

He smiled, exposing a row of perfectly straight white teeth and bright pink gums. "I confess I have a *wicked* sweet tooth!"

Lizzy laughed and handed him the pen. "By all means," she said. He took the pen and bent down to write his bid. "Your turn," he grinned, handing her the pen.

She read his name and bid, and gasped. "You win! Mr. Eldon Lange." She set the pen down. "I hope you like banana pudding. It's their specialty."

"Please," he said, hand to his heart, "call me Eldon, or El if you like."

"Eldon," she said with a slight head nod. "Nice to meet you. I'm Elizabeth Bennet."

He took her hand in his, lifted it to his lips, and planted a light kiss. "Lovely to meet you, Elizabeth."

They walked along the tables, commenting and laughing at the other offerings. "What the heck is wild game processing, anyway?" Eldon asked. "Sounds medieval."

"*Not* a hunter, then?"

"I've been on a fox hunt or two at our estate in Cornwall. Does that count?"

Lizzy looked up at him, trying to decide if he was man or boy. He did have mesmerizing blue eyes and a friendly smile. "Sure, why not?" she answered with a laugh.

He wagged a finger in her direction. "I think I like you, Elizabeth Bennet," he teased, making her smile even wider.

This feels good, she thought. So unlike the tense encounters with—. "Mind if I get in on the joke?" William Darcy appeared behind Eldon, his dark eyes locked on Lizzy. His chest rose and fell in a steady rhythm. Eldon clapped him on the back. "William! You didn't tell me how *beautiful* the women are down here. Have you met Elizabeth?" he asked with a wink. "She's *very* funny."

"Yes. We've … met."

Lizzy pulled away from his gaze. "Dr. Darcy and I teach at Delany," she said. "Although in very different departments."

Eldon's hand came to his chest. "Oh, thank god! Who needs another *boring* economics geek hanging around? No offense, mate." He placed a hand on Lizzy's shoulder and with his other hand, laid a single finger over his lips, as if he was pondering the world's deepest problems. "Hmmm. Let me guess. Theater? Art? No! Dance. That's it! You're a dance teacher!"

Lizzy laughed. "Hardly. No, I'm from the *boring* English department."

"Definitely not boring. Oh! You *must* come with me to the Globe next season! It's absolutely amazing!"

"And what makes you think she hasn't?" Darcy asked, his voice hard and even.

Eldon's eyes widened. "Have you?" he asked.

"As a matter of fact, I have," she said. "The summer of my junior year." From the corner of her eyes, she saw her mother looking their way. "If you'll excuse me. I need to return to my family." She hurried away, ignoring Eldon's protest. "Leave her," she heard Darcy tell him.

"Who was that?" Kitty asked Lizzy before she could sit down. "He looks like Hugh Grant!"

Lizzy smacked her hand on the table. "That's it! I knew he looked like some actor. It wasn't him, though." Kitty's face fell. "His name is Eldon Lange, and he has an 'estate' in Cornwall."

"A friend of Dr. Darcy's?" her mother asked.

Lizzy answered yes, but judging by William's coldness, she guessed it wasn't a close friendship. She had given little thought to how she could punish William for his crude dismissal of Jane, but the fiery jealousy she noted in his eyes was a good start. A wicked smile spread. *In the morning, glad, I see; My foe outstretched beneath the tree.*

"And what are you mumbling about, Miss Lizzy?"

Lizzy blinked, unaware that she had verbalized the infamous line. Her mother and father eyed her curiously. "Nothing. Ummm … think I'll go check out the serving stations. Is that where Jane went to?"

Mrs. Bennet sighed. "She went to the bathroom. Poor thing is still waiting for Charles to come back."

Lizzy's stomach churned. "I'll go see to her." She took her handbag with her, thinking her makeup might need a touchup.

Jane wasn't in the bathroom, at least not the one Lizzy had visited earlier. She stood in the small hallway, listening to the sounds of the gathering. An MC took over the mic and was doing his best to get people excited about the silent auction items. Eldon Lange's $1000 bid should make Mrs. Griff happy.

She walked down the hallway, in the opposite direction, hoping to come across Jane. A sign at the end pointed guests to another bathroom. She followed it and came out into the large entryway.

Seeing it brought back the memory of her grade school visit to the former plantation. She stood there gazing about the space, trying to get her bearings. The ballroom was on the north side of the house and tonight's guests entered through there. On the school tour, the guide had brought them through the front, pointing out the massive staircase and invited the children to imagine "an elegant Southern Belle cascading down in all her finery." He romanticized the place and its history, she remembers, shaking her head.

She saw the other bathroom on the opposite side. The family had placed a red satin rope barrier across stairs and hung *Please Do Not Enter* signs on a few doors. She couldn't fault them for that. This is their home, now filled with strangers.

Jane wasn't using that restroom either. A hint of panic came, and she turned back, hoping she would have returned by now. She was passing the staircase when his voice stopped her. "Looking for something?"

He was coming down the stairs, hands in his pockets, steps slow and deliberate. Damn, he looked good! She swallowed and found herself unable to move. When he reached the bottom step, he unhooked the rope barrier and stepped past, but stayed on the last step and gazed down at her.

"Jane," she said. "I was looking for Jane. My sister."

His eyes held hers for a few seconds before they traveled down her body, and then back. "You're looking exceptionally beautiful this evening," he said. "Dare I think it's for my benefit?"

Her hand clenched her black satin handbag as heat rose from her chest to her face. She willed her body to calm and tried to reignite the anger and hurt she had felt in the garden. "Think what you like," she said, hearing, but not recognizing, her own voice. She needed to leave him. Now. Turning and stepping away, she heard his footsteps, and he was in front of her before she had taken two steps. "I'm getting a little tired of you abandoning our conversations. It makes me wonder what you're afraid of."

She scoffed. "Afraid?" she asked, crossing her arms to still her trembling. "Of what?"

He took a tiny step forward. "You tell me."

He was so close. She could feel the warmth of his face and the scent of his cologne filled her nostrils. Her lids lowered as an involuntary and deep inhale carried the scent inside her body, leaving no room for her revenge. This was not the plan, was her last clear thought right before his mouth covered hers. The next thing she knew, she was being pulled around the staircase and through a small door that opened to a stairwell. He led, she followed. At the top of the stairs, he opened another door, and they emerged into a carpeted hallway. He turned right, never letting go of her hand. His breathing was heavy. Or was that her own? She scarcely had time to take in the large bedroom as he pulled her through, took her into his arms, and pressed her back against the door. His mouth covered hers and she ran her hands under his suit coat, up towards his broad shoulders, then down again. A groan escaped him as she pressed him closer. He moved a hand to the back of her neck, then to her hair and removed the pearl hair comb. He buried his face in the soft curls, inhaling like a man learning how to breathe. Impatient for the return of his kiss, Lizzy reached up to move his mouth back to hers, and with bodies entwined, they turned and then tumbled onto the waiting bed.

Although dressing for the evening had required assistance from her sisters and over an hour of prep time, her clothes fell away from her body with ease, and just a little help from him. He abandoned his clothes just as quickly. The moment before they reached the point of no return, her head turned sideways, and she spotted his very expensive suit jacket crumbled on the floor. He really should hang that up, she thought.

.   .   .

She expected the ceiling to be fancier. Perhaps with intricate plaster moldings, brass tiles, or, at least, impressive lighting. William lay beside her, eyes closed and resting an arm on his forehead. She couldn't tell if he was asleep, which wouldn't surprise her after that performance. "May I know what you're thinking?" he asked.

Not asleep. "The ceiling," she said.

He removed his arm and turned towards her, leaning on his side. He had an impressive chest, and she was sure his back now bore marks from her manicured nails. "What?" he asked.

She raised her arm until it was perpendicular to the ceiling and pointed. "It's kinda plain, considering." Her arm dropped, hitting the bed with a soft plop.

He followed her gaze, then turned back to her. "Sorry to disappoint you, but is *that* what's on your mind right now? My bedroom ceiling?"

No, but it's all I can bear to think about. His nightstand clock told her she had been away for almost an hour.

"I—we—should get back to the ball." This was the biggest bed she had ever seen, and the quickest way out was over him, which she couldn't do. She started scooting down towards the bottom, using the sheet to cover herself.

"Lizzy," he said, his voice anxious. "Are you okay? I didn't …?"

"No," she said, glancing back at him over her shoulder. "It's fine. I need to get back, that's all." The sheet was larger than the bed and she realized dragging it with her would look even more ridiculous. Her dress lay in a pile near the side, thankfully. She bent to retrieve it, feeling his eyes on her the whole time. "Bathroom?"

He pointed to a door behind her.

She closed the door and got dressed as quickly as she could. She avoided her reflection in the large mirror, believing her makeup probably resembled a Picasso painting by now. A soft knock came as she tried to zip up her back. "Yes?" The door opened.

In his hand he held her purse and hair comb. He handed them to her. "Thank you," she whispered. He stayed in the doorway. She turned to the mirror and released a sigh of relief. Not too bad, she thought. All she needed now was to return to the ballroom looking like a hot mess.

"You look beautiful," he said, as if reading her thoughts. "As always." Their eyes met in the mirror's reflection. He had put on his pants and shirt, but not completely buttoned, with the tie hanging loosely around his collar. Does this man ever *not* look sexy? She cast her eyes down and opened her purse.

"Lizzy," he said, taking a step into the bathroom and leaning on the wall opposite the mirror. "This may seem selfish, but I need to know. Are you … regretting what just happened?"

She lowered her head. "No."

His shoulders relaxed. "Neither am I. So …?"

"I just need to think, okay? That's all." She removed her lipstick and shook her head. "Because this was NOT supposed to happen. Especially …"

Their eyes met in the mirror. "I have been … drawn to you ever since I first saw you from my office window. You were in the garden, looking … lovely." He swallowed. "And every other meeting since, my … attraction to you has only grown deeper." He chuckled at her surprised look. "Yes, each one. Especially when we sparred."

"You did a good job of hiding it."

"Maybe. But that doesn't mean it isn't true."

She remained silent, and he took that as a sign to continue. "What you said when we were in that lecture hall is true. A relationship would be difficult." He shook his head. "And believe me, I tried to fight it. I mean, I even laughed at the thought of it— us—but as you see," he nodded towards the bed. "Some things are just too strong to ignore."

"*Things*?" she asked, feeling a different sort of heat rise.

"Yes," he answered, relaxing even more. "Think about it. I'm West Coast; you're firmly situated here in the South, although heaven knows why any straight-thinking Black person would be content living here." This first admission stunned her into silence, but seemed to produce the opposite effect on him. As if released from some self-imposed solitary confinement, he continued airing his concerns about her family (specifically Lydia), her father's naïve reliance on the Delany legacy and, most importantly, her chosen area of study. "Our firm won't even allow investments in anyone associated with violent rap music. How could I be involved with someone who …" his voice trailed off.

By this time, she was seething, her chest rising with each hot breath. Then she smirked. "Thank you … *Dr.* Darcy." He flinched.

"Why, here I was, all worried and wondering what to do, thinking, maybe? And then bam! You come in talking a line of *arrogant bullshit* and whoosh! Like magic. I know *exactly* what to do."

"Excuse me?" he said, looking confused.

She shook her head. "You have *no* idea, do you? And for that reason, I'm going to go easy on you and just say goodbye." She stepped through the door into the bedroom, but he grabbed her by the arm. "Is that it?"

She wrenched away, picked up her heels, and sat down on the bedside to slip them on. "Yep, and if you knew *anything* about us Southern Black girls, you'd be counting your blessings right now."

He looked down at her. "Oh, I see. You're offended by a bit of honesty. Maybe I should have flattered you with sweet talk and pushed aside what *I* was going through. But you should know by now that's not my style."

She stood up. "That wouldn't have worked either. I decided to kick you to the curb after I overheard your scheme to keep Charles away from Jane. How could I even *think* of caring for a man who is ultimately responsible for hurting my sister like that?"

His eyes told her he didn't understand. "I heard you in the Ancestors Garden this afternoon," she explained. "Do you deny it?"

"No, I do not. I was trying to help my friend—"

"By telling him to abandon Jane? Why? Is *she* not good enough for him, either?"

"You couldn't be more wrong," he whispered, and turned away. "I only wish I had someone to help set me straight in all … this." His last words came out as a sneer.

His back was to her, and she could have easily smacked him upside the head with her handbag. But she felt enough had been said. And done. *I told my wrath; my wrath did end.*

She placed her purse on the bed and brought her hands to her hair to try to get it back into the style she had a few hours ago. She lowered her head to secure the pearl hair comb. When she looked up, he was staring at her, his eyes soft and wondering. "Would telling you I'm in love with you make any difference?" he whispered.

Lizzy picked up her purse and tucked it under her arm. "William, I think it's time we end this right now. After expressing your *true* feelings, I really can't see the point. Can you?"

He took a hopeful step towards her. "I'm not ashamed of my feelings, and I know them to be sincere."

She shook her head. "I'm not that woman, William. I can't see how I could *ever* love you."

CHAPTER 38

Lizzy walked into a half-empty ballroom. Her family was still at their table, minus Jane. She glanced around but couldn't see her anywhere. "There you are!" Mary said. "We've been looking for you."

"Oh?" she answered, willing her voice to stay even. "I was wandering around and found myself ... outside. Have you seen the pool area? It's really nice!" She would have to rely on Jane's description of the place if there were more questions.

Mary squinted. "Really? I didn't see you there."

She offered a shrug and a lopsided smile. "Well, I'm here now. Where's Jane?"

Her mother smiled. "Off with Charles Bingley, who has said he will drive her home." She clapped her hands. "Hopefully with an engagement ring!"

Lizzy noticed a few heads turn their way. "Mother, you shouldn't jump to conclusions like that. Jane knows what she's doing."

"I know, I know. It's all just so exciting. To think! Our Jane, the mistress of Netherfield!"

Mr. Bennet stood up. "That's enough fantasizing Mrs. B. Lizzy is right, so let's leave it to Jane and go home." He turned his eyes on Lizzy. "We were waiting for you."

Lizzy's hand went to her chest, feeling a bit embarrassed. "Sorry. I, ummm, lost track of the time." This wasn't entirely untrue, she told herself. Her father kept his eyes on her for a few seconds more before leaving the table. The family joined him, and the Bennets began their exit.

Caroline Bingley was standing near the door, bidding goodbye to her guests. Next to her stood an older, distinguished looking woman using a cane for support.

"Thank you for a lovely evening. I am sure the Westside Clinic will benefit greatly from your efforts." Mr. Bennet smiled. "The entire community is grateful you all are here."

Caroline smiled awkwardly. Lizzy could guess why. No doubt she had plans to abandon them, just like her brother. "Well, thank you, and I am so glad you all enjoyed yourselves." She turned to the woman beside her. "Let me introduce you to Dr. Darcy's aunt, Dr. Catherine Deburge."

"Oh!" said Mr. Bennet. "Doctors must run in the family."

Dr. Deburge smiled thinly. "Yes, but I'm a medical doctor. Retired."

Mrs. Bennet nodded. "Ahhh …"

Catherine Deburge, though small in stature, possessed an imposing figure.

"Very nice to meet you, Doctor," Mr. Bennet said. "Sorry we didn't get a chance to chat earlier, but let me introduce you to my daughters."

Dr. Deburge nodded and offered a small smile to each of the now three daughters. She lifted an eyebrow when Mr. Bennet finished. "I understood there are *five* daughters?"

"Yes," Mrs. Bennet said. "Jane is with Charles. They've become quite close, you see. And our youngest, Lydia, couldn't make it, I'm afraid."

Caroline's slight smirk told Lizzy she probably knew the real reason.

"I met your Jane earlier. Quite a lovely woman. And a nurse. MSN," Dr. Deburge said.

Mrs. Bennet beamed. "Yes! We are very proud of our girls, aren't we, my dear?"

"Very," he answered. "But we won't keep you. It's been a long night, and I am sure an even longer day for you, Miss Bingley."

"Yes, it has," Caroline answered. "Good night then. So glad you could join us."

"She seemed nice," Mrs. Bennet remarked after the family was in their car, heading home.

Longbourne was dark and quiet when the family entered. "I'll go check on Lydia," Kitty offered as the rest of the family filed into the sitting room. "Tea?" Mrs. Bennet asked. She patted her middle section. "I know I could use some to settle my stomach after all that rich food." Lizzy suppressed the urge to run upstairs to her room and took a seat on the window settee. Her father had questioned her about her poolroom visit during the drive home. It hadn't felt like a cross-examination, but she began to wonder if he doubted her story. "I'll take one, Mother," she said.

Mary plopped down on the sofa. "Did you eat anything, Lizzy? *I* overdid it at that chocolate fountain!"

Kitty rejoined them. "She's asleep."

Mrs. Bennet had just returned with five cups of peppermint tea when Jane came home. She paused by the door. She had been crying. "I hope those are happy tears," Mrs. Bennet said, handing her husband his mug. Everyone else could tell they were not.

Jane shook her head. "I just said goodbye to Charles—"

"What?!" Mrs. Bennet exclaimed. "You mean for the night—"

"Let her finish," Mr. Bennet said.

Jane took a deep breath. "No. He has to go back to their offices in California for … awhile." She turned imploring eyes on Lizzy.

"Oh, is that all?" Mrs. Bennet said, taking her seat next to her husband. "Don't worry, Jane. You know what they say. Absence makes the heart grow fonder. When he comes back, well, you'll see."

Mr. Bennet, who had been watching his eldest, suggested she go up to bed. "You look tired. Maybe we'll all sleep in and skip church tomorrow."

"Yes!" said Mary.

Lizzy set her cup down. "I'm beat, too." She followed Jane upstairs and into her bedroom.

"He's not coming back!" Jane cried before collapsing into her sister's arms. Lizzy guided her onto the bedside. She let Jane cry and felt her anger at William Darcy rise. *I should have smacked him when I had the chance!* After a few moments, Jane pulled away and wiped her face on the tissues Lizzy handed. "Now," Lizzy said. "Tell me exactly what happened."

Jane took a deep inhale. "I should have expected it, you know. He's been acting so differently lately. More ... serious." She shrugged. "The hints, as they say."

Lizzy encouraged her to share what Charles had told her. "That's what matters, Jane. What he said."

Jane agreed and told her that Charles felt it would be better for both of them if he returned to his life, and she hers. "He kept talking about how he couldn't give me what I wanted," she said, sounding confused. "What do you think he meant?"

Lizzy shook her head slowly. "No idea. What else did he say? That he was giving up Netherfield? After all the money they put into it?"

"I did ask him about that, but he just dismissed it, saying the company could use it as an investment." Jane paused and Lizzy saw another tear fall. "He said it wasn't his *real* home!"

Lizzy's heart fell. "Oh, Jane. I'm so sorry. I don't know what to say. It all seems just so ..."

Jane brought her hands to her face. "My head is pounding," she said, massaging her temples. "I need to sleep, but seriously doubt any will come."

Lizzy stood up and told Jane to get ready for bed. "I'll bring you some tea and aspirin?"

Jane nodded. "Thank you. And Lizzy, please don't say anything to Mother. I'm not ready to talk about it. I may even call-in sick Monday so I don't have to face Mrs. Griff. Or anyone else."

When Lizzy returned with the tea and aspirin, Jane was in bed, but not asleep. She left everything on her bedside table and went to her own room. It was already Sunday when she finally made it to bed.

. . .

Darcy did not rejoin the ball. He stayed in his room, fell asleep, and when he woke up hours later, he went to his office. It was 3AM, and it took him 15 minutes to draft an email to Drs. Baei and Lucas, outlining his intentions to leave Delany after this semester. It was direct and offered no apologies. He gazed at the bright screen, hearing his father's reproach. "Darcys don't quit," or worse, "Always be a man of honor and principle." There was nothing principled about abandoning the university this way. He moved the email to his drafts folder and powered down the PC. In four hours, he would take Charles to the airport in Raleigh. His escape was of a different nature and one Darcy hoped would relieve his friend. Out of sight, out of mind, as the saying goes. But that night, he felt that an escape to the moon wouldn't do the same for him.

. . .

The sound of raised voices and pounding feet coming from downstairs woke Lizzy. It was 8AM. She heard pounding steps in the hallway and her mother's and father's voices. "What do you mean, she's not in bed?"

"Oh god," she moaned.

"I thought she was asleep," Kitty was saying when Lizzy joined them. Kitty pointed to the bed. "It looked like she was still in there!"

Mr. Bennet stood over the empty bed, except for the pillows Lydia had arranged to look like a sleeping body. His breathing seemed labored. "Did you hear anything during the night? Or early this morning? Maybe she left then, and not last night."

Kitty shook her head. "No, but I was pretty tired. I'm sorry ..." She cried.

"It's not your fault, Katherine," he told her, softening his voice. "I'm sorry I yelled." He looked at his family, who had crammed into the small bedroom. "I suggest we get dressed and meet in the kitchen to plan what to do next. She couldn't have gotten far."

Mrs. Bennet, who looked more angry than worried, shook her head. "She *wouldn't*," she whispered. "Our Lydia. She wouldn't do this to us ..." She gazed at her husband. "Would she, Harold?" Her mouth trembled, right before her eyes filled with tears. Mr. Bennet put his arm around his wife. "No, of course not. She's probably just out. You know how Lydia hates going to church."

Five minutes later, the daughters walked into the kitchen. Their mother sat at the kitchen table, the family phone book opened in front of her, their father on the phone. "Yes, sorry to bother you so early, James, but we were wondering if Lydia happened to be there visiting Amber." He nodded. "No, no, nothing wrong. She just left the house without telling anybody anything." More nodding. "Well, if you hear anything from Amber, let us know." He hung up the phone and looked at his wife. "Try the Wilsons," she said. "Lydia used to be friends with Michelle, back in junior high." She read out the number.

Jane went to the counter and started making coffee. Lizzy, Mary, and Kitty sat down. Once their father hung up the phone, he joined them and asked Kitty to make a list of any other people Lydia could be with. Kitty and Lizzy exchanged cautious looks, which their father saw. "Everyone," he added. Kitty got up to get a piece of paper from the kitchen junk drawer.

"Jane and I can take the Saturn and drive around town," Lizzy offered.

Her father agreed. "I was going to do that later, but I think you two going would be better. I should stay here with your mother."

The family discussed possibilities, keeping them light and benign. "She's probably just hanging out at the mall," Mary offered, ignoring the fact that Lydia was grounded. The ringing doorbell brought further conversation to an ominous halt. Mrs. Bennet reached out and grabbed her husband's hand. "Oh, dear God, Mr. B. My heart can't stand this."

"I'll get it," Mary said. A few seconds later, everyone exhaled when they saw Darren follow Mary back into the kitchen. Only Kitty noticed his worried look. "What's wrong, Darren?" she said, getting up to stand beside him.

Wickham was missing but was seen with Lydia late last night, about two in the morning. He shrugged. "One of my brothers happened to see them when he was coming home from the Crash Pad." He turned to Kitty. "I promised to I'd let you know, and when I saw your 911 message, I thought I should come over."

"Let you know *what*?!" Mr. Bennet rose slowly and stared down at the young man. "Kitty?"

Lizzy stood up too. "Father, you know how Lydia was acting ... infatuated with that Wickham. Darren was our look-out—"

Mr. Bennet turned searing eyes on Lizzy. "Are you telling me that my child has been hanging out with a grown-ass man, and no one thought to tell me? Her *father*?"

"Harold, George Wickham comes by the house now and then to see us, and Lydia, I suppose, but I've *always* been here. It can't be him," Mrs. Bennet said, sounding like she was trying to convince herself more than her husband.

Mr. Bennet turned back to Darren and motioned for Kitty to sit down. Darren made to move with her, but Mr. Bennet stopped him. "Not you. Stay where you are and tell me everything you know."

Darren shared how Mashujaa leadership had changed their minds about working with Wickham and asked him to leave, but because of another incident, they kept an eye on him. "We just didn't want any trouble, sir."

Mr. Bennet's face twisted in anger, and he brought his hand to his chest and rubbed it like he was trying to stop his heart from bursting through. "Well, you failed. I'm calling the police." He took three steps towards the phone, stopped as if he had hit a wall, then collapsed to the floor.

CHAPTER 39

Charles and William sat in the first-class lounge, sipping coffee. "You don't have to wait with me," Charles said.

"I know," Darcy answered, "but nothing's going on at home except for your sister and my aunt bickering over the party clean up."

"That's true." Charles gazed out the window. It was another overcast morning, but from his time in the area, he knew the sun would soon be out in full force soon. "I will miss this place," he said. "Especially the people. And not just Jane. Everyone is so … nice."

Not everyone, Darcy thought. "When will Caroline be leaving?"

Charles didn't know exactly, but it was sure to be before December. "She's on to her next project. Our big Y2K party."

On the drive to the airport, Charles had shared little about his talk with Jane. Only that she took it well and cried, but just a little. "It's better this way," he kept repeating. The lounge attendant came over to tell him the flight was ready to board. "Well, I guess that's it," Charles said, looking at Darcy. They embraced. "See ya in San Fran? We need to ring in the new century together!"

"I'll be there," he told Charles. He left the airport parking lot, but did not head back to Netherfield. Nothing for me there, he mused, driving in the opposite direction.

.   .   .

Everyone except Mrs. Bennet stood up when the ER doctor returned to the family waiting room. He nodded at Jane. "Good thing you were there," he said. "Or else it could have been a lot worse." Their mother released an achingly sad groan.

He turned to Jane and shared an update, speaking in medical terms and leaving the rest of the family worried and bewildered.

"In *English,* please," their mother finally moaned, causing the doctor to pause.

"I'll explain it all to them," Jane said. "When can we see him?"

Their father was going for a CAT scan, and then he could have visitors. "I'll send a nurse to let you know." He left them.

Jane took a seat next to her mother. "It's mild, Mother. Father will be fine. They'll run some tests and decide what to do next, depending on the severity of the blockage."

"Blockage! What do you mean?"

"His arteries, Mother. Father had a ... heart attack."

Her mother showered Jane with more questions, most of them she could not answer. "Mother, you—we all—will need to be very patient right now. These recoveries can take a lot of time."

Mrs. Bennet cried out, causing Jane to wrap a protective arm around her shoulders. "He'll be fine, Mother. I promise." Mary and Kitty stood around, offering their own encouragement. Lizzy sat away from her family, staring out at the blank space in front of her. All she could see was her father's anger-filled eyes staring back. Her well-intentioned plan to protect the family backfired in the most tragic way. Hot tears fell down her cheeks, and she knew she needed to make this right, whatever it took.

"Mother, I'm going to call Aunt Joyce," Lizzy said, standing in front of her family. "Now that we know more, we should inform them so that they can let others know." Her mother sniffed and nodded. Lizzy tapped Mary on the shoulder, who followed her into the hallway. Once outside, Lizzy reached into her purse, pulled out her wallet, and handed Mary some money. "Use this to get a taxi home if I'm not back by then. I'm going to see what I can find out about Lydia and Wickham."

Forty-five minutes later, she ran up the Netherfield front steps and banged on the door. A startled Miss Sarah answered after several more knocks. "Lizzy Bennet!" she gasped. "What's the matter?"

Lizzy walked past her and into the entryway. "Where's Dr. Darcy? I need to see him—now." Lizzy began walking towards the staircase.

"What's all that commotion?" Caroline asked, coming in from the back of the house. She saw Lizzy. "Excuse me. Did you forget something last night?"

Lizzy took a deep breath. "I need to speak to him right now," she said, then pointed upstairs. "Is he in his room?"

If Caroline was surprised by Lizzy's knowledge of Darcy's bedroom, she didn't show it. Instead, she took slow, deliberate steps towards Lizzy. "No, he is not. He took Charles to Raleigh this morning for his flight back to Napa." She checked her watch. "He should have been home hours ago, and I have no idea where he's gone to. Have you checked the university?"

Delany is locked up on Sundays, but she didn't want to waste time explaining. "Tell him to contact me as soon as he gets back. Please." She headed back towards the front door.

"Don't I get to know what caused you to come crashing into my home?" Caroline called after her.

"That's what I want to know." Lizzy turned to see Dr. Deburge slowly moving towards them.

Lizzy shook her head. "I don't have time for this," she said and continued out. "Forget them!" she mumbled. She was back in her Saturn, about to turn the ignition, when his car pulled up. She jumped out and was upon him before he could come to a stop and exit his car. "Tell me where Wickham is!" she shouted.

The following back and forth consisted of him wanting to know what was wrong, and her insisting that he must know Wickham's whereabouts.

"Lizzy!" he yelled in frustration. "You need to calm down and tell me what's going on. I can clearly see how upset you are, but I can't help unless I know more." He felt his heart clinch at the sight of tears streaming down her face. "Please."

She crossed her arms and used a finger to wipe a tear away. "You'll find out soon enough," she whispered. "Lydia ran away last night. And we think she's with … Wickham."

Darcy took a step back, stunned. "What? Are you sure? What's being done to get her back? Have the police been notified?"

The image of her father reaching for the phone, then collapsing, flashed before her, causing her shoulders to shake as a wave of convulsing tears broke free. Darcy pulled her into an embrace. "Dear god, Lizzy. Tell me what's happened."

Lizzy continued to cry, from worry and fear over her father and Lydia, and anger at herself. After a moment, she told him they hadn't had time to call the police. She pushed out of his arms, not wanting to tell him anymore. "We want to find her first. That's why I need you to tell me everything about Wickham."

He started to deny any knowledge of the man's whereabouts, but Lizzy cut him off. "You *knew* he had been in prison, didn't you? But you kept it to yourself. Maybe if *we* had known, this wouldn't have happened."

He placed his hand over his heart. "Lizzy, I swear to you that if I had any idea that he would do something like this, I would have tried to stop him. When I found out he was here at Delany, I went straight to Dr. Lucas to tell him my concerns."

That was true, but she still wasn't satisfied. "Just promise me that if you hear anything you won't keep it to yourself."

"Of course. And please, let me know if there is anything you or your family need."

Lizzy mumbled a thank you, then went back to her car. He followed. "You're in no state to drive. Let me take you back. We can get someone to take your car later."

"No. I'm not going back to Longbourne."

"Well, let me take you to wherever you need to go. You're too upset to drive."

"I drove here," she said. He looked genuinely concerned; she couldn't deny that. She sighed. "Don't worry about me," she said. "I'm okay now."

Darcy stood and watched her drive away. After her car turned onto the road leading back towards Merryton, he left the driveway and entered the house.

"What was *that* all about?" Caroline had been waiting for him. He pushed down the flash of annoyance and told her it was nothing.

"Really? It didn't seem like nothing. Why, you should have seen the way she burst into here screaming for you." Caroline emitted a ticking sound before continuing. "You would think she was yelling for her baby daddy or something." The bubble of laughter halted in her throat when she saw Darcy's cutting look.

"You've gone too far, Caroline," he whispered. He left, taking the stairs two at a time, leaving a bewildered and humiliated Caroline alone in the entryway.

After an hour of phone calls, talking to three different parties, and a hefty dose of begging, he finally got the name and contact information of the private detective the Kings had on Wickham. It was a local firm and Carlton promised to contact him right away and give him permission to share his findings with Darcy. "It *is* Sunday, you know?" Carlton King told him. "It may not be until early in the week." Darcy prayed it would be sooner. "Have him call me as soon as he can." He gave Carlton the house and his office number at Delany, along with his cellphone number.

Hours earlier, after leaving Charles and the airport, he headed east towards the Atlantic Ocean and ended up in a town called Washington. *The Original; 1776,* according to the welcome sign. He drove to the waterfront and spent an hour wandering around the docks, convincing himself that now was a good time to take up sailing. He would look into it. He invented other things to keep him busy as he walked, and when he finally made it back to his car, he had convinced himself that there was enough going on in his life that he needn't worry about anything else. But then she appeared, looking frightened and vulnerable. He abandoned his lists.

"There you are." His Aunt Catherine looked up from her reading as he entered the library. "I thought you fell in a hole or something."

Darcy bent down to give her a kiss on the cheek. "No, nothing like that," he said. "I just needed to clear my head. That's all." He went to the bar, reached for his Scotch, then stopped. He may need to drive soon. "Where's Caroline?" he asked, taking a seat.

Catherine closed her book and set it on the table in front of her. "She's upstairs. Claims she's tired from yesterday and … other things."

Darcy sighed. "I'll apologize."

Aunt Catherine grunted her approval. "Now, will you tell me what's going on? I saw the young lady, and she was clearly distressed." She peered at her nephew. "You didn't …?"

Darcy avoided her eyes and looked down at his hands. "The Bennets have a long history here. They are a well-respected family."

"I gathered that last night. Dr. Lucas spoke highly of them," Aunt Catherine said.

Darcy gazed across the room, his mind elsewhere. Finally, the elderly aunt tapped her cane on the floor to get his attention. "Respected *and* protected, I assume," she said. "May I speak bluntly, nephew?"

Darcy scoffed. "If I say no, will that stop you?"

She grinned and wagged a finger at him. "Ha! You know me well."

"So?" he asked, bracing for what she could say.

Aunt Catherine paused before continuing. "William, you're a young, eligible man. Elizabeth Bennet is a very attractive and smart young woman, but would it be wise for you to pursue—?" Darcy stood up suddenly, causing her to stop mid-sentence. He stuffed his hands in his pockets and walked to the cold fireplace.

"She doesn't want me, Aunt Catherine," he said, staring into the empty hearth. "She made that perfectly clear last night."

"Ahh," she said, nodding slowly. "And how do we feel about that?"

He turned around to face her. "Judging by what you were about to say, I'd say you must feel relieved. Me? All I can say is that it's too soon to tell."

Miss Sarah knocked on the doorjamb to get their attention. "I have a little dinner ready for you all, if you're hungry."

Aunt Catherine was ready to eat and pushed Darcy into joining her. "I can see you haven't eaten all day."

.   .   .

Darcy spent a restless night and wanted nothing more than to make an early escape from Netherfield. But having promised his aunt, he forced himself to sit at the breakfast table and make small talk, knowing Caroline would take the gesture as his apology. "I'm sort of looking forward to our tour today, Aunt Catherine," Caroline said as she finished her toast. "Should be fun to get a behind-the-scenes look."

"Fun? A free clinic in an impoverished part of town is fun?"

Caroline glanced awkwardly at Darcy, her eyes screaming, save me. But he was too busy worrying about what they could find out while there.

"I didn't mean fun as in funny, Aunt. I meant more interesting … fun."

Aunt Catherine smirked. "Well, it will be interesting." She looked at the nephew. "Why don't you come with us? And go to Delany afterwards?"

His morning was free, as far as teaching was concerned, but he needed to be close to a phone, and there were a few people on campus he wanted to talk to about Wickham.

"As much as I would love to," he said, getting up from the table, "academia calls."

When he arrived, the campus was just beginning to fill up, and walking along the path, he recognized a few faces. Everyone smiled and nodded. Charles was right. People here seemed to be friendly and more open. On the West Coast, everyone walked with their heads down, afraid to make eye contact. Before going to his office, he was drawn to the Ancestors Garden and allowed himself a few minutes to wander. Entering, he suddenly realized why Lizzy sought it out as a place of refuge. It was almost like stepping into another world; a sacred space away from everything else. The Bennet ancestors should be very proud of what they had created.

"Good morning, Dr. Darcy." He returned to the present to see Chantell walking towards him.

"Good morning, Chantell," he said, squinting at the sight of her face. "Have you been crying?"

Chantell nodded. "It's just so sad," she sniffed. "Poor Mr. Bennet."

The legacy. He glanced around the garden. "Yes, I agree. But I'm sure it has nothing to do with him personally, or with his family. It's most likely a strictly financial decision."

It was Chantell's turn to look confused. "What are you talking about, Dr. Darcy? Mr. Bennet had a heart attack yesterday and is in the hospital. *That's* why I'm upset, along with almost everybody else."

"Yesterday? When?"

"In the morning. It's crazy, you know? He had *just* called my house to ask if we'd seen Lydia." She shook her head. "My dad thinks the worry about her could have caused it."

"Mr. Bennet called your family hoping to find his daughter?"

Chantell nodded and explained how her younger sister, Amber, had been good friends with Lydia. "But they sort of fell out a few years ago." She lowered her voice. "Everyone says Lydia's gotten kind of wild."

Darcy agreed with that assessment.

Chantell waved a piece of paper. "I've got to go to the library and make copies before my first class. My mom and some other ladies from the church are putting together a meal train."

He nodded absently, his mind full of questions and frustrations. It was only when he was almost at his office that he wondered: What's a meal train?

At his desk, he went directly to email. Dr. Lucas had sent out a notice informing the staff of an unfortunate event.

Harold Bennet, our beloved groundskeeper, suffered a heart attack early Sunday morning. He is at Merryton General, recovering well. Doctors say the prognosis is good. Please respect the family's privacy at this time and route all correspondence through Family Services in our personnel office. Professor Elizabeth Bennet is on leave until further notice.

No mention of a missing Lydia. Had they located her yet? No, she would have told him if they had. If anything tragic happened with Mr. Bennet or Lydia, this would be the second time Wickham's immoral behavior brought a family to ruin. He banged his fist in frustration. Is Lizzy right? Was he to blame for this?

He had pulled open the middle desk drawer to search for the campus directory when Mrs. Hoffman buzzed. "There's a gentleman here to see you, Dr. Darcy. He doesn't have an appointment."

Darcy stood when he entered. A short, thin man, dressed in a cheap-looking tweed suit with a narrow dark brown tie. In his hand he held a worn, black fedora-style hat. The man looked like someone had plucked him from a 1950s cop movie. "Morning, Mr. Darcy. My name is Clint Wood of the Wood's Detective Agency. Carlton King asked me to share some … intel with you." He looked cautiously at the open door behind him.

"I was expecting a phone call," Darcy said, moving behind his desk to close the door. He took a seat in front of the desk and the detective took the other, and set an oversized brown envelope on the desk. "Yeah, well, I had to see you in the flesh," he said with a sly smile. "These days, you never know who's on the other end." He emitted a loud "Tksch!" by clicking his tongue against the top of his mouth. "Can't be too careful."

Darcy swallowed his impatience. "Very clever of you," he said.

Detective Wood took the compliment with a huge smile. "Thank you." He reached for the envelope and handed it to Dr. Darcy. "This is all we have on one George Thaddeus Wickham so far." He pulled a slim notepad from his upper suit pocket and flipped it open. "Last seen in these parts boarding the Raleigh Station Greyhound heading west. We assume his final destination will be somewhere in Northern California." He tucked the notepad back into its pocket.

Darcy opened the envelope and slid out its contents. "And was he alone?"

"That's a negative." Detective Wood leaned forward and took the stack of photos from Darcy's hands. He searched through them and then presented his find to Darcy. "This fellow and that young lady were with him. In fact, it was Wickham that bought the tickets. This one," he pointed to the young man, "is—excuse me, was—a member of that fraternity, *Maa-shew*, whatever. His name is Taylor Anderson. He and that little bird, one Lydia Bennet, have been spending a lot of time together, if you know what I mean." *Tksch!*

Darcy studied the photograph. He recognized the man to be the same one he saw Lydia fooling around with in the garden. "I thought they hired you to look into Wickham, not young lovers."

Detective Wood nodded. "Oh yeah, but these three have become thick as thieves lately. I think they were using Wickham's place for their little love nest."

Darcy set the photo aside to look through the others. He was tiring of this man's crude talk about Lizzy's younger sister. "Did it seem like Lydia was being taken against her will, or anything like that?"

He shook his head quickly. "Not at all. We figure with both Wickham *and* Taylor now persona non gratis at that frat house *and* Delany University, they decided to vamos out of here and take the chickee with them." He shrugged. "'Cause, why not?'"

Darcy looked at him coldly. "Her name is Lydia Bennet." He took a deep inhale to calm himself; as revolting as this man was, he needed to keep him talking. "You seem to have discovered quite a lot about the situation."

Another proud smile. "Oh yeah. Once I got a guy in here working undercover and such, it was pretty easy." *Tksch!*

"Undercover? That seems extreme."

Detective Wood laughed. "And necessary." He held his hands up to his sides. "I mean, look at me. I *hardly* blend in."

Darcy reluctantly agreed. Detective Clint Wood was white.

The distinct sound of a cell phone ringing caused both men to pat their pockets in search of their devices. "That's me," Detective Wood said. He tucked the phone between his ear and shoulder, leaving his hands free to take out his pad and pen. "Talk to me," Detective Wood said into his phone. He used Darcy's desk to take notes.

While he talked, Darcy looked through the remaining photos. Mostly benign; Wickham jogging, sitting with others he assumed were members of the fraternity, walking with Taylor, sometimes alone with Lydia and then one that caused Darcy's heart to drop. George Wickham and Lizzy Bennet, together at what appeared to be a bar, sitting close, drinks on the table, and smiling at each other. There was one more of the twosome, this one taken from the outside, looking in through the large window. They sat at a diner, enjoying a meal. It looked like Lizzy was laughing. He tossed the photos on his desk as if they were burning his fingers.

"All right, thanks. Good work." Detective Wood closed his phone. "That was my guy. He's on the Greyhound with Wickham, et al."

Darcy folded his hands together and turned his head to stare out the window. He could easily wash his hands of this matter, send that email to Dr. Lucas, and leave, with no need to return. But he promised her. He turned back to Detective Wood. "And?"

"They're in Houston. Apparently, that's as far as Wickham's money would take them. The girl—Lydia Bennet—is mad as hell and screaming about wanting to go back home."

Darcy thought for a moment. "Lydia's a minor. Do you think the authorities could get involved?" An interstate scandal such as this would only exacerbate Mr. Bennet's health issues.

"You ain't from around here, are you?" The detective smirked. "Sixteen. Once that happens, these kids can do pretty much *anything* they want, and their parents can't do a damn thing to stop them. Plus, since she's technically with Taylor, *not* Wickham, their age difference is A-Okay with the law here." *Tksch!*

Darcy walked to the window and gazed down at the garden, knowing what he had to do. "Would it be possible for 'your guy' to keep me informed of their movements?"

Detective Wood agreed, and they exchanged numbers. He held out his hand. "Good luck to you, Mr. Darcy." He looked down at the photos. "You can have those."

Before he left, Darcy had one more question. "They hired you to locate any assets Wickham may have hidden from the Kings. Any luck?"

Detective Wood eyed Darcy suspiciously. "Not yet, but we—me and the west coast firm they hired—think he may have them socked away in 'Frisco. Does Wickham owe you money too?"

Darcy shook his head.

"That guy's a piece of work!" Detective Wood said. "I looked into the case and wow! Too bad he was dumb enough not to check that little fairy for a wire." *Tksch!*

Darcy spoke through gritted teeth. "You seem to be collecting a lot of fees while failing to produce results. Mrs. King must really trust you."

Detective Wood replaced his hat. "The Kings ain't paying me, although I do report to them, too." He shook his head at Darcy's questioning look. "Can't reveal that, confidentiality and all." He turned to leave, then stopped. "But let's just say it's someone else who was *intimately* involved with the case." *Tksch!*

After he left, Darcy gathered the photos and slid them back into the envelope. *That's* Dr. *Darcy, asshole.* He put the envelope in his satchel, then buzzed the front desk. "Could you come into my office, Mrs. Hoffman? I need your help with something."

CHAPTER 40

Claire Hoffman's heels clicked on the hospital's gleaming white tile floor. The lobby receptionist told her that Harold Bennet was on the second floor. She walked to the elevator and pressed the call button. A few seconds later, stepping into the empty elevator, she still couldn't believe that Dr. William Darcy had enlisted her help in his Lydia Bennet rescue mission.

The request to enter his office was an unusual one, but then again, it had been an unusual morning. Greeted with the news of her dear friend and former classmate Harold Bennet's medical emergency, she was already primed for a stressful day. In his office, when Dr. Darcy asked her to sit, she worried more.

He was standing by the window. "The man who just left is a private detective hired by some acquaintances of mine in the hopes that he could discover any hidden assets of a man called George Wickham." Mrs. Hoffman nodded. "Do you know of him?"

"No, not as in the *we've-met* sense, but there's been talk. Apparently, he is really good at borrowing money, but loses his memory when it's time to pay it back."

Darcy sighed. "That's him." He wanted to share as little as possible, but he also knew Mrs. Hoffman was close friends with the Bennets. "You've heard about Mr. Bennet's heart attack?" She had. "And do you know anything about his youngest daughter, Lydia?"

She nodded. "My brother is the father of one of Lydia's school friends. Her name is Amber."

Darcy looked incredulous. "Is everyone in this town related? Amber is ... Chantell's sister?"

"Yes, my nieces."

"So you're aware she went missing Saturday night? Well, that man told me where she is, and I plan to go get her."

.　　.　　.

And get her he did, Mrs. Hoffman thinks as she searched for the correct hospital room. Money sure can make things happen. And quick. She spied three of the daughters sitting in the waiting area. "Hello girls. How's your father?" They all looked exhausted, and even more worried.

"Mother and Jane are in the room now, talking to the surgeon," Mary told her. "Father's bypass surgery is tomorrow."

Mrs. Hoffman's hand flew to her mouth. "Oh, girls, I am *so* sorry. But don't worry! There isn't a man stronger than your father and between the doctors and our prayers, he'll pull through." She looked over at Professor Bennet, who sat quietly. Truthfully, she hadn't been too surprised by Dr. Darcy's intentions. She had seen these two together around campus, and although neither probably had a clue, she could see exactly what was, or would be happening between them. "Well, I have good news," she said. "Lydia is found and will be back in Merryton," she checked her watch, "in about two hours." Dr. Darcy had called from the Houston airport to let her know they were about to board. "You can tell the Bennets she's coming home, but please don't mention my involvement," he requested.

Lizzy jumped up. "What do you mean? Who found her? Where is she, and how is she getting home?"

Mrs. Hoffman held up her hands. "I know you all have a ton of questions, but just know that she is in safe hands. We can talk about the details later."

"Is she all right?" Kitty asked.

"Perfectly." She let the news digest before continuing. "Now, what I need to know is, do you want her to be taken directly to Longbourne, or here, the hospital?"

"Here," Lizzy said. "Father will want to see her before ..." She started crying. Mrs. Hoffman hugged her and said she thought that was a good idea. She left a few minutes later, but while waiting for the elevator, she heard Mrs. Bennet's jubilant cry at the news. "You done good, Dr. Darcy," she whispered as she entered the elevator. "Very good, indeed."

.   ▪   ▪

Dr. Darcy pulled his Lexus into the circular driveway of Merryton General Hospital and stopped at the front entrance. It was almost 9PM, but Mrs. Hoffman had told him that the Bennet family would still be there. They had taken to sleeping in the family waiting area and took turns sitting with their father. The hospital staff had given up on asking them to go home. Lydia unbuckled her seatbelt, picked up her backpack and laid it in her lap. She stared at the entrance like she was looking down a deep well. "Do you think they hate me very much?" she asked, her voice barely audible. Darcy followed her gaze. Since picking her up almost five hours ago, this was the first time he had seen or heard her display any regret or remorse. She had the uncanny habit of being completely oblivious to the effect her actions may have on others. It took little convincing to get her to come with him, and on the flight back, she spent the first 20 minutes fawning over the first-class cabin, and then fell asleep, only to wake up after they landed in Raleigh. Darcy suppressed a yawn and turned to her. "They may be upset, and a little angry, but I am also sure that the relief and happiness at seeing you back safe will overcome all other feelings."

Lydia swallowed and looked down at her hands perched on top of her stuffed backpack. "Do you think I caused it? The heart attack?"

Darcy placed his hand on top of hers and squeezed. "I can understand how you would feel that way, but no, I do not think you caused it."

"Thank you. And thanks for coming to get me." She hugged her backpack to her chest. "It started out as a good idea, but then it just …" She turned to him, her hands expressive. "I felt like I was watching myself from above, you know? Looking down and I couldn't speak or do anything. It was *crazy*. Have you ever felt like that, Dr. Darcy? Ha! Probably not, you being so rich and all." She sighed. "I need to get rich, so I don't have to worry about *anything* and be happy all the time!"

Darcy marveled at how quickly she moved from deep reflection to rambling teenager. He smiled. "I'm sorry Lydia, but what they say is true. Money does not buy happiness."

She squinted at him. "It doesn't?"

"No," he answered slowly. "It most certainly does not."

After a moment, he told her it was time to part. "Your family is waiting for you." He watched her run inside and drove away when she was out of sight. He needed sleep. Desperately.

CHAPTER 41

Darcy's eyes opened slowly. He blinked at the morning sun and rolled onto his back. It was a plain ceiling. Very different from the one in his bedroom at Pemberley Towers. That one has a sunken ceiling with soft, recessed lighting around the perimeter and the original Tiffany ceiling light hanging directly over his California King sized bed. He closed his eyes and rolled back to his side. Two long days ago she was here with him, and for a few blissful moments, he had believed his months' long agony was coming to an end. "What a fool!" he scolded himself before sitting up.

"Oh god. You look horrible!" Caroline's shocked look greeted him as she entered the breakfast room. He was more hungry than usual, having eaten very little yesterday. "Thank you," he said, his voice thick with sarcasm. "What's for breakfast?"

As if on cue, Corrine entered with his coffee and orange juice. "Thank you, Corrine," he said, downing his juice. "You're an angel." She giggled before going back into the kitchen.

Caroline eyed him curiously. "What happened to you yesterday? And last night? Aunt Catherine and I were wondering."

He didn't want to lie, but telling her the entire story would be an even worse mistake. He met her eyes. "All I can tell you is that some personal and urgent business came up that I had to tend to. Can we leave it at that? Please?"

To his relief, she reached over to give his hand a reassuring squeeze. "Of course, William. I know how *hard* it's been for you these last few months." She smiled. "In fact, I decided to stay at Netherfield to keep you company. What do you say to that?"

"I think it's an excellent idea," Aunt Catherine said, entering the breakfast room. Darcy stood to pull out her chair. "I'm leaving this afternoon and I will feel much better knowing you are not alone here, rattling around in this enormous home."

"My thoughts exactly," Caroline said with a huge smile. "So, what do *you* think, William? Shall we be roomies?"

He thought it was a good idea. "Thank you, Caroline. I appreciate that." He gazed through the breakfast-room window. The sun's rays were lighting up the wooded area that sat on the west side of the mansion. Hints of fall color glowed on branches and shrubs. "With your ball over and the semester winding down," he said, "perhaps we can do some exploring."

"Amen to that!" Caroline cheered. "I *do* believe a weekend on the coast is in order."

They were silent as Corrine came in with the rest of breakfast. After she left, Darcy asked about the tour of Westside. "Was Jane able to show you around?"

Caroline set her coffee cup down. "No, she wasn't, and all we got from them was that she had a family emergency." She sighed. "Poor thing is probably still upset over Charles."

Darcy didn't contradict her, knowing that by lunchtime, Caroline would learn most, if not all, of the Bennet family business. For all her grumbling over Southern life, she sure had taken to Southern gossip.

After breakfast, Aunt Catherine walked him to the door and reminded him not to hide himself away. "I worry about how you get if there's no Charles Bingley around to keep you occupied."

He bent down to kiss her cheek. "Don't worry about me. You just have a safe flight home," he said. "See you at Thanksgiving?"

Her eyebrows lifted. "Oh? I get you for the holiday then?"

He picked up his bag. "Of course. We're family, remember?" he said, giving her one last hug. The only family I have, he thought, walking to his car.

. . .

Mr. Bennet was ready to be discharged and Lizzy, Kitty, and Lydia busied themselves with cleaning the house, shopping for groceries, and getting their parents' room ready. It had been the longest four days in their young lives. Mr. Bennet got to see his youngest daughter before his surgery, and it seemed to make all the difference. Lydia had very little to say about her adventure, and the rest of the Bennets were content to keep it that way. There would be time later.

The day after Lydia's return and Mr. Bennet's successful surgery, Mary and Kitty accompanied Lydia to her school and helped her collect all her missing assignments. "It's going to take her forever to get caught up," Kitty told Lizzy. "She probably won't have enough credits to graduate."

Lizzy had suspected the same, but everyone was relieved Lydia was showing interest in school again and discussing reasonable post high school plans. "I guess Merryton JC is a good place to start," Lydia mused as they made up their parents' bed. "They have a cosmetology department."

Between it all, Lizzy found a few hours to catch up on grading, reviewing her syllabus and deleting assignments and readings she was sure the students would not complain about. All she wanted was for this semester to end. Dr. Wright checked in with her a few times, bringing cards and well wishes from the staff. "Seems like we won't need to contend with that plagiarism mess," she told Lizzy as they sat in the family room one afternoon. "Mr. Taylor Armstrong is MIA and dropped—with failing grades—from all his classes." Lizzy offered a noncommittal response. The little Lydia had shared was that she had left with Taylor, not Wickham. "Wickham!" Lydia gasped. "Why would I want to be with that old man? He's like ... thirty!"

Lizzy decided to take the next semester off, although she wasn't ready to share this with anyone. Between the hospital, helping Lydia getting back on track in school, and preparing the house for her father's return, she hardly had time to think about anything else. Except William Darcy. She often found his strong, proud, and beautiful face staring back at her. He told her he loved her, but how could he really, after sharing his apprehensions? That's not love, she kept telling herself.

"Lizzy?"

She gave her head a quick shake and returned her attention to Dr. Wright. "Sorry, Laura, I was just ..."

Dr. Wright stood to leave. "No worries, my friend. It's time I leave, anyway." She gave Lizzy a huge hug. "Can't wait to have you back!"

Lizzy stood on the front steps of Longbourne and watched her friend disappear into the campus. Her reverence for the university had definitely waned, but she wasn't sure where to lay the blame. The dismantling of the legacy, for sure, but was there more to it than that? The phone ringing interrupted her reflections. She pick up the call on the entryway phone. It was Jane. Father was coming home.

. . .

"Stop fussing! I'm fine." Mr. Bennet looked around at his family. Six women, all focused on seeing to his every need. "Please," he said, softening his voice. "All I want is for everything to get back to normal as quickly as possible, so you all go about doing your own thing and ignoring me just like you used to."

"Father!" Jane gasped. "How can you say that?"

Mr. Bennet laughed. "Well, as you can see, I'm getting my sense of humor back, so everything must be okay."

Mrs. Bennet stepped forward and began readjusting her husband's pillow. "I can take care of your father, girls," she said. "Jane, Lizzy, I know you both have enough to do with getting back to work and everything. You too Mary and Kitty." She straightened up and looked at Lydia. "Now, if you all will leave us with Lydia, there are things to be said."

Kitty and Mary went up to their rooms, Jane and Lizzy walked into the family room. "This is all my fault," Jane said, sinking down onto the sofa. "I'm a NURSE! How could I not see Father was …?" She lowered her face into her hands.

"Jane, you're being too hard on yourself. The doctor said—"

"My mind has been elsewhere, Lizzy. I even miscalculated a patient's meds at the clinic!" She straightened up and squared her shoulders. "I'm beginning to resent Charles Bingley! I mean, how dare he fly in here, mess with a girl's heart, and then just leave!" She folded her arms and leaned back onto the sofa. "Sometimes I wish he had never come here."

Lizzy had the same wish, but for Dr. William Darcy. She sighed.

"Lizzy," Jane said, "I've been meaning to ask about you and William."

Lizzy looked at her hands and shrugged. "Not much to say, really. We had … words at the ball and I probably won't be seeing him again. At least not in any way romantic."

"Words?" Jane asked. "Did he tell you he was leaving, too?"

Lizzy stared over Jane's shoulders at the bookshelves that lined the wall. The sisters typically had no problem sharing intimate details of their relationships, but she couldn't bring herself to tell Jane about what happened with William at the ball. Especially after Charles practically dumped her that same night. Fortunately, the entrance of Lydia, who plopped down on the sofa next to Jane, saved Lizzy from her confused state.

"Well, that wasn't as bad as I thought it would be," Lydia said, laying her hands across her middle section. "Grounded. Of course. Plus, they want me to do community service somewhere. Fifty hours! Claim I must have too much free time." She huffed.

Lizzy nodded. "Sounds like a good idea to me."

"I agree," said Jane. "We always need volunteers at the clinic."

Lydia rolled her eyes. "I *knew* you would say that." She slapped her hands on the sofa. "I wish I had enough money so I could just pay someone to do it for me." The fantasy made her smile. "And my homework."

"Paying someone else to do your homework won't help you get ahead, Lydia. You can't buy happiness, you know."

"That's what Dr. Darcy said. Although he said it all serious and stuff."

"*Dr. Darcy?*" Lizzy asked. "When did you see him?"

Lydia gazed blankly at her sisters. "What do you mean? It was Dr. Darcy who came and got me in Houston. He flies first-class! All. The. Time. It was so cool, except they wouldn't let us wait in the first-class lounge at the airport 'cause I wasn't dressed appropriately. What snobs."

Lizzy's head spun with so many questions that she didn't know which to ask first.

"Slow down, Lydia," Jane said. "Tell us exactly what happened."

Lydia began relaying the story; how they got stuck in Houston, Dr. Darcy just "showing up out of nowhere," and then flying her back home. "You know, he just *gave* Taylor $200 and told him to get home, too. Just like that!" She snapped her fingers. "Must be nice."

"And Wickham?" Lizzy finally asked.

Lydia scoffed. "Him! As soon as he saw Dr. Darcy, he took off, even though he had promised Taylor and me jobs if we went with him. Ha! I guess he was afraid of getting punched again!"

"Lydia," Lizzy said, exasperated. "You've been back for four days. Why are you just telling us *now*?"

Lydia raised her shoulders until they met the bottom of her ears. "I *assumed* you all sent him. I mean, why else would he come get me?"

.   .   .

Mr. Bennet got his wish, and his home, Longbourne House, went back to normal, except for his wife's obsession with preparing healthy food for him. "*Turkey* bacon?" he asked. "That's got to be against some kind of North Carolina law."

She ignored him. "Well, there will be more changes, my dear, so it's best you get use to them."

Jane picked up more shifts at the clinic, and Lizzy poured herself into making the last weeks of class something her students would never forget. On a sunny Thursday, one week before finals, she gathered her hip hop studies class in the Ancestors Garden to listen to Ice Cube's *Today Was a Good Day*, and Tupac's *Dear Momma*. "Forget what you may have seen in any music videos," she told her class. "And try to experience the song, the lyrics, through a different lens."

Leaving the garden, she glanced up to see Dr. Darcy peering at them from his office window. She had been putting off thanking him, but knew it needed to be soon. He, too, was making this his final Delany semester.

.　　.　　.

The long-awaited Y2K celebration was happening the Saturday before finals week. Too late, some complained, too early for others. The whole affair blew out of proportion, and Dr. Lucas just wanted it over. "I really wish the board had never agreed to this," he had shared with Mr. Bennet during one of his visits to the house. "But don't you worry, Harold. You trained your guys well and the stage area is all set." Since his heart attack was close to the end of the semester, everyone agreed that waiting until the start of the spring semester to return to work was the best way forward. Everyone except Mr. Bennet, of course.

Nate ended up getting his wish. The other Y2K committee removed Mashujaa from the lineup after their president came back from his study abroad in Costa Rica. Lizzy heard he ordered the withdrawal to punish the house over their inappropriate behavior and poor judgment. When Darren finally got the nerve to make a re-appearance at Longbourne, he told Kitty how he was leaving the house. "Frat life isn't for me," he said. This news brought great relief to Kitty.

Mr. Bennet made an exception to Lydia's grounding, and the whole family attended the celebration. Nate and Charmaine sat with the family, along with a few of Mr. Bennet's groundskeepers. Everyone was especially happy to see their Mr. Bennet back again.

After the jazz-blues act Lizzy had liked during the auditions, Nate returned to his seat after a snack run. He handed Lizzy a bag of popcorn. "Yo! Did you see that *fine* looking woman with Dr. Darcy? The same one he was at the ball with?" he asked while tearing off a piece of his Red Vine licorice with his teeth. "Looks like she's dipped in money; wearing designer *everything*!"

Lizzy felt her face tighten. Good for him, she tried to tell herself. Thankfully, the performances were almost done. After the last act, Dr. Lucas came onto the stage to thank the students and staff for their efforts. He offered a pre-holiday greeting and affirmed that Delany University was more than ready for the turn of the century. "The year 2000 will be Delany's greatest year yet!" he said to a cheering crowd. After the cheers died down, he turned serious. "We have a lot to be thankful for here at our little university, but this year, we are especially thankful for the good health and recovery of our beloved groundskeeper and dear friend of Delany, Mr. Harold Bennet" This announcement took the whole family by surprise as the crowd erupted in cheers. "Stand up!" Dr. Lucas said from the stage. "All of you!" Lydia was the first to pop up, waving like she was in a Miss America pageant. The rest slowly joined her, smiling and nodding as they took in the crowd. About four rows back and to her left, she saw them. William Darcy and Caroline Bingley, her arm securely entwined with his. Tears filled her eyes, and she told herself they were for her father.

CHAPTER 42

Dr. Darcy,

    I would like to speak with you before the end of the semester.

    Would it be possible to meet at Kahawa Cafe? The one near the liberal arts building?

    Tomorrow at noon? It shouldn't take long.

    Sincerely,

    Professor Elizabeth Bennet

He read the brief message again, and then once more. He hit reply. *Certainly. See you then.* He pressed *SEND* and tried not to hope too much.

She was sitting at an outside table, wearing a gold-colored sweater and dark blue jeans. Her hair was loose, and a light breeze made the curls dance around her lovely face. He took a deep breath as the memory of its scent and the feel against his face returned.

She stood up when she saw him approaching. "Thank you for coming," she said, smiling. "Can I get you anything?" She motioned towards the coffee shop. She had ordered nothing for herself, he noticed.

"No, thank you," he said. They sat. "Is it true that you are not returning next semester?" he asked.

The question took her off guard. She had rehearsed the conversation, over and over, but his first question had not been in her script. "Ummm, yes. I plan to use the time researching and applying to doctoral programs. As I mentioned before …"

"Really?" he asked, looking surprised. She braced herself for his rebuke. "That's good, and I'm sure any university you choose to attend will be lucky to have you."

She watched him. No, he wasn't being sarcastic. "Thank you," she whispered.

He leaned forward. "Professor Bennet—Lizzy—I know that at the beginning—"

She held up her hand. "It's okay. I didn't call you out here to talk about me or my future studies." She took a deep breath. "I wanted to thank you, for myself and my family, for what you did for Lydia." Their eyes met. "You have no idea how much it meant to have her back safely."

"Yes, I think I can, and you don't have to thank me."

"Yes, I do—"

"No, you don't." His eyes flashed. "What you said about it being my fault is true. I should have been upfront with everything, but I let my pride get in the way of doing the right thing." He sighed heavily before continuing. "My father practically raised George Wickham, and I guess a part of me wanted to believe that my father's efforts weren't all in vain. That even George Wickham was capable of reform."

Lizzy thought about Jane telling her how Wickham had done something terrible to Darcy's family. She looked down at her clasped hands. "I feel foolish now, after you tried to warn me."

"Don't," he said. "There's much you can't understand right now, but that's a story for another time."

"Yes, I can see that. But it doesn't mean you didn't do my family a great service. I don't know how we can repay you."

"How is she doing? Lydia?" he asked quickly.

Lizzy told him she was doing well. "Longbourne is a lot more peaceful now," she said, smiling.

"I'm glad. And that's all the payment I need."

Lizzy's nerves threatened to overcome her. She twisted her hands in her lap and glanced around the campus, but everything was a blur. She cleared her throat. "Well, thank you for meeting me. I know you're busy, like everyone else."

"Yes," he replied, standing up. She stood, debating whether to offer her hand. Instead, they clasped in front of her. "Goodbye then."

He hesitated. "Yes—no! Wait." She stopped. "I may spoil the surprise, but did you know that Charles is on his way here? Today."

"No, but then I haven't seen Jane since last night." She paused. "Is he coming back to see her?"

"Yes. It turns out that he can't live without her, apparently." His smile widened.

She watched him, trying to decide how he felt about the decision. What he said next solved the mystery. "I'm happy for him. They make a good couple."

What changed your mind was on the tip of her tongue, but she held it in. She was just happy for Jane. She checked her watch. "What time does he get in? Will he come to Longbourne directly? I should go warn her."

Darcy chuckled. "I think we can leave it up to them to work it out."

She relaxed. "Of course." Then she laughed at herself. "So much for my goal of keeping out of my sisters' business!"

"You care about them," he said, his voice soft and warm. "Nothing wrong with that."

She gazed off into the distance before responding. "I know, but I realize now I was using them as an excuse to *not* take care of me."

He asked her to explain, but she told him she couldn't. "I'm just beginning to understand it myself."

They were both silent for a few moments. When their eyes met, his piercing gaze caused her to turn away quickly. "I've kept you too long,"

He cleared his throat. "I'm glad I got to see you before I leave."

"So, you're not planning on coming back in the spring?"

He looked away. "I had agreed to teach one semester, and the work Dr. Baei and I still have to do can be done through conference calls, emails, and such." He turned back to meet her eyes. "Unless there's something for me to come back to … "

The clock tower gonged. Her short meeting had taken almost half an hour. "I think that's something you'll have to answer for yourself … Dr. Darcy."

"Thank you for that." His eyes flattened. "You've made yourself perfectly clear." He gave a curt nod, said goodbye, turned, and walked away. She watched him for a few seconds before departing for Longbourne.

•   •   •

"Lizzy! He has come! He has come!" Not two feet inside the house, her mother came barreling down the entryway, smiling and crying at the same time.

"I heard, Mother. Where are they?"

Her mother hooked her arm inside Lizzy's. "He's in your father's study, asking for Jane's hand! Oh, isn't that soooo romantic?"

Lizzy laughed. "And unnecessary! Where's Jane?"

Mrs. Bennet led her to the family room. "Yes, I know, but he insisted." She sighed. "Such a lovely young man and our Jane will be so happy!"

Lizzy entered the family room to see a beaming Jane. She got up and met Lizzy at the door, embracing her in a grateful hug. "Oh Lizzy! He loves me and always has!" Tears of joy streamed down her face. Lizzy hugged her back. "Yes, of course he does," she said. Then, peeking down the hallway to make sure Charles wasn't returning, she asked: "But it's how *you* feel that I care about, Jane. Are you sure?"

Their mother scoffed. "Oh Lizzy! Always the downer! Of course she loves him! He's perfect!"

Jane laughed. "Well, he certainly *isn't* perfect, but that just makes me love him more!"

Lizzy covered Jane's hands with her own. "Well then, I am very happy for you, sister. And Charles!"

There was much laugher and cajoling at Longbourne that evening. Mrs. Bennet insisted Charles stay for dinner and the family talked about wedding plans and Jane's future. Her younger sisters peppered her with questions about work, where she'll live, and babies! "I can't wait to be an aunty," Lydia said. "I'm tired of being the youngest Bennet."

Jane's face grew hot, and she pressed her hands against her cheeks, causing Charles to grin playfully at her.

"Now, now," Mr. Bennet said, "there is plenty of time to talk about that. Let's just get through the holidays, survive this Y2K business, and then start planning. Guess I'll have plenty of time to help with that ..." His voice wavered. Everyone fell silent and turned to him with looks of concern. He waved off their worries. "I'm fine. Just a father filled with happiness."

Charles cleared his throat. "Same here!" He looked around at the people who were soon to be his in-laws. "And thank you for welcoming me into your family. I hope I live up to your expectations." He took Jane's hand and gazed into her eyes. "Your daughter and sister is very special to me. I'd be lost without her."

Lydia grinned mischievously and picked up her knife to clink it against her water glass. "Kiss! Kiss!" she shouted. And they did.

CHAPTER 43

It was decided that Christmas would be at Longbourne, and Jane would fly to California to welcome the year 2000 with Charles. Bingley Wineries was hosting an event, and as the soon to be wife of the CEO, she should be there. Of course, she was nervous.

"What if I say the wrong thing, or make a fool of myself by ... I don't know ... using the wrong fork or something!" Jane covered her face with her pillow and screamed, making Lizzy laugh.

"Please tell me you're joking. You'll be fine. Better than fine, and it's them who need to worry about making a good impression on you!"

Jane set the pillow back on the bed. "That's what Caroline said. She's been really helpful."

"You sound surprised," Lizzy said.

Jane nodded slowly. "I am, but you know it was Caroline who eventually told Charles about Father's heart attack. After he heard, he felt so awful that he hadn't been here for me. He said it was just the slap in the face he needed to make him see sense."

"There's our silver lining, I guess," Lizzy mused. She remembered something. "But Jane, did he explain to you why he left in the first place?"

Jane's mouth twisted to the side in thought. "He only said he was sorry and that he was afraid of hurting me or that I'd find him lacking." She paused. "I hate to think I made him feel that way."

Lizzy shook her head. "You didn't. But I can sort of see how he *would* feel that way."

"How?"

Lizzy smiled. "Jane! I know you don't think so, but you're an excellent catch!" She ticked off her sister's qualities. "Smart. Beautiful. Caring. *Independent.* And Charles sees that in you and probably understands how it's going to take more than his bank account to impress *and* keep you."

Jane thought for a moment. "He has so much more to offer than just money," she whispered.

Lizzy hugged her. "I know. And that's why, big sister, you fell in love with him."

The two chatted some more about Jane's upcoming travels, wedding dates, and Christmas. "Charles and Caroline are coming to the Christmas Eve service and potluck at the church," Jane said. She glanced at her sister. "William won't be there. Charles says he'll be in Chicago at a board meeting for Darcy Finance."

Lizzy nodded. "I figured he'd be gone by then. He couldn't wait to leave."

"Lizzy, why don't you come to California with me? William will be at the New Year's Eve party. You can talk to him some more."

"And say what?" Lizzy said. She stood up, placed a hand on her forehead, and paced the small bedroom. "We've said all there is to say, Jane. He knows my feelings, and I know his, and they are simply not compatible."

"He must care, Lizzy, after what he did for Lydia."

Lizzy stopped pacing and turned to Jane. "He did that out of guilt, not caring." She shook her head. "I doubt that man cares about anything."

Jane, who had been spending more time at Netherfield, told her sister that her assessment of Dr. William Darcy could be off. "He has a gentle caring side and is passionate about his work in micro-loans. He believes it could help to lift millions out of poverty." She paused, waiting for Lizzy to respond. When she didn't, Jane continued. "What he's doing is really important work, Lizzy, and he gets nothing financial out of it."

Lizzy knew all this. She had done her own research into Dr. Darcy's work and studies. She doubted he had done the same for her's. "Look, I know all that, but I really need to focus on me! Getting into a program and then it's going to be just research and study. Plus a whole lot of writing. No time for anything else."

Jane felt her sister had had enough of the topic. She started to leave her bedroom, glancing at the two Banker's boxes tucked in the corner. "Is that all your things from the office?"

Lizzy shook her head. "Just a few more. I can't believe how much stuff I've collected there. Mostly books." She glanced at her bedside clock. "Which reminds me. I'm supposed to meet Jake. He's going to help me with the last of the boxes." She grabbed her jacket and headed out.

The campus had returned to its pre-semester emptiness. A few years ago, Delany began offering three-week Winter sessions, but those would begin in January. She poked her head into the groundskeepers' building to let Jake know she would be ready in about a half hour. "Just come up to my office when you get there."

Dr. Wright greeted her at the Liberal Arts Department door. "Coming or going?" Lizzy asked.

"Going. But I can stick around to keep you company if you like."

Lizzy thanked her.

"I sound like a broken record," Dr. Wright said, entering Lizzy's nearly empty office, "but I am going to miss you."

"And I you," Lizzy said, taking the last of her books from the shelf. "But we will see as much, if not more, of each other, since you'll be helping me with my proposals."

Dr. Wright flashed a mock salute. "Sir! Yes, sir!"

Lizzy laughed. "That's Ma'am, if you don't mind."

Dr. Wright leaned against Lizzy's old desk and folded her arms. "Well, they weren't here long, but they sure made an impression on our little community. Fancy ball and now a fancy wedding." She cocked her head to the side and pointed. "Make sure I get an invitation!"

Lizzy didn't respond. It was funny how others could easily make light of the major changes that were coming to Jane and the rest of the family. While she was immensely happy for Jane and Charles, she worried how it would forever alter her life.

Dr. Wright watched her carefully. "Hear anything from Dr. Darcy?" she asked.

Lizzy dropped the book she had been holding, an Audre Lorde biography. She picked it up. "No. Why would I?"

She shrugged. "Just wondering. You two were on that committee together and his best friend is marrying your sister. I thought ..."

Lizzy slipped the lid on her final packed Bankers' box. "I saw him right before the end of the semester. All that needed to be said was said." There was a soft knock, and both women turned to see Jake standing in the doorway. "Ready?" he asked. "I got the cart downstairs."

Dr. Wright gave Lizzy a hug before leaving. "We'll touch base first of the year," she said. "*If* the sky doesn't come crashing down!"

After Jake carried the boxes into Longbourne, he asked to see Mr. Bennet. "Make it short," Mrs. Bennet told him. "Claire Hoffman just left," she huffed. "These people must not know what bedrest means."

Jake promised he'd keep it short, and Lizzy went to take her boxes into the old carriage house that sat behind Longbourne. When she returned, Jake had left. She was heading upstairs when she heard her father calling her.

He was sitting up in bed, magazines and newspapers scattered about. On the nightstand was a small stack of books. He motioned for her to sit.

"How are you feeling today?" Lizzy asked. "Can I get you anything?"

He shook his head. "I didn't call you in here for that." He picked up an envelope and handed it to her. "Claire came to give this to me." After she took it, he said, "Read it."

Lizzy slipped out the letter and read. Her eyes widened as the letter's contents were revealed. After she finished, she dropped it on the edge of his bed. It was a full account of Darcy's involvement in getting Lydia back home.

"You knew, didn't you?" Mr. Bennet asked.

Lizzy nodded. "Lydia finally told us the day you came home. But I didn't know about the private detective or Mrs. Hoffman's part in it." She tilted her head to the side. "Although it makes sense, she was the one to tell us Lydia was coming home."

Mr. Bennet nodded. "She was very helpful, and I thanked her for that. She told me she had to convince Dr. Darcy to agree to her telling us everything. Apparently, he's pretty humble and didn't want to draw attention to himself." He paused. "Make sure you offer our thanks to Dr.—"

"I already did. A few days before the semester ended."

Mr. Bennet's eyebrows rose. "Really? Is that ... all?"

Lizzy rubbed her hands on her thighs. "What do you mean? I thanked him. He said don't worry about it, and that was that." She looked at her father. "What else is there to talk about with him?"

Her father shifted, looking uncomfortable. "Lizzy, I saw you ... leave with him during the ball, only to return an hour later, looking ..." He shrugged. "Well ..."

Lizzy's hands covered her face. "Oh god!" she groaned. "That wasn't supposed to happen!"

"What? Me seeing you, or you and him going off to do whatever it was you two were doing?"

"Both!"

Mr. Bennet looked at her carefully. "Elizabeth, did he take advantage of you?"

"No!" she stood up and moved behind the chair, creating a barrier between herself and her father. "He didn't," she whispered.

Mr. Bennet thought for a moment. "Charles told me he and Darcy are like brothers. Will you be okay with seeing more of him, which is bound to happen."

Lizzy folded her arms. "I know, but after the wedding, he'll go back to his world, and I will start a PhD program, hopefully, so ..."

Mr. Bennet reached out his hand. "Come here, Lizzy."

After she was sitting by his side, he held her hands. "Your mother and I have been waiting for you to move on. We understand how much you love Delany and your family, but always thought there was so much more for you out there beyond Delany and Longbourne." He sighed. "But please make sure you're doing it for the right reasons, and not just running away."

.　　.　　.

After Christmas, Jane left them with a teary goodbye. "See you next year!" she waved from the car as Charles drove them away.

The only Bennets to have New Year's Eve plans were Kitty, and to everyone's surprise, Mary. "What? Can't I have a boyfriend too?"

On December 31, 1999, at 11:55pm, East Coast time, Jane called from the party at Bingley Vineyards to wish her family Happy New Year. She had to shout to be heard over the party goers. Lizzy put the phone on speaker. "We have three more hours to go here!" Jane said. "How's everything there? Any mishaps?"

"Nothing!" Lydia shouted. "Something *better* happen after all that fuss!"

Jane laughed. "Well, hopefully, nothing too bad." They heard her name being called. "I have to go, but I love and miss you all! Happy New Year!"

Outside Longbourne, they heard the sounds of party goers, firecrackers, and a few rifle shots. Lizzy walked to the living room window to take a peek. Over Delany, a fireworks show had started. "Happy New Year," she whispered into the dark, cold windowpane.

.　　.　　.

Jane handed Charles his phone. "Thank you," she said. "Everyone says hello and happy new year." Charles pecked her on the cheek. "Are you missing them?" he asked, looking worried.

Jane smiled. "Just a little. But I am also very happy to be here. With you." Charles smiled and bent to kiss her.

"I thought you were supposed to wait till midnight for that?" Darcy said, coming up to join them. He had been outside on the balcony that overlooked the vineyards. He needed a break.

"We'll kiss again then, too!" Charles said with a sly grin. Despite his mood, Darcy was genuinely happy for Charles. Back at Netherfield, when Caroline confessed that she had broken down and told Charles about Mr. Bennet's heart attack, he was relieved, but curious. "I thought you had objections to Jane," he had asked her. "What changed your mind? You must have known telling him would spur him into action."

Caroline threw up her hands. "*He* changed my mind! Every time we talked, he sounded like a sick puppy. I couldn't take it anymore, and everyone kept telling me how changed Charles was and how he was finally acting like a real CEO, instead of just playing at it." She sighed. "I guess a woman can really change a man."

Darcy didn't agree with her change-a-man assessment, but he now understood how the right woman could help a man release the better parts of himself; the ones he's kept tucked away and safe from those who could do him harm.

Jane, Charles, and Darcy chatted with each other and some guests. Caroline sought them out, only to pull Jane away. "You must meet the Ramirez's. Their family owns a small, but fabulous winery near Santa Barbara." Charles watched them vanish into the crowd, then turned to Darcy, who was empty-handed. "Drink?"

Bingley ordered tequila shots and as they waited, Mr. Eldon Lange appeared. "Well, well, well," he said, arms open wide. "If it isn't my two favorite Black multi-millionaires." He laughed. "Wait, make that the *only* two!" He continued laughing, patting Darcy and Charles on the back.

"Eldon," Darcy said. "Looks like you'll be walking into the new millennium drunk and … well, just drunk."

Eldon, unable to comprehend how these two gentlemen could do anything but hold someone like him in high regard, missed the insult. "Yep!" he crooned. "The only way to do it, if you ask me." He released a loud burp, which seemed to sober him up a bit. He squeezed between Darcy and Charles, turned around and leaned his back against the bar, propping up on his elbows. He surveyed the room. "Delightful party you got here, Bingley. *Very* nice. And that fiancé of yours is something to look at!"

"Careful, Eldon," Darcy whispered.

Eldon jolted upright. "That's right! I wanted to ask you guys about the *very* lovely Bennet sisters!" He turned and patted Charles on the chest. "Looks like you scored the pretty one, Bingley, which is fine by me 'cause I still got my eye on the other one, that professor chick. Man, she was hot! And so exotic!"

Charles looked nervously at Darcy. "Eldon, I think I hear your brother calling you," Charles said. "Over there." He pulled Eldon away from the bar and attempted to push him into stepping off. And quickly.

Eldon took a few wobbly steps from the bar, only to stop and swing back around. "Hey! I gotta be in Philly next week and thought I'd take a little detour through Merryton. Do you think she's into white boys?" He licked his lips. "Cause I wouldn't mind getting a little Oreo action going, if you know what I mean."

Before Darcy could take a swing at the obnoxious prick, Charles stepped forward and knocked him to the floor with one, solid hit. The crowd gasped, but after a few seconds, everything went back to normal. Eldon's brother appeared from the left, took one look at his younger brother lying on the floor and shrugged. "It was bound to happen eventually," he said. Charles looked up to see Darcy striding out of the room.

"Woo woo woo, Darcy!" Charles followed him out into the lobby area. "Where are you going?" Charles grabbed him by the arm. Darcy's face had contorted into the angriest look Charles had ever seen. It almost frightened him. But there was something else there. Fear. "What's going on, Darce? I took care of Eldon."

Darcy stopped pacing. His breath was coming fast, as if he had just finished a marathon. "I can't do it, Charles. I can't." He shook his head. "I tried, but after hearing that moron talk that way about her. No. I can't and I won't."

"Can't do what, Darcy? What's going on? Eldon was a prick, but—"

"Can't live without her." He took a deep breath. "Elizabeth Bennet. I'm in love with her. Desperately in love."

What Darcy thought was a confession, turned out to be confirmation of what Charles Bingley had suspected for a long while now. Plus, Jane had confided in him. He smiled slowly. "So, what are you waiting for? The world to fall apart?"

Darcy's mind spun. But after weeks of tortured uncertainty, he finally saw a path forward. He didn't know how, or if, it was even possible to convince her, but he had to take that chance. He patted Charles on the back. "Thank you, my friend. Will you make my excuses to Jane and Caroline?"

"Yes, of course. But don't worry about them."

Darcy checked his watch. "Do you think there's a flight out soon? I need to get to Longbourne as soon as possible. I've wasted too much time already."

Charles agreed, but shook his head at the flight possibility. "Just get to the Oakland airport. You can take the jet. I'll call ahead and by the time you get there, everything should be set." Darcy hesitated. "Go man! What are you waiting for?"

.   .   .

In Merryton, North Carolina, as in every other part of the world, the year 2000 rolled in uneventfully, which disappointed no one except Lydia Bennet. "The lights didn't even flicker!" she complained. For her part, Lizzy was thankful for the uninterrupted electricity and the World Wide Web. She planned to get started right away and sat at her computer in her bedroom on New Year's morning in the year 2000. There was an email from Dr. Wright with the subject line: *Guess you did have an effect*. Lizzy opened it.

Darcy Finance Announces End to Ban on Rap Music Investments. It was a link to an article in the New York Times Business Section. *Dr. William Darcy, the company's senior board member and son of founder, James Darcy, brought the controversial initiative to the table late last year. After a heated debate, the resolution passed with a slim margin.*

Lizzy stared at the article until a knock on her bedroom door called her down to breakfast. Mary, still wearing her shiny silver 2000 party crown, Kitty, and her father sat at the table. A platter of pancakes and what smelled like real bacon sat in the middle. Her father grinned as he loaded strips onto his plate. "Now don't you overdo it, Mr. B. This is a special occasion and if your cholesterol ticks back up, then—"

"Back to that fake bacon," Lydia said, sitting down. She popped right back up. "Forgot the butter." After retrieving it from the refrigerator, something outside the window distracted her. She went closer and pulled back the curtain. "Oh god!" she gasped. "What's *he* doing out there? Standing out on the sidewalk like he's lost or something?"

"Who is it, Lydia?" Mrs. Bennet asked. Lydia dropped the curtain and faced her family. "You'll never guess!" she said, moving back towards the table.

"So, you better tell us," Mr. Bennet said.

Lydia set the butter dish on the table and winked at Lizzy. "It's Dr. Darcy, that's who!"

CHAPTER 44

SPRING 2002
LONGBOURNE HOUSE

Lizzy stood in front of the full-length mirror, still unable to believe the image that stared back. The wedding dress was simple, yet elegant. An A-line silhouette made of gleaming white tulle, embellished with floral appliques and tiny pearls. Spaghetti straps and a V-neckline added just a hint of sexiness that would drive her soon-to-be husband mad. She smiled, imagining his reaction as she walked down the aisle.

"August! Stop running!" Jane stumbled into the bedroom, following her active almost two-year-old. She scooped him up before he could reach his aunt, which could have proved disastrous. Jane was dressed and ready in her rose pink matron-of-honor dress. She held up a little black clip-on bowtie. "I don't think he'll keep this on, Lizzy. He keeps tugging it off."

Lizzy smiled and reached for her nephew, who giggled and fell into her arms, despite Jane's warning. "Be careful or you'll damage the dress!"

August peered into the full-length mirror at his auntie. "Pwretty!" Lizzy pecked him on the cheek. "Why thank you, handsome!" She set him down and watched him scurry off to the corner where some of his toys were.

Jane stepped around the bride, checking to make sure everything was in place. "I am so glad you went with this one, Lizzy. It looks so good on you. William is going to die!"

Lizzy laughed. "I know! Have you seen him? Are they here?"

Jane nodded. "And you," she said, pointing at her sister, "are going to die, too, once you see him in that tux." The sisters' eyes met in the mirror. "No crying, Lizzy, or we'll have to do your makeup again."

"Don't worry," Lydia said, entering the bedroom. "I used waterproof everything!" She stood behind her sisters and nodded. "Not bad, ladies."

One of the more surprising developments to come from the Bennet-Bingley family merger was Caroline Bingley's interest in Lydia. "She's a feisty one," Caroline said. "I like that, but we need to work on redirecting some of that energy." Lydia walked the stage her senior year but didn't officially graduate until she completed make-up classes that summer. Soon after, Caroline began introducing Lydia to the behind-the-scenes fashion world, stressing the importance of an education. "Business," she told Lydia. "You must learn all you can so *no one* can take advantage of you." Lydia is now studying and working on getting accepted into the New York Fashion Institute, and no one doubts she will.

Kitty graduates from Delany this year, but she's still unsure of her next move. She and Darren eventually grew apart but remain friends. Tanzania proved to be a good move for Mary, and her three-month study tour turned into a full-time job at an NGO with a mission to save certain insects from extinction. The family sees her about once a year, but Jane and Charles always arrange to meet up with her during their visits to South Africa.

Jane and Charles divide their time between Netherfield and Napa. Jane continued to work at the clinic, but after she became pregnant with August, she resigned. In California, she convinced the Bingley Charitable Organization to sponsor a free clinic in

Oakland. Jane mentors junior nurses there and at Westside whenever she's in town.

The Delany-Bennet legacy ended as planned. Fortunately, the excitement over Lizzy and William, and the busyness of Jane and Charles' wedding, allowed little time for sorrows or regrets. Lizzy and William were able to convince the Delany board to let Mr. Bennet remain in charge of the Ancestors Garden, which Mr. Bennet greatly appreciated. Between that and traveling, volunteering at church, spoiling their grandson, and the knowledge that all their daughters were safe and happy, the senior Bennets had no complaints.

"Dad says he's ready when you are." Lydia told them. The sisters were Lizzy's bridesmaids and little August, if he cooperates, the ring bearer.

The nuptials were to be exchanged in the Ancestors Garden in front of a small gathering of family and very close friends. A much larger reception will follow at Netherfield. Lizzy took one more look at herself, placed her veil, and followed her sisters outside, where their father waited to escort her to the garden. Lizzy laughed at the row of golf carts decorated with flowers and streamers.

Mr. Bennet made a show of looking at his watch. "Come on, now," he said. "Don't you think you've kept that man waiting long enough?"

Of course, William had proposed to Lizzy that New Year's Day. In between kisses, hugs, feelings of relief, and grateful laughter, he dropped to one knee. They both heard Mrs. Bennet's delighted screams coming from inside the house, where everyone was watching through the family room window.

And of course, Lizzy said yes, but with a condition.

William would have preferred to be married right away, but he also understood her desire to move forward in her education. He pressed her hands to his heart and pledged his support. "I'll wait a thousand years if I have to," he said.

Her face shifted into mock insult. "You think it'll take me *that* long to get a PhD, huh?!"

He turned serious. "Please forgive me for what I said that evening. My words were thoughtless and cruel. I couldn't blame you for what you said, how you could never love me, although hearing it was … devastating." He lowered his head, and she reached up and placed her hand lightly on his cheek.

"I'm sorry," she said. "I had no idea my words hurt you so much, but part of the blame falls on me, too." She sighed. "I confess I had revenge on my mind that night."

"Yes," he nodded. "I can understand why—"

She held his face between her hands and gazed into his eyes. "William, I *do* love you, and none of that matters now."

He bent to kiss her once more but stopped at the sound of the front door opening.

"Y'all need to get inside and stop messing around out here!" Lydia screamed.

William chuckled. Lizzy took his hand and led him towards the front door.

"Welcome to the family," she said.

THE END

AUTHOR'S THANK YOU

I first want to thank the BBC for introducing me to the work of Jane Austen. Another big thanks to my writing group: Amber, Laura, and Karimah. Thanks for keeping me motivated and sticking with me throughout the long process. Thanks also to Melissa J., Darlene E., Steve the bartender, and the BRW community. Finally, thank you Sarah Rose, my daughter. Your faith in me keeps me going. I Love you!

ABOUT THE AUTHOR

Photo courtesy of Nicole Moore

Desiree Kannel is the author of *Lucky John*, also published by BRW in 2020. She is the founder and facilitator of Rose Writers Workshops, leading creative writing classes and workshops for adults and youth. Her other publications include *Running Wild Anthology of Stories*, Vol 3, *Tall Tales and Short Stories*; a Flash Fiction Anthology, and others. Her literary affiliations include Women Who Submit, Amherst Writers & Artists, and Gemini Ink. A native of Long Beach, California, Desiree currently lives in San Antonio, Texas with her cat, Malcolm.

Desiree R. Kannel

Lucky
John

NOTE FROM DESIREE R. KANNEL

Word-of-mouth is crucial for any author to succeed. If you enjoyed *The Delany Bennets*, please leave a review online—anywhere you are able. Even if it's just a sentence or two. It would make all the difference and would be very much appreciated.

Thanks!
Desiree R. Kannel

We hope you enjoyed reading this title from:

BLACK ROSE
writing™

www.blackrosewriting.com

Subscribe to our mailing list – *The Rosevine* – and receive **FREE** books, daily deals, and stay current with news about upcoming releases and our hottest authors.
Scan the QR code below to sign up.

Already a subscriber? Please accept a sincere thank you for being a fan of Black Rose Writing authors.

View other Black Rose Writing titles at
www.blackrosewriting.com/books and use promo code
PRINT to receive a **20% discount** when purchasing.

Printed in the USA
CPSIA information can be obtained
at www.ICGtesting.com
JSHW021914101023
49641JS00001B/2